The Prophecy Of
SERONDHEL

"Hero's Trial"

"...when the poor are hungry, they will not hesitate to eat from a dirty hand."

~Bondor, Councilor of Riverock

The Prophecy Of
SERONDHEL

"Hero's Trial"

By
Jason L. Garner

RUTLEDGE MOUNTAIN PUBLISHING

HERO'S TRIAL

Published by

Rutledge Mountain Publishing

Vernal, Utah 84078

www.rutledgemountain@gmail.com

Printed in the United States of America.

ISBN: 978-1-7334700-0-1 *(Paperback)*

ISBN: 978-1-7334700-1-8 *(Hardcover)*

ISBN: 978-1-7334700-2-5 *(eBook)*

Library of Congress Control Number:2019914537

To my sweet Rebecca,
for giving me the motivation
to see this through.

THE PROPHECY

As was told in an age long past
The wolf's dark cry shall spark anew
The path of light for us that last
A champion will rise to uncover the true

Orphaned in infancy on the one moon night
With the everlasting name of Obah-a-Tou
Shall the kingdoms of old once more unite
To battle the tyrant invading foe

Ancient saints shall awaken as signs
To guide and foretell on the path of destruction
By an arrow pierced in the heart of Divines
The clues are restored which were bound by obstruction

As the land once was it again shall be
All the clans shall accept him as fate
With a message of fire for all to see
A champion will come to unlock the gate

Past the treacherous swine who know in denial
The secrets of old shall begin to cascade
Guidance and witness shall end in betrayal
Three false gods shall be struck by his blade

Wandering alone in the chasm of hell
A champion will stand where all else would fall
To clear way for the truth generations will tell
He discovers his destiny and that of them all

By blood of the old Obah-a-Tou enters the fray
With the ancients demise he rejects the past
The tyrant cries and becomes the prey
The heirs of Serondhel shall be free at last

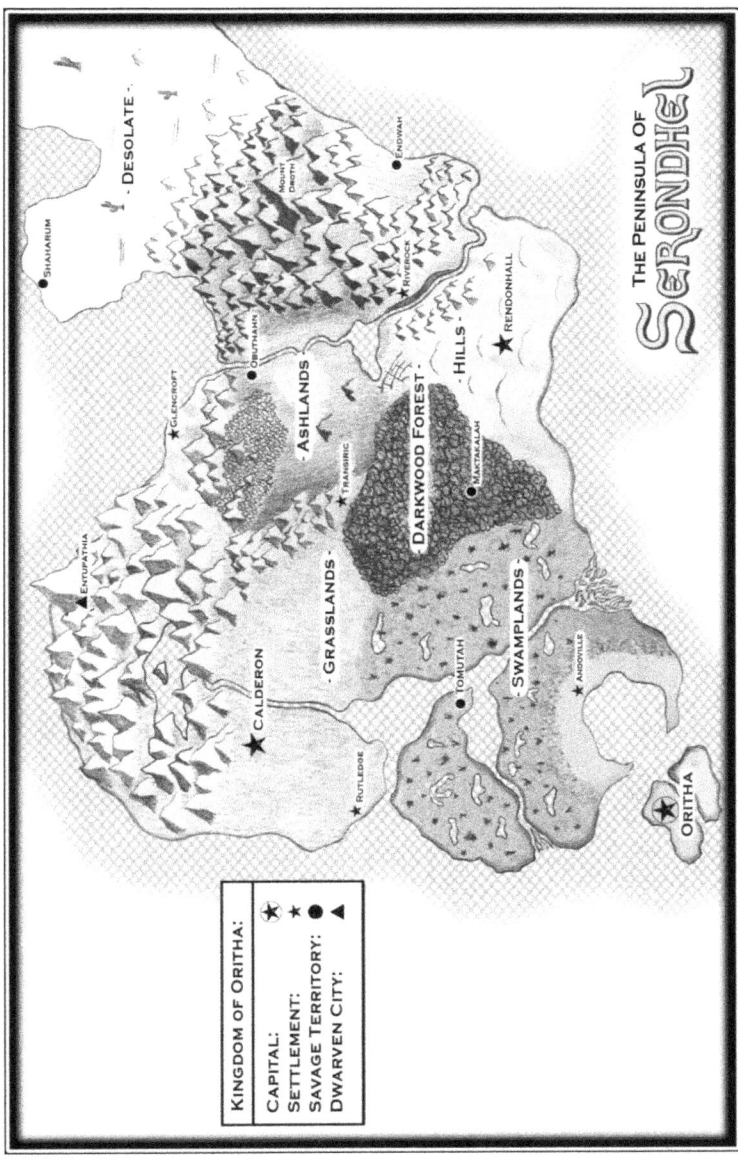

THE PENINSULA OF

Serondiel

- DESOLATE -

SHAIARUM

MOUNT DEITH

ENDYAH

RIVEROCK

GLENCROFT

ORUTHANN

ASHLANDS

EKITUPATHA

TRANSARIC

DARKWOOD FOREST

MAKTARALAH

RENDONHALL

- HILLS -

CALDERON

- GRASSLANDS -

TOMUTAH

SWAMPLANDS

RUTLEDGE

ANDOVILLE

ORITHA

KINGDOM OF ORITHA:

CAPITAL: ★

SETTLEMENT: ★

SAVAGE TERRITORY: ●

DWARVEN CITY: ▲

Order by Blood

Nobles: a fair race of man, higher than them all

Shaharans: second to the throne, preferable to elves

Endwans: greatest of the heathens, elves none the less

Darkwood elves: short and fair, buried in the darkness

Bog elves: blue-skinned, writhing in muck

Ash elves: black and disgraceful, lower than them all

~The Great King Scharric

PROLOGUE

I t was another storm. Thunderous booms erupted in the sky above Calderon like they had so many times before. While the wind menaced beyond the windows, sporadic flashes filled the castle hall with light.

Duke Roland, sitting steady at his large dining table, ran a hand down his face and across a short graying beard. His broad shoulders slumped, and his chapped lips forced a smile as he lovingly viewed his daughter sitting across from him. She looked just like her mother, but perhaps even more beautiful. Adalyn had long blonde hair and extraordinary deep blue eyes, resembling far too closely the woman he had once loved.

Unfortunately, she now wore the same disappointed pout that her mother often had.

"Would you like more to drink?" Roland asked her sincerely.

The girl refused to respond, upset with him for denying her request to take part in an upcoming trip to Oritha, the capital. He had told her repeatedly that these were dangerous times, but she wouldn't listen. The roads were no place for a sixteen-year-old princess! The Natives had become dangerous and unpredictable. Whether they were evil or just irritated prisoners of the kingdom, Roland didn't know, but he would die before subjecting Adalyn to their ways.

"Etnah, would you fetch my daughter more to drink?" the duke asked, turning toward his servant.

"Certainly, my lord," the black skinned elf responded, immediately motioning toward Adalyn. For a Native, Etnah had always been a faithful and responsible friend to Roland. He never disobeyed and was perhaps the duke's most reliable confidant. In turn, the elf had entrusted his master with many opinions and observations. They both looked forward to a day when a friendship such as theirs could be displayed without all hell raining down.

"I do not need more to drink," the princess ordered.

"Very well, my lady," said Etnah, giving Roland a reassuring glance. The servant had large tall ears — as typical to most elves — that were pierced in several places. He was lanky, perhaps six and a half feet, and slender, but strong.

Roland shook his head in amusement. With everything going on in the kingdom, he sat idle and stressed over his daughter being angry! At least he had the support of Etnah, the elf of the Ashlands. If the other Natives could be anything like this one servant, then Roland knew that the Legion was fighting the wrong war. It wasn't a far thought to question who was really in the wrong: was it the Natives, or the Nobles? The elves had possessed the peninsula for centuries before the Nobles showed up to claim a right to the lands long held sacred by their predecessors. An enduring and horrific conflict, the Lurid War, had ravaged the primitive forerunners, ending in their slaughter and eventual quarantine. Though they had done nothing but defend their homes and nations, the 'savages' were now seen as a backwards and heathen people. Somehow, the invading kingdom, led by a power-hungry King Scharric, was regarded as Noble. The logic did not make sense.

"Mother would have let me go to Oritha," said Adalyn, dropping her fork.

"Well your mother isn't here," stated Roland on the defensive, "and I'm sorry, but I do not expect her to come back."

"Yes, and I believe that was your fault too, was it not?" accused the angry girl.

"Adalyn, I loved your mother," said Roland, putting a finger to the table, "and you know that. It was her decision to go back to the homeland, not mine."

"We could have gone with her."

"I have responsibilities as the duke!"

A loud roll of thunder echoed through the spacious room, interrupting them. Roland looked to the window as a bright streak of lightning cut through the dark of night. The storms—another problem that he had absolutely no control over. They had seemed to grow more frequent over the past few months, now numerous but irregular, fierce, and a blight to anyone wishing to keep peace in a city as large as Calderon. Roland did not believe in the three divines, no Noble did, but if they truly were there, he wondered what evil had been done to engender their wrath.

Adalyn rolled her eyes and looked back to her plate of fried turkey and potatoes.

How can I make her understand? Roland asked himself. Everything that he had ever done was for the benefit of his family. He had already lost his bride. If he lost Adalyn too, then what would be left to fight for—to live for?

Abruptly, the tall wooden doors of the hall burst open and caused him to jump. Barreling through the entry was a thin man with black hair, soaking wet from head to toe. With a smug look on his face, he approached the duke in quick stride. He was closely followed by two of Roland's personal guards.

"I bring a message from King Scharric!" the man announced through deep and heavy breaths. "He sent me in urgency!"

Roland rose to his feet promptly, fear and anticipation gripping his edges. Had the elves in the Swamplands broken the truce? Did they now march on Calderon? Or was there an assassin making his way to this very hall, bearing in heart the common Noble hunger for power?

Looking at once to his daughter, he commanded softly, "Go to your quarters."

Appearing offended, Adalyn tried to retaliate. "This isn't fair! Why can I never know what is going on in the kingdom?"

"Adalyn—"

"No! You keep me cooped up in this castle like I'm some sort creature not allowed to see the light of sun. I know not where to let my mind wander!"

"Adalyn, go to your quarters!" Roland repeated sternly. "Do not make me ask again!"

Groaning, the princess complied. She stood up in frustration and threw her napkin to the floor before stomping out of the hall. When she had gone, Roland sighed and refastened the silver bracer on his wrist. Tugging at his fur coat, he turned back toward the messenger.

"What news have you, steward?"

The drenched man took a moment to catch his breath, wiping water from his brow. With dead eyes and a serious composure, he stepped toward the duke and gave a halfhearted bow.

"Your highness, our king has sent me regarding an enemy that must be dealt with. There is a boy living in the mountains, not far north from here. The king has ordered that he be eliminated and has given you the responsibility of seeing it through."

After picking up Adalyn's napkin, Etnah gave a keen ear to the messenger. Approaching Roland's side curiously, he seemed to tune in to every word.

"Just a boy? How old is he?" Roland inquired.

"I was told that he has just passed his seventeenth year."

"Just a child," Roland scoffed. "What wrong has this boy done?"

"King Scharric simply stated that he is a threat to the kingdom and perhaps a hindrance to the future power of the Nobles. That was all I was told, but the boy's death is essential. As you know, the king does not respond kindly to those who question his motives."

Roland looked taken aback. He knew better than to question Scharric, but this was without a doubt the most far reaching order he had ever received. What could this poor child have possibly done to offend the king himself?

Etnah seemed intrigued. He looked to his feet before reluctantly deciding to speak, "Does this boy live with his parents?"

As if tortured by the screeching cry of a Swampland bird, anger flooded the face of the messenger.

"Learn your place *savage!*" he spat with hatred.

Roland calmly grabbed Etnah by the shoulder as the elf stepped forward in reprisal.

Rebuking the messenger, the duke scolded, "I will not have such talk here! This is a servant of my household, and you will answer his question!"

The man looked to Roland in disbelief, but through clenched teeth he obeyed. "The boy lives alone. Apparently, he was raised in the Calderon orphanage."

Etnah's brow elevated as he took a step back. Bewilderment and exhilaration were the only words that could define the look on his face.

"Here is the official writ from King Scharric," the messenger noted, handing over a drenched parchment scroll. "It should explain in detail your assignment and the boy's whereabouts."

"You are dismissed!" Roland commanded, receiving the order. "Though I do not yet see reason to kill this target, I am not ignorant of Scharric's ways. Inform him that I will carry out his command.

"Now be gone! You may stay the night at the Westmore Inn if you wish. Tell them I demand the best of service for you."

Once again, the messenger bowed with lackluster, and after casting a degrading glare to Etnah, he departed back into the storm. The moment he and the guards had cleared the room, Etnah turned to his master.

"You must not kill this boy!"

"What do you have against it?" Roland asked perplexed. "This is an order from the king himself. You know what that entails."

"It is most likely intuition," said Etnah nervously, looking around for prying ears through an open door or window, "but I feel it in my bones! We must not kill him."

"Etnah, the king commands it, *the king!* If this young man has produced enough of a stir to gain Scharric's attention, then he must be more of a danger than we suspect. He could be trained, elusive. He could have a following, waiting to wage war against us at the first opportunity. There are many variables, but every outcome must end with us killing this boy."

Etnah shook his head, disagreeing with every word. He clearly had more cause than he was letting on.

"You remember our conversations?" the elf asked. "The talks of a world free from the hate that fuels our societies? Do you remember the prophecy of my people? This boy by all counts matches the description of our hero! He can make our dream a reality. I can hardly believe that the time may have come!"

Roland was well-aware of the prophecy and source of Etnah's elation. The Natives believed emphatically in their sacred scripts, and if what Etnah suspected was true, then maybe it could mean all the difference in the world. A hero, come to unite the peninsula under one banner, could fix everything! Perhaps this boy was a threat to Scharric, and not to the kingdom as a whole. But what if he was not a hero?

Scharric would not take kindly to Roland's defiance. If the boy was not a fulfillment of prophecy, then any showing of mercy would act as another nail in Roland's coffin. And who was to say the prophecy carried even a hint of truth? Could it honestly be valid? The Natives claimed it was given to them of the divines, but where had the gods been in the last fifty years?

"I remember our conversations, but what do you propose we do?" Roland asked. "We cannot just ignore the order. I already gave my word that I would fulfill it. If I were a wise man, I would send Captain Earnst and his men immediately."

"Ah, but your lack of wisdom makes room for courage and morality!" Etnah exclaimed in eagerness. "We must do *something*."

"Yet I must send men after him, if not only to *look* as though I were obedient to the king."

The ash elf stared at the floor and flicked his tongue like a cat lapping milk. The duke had to chuckle at Etnah's curious personality. The elf was intelligent, but strange did not even begin to describe him.

"If that is the case, then we must compromise. There must be a method to get the boy away unscathed," mentioned Etnah. "Allow me to visit him before you send the Legion, to warn him if nothing more. No one else need ever know."

Roland's eyes narrowed. "Etnah, if I release you, you will never be allowed back into my court. There must be another way."

"I know the law," agreed the elf, "but it is best that I go myself. Who else can we trust with information such as this? I have been in your service for nearly two years and will forever be in your debt. You have treated me well, but in that span, I have never asked for anything save this. The boy is an orphan, Roland, possibly since the one moon night seventeen years ago. If this is fate, then I must be the one to seek him out."

"I do not expect the boy is a Native."

"Perhaps he is not, but if I have learned anything from my years in this castle, it is that goodness exists in everyone, regardless of belief or color. Some people just choose to discard that goodness for fouler paths. Grant me this request."

"You've been a good friend to me, Etnah," said Roland, placing a hand on his servant's shoulder. "Understand that this is the last thing I can do for you. Once you go, I may never see you again, and if I do, I pray the moment is right. Until then you cannot set foot in Calderon."

"I understand," said Etnah, a look of total conviction on his face. "The greater head start you can give me the better."

Roland looked into his friend's eyes, knowing what he would say but not wanting to allow time the pleasure of bringing it to reality. With sincerity and purpose, he granted the elf's request.

"Etnah of Obuthahn, I release you from my service and command you to depart. You have two days. Take care my friend."

CHAPTER 1

I n full force the pickaxe landed. Slowly it ate away, chunk by chunk, at the mine's wall. Drenched in sweat, Lancen let the tool slip in his hands. With his bare torso glistening, he stopped to look at the mess around him. A thousand pieces of ore and clay surrounded, but no gold. With a sigh he stared dolefully at the stone wall flickering along with the torchlight. He had been working in the same spot for hours. The air was uncomfortably hot and notably thin. Lancen was weary, and seeing the material piling around him did nothing to soothe his angst.

I'll haul it all tomorrow, he thought. *Just one more swing and I'll call it a day.*

Gathering his strength, Lancen poised himself for a final hammer. The muscles in his back tightened as he asserted all the effort he could into the throw. The pick fell and struck solid into the wall, dust shooting from its point of contact. As it broke through the stone and into a small hollow, a subtle glimmer of precious metal flashed in the torchlight.

His heart raced at the sight. It was definitely gold, and it was no mere flake! At first glance it looked as large as a nugget, or even an entire vein! Pulling out his chisel and hammer, he quickly chipped away at the rest of the small opening, but as he got a better look, he knew that something was off. The find was far too glossy to be natural. Reaching his hand into the cavity, he rested his fingers around a smooth object.

Cursing to himself, Lancen pulled it free and looked the item over. In his hand was a small and finely crafted key, about the length of a finger, having on one end a tiny ringlet, and on the other, three jagged teeth.

Setting down his tools, he was unable to take his eyes off the discovery. What was it doing buried in the wall? Making his way out of the tunnel, he studied it intently, nearly running into the stopper for his sliding mine cart. In the entire year that he had worked in the mine, this key was without a doubt the most absurd thing that he had ever found. When light from the outside world began pouring in, he discovered a strange insignia etched into its side. It looked somewhat like an arrow.

At the end of the tunnel he gave a hopeless look at the cracking support beam above his head. One day the whole mine would come down on top of him, but he wasn't going to worry about it today. Instead, he stepped outside to take a deep breath of mountain air. The sun was already on its descent, and a nightly mist was beginning to settle into the small bowl of his homestead. The chill of autumn instantly bit at his skin. It had been a long day.

Quickly throwing on the shirt he had left by the mine's entrance, Lancen solemnly surveyed his home. He lived within a decent sized clearing in the Northern Mountains, about a day's journey from Calderon, the pinnacle city of the Grasslands. A small stream ran through the center of the homestead, his humble one room cabin only a stone's throw away. Lancen now stood on the western side where his mine and chute system were, but to the east, a lowly open shed, a wood pile, and a chopping block were the extents of his property — and his life.

"Rune! Come here boy!" Lancen yelled, watching as his wolf-like husky came running. The white dog barked and smiled, excited to see its master.

"Check it out, boy," said Lancen, showing Rune the mysterious key. "What is that, huh?"

The dog barked and panted, tongue flailing.

Lancen smiled and scratched behind its ears. Rune was the only companion he had had over the past year, and although he loved the animal, it seemed like ages since he last saw his Calderon friends. Had it really only been a year?

For a moment he closed his eyes and grit his teeth. The loneliness was wearing on him, and it had been for some time now. Yet if there was ever a thing that was certain, it was that he could not return to the city. He could never see his friends again.

Opening his eyes, the boy forced a smile and clapped his hands. "Don't worry, buddy. You are excellent company," he told Rune as they walked back to their one room abode. The cabin was small, barely containing a fireplace, a bed, and a table, but it was warm, and it was home. Untying a rabbit that had been hanging just outside the front and only door, Lancen went straight to the table and began to prepare their supper.

Whenever he thought about his past, disappointing feelings and memories would quickly stroll back to him. He had been dropped off at the steps of an orphanage when he was only a few weeks old. As far as he was concerned it was on that day that he was born, and it was from that day that he celebrated. The day after tomorrow would be his seventeenth birthday. He wished he could spend it with loved ones. He wished he could spend it in Calderon, but there were too many wounding memories there, too many dangers, and too many regrets. The mountain was where he needed to stay. It was peaceful up in the cold, and it was safe.

When he allowed himself to think of them, there were obviously some things he missed about the city. In fact, there were numerous things. For one, he thought about his best friends Hans and Avik daily, and their work at the lumber mill just outside of the city walls. The three had always dreamed of adventures and riches in the King's Legion, and with sparring and archery they created their own fantasies of the Noble army. It was hard to believe they were all of age to join. After so many years of avoiding work for training, it was a given that his friends had already signed on without him.

Another of the great recollections from Calderon was Adalyn, the duke's daughter. The beauty she possessed was unbelievable. Every day he used to pass her on his walk to the mill. She was usually coming out from behind the old chapel on the corner of the castle grounds, and occasionally their eyes would meet. He could have sworn that she would sometimes smile at him, but why would she ever care about a peasant orphan?

Lancen was a decent looking character, sure, but in no way saw himself as kingly. He wore dark brown hair and stood around six feet tall. He had blue eyes and strong athletic ability, but Adalyn never saw it. Too bad she had never wandered out to the mill. Perhaps there she would have been impressed in reality, and not just in the creations of his mind.

Bringing his mind back to his meal, Lancen proceeded to dice some onions and potatoes and throw them into a pot, reminding him of the one person he missed most of all, the one who he had longed for more than any. Looking at Rune he spoke his mind, "Mother would kill me if she found out I was skipping the carrots in rabbit stew."

He missed the woman who had raised him, Sidna, like crazy. She wasn't really his mother but…as always, as soon as the thoughts came, he had to force them from his mind. He could never dwell on the subject. *She's gone*, he always told himself, *forget it.*

Rune barked and pawed at Lancen's leg.

"You are just always happy, aren't you?" Lancen said, scratching behind the dog's ears and looking briefly to his bow on the wall. Trailing off and speaking more to himself than the animal, he concluded, "Well maybe one day I will be too."

Setting the pot of stew over the fire, Lancen reclined on his wooden chair, sore from the long day of work. Turning the golden key over and over in his hand, he allowed thoughts of the lumber mill, events of a previous life, to overwhelm his conscience before he drifted into a peaceful sleep.

*   *   *

CRASH! Lancen awoke at once. Rune growled and stiffened in the doorway, ready for a fight. Looking at the dog, Lancen felt a bitter uneasiness.

"What was tha—" *CRASH!* It was coming from the shed on the eastern side of the homestead. He could hear bottles rattle and glass breaking. Jumping to his feet, Lancen looked past the open front door to the darkness beyond. Hairs stood up on the back of his neck as the sound of a terrifying howl echoed through the forest clearing.

"Wolves," he said aloud, "they must smell the stew."

Rune growled, threatening with barred fangs. Immediately there was a second howl, and then another. There was more than one beast. It was obvious, wasn't it?

"Shut up, dog," Lancen said through clamped teeth as Rune continued to snarl.

He had never dealt with wolves before, nor any other beast of threat, but he was skilled with a bow and practiced in hand-to-hand. Unfortunately, the butterflies in his stomach tried to convince him otherwise.

"Get in your cage, boy," he told the dog.

Rune didn't listen but remained composed for an attack. The dog's hair pricked up stiffly, alert to the danger.

"Rune, get in your cage!" Lancen yelled. Quickly he resorted to pushing his pet into its metal kennel below the table and locked the door. "I don't want you getting hurt."

Rune looked at his master with wide and frightened eyes, as if to say, 'I don't want you getting hurt either.' Pawing at the bottom of the door, a small but earnest yelp escaped the dog's mouth.

"I love you, boy."

Lancen grabbed a torch from beneath his tattered bed and lit it in the dimming fire. He then grabbed his bow from its mount on the wall and slung a quiver of arrows over his shoulder.

"Watch the stew for me, huh?" he told Rune at the end of a deep and shaky breath.

Stepping out into the chill air, he started toward the shed where rustlings were still apparent. The night had fallen in its fullness and felt unusually dark in the present circumstances. It was a darkness that seemed to enter his pores and wander through the vessels of his being. Walking slowly, he could make out only the quiet rush of the nearby stream. Had they gone?

Regardless, he continued toward the shed. As he passed the stump of his wood splitting area, he nodded reassuringly.

Must've been spooked off.

Yet just as the thought crossed his mind, a clear and definite rush of air moved behind him. The darkness was breaching into his heart. He was now entirely encumbered.

Trying to remain calm, Lancen breathed slowly and whispered, "Where are you?"

As if on cue, the snap of a stick sounded to his left. Without a second thought, Lancen dropped his torch and swiftly pulled an arrow from its holster. Immediately he launched it into the darkness, toward the sound. The projectile struck solid to the ring of a loud cry, and a thud as the beast hit the ground.

Out of nowhere a second animal pummeled the boy to the earth. There was a fierce growl, and claws shred apart his clothing. It took Lancen a moment to catch up to what was happening. The creature atop him was like no wolf he had ever seen. It was shining black with a short, clipped coat. It was far too large to be a wolf, but there was no mistaking its canine nature. After the initial glance, the only feature Lancen could manage to focus on was the sharp and ferocious teeth dropping below the beast's lips. The monster continued to claw.

Finally, Lancen felt the pain and released an agonized cry. There was a tearing feeling in his right leg as the hound quickly turned and bit into his flesh. He struggled to kick it off, but to no avail, receiving nothing but dangerous claws to his other leg.

Snarling in a painful adrenaline, he battled for the wood-splitting axe just a few feet away. The monster released its hold on his leg and at once dove for Lancen's neck, sinking long fangs into his flesh. A shocking flash flew across his face as the animal scratched with ferocity.

At last his fingers found grip around the axe's wooden handle, and he swung it without delay, roughly catching the huge leg of the violent beast. Yelping, it released its bite and backed away in anguish. Lancen's vision blurred and darkened. He felt warm, warmer than he ever had before. It was a comfort unmatched, like a terrible but brilliant bed that would not allow one's departure. Faintly, he heard the whimpering hound scream and then fall. There was a man's voice, and then footsteps...

CHAPTER 2

Visuals of black and white raced through Lancen's quiet thoughts. Pulsating pictures grew brighter and brighter before diluting into a single image. As if looking through an open window into another dimension, a small and barren room came into focus, where he saw a dark hooded figure rise from the dust of the ground. Though he had never laid eyes on this being before, Lancen knew him instantly. It was *the Master*, standing before an ornate and curious door. Something about this man, or creature, was unmistakably familiar, and yet as a whole, completely and absurdly foreign. After only a moment, the image slowly faded from his concern and recollection, and he drifted once again into a restless unconsciousness…

Lancen's entire body ached. His head pushed and pulled under pressure as if being squeezed. Slowly, he forced his eyes open and willed himself to life. His vision was clear and his senses sharp. He smelled the comforting smoke of his fireplace, mingled with something wretched. He heard a calm breeze moving outside, and Rune playing joyfully. A soft morning light poured in through the gaping doorway. He was comforted to be lying in his own bed, in his own cabin.

Painfully, he raised to a seated position, grimacing at the throb that echoed behind his eyes. What had happened to him? No dream could have caused such a beating. No nightmare could leave an authentic wound. It came in waves, but gradually he remembered the events of the previous night. Wolves, or perhaps something worse, had attacked him — a nightmare indeed. What type of monsters were they, and where did they come from? And how did Rune get out?

As Lancen looked to the world outside his door, he saw a peculiar figure approaching in quick stride. Dark and tall, it neared his cabin, a stranger, with black skin and a gaunt face. His large pointed ears were decorated with polished rings of stone and bone. Drawn on his neck and arms were several red-lined tribal tattoos. It was clear that this was a Native from the Ashlands, but it was odd for an elf to be in the Northern Mountains, and even more, in *his* home! The elves were savages that performed horrible rituals and witchcrafts, using bones as jewelry...

"You're awake," said the Native, having to cock his head to walk beneath the cabin door. "It is about damn time."

Lancen was surprised at the elf's words. He had never spoken to an Ashlander before. The stranger spoke with a unique and unfamiliar accent. In astonishment, Lancen couldn't respond.

The creature leaned in over the bed and brought his face within inches of Lancen's. Clicking his tongue several times, he stared the boy down with large red eyes.

"What's the matter, too much gunk between your teeth?" the savage asked. "Don't worry, we'll take care of introductions in a moment. First, we need to re-wrap your leg and discuss the events that would bring me to this strange abode. Raise your foot, would you?"

Lancen cautiously processed the black elf's words, contorting at his horrendous breath. What was this savage doing here? He was still too confused and concerned to respond.

"Go on, lift your leg!" the stranger repeated.

Reluctant, but sensing honesty, Lancen exerted strength to raise his right leg. It was only then that he observed himself and saw what poor condition he was truly in. A cloth bandage wrapped his neck and shoulder where the hound had sunk its teeth. Thrashings of cuts painted his torso and waist, most of which seemed to be healing, but as the elf unwrapped his calf, the grisly image of a still-open wound was revealed.

Careful as he was precise, the savage began to clean the bite. Taking in the moment, Lancen further observed the stranger in his home. The Native man was dressed in an open black vest of tanned hide. He wore interesting pants and boots that seemed to be armored with bone, and appeared to be an older man, but in formidable shape and health.

The creature reached to the fireplace and removed the lid from one of Lancen's metal pots, releasing a putrid smelling vapor. Dipping into it, he retrieved a stringy looking weed, popped it abruptly into his mouth, and began to chew. *Disgusting!* After a moment, he spit the foul mush into his hand and pressed it into Lancen's open gash. The boy fidgeted.

"Don't strain yourself," said the elf. "It's only pit karp from the Swamplands. It's excellent for wounds such as these."

Lancen closed his eyes, grimacing at how the weed stung. Leaning his head against the wall, he sighed in overwhelming confusion. After a few seconds of silence, he stared blankly into the fire, hoping to wake up from this headache of a dream. He didn't know who this savage was. He had no idea how he had been found or why the stranger had saved him, and on top of everything, he felt incredibly hungry.

"How long was I out for?" he asked, attempting to make at least some sense of things.

"Just through the night and morn," answered the Ashlander, finishing the new wrap of Lancen's leg. "For a while I thought you would not survive the night, but this morning you have recovered with ungodly speed!"

"Well, is that not a good thing?" Lancen asked.

"It is a strange thing! Do you have any idea what it was that attacked you last night?"

The boy responded honestly, "I don't know. It had to be some sort of dog or wolf."

The savage smirked. "Yes, that is for sure. Only were it a mere wolf you would not have healed so quickly! No, the creatures that attacked you were something more. I had never seen them before, but I have every reason to believe they were death hounds. Ever heard of them?"

Lancen shook his head. "Never."

"I only know of them from legend and tales of paranoid hunters. The problem is that every occurrence I've heard of has placed them in the Ash Mountains. That is why my eyes are crossed like a doped-up cow. What would they be doing in the North?"

Lancen was speechless yet again, he didn't know whether to laugh at the elf or take him seriously. Death hounds?

"According to stories, death hounds are known companions of skoles. Yet another fable I've never believed in, but after last night I suppose that anything is possible. The dogs are said to carry the same metamorphic disease. Not only is it a miracle that you are alive, but if the legends are accurate, it is a miracle you are still human!"

Metamorphic disease? Skoles? Lancen lowered his brow in confusion.

"You've never heard of skoles?" asked the Native, surprised. "How long have you been living on this blasted mountain?"

"What are they?"

The stranger shook his head and ran a black hand down his face before responding. "Everything I know on the subject," he began, "and I mean everything, has only been told me of legend. Skoles are predators of the dark. They are thirsty for blood and are never at peace until they get it. They are strong and fast, nothing but evil shadows in the blackest reaches of night. Perhaps your recovery *is* coincidence, but more likely you have contracted their disease. You have inherited the beast. Had you seen your state last night you would have been as wide eyed as a baby Ashlander! And now you are pale, but not ghostly. Your eyes have grayed but are not white as described in tales. Though I sound ridiculous saying it, I believe you are *becoming* a skole, and are not one yet."

Lancen refused to believe the garble he was hearing. Him a skole, a creature of the night? That was ridiculous! It couldn't be true. He desperately wanted to find a mirror and confirm the horrendous suggestion. Had his appearance really changed?

"My name is Etnah, by the way," said the elf, extending a hand in courtesy.

Lancen widened his eyes and ignored the gesture. "Is this serious?" he asked intensely. "Am I going to change?"

Etnah looked to the roof and chuckled. "Perhaps we should start with your name and spare the details. I have other business being here."

What other business could this stranger have?

"Come on, name boy!"

Lancen widened his eyes. Refusing to believe this was serious. Holding out a hand in incredulous gesture, he eventually submitted. "Lancen."

"Perhaps," said Etnah, taking his hand with a curious stare. "Lancen, son of who?"

"Son of none," said Lancen, now giving in to the insanity of the Native. If he wanted answers, maybe he needed to play this game.

"How so?"

"Well I'm sure I had parents somewhere along the way."

"Interesting," said Etnah. "So you're a stray, a bird, a flyer. Why is that?"

Lancen scoffed. *A bird?* "You know, that is a good question. I was left at an orphanage when I was an infant, and that is all I have ever known. Now can you tell me why you are here, Etnah?"

The elf rolled his eyes. "I am not aware of how much you know of Native lore, child, but I assume it is not much?"

"That's right. I know only rumors. I had a friend that is Shaharan, sort of, but I know next to nothing of elves. I have never spoken to a true Native before."

"Nor I to an orphan boy living in the mountains."

"Fair enough," Lancen admitted to his eccentric guest.

"Well allow me to educate you," said Etnah. "I'm sure you know of the five Native camps? The Shaharans share a blood very similar to yours, but the rest of us are elves. Each of the five clans has appointed a chief to lead them, although we respect our wise women, the vatises, as prophetic and authoritative. I am from Obuthahn, the largest and most diverse of the five. We are god-fearing people Lancen, and we hold fast to our traditions and rituals that honor the three divines."

"So how does this concern me?" Lancen asked.

"Oh, far more than you know! One of our traditions, and by far the most sacred, is the recitation of an ancient and divine prophecy by the clan vatisus." Etnah paused and cocked his head before looking to the floor. "Let's just say that you 'fit the profile.'"

Lancen hung his head, trying to process what the elf was saying. He fit the profile? Of what, some prophecy?

Laughing, Lancen shook his head. "This is ridiculous!"

"Yes, probably so, but I have never had more reason for faith!" Etnah exclaimed. "Lancen, the prophecy tells us of a future hero that will come and save our people from all tyranny. If I only told you the first stanza, you would leap from your seat due to the impossibility of it all! Now, however, is not the time for you to know sacred details."

"You believe that I am your hero? Are you insane?"

"No, I do not believe you are the hero, but yes insanity is probably the reason for me being here. When I caught wind of an orphan in the mountains, my intrigue was peaked. The death hounds only strengthen that suspicion, but that isn't important. Tomorrow, however, is. Do you know what tomorrow is, boy?"

Lancen thought for a moment, and although he couldn't come up with anything relevant, tomorrow did hold *some* significance to him.

"Tomorrow is my birthday," he stated with heavy sarcasm. "I mean not exactly, but it does mark seventeen years since I was found at the orphanage."

Etnah dropped his head and laughed loudly, taking a moment before responding, "Well then you ought to know that tomorrow is also the night of one moon! Tomorrow the vatises will present the prophecy to each clan, and in exactly fifteen days, each camp will hold what is called the Hero's Trial. That's why I am here, bird.

"The Hero's Trial is a revered practice among Natives. It is a challenge of strength and valor for young warriors. I want you to test that tradition! Travel to Obuthahn and complete the trial!"

Again, Lancen was taken aback. It felt as if each surprise was a subsequent wave hitting him with greater force than the last. There was no way he would wander anywhere near Obuthahn! This elf was crazy! Skoles and prophecies! What was next, faeries and leprechauns? He had too many questions. Who was this crazy elf? What was this prophecy? How did death hounds factor into it? And why would a savage *ever* invite a Noble to a Native camp? That would be suicide!

"You are talking to the wrong person, I'm certain!" Lancen insisted.

"And I am certain that you are exactly who I have been looking for."

"I can't go to a Native camp!"

"I understand the risk, but you must accept the challenge!"

"I would be killed on sight!" Lancen argued.

"Oh posh!" cried Etnah, a smile forming on his face.

"Well what is the challenge like?" asked Lancen.

"No one knows!" said Etnah manically. "Every year it is decided by the chief and vatisus the day before the trial — usually it is rather dangerous. So, will you come to the Ashlands?"

Lancen considered the spontaneous absurdity of this, all the while chuckling to himself. Could he, by any chance in heaven or hell, be a hero of prophecy? Could he journey to a Native camp, where he would be hated, and take part in one of their most revered traditions?

"No," he eventually said, "I will not go to Obuthahn! I would be ridiculed and very likely killed! I know how the savages feel about Nobles because I know how the Nobles feel about savages!"

Etnah flinched at the word savage but held his temperament. "Boy, it may not mean much to you now, but if you are the fulfillment of the prophecy, then you could free my people. That would affect not only the Natives, but every living soul on the peninsula. You could bring a peace to this land that has never been matched! The Natives only hate the Nobles because of the tyranny they put us under. If you end that abuse, imagine the prosperity!"

"Why should I care about the Natives?" Lancen questioned.

"I suppose you have never been given reason to," said Etnah, pulling at a small sack tied to his belt. Raising it with a wink, he emptied its contents onto Lancen's table. A dozen or so fingernail-sized emeralds fell like colored ice to the wooden surface. "Perhaps this will make your journey worthwhile? You will get this now, and double it after the trial, pass or fail."

Lancen eyed the jewels with doubt. Avik and Hans would have jumped for them without giving it a second thought. He and his friends had often dreamed of riches and glory while working at the mill, but now Lancen had to be more cautious. His life was at stake if he accepted. Although, perhaps his life was also at stake if he didn't.

"I can assure you; a bag of gems is nothing compared to what you will receive if you are our champion," said Etnah. "So?"

Lancen couldn't decide so hastily. The ash elves were wild and necromantic. Why would he trust Etnah? Would the compensation be worth the risk? Lancen would never return to Calderon to spend his wealth. What would he even do with it? And though all of these questions riddled his mind, his heart craved something more than his current existence. It was possible that this was a second chance for him, a prospect for redemption, and on the edge of his memory hung three words from his late mother Sidna, '*serve the divines*.'

Lancen finally opened his mouth, still unaware of what would depart from it.

"Okay," he said, barely comprehending the path he had just committed to, "I will do it, but I do not expect that I am your hero."

"Nor do I," agreed Etnah, not displaying the least bit of emotion, "and I am sorry, but we cannot travel to Obuthahn together. You are not healthy, and I must leave at once. I do not know if you contracted skolism, but quite frankly I do fear what you may become."

"I do not know the way," said Lancen weakly.

"I figured as much. I shall leave you with a map of the peninsula. It is about a twelve-day journey from Calderon, directly east in the Ashlands. That is on horseback boy, so you had best purchase one before you depart. I have given you plenty to cover any expense that you may have.

"Now, I must be off immediately. I still may not make it in time." Etnah looked exhausted but rose to his feet and stepped to the door.

Looking back, he left the boy with a final thought, "Lancen, there are a lot of differences between Natives and Nobles, but they are only differences. They have never produced a need for hostility. You *must* be to Obuthahn in fifteen days! Koto mei, goodbye and good luck."

And with that Etnah turned and moved briskly away from the cabin. Lancen listened as the stranger marched away and called out words in a strange and foreign tongue, 'lehket rah,' and then all was silent.

CHAPTER 3

The next afternoon Lancen wandered north along the mountain stream. He was treading lightly on his injured leg, but overall it was nothing short of miraculous how he had healed. His neck was smooth besides a thick pink scar. His upper body was stiff and bruised, but considering the manner of the attack, he felt lucky to be upright.

The only thing he knew that wasn't functioning properly was his mind. He couldn't stop thinking about the strange events that had followed him like a shadow the last two days. Why was there a golden key in his mine? Why had the death hounds attacked him? By Noshera what did their bites do to him? And finally, why had Etnah journeyed all the way from the Ashlands just to tell him about some prophecy?

Internally, he still debated on whether he would travel to Obuthahn. The venture would carry so much risk and provide such an uncertain reward. It would be his first experience leaving the western region, going to lands wild and foreign. He would be stepping into the most dangerous escapade of his life, and yet somehow, there lingered a strong sense of importance in Etnah's proposition that he just couldn't get past.

As he followed the creek northward, he stopped to get a drink. Crouching over the water, he guardedly viewed his reflection and hardly recognized the person looking back. His eyes had truly grayed, hair lightened, and subtle scars from the slash of the hound crossed his left eye. Overall, his facial structure had carved and hardened. The golden key dangled from a string around his neck, casting a bright shimmer. He was still Lancen, but he could hardly imagine retaining that identity. He appeared tired and starved — because he was — and he appeared angry. Beyond all else, he *was* angry.

His image abruptly rippled and blurred before him as Rune approached, attempting to lick his face. Lancen laughed and held off the dog. "What do you think, bud, do I look better?"

Rune barked in response as Lancen ruffled the hair around the dog's head.

"Was that you telling me happy birthday?" Lancen asked, patting Rune's back. "I know you like surprises, but this year you ought to just tell me. We might be taking off tonight and I'd hate to ruin your plans."

Rune smiled and stuck out his tongue, helping calm the nervousness that Lancen had been bottling. The dog proceeded to try another quick lick on the boy's face.

"Settle down, dog. How about we check our traps?"

Lancen rose and continued walking along the creek toward a small snare that he had placed earlier in the week. As he strode, he contemplated the beauty of his surroundings. The tall aspens and scattered pines seemed to mingle and play. The sky gleamed a shallow blue, as if to produce a goodness and safety that only the soul could receive. Vibrant reds and yellows accentuated the utter magnificence of the season. How could he ever leave this place?

As he looked to the dark soil beneath him, he saw the repetitive back and forth motions of each footstep. His boots moved steadily, each new step precisely cloning the one before. In this limited view they seemed to be going nowhere, only repeating the same duty step after step. Maybe that was why Lancen knew he could not only leave it all behind, but a large part of him needed to abandon the present and do something to create a future. It seemed like his life was a continuous and tedious effort that persisted day after day. Something needed to change. Perhaps everything did.

As he approached the first trap, Lancen and Rune were quickly disappointed. The second and third were to the same effect, and after the fourth Lancen bit his lower lip and clapped his hands in discontent. It took a conscious effort, but he was not going to allow the brooding hunger to overwhelm him. It was a coincidence, or it was his recovery. He refused to believe that the hunger was caused by the death hound.

"Well, we're out of luck today," Lancen said to the dog. "I suppose we'll eat the jerky back at the house. Should we get going?"

Returning to his calm and steady stride, Lancen again watched the rhythm of his boots, too deep in thought to focus on much else. He had been at the mine for an entire year! It wasn't much, but it had become his home. Yet even though he felt so safe, his inner debate persisted. Though the world beyond his homestead may not have much to offer him, it could at least provide opportunity. It would be possible for him to find riches, companionship, and accomplishment—everything that Lancen craved and desired. For once in his life he knew that he needed to reach for the stars. The odds were slim of course, but it remained that if a person could only get close enough, they might actually grasp a heavenly light.

As Lancen grew nearer to his homestead, the smell of smoke triggered an alarming concern. He could feel that something was wrong, his gut wrenching as if to anticipate tragedy. Rune let out a sharp bark and trotted more hastily toward home.

"Do you feel it too?" Lancen asked.

Suddenly, Rune set off at a sprint along the stream. Lancen immediately followed, eager to see the cause of his heart's uneasiness. His legs warmed as he willed himself to run faster and faster, the ground rushing beneath him as he kept remarkable pace behind his white hound. Above the trees ahead of them he could make out a dark cloud of smoke. Before reaching the clearing, he slowed to a stop. He knew without even seeing that his cabin was beyond saving.

Just then he heard a voice yelling, and then another. Rune

growled and sped toward the source.

"Rune, *STOP!*" Lancen hissed, chasing after him.

But as they reached the line of trees, he halted dead in his tracks. At the bottom of the mild slope before him, his one room home was engulfed in flames, sending sparks and ash on all its surroundings. A small group of eight soldiers gathered near the structure. They were equipped in the typical attire of the King's Legion. From head to toe they were armored in steel. The standard Legion insignia, a depiction of the two moons both at half-sphere, shown plainly on their breastplates. Rune continued with fervor toward them as Lancen leapt for cover behind the nearest tree.

The men were soon aware of the charging dog.

"*WOLF!*" they yelled, as the largest among them pulled a knife and immediately threw it toward the threat. Hitting its mark, the dagger struck solid into Rune's lower chest, and at once the dog yelped and tumbled. Lancen watched in horror.

The large man moved forward and drew his sword. Rune was whining and made a futile attempt to get up. Before the legionnaire had even reached the animal, he let out a small chuckle before hollering, "It's just a sissy pup! Probably belongs to the boy!"

The man cackled arrogantly and triggered ensuing laughter from the others. Clearly the leader among them, he looked down at the wounded pet with a sadistic smile. Lancen internalized the ugliness of the man's face. His jaw was broad and jutting, his hair nothing but stubble on a recently shaven head. A large bubbling scar extended from his forehead to the very bottom of his face and shining in his mouth was an eye-drawing golden tooth.

With no further word the man raised his sword and thrust it down into Rune's side. The dog twitched and fell limp.

Lancen's heart dropped, the sound of wind moving through the trees ceasing in an instant. The world surrounding him seemed to diminish and blacken, engulfing everything but the demented image of his friend's killer. An immediate fill of burning hatred caused him to shake, while a cumbersome passion overcame him.

Scarcely breathing, he rose from his hiding place and ran down the hill toward the legionnaires. Startled, the men promptly turned toward him and drew their weapons. Without stopping, he pulled an arrow from its quiver, and in fluid motion released it en route to the man with the golden tooth. In the scuffle another soldier stepped into its path and the arrow ricocheted off armor, knocking the man from his feet.

"*GET HIM!*" Goldtooth cried. "That's the boy!"

As the attackers rushed toward Lancen, he swiftly fired another arrow, unintentionally hitting one of them in the throat through a small hollow in the steel armor. He turned quickly to evade, but his enemies were already on him. To his left, a soldier raised a sword, and gave him just enough time to counter and swing his bow, connecting it full force into the opponent's head. The wooden arc snapped on impact, jarring his hands. Without a second to waste, he shoved away the next challenger and dodged the axe-blow of a third. He had no time to marvel at the sharpness of his reflexes, but as his adrenaline pumped faster and faster, the existence of time seemed to disappear completely. He could feel the incoming force of the next blade, and leaping backward, was able to narrowly avoid its killing blow. Ducking his head, he barreled through two more men and into the clear.

Screaming, Goldtooth chased desperately behind him. Discarding the quiver from his back, Lancen ran past his burning cabin, beyond his mine and chutes, and into the southern woods that followed. The ground flew in a blur beneath him as he sprinted, leaving the legionnaires further and further in the distance. He felt a cold rush of wind against his face and small beads of sweat forming on his brow. Thoughts polluted his mind as a merciless anxiety swept over him. Why had they come? Hadn't they gotten their justice a year ago? Just as when Lancen fled Calderon, his life was now completely mangled and distorted, so he ran, not once glancing back at what he was leaving behind.

CHAPTER 4

Keira took flight through the burnt trees of the western Ashlands. Her brown hair waved like a flag behind her as she dashed beneath the darkening sky. Turning her gaze to the heavens, she watched the two moons, one full and bright, the other nearly covered in shadow. She was running out of time.

A tall young man named Engle ran beside her. Although he was one of the fastest warriors of the tribe, he kept a slower pace to remain at her side. It was his fault they were late. His constant invitations to go hunting just the two of them had finally gotten to her, but why did she have to say yes tonight of all nights?

"I swear, if you made us late to the recitation, I'll never hunt with you again!" Keira threatened between short breaths. "Of all the times we could have been late it had to be tonight!"

"No one made you say yes, you know," Engle responded with a smirk grin, "although I know I'm not easy to refuse."

Keira rolled her eyes. Engle was very handsome, but she would never let him know it. He was also tall, strong, and a great hunter.

"Oh, I have no problem refusing. I'm just trying to figure out if there is anything going on in your big head." she responded, trying to keep his ego at bay.

"Well of course there is! I'm always thinking of your amber eyes!"

Keira couldn't help but blush. As well as boosting her self-esteem, Engle helped her feel safe and comfortable. It was perfect. Being the only other Shaharan close to her in age, Engle was destined to one day take her in marriage. Keira would end up with one of the best men the clan had to offer, so how could there be any apprehension whatsoever?

She had been trying to answer that question for years. The older Shaharans drooled over him, but Keira never completely allowed him to swoon her. Perhaps it was the lack of options, the absence of freedom to choose for herself who to love.

As for now, she and Engle were late to the most important event in their culture. The night of one moon came only once a year and marked the future birth of Obah-a-Tou, their hero. On this night the entire tribe would celebrate and glorify the coming liberation of the five Native clans from the tyranny of the Nobles. Always beginning with the recitation of the prophecy by the vatisus, the ritual would consistently draw the largest crowd of the year. The amphitheater would probably be filling up by now. Keira had to move faster.

Brittle grass crunched beneath her feet as she moved past the outlying trees of the western woods. Before her, she beheld the vast valley of dust and ash that she called home. In the distance, she could see the torchlights of camp, the majority of which were moving toward the same general location — the central amphitheater, the pit in which all major events took place.

Stopping to take a deep breath, she put her hands on her hips and glanced at Engle only to shake her head at his unfatigued appearance. Digging deep, she overlooked the valley for only a moment before taking off toward her home — Obuthahn.

Lancen's legs moved rhythmically as he slowed to a jog. He had run through the dusk and into the night in relentless pace. Everything inside of him burned, partly from anger and shock, but mostly from exhaustion. Throughout the evening, whenever he had wanted to stop, emotion rolled back to his conscience and he re-established his speed. Now, after the many miles he had placed between himself and his enemies, he stumbled to a halt. His body could take no more. Falling to his seat, he shimmied to rest against a nearby tree.

After everything that had happened, all Lancen wanted to do was cry. He wanted to release the pain and hatred that had taken residence in his chest, but his eyes would not provide him the luxury. An engulfing and degrading sense of loneliness had overwhelmed him. He had nothing left, nothing at all.

Gasping, he felt no air enter his lungs. All desire for life had left him as he buried his face in his hands. He had now lost everything! His home, Rune, Sidna, his friends, his mine, everything that he had ever loved had been taken from him, ripped from his very grasp. And there was but one culprit, not the Natives or the death hounds, but one evil force that had stolen it all — the King's Legion.

The unusual darkness of the one moon night was matched only by that in his heart. He wanted revenge more than he had ever wanted anything. He wanted justice brought upon Goldtooth, upon Duke Roland, and even upon 'The Great' King Scharric. Lancen's hostility would not be silenced until he enacted vengeance, and if he were to die in the process, then he would do so with Legion blood on his blade.

What would his first move be? He had several options. One, he could try to circle around and follow Goldtooth and his men. Perhaps if he was careful, he could isolate the ugly leader, and slit his throat. At his waist, Etnah's bag of emeralds still hung. It would be possible to go to Calderon and purchase weapons before mounting an attack. Or maybe he could wait beside the castle grounds until Goldtooth arrived, follow him to a place of solitude, and then put a blade between his eyes. He grasped a handful of cold earth at the thought.

Yet after a moment he let the dirt fall and hung his head. Who was he kidding? He was no assassin. The truth was he was lost. He had no idea what he would do. It seemed he had nowhere to turn, but then the voice of Sidna once more echoed in his mind. He could see her soft face, her dark hair falling over her cheeks, and her lips as she mouthed the words, '*serve the divines*.'

"Well it is kind of hard to serve someone that isn't there!" Lancen whined breathlessly to the obscure memory.

He was resentful. The three divines, Athleon, Noshera, and Yehawa, sure didn't seem to do much. One would think that a 'god' would actually intervene in the world below to achieve some purpose, whether it be righteous or malicious, but Lancen had never felt them nearby. There were no divines, and if somehow there were, then they only required the misery of all inferior beings.

Whatever Lancen would end up doing next, he wouldn't receive the help from a 'god.' Perhaps he must journey to Obuthahn as Etnah advised. If he could find a horse over the next few days, there would still be time to get there before the trial. That would put hundreds of miles between himself and the Legion, and if by some small chance he was the fulfillment of their prophecy, it would land him with a small fortune and better means of exacting a proper revenge.

In order to get to Obuthahn he would have to first visit Calderon, and the thought of that seemed worse than anything the elves could do to him. For so long he had convinced himself that he would never walk those streets again, and now he was plagued with only a few options, all of which required him to enter the city. The last time he stood on those grounds he had watched his foster mother die, and it was all his fault.

Lancen shivered and bundled up inside of his hooded tunic. As he closed his eyes, he knew that he needed to go. He had no other choice.

The autumn nights were ruthless in the mountains and it was proven with the mist of every breath. Comfort was a foreign concept that Lancen knew he may never again experience. Longing for the warmth of a flame, he curled into a ball beside the tree. If only he still had his cabin. If only he still had a lot of things.

*   *   *

Flames of all different colors danced in a line around the pit below. Keira found her seat beside Engle on an old wooden bench near the top of the amphitheater. It wasn't the best view, but at least they had made it in time! Below her, center stage, and surrounding a ceremonial stone altar were the eight members of the chief's council. They all stood still, like incredible cloaked statues erected from the dark earth.

As the people of Obuthahn settled, whispers rolled with the mild wind. Keira looked around the crowd of several hundred. Every soul of the tribe had come to witness the sacred ritual. Men and elves of all different sizes and colors sat side by side, united in purpose. They were gathered for the same reasons and shared the same dream. Unlike the tyrant Nobles, these people would never victimize others based on culture alone.

The most prominent race in attendance was native to the land where they now gathered, the ash elves, a black-skinned and proud population. Mingling among them, were the blue-skinned bog elves of the Swamplands, elves from Endwah in the Eastern Region, and the pale, short wood elves from Darkwood Forest. Also in attendance were the people of her own descent, a tan-skinned, dark-haired race of man come down from Shaharum in the North.

Keira could scarcely believe that in only fourteen days she would stand before this very audience as a subject in the Hero's Trial. Typically, only the best young warriors were selected, but perhaps being an orphan, brought in from a foreign land, gave her somewhat of an advantage, considering the words of the prophecy. At fifteen years old, she would be among the youngest to ever compete, and she reveled at the opportunity.

Suddenly, the crowd fell silent, and each Native turned their attention toward the pit. Keira quickly followed the others as they raised three fingers of their right hands to their brows. That could mean but one thing, and as Keira looked to the altar, she saw her, in her wisdom and glory, the clan vatisus — Lady Nihwiah. The multitude in near unison removed their hands from their faces and extended the three fingers toward the wise woman as a token of greatest respect.

Nihwiah was dressed in a long leather gown, so tall that its bottom dragged across the dirt as she approached the councilmen. Her sleeves dropped like shadows past her wrists, where thin black fingers extended from the darkness. She was decorated from head to toe with thousands of beads of every color under the sky and in her hair was a finely crafted stone and glass tiara. The woman was old, but to Keira, she was the definition of beauty.

Nihwiah slowly raised her arms and the eight ash elves of the council dispersed from around the altar. A small flame burned at its base, where Keira could make out the hilt of a ceremonial blade. The foremost of the eight stepped forward. It was Shikobin, chief and leader of clan Obuthahn. Keira was taking in every moment.

Shikobin approached the crowd and spoke with a firm authority, "I welcome all you children of ash! You have been summoned here on this one moon night to witness that of tradition and divine prophecy. This night, you will be reminded of the promise of the ancients by the passed down ritual of the gods. Tis the same ritual performed by our ancestors. Tis the same prophecy that has survived the generations. Tonight, our dear Lady Nihwiah will recite this promise that has been made by them of old. These ancient words *will* come to pass! The day of our liberation is nearing, and we, the Natives, shall soon be the sole possessors of this our rightful land! Tis the prophecy of Serondhel!"

At once the camp exploded into cheers, with Keira yelling as loud as any for the freedom of her people. She couldn't help but think of how the Natives had once lived bountifully on the peninsula, a long time ago, before the day of the Nobles. They were spread across Serondhel and traded freely with the dwarves, who were at that point numerous upon the land. In those times there was no unwarranted bloodshed, no hatred and prejudice, and most importantly, no Nobles.

Eventually the dwarves began to exodus to the unknown lands of the North, and the Natives were left alone to many years of peace. Although civil war did break out among the clans, it was nothing compared to the hell that was to come.

When the Nobles arrived in Oritha, no one could see them for the tyrants they were. Some even expected that General Theroll, later known as King, was the fulfillment of the very prophecy that they had gathered to witness on this one moon night. However, all who had believed that were drastically wrong. The Lurid War enveloped their sacred lands and destroyed much of what the gods had ordained. Natives were driven and tortured with many being taken as slaves. After much persecution, the tyrant quarantined the remaining Natives into five tribes, and ever since, they had been in total compliance to the evil King Scharric.

The Nobles were the tyrant, and Keira knew in her heart that justice would eventually be served. The prophecy to be read tonight foretold the future liberation of the Natives. Keira could only hope to be a part of the resistance and see the monsters overturned once and for all.

As the cheers died, the audience began to chant in the Native language. Intently, Keira watched the dagger beside the fiery coals of the altar-flame, anticipating what was to come. The fire began to fade and extinguish, causing the uniquely dark night to become more dominant. On the altar was a fist-sized glowing mushroom, resting next to a ceramic bowl.

Lady Nihwiah, the glorious prophetess, gracefully retrieved the dagger which illuminated a bright orange hue. Grabbing the mushroom, she gently cut into its soft side. Immediately it oozed a neon blue liquid that dripped slowly into the bowl beneath it. Nihwiah dipped a finger into the substance and swiftly drew a luminous line from the center of her widow's peak to the tip of her nose. Then, after adding two horizontal lines to each cheekbone, she rubbed her hands together in the ooze, causing them to shine through the darkness. Throwing her head back, she stretched out her arms to call to the divines in the Native language.

The woman yelled harshly, *"ATHLEON, NOSHERA, YEHAWA!"*

Two men on each side of the vatisus promptly emptied large baskets of glowing mushrooms across the pit, setting the amphitheater apart from the sheer blackness of the night. Drums began to beat steadily behind the audience. Everyone was transfixed on Lady Nihwiah. Looking across the clan with red and twinkling eyes, she commenced to recite the prophecy:

> As was told in an age long past
> The wolf's dark cry shall spark anew
> The path of the light for us that last
> A champion will rise to uncover the true

> Orphaned in infancy on the one moon night
> With the everlasting name of Obah-a-Tou
> Shall the kingdoms of old once more unite
> To battle the tyrant invading foe

> Ancient saints shall awaken as signs
> To guide and foretell on the path of destruction
> By an arrow pierced in the heart of Divines
> The clues are restored which were bound by obstruction

> As the land once was it again shall be
> All the clans shall accept him as fate
> With a message of fire for all to see
> A champion will come to unlock the gate

> Past the treacherous swine who know in denial
> The secrets of old shall begin to cascade
> Guidance and witness shall end in betrayal
> Three false gods shall be struck by his blade

Wandering alone in the chasm of hell
A champion will stand where all else would fall
To clear way for the truth generations will tell
He discovers his destiny and that of them all

By blood of the old Obah-a-Tou enters the fray
With the ancients demise he rejects the past
The tyrant cries and becomes the prey
The heirs of Serondhel shall be free…at last

CHAPTER 5

Lancen opened his eyes to a dull but brightening sky, releasing breath that immediately vaporized into the chill morning. Judging from the sun and misty air, he knew that he hadn't slept long, but it was time to move. He needed to keep distance between himself and Goldtooth. If he hurried, he could reach the city by early afternoon.

Climbing to his feet, he attempted to shake off the cold. After regaining his bearings, he began to move south toward the tree line where the world would open-up to the expansive rolling hills of the Grasslands. He tried to keep his mind away from the city, but the more he tried to avoid it, the more it persisted itself into conscience. How could he return to Calderon? He had been avoiding it for so long and was afraid of what would happen when he once again beheld the stone and sand metropolis of his upbringing.

The memory of Sidna's death remained vivid and consuming. There were so many ways it could have been prevented, and Lancen knew that his hands hadn't been bound. He could have acted somehow to stop the proceedings. He could have done something to save her, but instead he just sat by in an emotionless state, watching. When it all came down to it, he supposed that she died for her belief in the divines. Once upon a time it wasn't unusual for people to believe in them. The early settlers adopted pieces of Native culture before beginning their conquest, but when Scharric took the throne everything changed. He outlawed the worship of any deity, with an emphasis on anything derived of the

Natives. Sidna was killed because of her refusal to give them up. If only the gods had been as loyal to her as she was to them.

The Faith of the divines was straightforward enough. Athleon was the god of strength, mythically known for hand-picking the winners and losers of war. Noshera, the goddess of love, watched over all forms of romance and was rumored to have deep interventions regarding diplomacy. Yehawa was the god of guidance, and allegedly aided in the decision making of all believers. Chapels for worship had been erected in every Noble city of the peninsula before being rendered obsolete. After the Lurid War, Scharric annihilated all aspects of savage culture among the civilized, and rightfully so in Lancen's opinion. The gods were a waste of energy.

What they stood for on the other hand, he could understand. Finding hope during conflict was something Lancen was now in need of. The god Athleon could intervene and help him to defeat his enemies. Guidance in decisions from Yehawa would be a welcomed charity, and as for the god of love: he *was* going to be in Calderon. Perhaps Noshera could touch him with her magic and allow him to woo Princess Adalyn.

Though that dream was as far-fetched as becoming a champion among the Natives. He could dwell on the good memories of Adalyn for now. Her long blonde hair was smooth and wavy. Her eyes were blue like dawn, her skin white and fair, but she was only a memory. He knew very well that the thought of them together was as dust blowing in the wind. It would diminish and disperse until there was no trace that it had ever been airborne. Her father was the duke! Not only had he personally made the call to execute Sidna, but the man was kingly. He would never allow his daughter to end up with a slummy commoner.

Several morning hours passed before Lancen reached the base of the mountain forest. It was there that he could finally see the great city of Calderon towering high above the brown plains of wild grass. He had to admit that the site was magnificent. From a distance, the city appeared to be crafted entirely of stone, and was surrounded by an enormous fortified wall.

At once the thought struck him that gaining entrance could prove a challenge. Assuming Goldtooth had come from Calderon, the guards at the main gates would likely be aware of Lancen's alleged crimes. He didn't know who gave the order to have him killed, or why it had taken so long, but until he had answers, he needed to be the most careful person in Serondhel.

The nearest gate along the northern wall would probably be his best bet. Relatively small and wooden, the entry was typically only manned by a few soldiers, and they were usually put there as a punishment. Whether they too would be a problem, he did not know, but reluctant as he was his options were few to nil.

As he viewed the place of his upbringing, a surprising motivation crept over him. Along with an overwhelming dread, the thought of his true home also brought a hope to his being that had been lost for far too long. Calderon was a place of creativity and wealth. There were people in the city that deserved every morsel of happiness prestige could offer, and with a little hard work, both happiness and prestige were possible to obtain. Hans and Avik had dreamed of just that. Not seeing them during his quick stay wouldn't be easy, but it did not seem logical to visit a couple of legionnaires. He would rather never see them again, retaining the memory of their friendship, than meet them only to stare up the edges of their blades.

Reaching to the ground, he grabbed a handful of dirt and powdered his face. Throwing on his hood, he traversed the valley before him and approached the northern wall. Finding his way to the road, he contemplated his plan of action: get in, get outfitted, get out. As he neared the gate, he could make out four guards, each toting tall iron pikes and cheap rounded shields.

"Halt, traveler! What business have you in Calderon?" fired one of the four. He was a vile looking man with a rough beard and rotting smile.

Lancen feared to raise his gaze. What if they recognized him? He was armed with nothing but a small dagger. He would never win the fight.

Trying to keep his face down and hidden in the shadow of his hood, he responded steadily, "I come from Glencroft. I only wish to trade in the markets."

"Ah, Glencroft is no easy journey. Where are your supplies?" the bearded man asked, stepping slowly closer. "What is it you bring to trade? You are little more than a boy."

Lancen hid his nerves and remained still. "We are camped a few miles north. My crew is waiting there. I come to buy food for the evening, but the bulk of our trading will be done tomorrow."

The guard eyed him with suspicion. "Sounds reasonable I suppose, but if you wish to enter, you must pay the toll of ten drachmas."

"There has never been a toll before," Lancen answered, concerned.

"Well today there is," grumbled the guard.

"Either way, I can't pay you now, but perhaps I could upon my exit?"

All four of the guards laughed. The one nearest the gate hollered, "These are dark times, friend. You really expect us to just let people in on their word?"

The guard next to him chuckled, "You do seem pretty shady!"

"I agree," chimed the bearded man, now only inches from Lancen's face. "We can't let just anyone in. At least not until they contribute to the Nobles' general welfare! How are you going to trade without any money? You must be carrying *something* of value?"

Lancen immediately thought of the key around his neck. Was it worth hanging on to? And then there were the emeralds at his waist. Perchance he did part with just one gem, he would still have plenty to purchase a horse and weapons, but would the guards be satisfied? The four strolled forward and encircled him. Bringing his hand to his pant leg, he debated on whether to grab the gems or his dagger.

"Just let me through," he said bluntly.

The guards laughed as they moved closer, evil smirks contorting their faces. "And what are you planning to do if we don't? Why don't you tell us what's in that pouch?"

Without thinking, Lancen drew the dagger and swiftly slashed at the bearded soldier. The strike was denied and in a fraction of a moment the broad side of a spear slapped him across the head. The knife flew from his hand as he tumbled to the ground, disoriented. Before he could react, he felt the sharp jabs of steel boots meeting his side, his back, and his stomach. Tasting blood, he fought to his knees, but was abruptly pushed back into the dirt. Similar to his encounter with Goldtooth, as his heart raced, time began to slow. Only this time there was no escape.

When the thrashing finally ended, the foreman searched Lancen's persona. Inspecting the sack at the boy's side, he discovered the small and flawless jewels.

"Well what do we have here?" he shouted joyfully. "Mr. Glencroft has something to cover the toll!"

The guard kissed a stone and tossed it to one of his cronies, then continued to distribute gem after gem until the bag was nearly empty.

"Those are mine!" Lancen groaned.

Laughing, the man grabbed Lancen by the shoulders and lifted him to stand. Arrogantly, he placed the ravished pouch of emeralds into the boy's shaking hands. Crudely being shoved through the gate, Lancen stumbled and fell, his face landing roughly on the cobble stone of the city street.

After giving him a brutal but final kick to the side, the guard hissed, "Welcome to Calderon," and closed the gate behind him.

CHAPTER 6

Out of breath, Lancen rested against the wooden post of a corral in the market region of Calderon. He tenderly felt his cheek bone and grimaced at the touch. His stomach ached while sharp pains bolted up and down his back, all more reasons to be furious with the Legion. Of the dozen emeralds Etnah had given him, only three remained. Though he knew the odds of buying a horse with them were slim, he had no other choice.

In front of him were three fine animals, two brown mares with a younger chestnut steed beside them. If Lancen could somehow convince the trader into selling one of them for two gems, he could still purchase a bow and arrows with the third. Approaching the youngest animal, he held out his hand to stroke its neck. His longing for the horse was strong. To obtain it after everything he had been through would be an incredible change of pace.

"Ah, that is a fine beast!" noted the trader joyfully, approaching Lancen's side. "She's four years old and friendly as can be. This one was trained by Mathis himself, the old gag, finest horse coach in the region! I can guarantee she won't do you wrong. You looking to buy?"

Lancen eyed the steed with desire and responded, "I am. I was hoping to trade for her."

The dealer smiled and rested a hand on the horse in discussion. He was an old man with a long white beard and twinkling eyes. "Well what have you got for me, son."

"I have some very valuable gems," said Lancen pulling out two of the emeralds. "I'm not sure their exact worth, but I know it's a fair deal."

The trader eyed the jewels and clicked his tongue. With a frown, he answered, "I'm afraid I can't agree with you. What are you needing the filly for?"

For a moment Lancen couldn't answer the question. He considered telling the truth, that he needed to be in the Ashlands within a fortnight, but very quickly saw the stupidity in it. "I am on my way to Rutledge. I have an uncle there with a load of skins to take back to Transiric."

"Transiric, huh? Interesting town that, built buy the dwarves it was. I wouldn't take you for a midland folk, but who am I to judge," the trader rambled. "Well, bud, I wish I could do more for you. There was a time not long ago that I'd loan her to you for less than one of those stones, but you can't trust anyone these days. More than once I've been jellied into a sour deal."

"You have my word. If you just loan her to me for two or even three gems," Lancen reached into his shirt and pulled out the golden key, "and this. I'd take any of these mounts, I promise that I will bring them back within the next two months," pleaded Lancen, beginning to feel desperate. "Please."

If he couldn't get to Obuthahn in time for the Hero's Trial, he had no idea what his next move would be. He was alone and had absolutely nothing. The feeling of being lost ate at him constantly. He needed a horse!

The trader looked truly unhappy about it, but his decision was not swayed. "I'm sorry, boy, I really am, but I've got a family to look out for and can't let any of my nags walk out of here for nothing. Take a carriage to your uncle and see if he can help you get some coin together. Then come see me."

Patting Lancen on the back, the old man gave a weak smile and walked off toward another potential customer. Immediately Lancen's heart sank. Everything seemed to be pitted against him.

He felt as though he were meant to lose, to be beaten and robbed. What was he to do now?

Keira crouched low in the tall brown grass of the burnt forest. Readying her bow, she aimed for the heart of the unaware atling before her. Very similar to a deer, it was covered in gray fur, had a bushy white tail, and jutting from its small head were two long and curved horns. Keira hoped that it would soon be her dinner.

She steadied herself and inched forward, trying desperately to be silent. The male atling turned and looked directly at her, wide eyed and alert. Keira held her breath and focused intensely. Biting down on her lower lip, she carefully aimed her weapon and released an arrow. The deadly projectile zoomed forward, just missing the animal's neck and triggering its instinct to run. As it turned to flee, Keira jumped erect and as swiftly as she could, launched another arrow. Broadly missing her target, she watched the atling bounce off and into a thick of burnt woodland, fully concealing itself from her view.

Frustrated, she threw her bow aside and took a heavy breath, a drop of sweat rolling down the side of her face. Judging by the sun in the western sky, it was now late afternoon. Once again it appeared that she would be going home empty handed. Disheartened, she dropped to a seat in the grass. As she leaned back, she noticed her tanned skin gleaming with sweat in the sunlight. It seemed the Ashlands had only a few weeks of winter, and then months on end of a temperate summer. She couldn't complain, but a little variety would certainly be welcomed every once in a while. Brushing her hair away from her face she sighed dismally. How was she supposed to win the Hero's Trial if she couldn't even down an atling?

It was hopeless. She had waited her whole life, praying she would be selected for the trial, and now, at a mere fifteen years old she would get her chance. She hoped for the best, but in her heart, she knew that she lacked the valor required to succeed. In a handful of days, she and other young warriors of the clan would embark on a task of courage and strength. The challenge would be of the highest difficulty, to be completed by few if any at all. Far too often clan warriors would never even return from the venture. These thoughts that should have brought joy and anticipation, instead placed only fear in Keira's heart.

A typical trial varied in substance and danger. Often the subjects were required to journey to the perilous Ash Mountains and retrieve a well-hidden totem. Other times, they may be commissioned to slay a wild beast that had been a nuisance to the camp. In fact, the most frequently presented challenge was to find an ash troll and bring back its head. Any number of subjects could win the trial, though few ever did, and all who succeeded were regarded as the most honorable members of the culture.

It was an accepted idea that eventually Obah-a-Tou himself would complete the challenge. Vatises throughout the ages had declared that the champion would be of Native descent. 'The blood of the old' could mean nothing else, especially since the Nobles were clearly the 'tyrant.' Keira would sometimes play with the thought that she herself might be the prophesied hero. To personally bring down their oppressors would be the most fulfilling experience imaginable.

Falling to her back, she looked up at the dark clouds. Everything was gray in the Ashlands: the dirt, the rocks, and the animals. Even the sky was bland and lifeless. Sometimes she grew tired of her dull surroundings. She longed to visit the other tribes, like Tomutah in the Swamplands, or Endwah on the coast with its stilted wooden structures, but most of all she yearned to see Shaharum, the land of her ancestors. At the end of the Lurid War, just before the treaties were made, her homeland was attacked, and her parents murdered. Keira was taken in by a loving ash warrior who found her among the wreckage. She could scarcely recall a memory of the white sands and blue waters that she had been born to.

The people of Obuthahn had grown distant from them in Shaharum, as well as from most of the other tribes. The quarantines had made trade and communication very difficult. It was also a dangerous road to Desolate, and Keira knew that the clan would never let her go, but maybe if she completed the Hero's Trial…

Keira jumped affrighted as a movement to her right surprised her. She sat up at once. Sneaking up on her, were her friends and soon to be competitors, Engle, Eltou, and Yantik.

"I told you to move softly wide-eyes!" Eltou chastened.

"Do you forget that I am from Darkwood Forest?" shot back Yantik. "Perhaps it was you that she heard!"

"They were going to scare you," said Engle from behind the others. He looked Keira in the eyes, with a grin forming on his face. Her cheeks flushed.

"You seem startled enough though," he laughed.

Keira smiled and averted her eyes. "I knew you were coming the whole time," she lied. "I was just caught thinking about the trial is all. I wasn't expecting you back so soon."

Her friends were all testing their strength in the trial as well this year. Eltou was a tall and strong ash elf, and the oldest among them at eighteen. He was the son of the chief and having competed in the last three trials, he was already a proven contender. Though he had yet to complete the challenge, he had established himself as a well-respected member of the tribe.

Yantik, at sixteen, was a first-year subject, a Darkwood elf from Maktakalah. They were a short and fair people with wide eyes and nocturnal instincts. As innocent and pathetic as Yantik looked, Keira knew that the elf was a swift and brutal force to be reckoned with.

Then there was Engle, of course, the tall broad-shouldered Shaharan. At seventeen, he was nearing manhood. It was only a matter of time before he would ask for her hand in marriage. At this point Keira struggled to decide if that was what she really wanted. Although, were he to complete the Hero's Trial, to marry a victor was considered the greatest of honors.

"We were able to finish the day early," said Eltou with a smirk on his face, "thanks to you!"

"What do you mean?" she asked.

"What do you mean what do I mean?" Eltou laughed. "You spooked a beauty of an atling right to my perch over the hill! I shot him dead at a stone's throw."

"I got a young doe about an hour ago," said Engle.

"And I cornered a black swine around the same time," chimed in Yantik. "This is the biggest haul we've had in a month! It will take some time to carry it all to camp. We could use your help."

"So I am the only one without spoil? Again?" Keira stated with dismay.

"Don't worry, girl, it's alright," said Engle extending a hand to his future bride. "Yantik's hog is big enough to count for two. Now help us transport the game."

Keira reluctantly took his hand and climbed to her feet. If it were anyone but Engle, she would have had a smart response. She was certainly glad it was he that was the Shaharan and not Eltou or Yantik. Marrying one of them? Frightening. Eltou was the son of Chief Shikobin, and though a valiant individual, he seemed to care little for anything other than hunting and fighting. Yantik was a Darkwood elf through and through, with the attitude to prove it. The forest elves had always been cruel and merciless, even with their own kind. Since the Lurid War they had kept to themselves more than any other, and with the cruelty of the forest there were few that ever traveled to their camp, Maktakalah. Yantik had only relocated to Obuthahn because of his parents. It was no secret that he didn't belong.

"One of these days I will down the biggest kill of the year," joked Keira, trying to play off her failure.

"One of these days you will learn how to shoot an arrow!" Engle said, putting his arm around her.

Keira shook her head and leaned into him. Remaining deep in thought, she helped begin preparations for the long walk back to Obuthahn.

CHAPTER 7

L ancen clenched a fist and hit it against the stone wall surrounding the barracks. It was certain now that he had lost his mind. Yes, he was in dire need, but to walk into the training facility of the very Legion that had ruined his life, the same Legion that had tracked him down in the mountains to kill him, was insanity. If he could think of anywhere else to turn, he would go there in a heartbeat, but the time had come when decisions needed to be made and risks had to be taken. It was a long shot, but he had now made up his mind to enlist in the help of Hans and Avik.

They would have no reason to help him. In all honesty, he expected them to arrest him before providing aid, but what other option did he have? After all he had been through, he refused to give up now. His hunger for revenge would not sleep. It was as softly burning coals, glowing red and never to cool. If a solution was out there, he would find it by travelling to Obuthahn. He had thirteen days until the Hero's Trial, and nothing, no obstacle, man, or beast, would prevent him from getting there in time.

It had been more than a year since the last time he had seen his friends. His memory of their final day together was blurred and distant. They had been working at the mill, dreaming and sparring as per usual. Lancen had left them in a good mood, but later that day his entire life would change.

As always, the thoughts were too painful to dwell on, and he pushed them from his mind.

Removing his hood, he looked up at the impressive scene before him. Within the walls, a tall building and its extensive grounds once provided an excellent location for the gathering of soldiers to be briefed on their duties of war. Now, in times of 'peace,' the location collected dust and produced warriors with the sole purpose of intimidating Natives and Nobles alike. Walking toward the large wooden doors at the front of the structure, Lancen tried to contain the fury that was building in his chest.

Wiping the anger from his face, he nodded to the guards at the entrance and moved inside. In the front room, a tough looking woman sat behind a massive desk.

"May I help you?" she asked routinely, her eyes not moving from the ledger she was working on.

Lancen gave the best smile he could force and answered, "Yes, ma'am, I hope so. I am a traveler looking for two recruits. I have business with them."

"Very well, all the recruits would be in the mess hall for supper. What are their names?"

"Avik son of Ramdor, he is a big Shaharan. And the other is a shrimpy one, Hans son of Gong," Lancen replied politely.

"I will see to fetch them, and who should I say bids them, traveler?"

"Tell them it's Redd, an old friend from the mill. They will know who I am."

"Good, I will be just a moment." The woman smiled kindly and stood to leave, but on her way out of the room she turned and asked quickly, "Are you feeling alright? You look like you've been hit by a troll."

"Fine, thank you," Lancen answered, faking a grin in assurance.

When the woman left his expression immediately changed. Truthfully, he *was* in pain, he was tired, and he was hungry. His world had been flipped upside down and he was hanging on by his fingertips. Worry continued to eat at him, exhausting him both mentally and physically. What were the odds that his friends would help him? Would they even recognize him?

And what was he supposed to say? For some reason, "Hello friends, I'm going to play games with the Natives, and if I win, I'm going after the Legion" didn't sound so good. How was he supposed to convince them of anything? Certainly the truth was not going to be adequate!

After just a few minutes the door to his right flew open. Avik entered first. He had grown in the last year from large to massive. The Shaharan wore a hopeful smile, sporting a new black beard beneath his chin. Shortly following him was an anxious looking Hans, still lightweight and pale as he had always been. Both of them were garbed in light leather armor. Once they realized who they were looking at, Avik jumped forward and threw his arms around Lancen.

"Where have you been?" Avik muttered.

After the embrace there was a brief silence. The two recruits seemed slightly hesitant, and Lancen's curious demeanor didn't help matters.

"You look different," Hans said flatly.

"Yeah I do," Lancen laughed, leaving it to Hans to greet an old friend in such a way.

"I meant you look sick. It's not a good thing," said Hans, holding back a smile. "Strong, but sick, and look at your eyes. You're repulsive."

"It's good to see you too," said Lancen smiling, glad that his friend hadn't changed. "I see you haven't eaten since I saw you last."

"We missed you," said Hans shaking his head.

"I missed you too," Lancen said soberly.

"Then why didn't you come back?"

"I can explain if you have some time," Lancen answered. As he spoke to them, he thought of abandoning his mission entirely. It seemed that the maladies he had gone through were all suffocated by the voices of friends, but he knew that it wouldn't last. The hunger inside of him would, the ache for sustenance as well as for revenge.

"We just finished up for the day. We have plenty of time," Avik responded, looking to Hans for approval. The shorter boy nodded in the affirmative.

"Mind if we find somewhere private?" Lancen asked.

"Lead the way boss," said Hans motioning them out of the building.

As they walked Lancen felt incredibly comforted, the best he had in days. For one, his friends were willing to give him a chance. They didn't recognize him as an outlaw, which brought peace, but also more questions. Why then had Goldtooth come after him? Why was no one else aware of the warrant?

"You don't know how good it is to see you," Lancen said when they had reached the city street. He continued to lead them east toward the duke's castle.

"We thought you were dead," said Avik. "We can understand why you left, but not why you never returned. Where did you go? We thought maybe Glencroft. When the woman came in saying Redd was here to see us, we thought it was your uncle bringing news."

"Well you have it mostly figured," said Lancen trying to think of how to answer appropriately. He thought of Redd, Sidna's brother. He had only met the man on two occasions. The first time he was only a young child, and Redd had taken him to the market for some sweet bread. The second occasion came just a few weeks before Sidna died. He had come to Calderon to sell his final haul from the mine and visit the orphanage to announce his retirement. On that day he brought gifts for all the children, and left Lancen with a bow and arrows. It was that very bow that was recently broken across the head of a legionnaire.

"I knew that my uncle had recently left his mine in the mountains just north of here. He had retired and gone to Glencroft for their fishing. I figured it would be a place of solitude, so I took Rune and went there. I have been working in the mine ever since."

"It feels like you are back from the dead," said Hans solemnly.

"I wanted to come back," said Lancen. "I wanted to every single day, but I couldn't bring myself."

"Well did you at least have success in the mine?" questioned Hans, ears perking up at the prospect of wealth.

"No, I never found a thing," Lancen said, noticing the golden key softly touch his chest with every step, "and honestly, I never expected to. Redd wouldn't have retired if he thought there was anything left in there, but I worked every day without fail. I filled carts with rocks and ran them through the chutes. I swung that pick so many times I would find myself walking back to the cabin and my arms still trying to swing. There was just something therapeutic about it, but I wish I would have come back."

"Well, you are back now, and that is what matters," said Avik. "'The valiant three united to save the weak and protect the strong!'"

Lancen laughed, recognizing the saying. The three used to use it frequently while talking about their future adventures in the King's Legion. He couldn't yet bring himself to tell Avik that he wouldn't be staying.

Lancen looked around in wonder as they walked through the city. Nothing had changed. He still knew every street and building as though he had never left. As they passed the Westmore Inn, a tall stone structure on a corner, he could see across a courtyard to an alleyway that led to the city orphanage. A young boy that Lancen didn't recognize sat in the passage, looking clean and well-fed with a half-eaten apple in his hand, but in the child's eyes Lancen could see a desire, mixed with discouragement. It was a look of positive dissatisfaction, a look of hope.

Trying to avoid the trip down memory lane, Lancen kept talking to his friends, "So how have you two been since I've been gone?"

Hans answered, "Things were quiet at the mill after you left. The day I turned seventeen we joined the Legion together. We are just about to finish our training."

"And where do you go after training?"

"It's difficult to tell," said Hans. "It could be anything from working as a guard, to patrolling the roads or collecting taxes."

"From what we hear things are getting pretty tense in the Swamp Region," noted Avik.

"Those blue-skinned freaks have been causing serious problems in Rutledge," continued Hans, as if he and the Shaharan operated within the same mind, "and not to mention on the roads to Andoville. I hope they send us there. Things are escalating, and the way I see it, war is coming. It's only a matter of time before we finish what the Lurid War started."

"You should join us," Avik mentioned quickly.

"I could never," said Lancen somberly as they approached the castle walls, "not after everything that has happened."

"You have to let that go!" Hans shot intensely. "Obviously it's why you left, but you must admit how convincing the evidence was."

Lancen stopped in his tracks and bit his tongue. Holding back a curse, he forced a controlled reply, "She didn't do it."

Hans looked at the building they were nearing and chortled, "Is this not the very place where it happened?"

Lancen nearly doubled over as a wave of guilt attacked him. He had done his best to block out the memories of what had happened here. They were standing in front of an old white chapel just outside of the castle grounds. The building was now obsolete, of course, but its beauty remained. Tall glass windows extended from the bushes several stories upward. Above them, grasping at the clouds, shot three tall spires, symbolic of the three divines. Lancen remembered clearly the many times he had come here to worship with Sidna. If there was ever a place for solitude and peace, it was here.

"Drop it," said Lancen, thinking of nothing better to say. "That isn't why we are here. Around back there is a garden with lots of trees and shrubbery. If there is a single place in the city to talk without prying ears, it is there."

Hans shrugged and waved for Lancen to keep moving. Once around back it was apparent that the groundskeepers had not kept up the place. Weeds grew over every flower, out of every statue, and behind every tree. With maybe twenty feet between them, the giant city wall stood much closer to the back of the chapel than Lancen had remembered. It was sad to see the garden in such condition, but at the same time, being unaware of how much information he would disclose, it was probably best that there would be little chance of visitors.

Once Lancen deemed the place safe, he began to explain himself, specifically omitting a good amount of information, "I do not expect you will believe everything I tell you, but I only hope that as an old friend you will give me a chance. Three nights ago, I was attacked by wolves. The details are not important, but for some reason an elf from the Ashlands saved me. I don't know how he found me, but he arrived just in time."

"Wait, a *savage* saved you?" Hans interrupted.

"Well I think so—or he may have brought the wolves. I don't know, but he nursed my wounds and seemed cordial enough. He was very strange. He said there is a prophecy among the Natives that I fit the description of and asked me to travel to Obuthahn for some event they call the 'Hero's Trial.'"

"And you told him to step-off, right?" asked Hans, seeming a bit anxious.

"Not exactly," answered Lancen, "well I did, but then he emptied a bag of emeralds on my table and I started taking him seriously. He said I would get double after the trial, win or lose."

"How much exactly are we talking about?" asked Avik, not immune to his share of greed.

"There were twelve or so to begin with. The guards at the northern gate robbed most of them. The horse trader seemed to think it would take at least a few to buy a young chestnut," Lancen responded.

"A good horse would go for a hundred drachmas. So altogether they must have been worth a half-thousand!" Hans said computing the figures swiftly. He was always the smart one, as rude and arrogant as he could sometimes be.

"Buggers at the gate!" exclaimed Avik. "I've met that crew. They're scum. We could try to get them back for you."

Lancen smiled and shook his head. "Don't worry about it, and if you do, then keep it for yourself, but that is why I'm here. I intend on going to Obuthahn, but I need a horse. I was hoping the two of you could help me find one."

"Hold on," said Hans quite loudly, "you actually plan to go to the savage camp! Did you lose your mind up there?"

Suddenly, Lancen thought he heard branches moving to their left along the church wall. Waiting several moments, he listened intently for further disruption. After a moment, and somewhat paranoid, he threw on his hood and looked back to Hans with conviction. "I have to go," he said confidently.

"Why?"

"You probably wouldn't understand."

Hans smirked and threw his arms up. "Try me!"

Once again Lancen was tempted to tell the truth. He wanted to explain that he had been attacked by legionnaires on the mountain, that they killed his dog, and that he would not rest until he got revenge. He wished they could know the pain that he had been through so that they could understand, but again, he knew that the truth would not be wise to share.

"It is time for me to make my mark on the world. If those emeralds were worth hundreds of drachmas, then two bags would be worth a thousand," Lancen reasoned, "and if one Ashlander can produce that so easily, then imagine how much wealth can be found at his camp. They have no use for it besides paying taxes. They can hardly trade, so I plan to take it off their hands. Will you help me?"

"How do I know you are telling the truth?" asked Hans suspiciously. "Show us the gems you have left."

Lancen undid the pouch at his waist and emptied the gleaming stones into his hand. "This bag was full. The elf promised double in Obuthahn, *double*!"

"Why would we trust a savage on his word?"

"You don't need to trust him. Just me," Lancen answered, now beginning to lose hope. "Please."

"You *did* lose your mind," Hans immediately responded, exasperated. Looking around curiously, he hushed his tone. "You show up out of nowhere and expect us to help you play games with a savage tribe? We haven't seen you in a year! Listen, I am sorry about what happened to Sidna, but for all we know you are a drunk and an outlaw."

"This is not just a game," defended Lancen. "The victor of the Hero's Trial is immediately placed in high rank in the tribe and rewarded with who knows what riches. If I win, I may even gain access to their entire treasury. This is an opportunity. It is an adventure!"

Hans rolled his eyes. "Adventures are for children. You seem to be forgetting that the savages are the enemy. They are who we should be fighting, not joining!"

"Hence why I want to rob them!" Lancen exclaimed, losing his nerve. It was a bluff, but he knew Hans, and in this case the truth wasn't going to fly.

"The savages are a mindless and cruel people. They deserve no breath for all they want to do is steal ours. I won't help you unless you plan to spill their blood."

"We believe that because it is all we have ever been told, but what is the real truth?" Lancen suggested.

Hans seemed taken aback. "That sounded an awful lot like you were defending them! Do it again and I will arrest you!"

Lancen bit his tongue and clenched his fists. Speaking slowly, he held a calm demeanor, "I am sorry, Hans. I am sorry, Avik. I never should have left you, but you must understand to some degree what I was going through. My mother had just been killed — by the Legion, and I couldn't stand the thought of staying. The pain in this city is thick as steel, but I am here now, and I need your help."

Avik caught Hans by the shoulder as the boy turned to walk away.

"I believe him," argued the Shaharan, "do you remember the times at the mill when we said nothing would tear us apart? We spoke of riches and fame. Now we have an opportunity to help Lancen achieve that. Legion or not, Nobles or not, the important part was always that we were in it together."

Hans shook his head and stared at the ground, looking upset.

"Please help me," Lancen pleaded to Hans. "All I need is a horse."

Hans closed his eyes and contemplated. "That isn't true," he finally stated.

Lancen dropped his head. It was over.

"You are going to need three," said Hans.

"What?" responded Lancen and Avik in near unison.

"You are going to Obuthahn, and we are coming with you. Our goal was always wealth and power. The Legion was just a stepping-stone to get there…well, we don't need that step now so screw it. You said double that sack of emeralds, right?"

Lancen nodded and laughed, "That's right."

"Avik and I get a sack and a half, plus the majority of whatever we steal. Then we all come back to Calderon."

"Done," Lancen stated. He disagreed about returning to the city but wasn't about to argue now that he finally had them. He would cross that bridge when they got there. "So you are with me?"

A small grin formed on Hans' face. "It looks like we are."

Lancen sighed in relief, but then quickly turned his head. Once again, he thought he heard a branch move to his left, only this time it was followed by the crunch of a footstep.

"Did you hear that?"

Lancen turned from his friends toward the sound. Before him was a thick of trees and foliage. An old moss-covered statue of King Theroll was barely visible through the vegetation. There was movement behind it, and Lancen was swift to investigate. Pulling the dagger from his thigh, he stepped toward the eavesdropper near the chapel wall. Moving carefully, he jumped around the statue and in the same motion swung his knife to point at the intruder.

Jaw dropping, he let the weapon fall and stepped backward. His breath left him as his eyes widened. Before his face and sitting in the dirt, was Princess Adalyn, daughter of the Duke of Calderon.

CHAPTER 8

How could this be happening? It made sense that Adalyn would be here. When Lancen had seen her in the past, she was often coming out from behind the chapel, but he had trouble comprehending her being here now, dressed in commoner clothes, and within two feet of him. What had she heard? What should he say? There was no way she would recognize him like he recognized her, and now he was just standing there, saying nothing, with his mouth wide open and breath cut off. This was going to be terrible.

Noticing his state of shock, Adalyn spoke. Her voice was sweet as honey, her gaze locked on Lancen. "Forgive me, I didn't mean to startle you."

Lancen's heart pounded as Hans and Avik approached his side. He tried to speak, but no words could find their way past his tongue.

"How much did you hear?" Hans fired immediately.

Adalyn's blue eyes dashed to the ground and then up to Hans. Lancen was transfixed.

"I heard very little," the princess said flustered, "just a little regarding a journey to the Ashlands, and…okay I heard everything, but I will not tell anyone at the castle, I swear!"

"Wait, the castle?" questioned Avik bluntly.

Before she could respond, Lancen nervously spoke for her, "This is Princess Adalyn, Duke Roland's daughter."

Hans' brow raised. A wry smile began to form in the corner of his mouth. He and Avik exchanged a quick glance. In the past,

Lancen had spoken frequently of the beautiful girl he would see on his way to the mill. Of course, they would have recognized her from public appearances, but with her hair down, clothed in a dirty blouse, she looked like a commoner.

Adalyn eyed Lancen curiously, "I recognize you as well, but I am afraid I haven't learned your name."

Lancen looked back at Adalyn in amazement. His face flushed red. He still couldn't breathe. *Speak, Lancen, SPEAK!*

Laughing, Hans patted him on the back, "This is Lancen Wolf-slayer."

Wolf-slayer! What? Panicking, Lancen bowed and forced words past his lips, "G-good to meet you Prince Adalyl." His tongue twisted in his mouth. This was humiliating! "I mean Princess…Adalyn. These are my friends, Hans and Avik."

The two young men bowed tediously.

Adalyn waved her hand, and protested, "Please don't. I am so tired of people bowing! I would ask that you call me Adalyn, and just Adalyn. No more princess, or highness, or royal hogwash."

Lancen fought to remain calm, but his heart was beating out of control. His adrenaline pumped and his vision focused. Absolutely nothing was going to help him through this. Surrealism, shock, horror, excitement, elation all fell short of describing the emotions coursing over him. He was speaking to Adalyn! She was prettier than he had ever recalled, and she was looking directly at him. She remembered him! He *knew* that she had smiled at him on his many walks to the lumber mill!

"Did you hear anything about the treasuries of Obuthahn?" Lancen asked coolly.

"No," she said quickly, "well, yes, but I swear I will never tell a soul. I promise!"

"Good," said Lancen trying his best to keep eye contact, "and it is good to see you, but if you will excuse us, we really need to be getting on our way."

As Lancen nodded to his friends and turned to leave, Adalyn

grabbed his arm and pleaded, "I want to come with you!"

A chill ran up Lancen's spine. She what? He had fully intended on going alone. Journeying in Serondhel was dangerous and having so many others along would only slow him down. The Natives were highly unlikely to receive him alone, much less an entire company! It wouldn't be wise to bring her, but as he turned back and looked into her longing eyes, a conflict raged inside of him.

This was Princess Adalyn! It was better than anything Lancen had ever dreamed of, but to have the duke's daughter riding along with them, on a cross country adventure, was madness. Surely Roland would not approve of her leaving and would likely send the entire Legion after them. Lancen looked desperately to Hans but received no answer.

"Don't ask me," said Hans. "This is your quest."

Lancen sighed and dropped his head. "I'm sorry, Adalyn, but I can't let you come with us. Believe me, there is nothing I would like more, but it will be too dangerous."

"Danger does not scare me," Adalyn responded eagerly. "And I do not care if you are thieves or killers or anything. All I want is to get as far away from that castle as possible."

Lancen looked again to Hans.

"Brother, this one is on you," Hans responded. "We will follow you either way."

Gritting his teeth, Lancen held his ground, "We can't have the princess of Calderon along with us. It is much too risky. Your father will send who knows how many soldiers after us, and we do not need that target on our backs. Bringing you would be too much of a burden."

"No, I promise I won't be a problem," begged Adalyn. "As for my father, he is on his way to Oritha, a thousand miles away. He is not due back for a month, and even if a messenger is sent to him, it would take weeks for a response to be made. By the time they come after me, we will be far out of range."

Lancen looked at her solemnly and shook his head.

"Lancen, please," said Adalyn, "you don't know what it is like to be cooped up in that castle. My entire life, every decision I have ever been faced with was made for me. I would dream, but I have seen nothing outside of a book! They keep me as a prisoner and then present me to Calderon as majesty. Let me go with you!"

Lancen's heart ached. He wanted so badly to say yes and allow her access to the freedom she craved. It seemed that every part of him wanted to spend time with her, but at what cost? The lives of Hans and Avik? There was no way for him to justify her request.

"I am so sorry," Lancen answered. "There are just too many variables with you in the picture. The Legion would surely come after us. Every city of Serondhel would receive word of your disappearance. You would be a great burden."

Adalyn's expression softened as she nodded and looked away from the boys. Tears formed in her eyes and soon began to roll down her cheeks. Lancen had talked to her for five minutes and had already made her cry. Perfect.

"I would rather die in the wilderness than spend one more night in the castle," she said gloomily. "You said you need horses. I can provide you with the best mounts in the region. I can get food from the pantry, and clothes from storage, blankets, and packs, anything we will need."

It was a last stage effort, but she looked to Lancen with hope in her eyes. He saw the hurt in them, the longing for something more than her current existence. It was the same longing he had felt himself so many times on the mountain. She needed this as much as he needed revenge, and horses. Perhaps the pros could outweigh the cons. Or maybe he was about to make the poorest decision of his life.

"Okay," said Lancen, "you've convinced me. If you can get us horses and weapons, we will receive you as one of our company. Adalyn, I would love for you to join us."

Without warning, the young woman leapt forward and threw

her arms around Lancen. He felt the warmth of her body against his, the soft skin of her arms around his neck. He could smell the sweet floral fragrance of her hair. Releasing him a moment later she followed suit with Avik and Hans.

Brushing off the daze that had enveloped him so rapidly, Lancen picked up his dagger and returned it to its holster.

"Well come on," he said. "We have a lot of work to do."

Adalyn wiped the tears from her cheeks, and a contagious smile spread across her face. Lighting up like a candle, she stood up straight and put her hands on her hips. "So what's the plan?"

CHAPTER 9

The afternoon turned swiftly into night, and black clouds settled in over the city. By sundown, lightning was flashing in the sky, and heavy rain pounded the earth. Roaring like the beast it was, the storm threw fierce wind across all things living. The streets of Calderon were vacant. Citizens hid beneath their various shelters as the guards ran to and fro, helping people escape the divines' wrath.

Lancen stood drenched with Hans and Avik just outside of the castle walls. They had spent the last several hours gathering essentials for their journey and planning their course. Seeing as there was no road in direct route to the Native camp, crossing the many miles of grasslands and mountain forests in so short a time would prove an incredible challenge. They needed horses, and because of Adalyn, they were getting the best in the region.

"You are sure she will be there?" called Hans over the storm. It had been made more and more evident how afraid he was of being caught by the Legion. Penalties for soldiers gone rogue were greater than that for an average citizen. If they were to be caught taking horses from the duke's stable, the consequences would be severe. Lancen, however, had nothing to lose. He did not fear the Legion.

"She'll be there," he hollered back, turning the corner to move onto the castle grounds. His friends followed closely. The legionnaires normally defending the premises appeared to have taken shelter. With the castle towering on the hill ahead of them, Lancen could see no obstacles between himself and his destination.

The three moved hastily toward the stables.

Once inside, they counted eight stalls on both sides of a long median, nearly every space occupied by a fine steed. Bearing heavy shadows, the building was dark, except for a single lit lantern near its center. Working swiftly in the flittering light was Adalyn, soaking wet, but clad in an elegant violet gown. She had already finished dressing two horses, both strong-looking roans, and was now working on the third, a tall and black thoroughbred.

"Come quickly," she said as they entered, "we do not have much time. They already know that I am up to something."

Lancen waved Hans and Avik to the prepared mounts. "Get them ready, those are yours."

"I have strapped an iron sword to both of them. I know they aren't great, but they were all I could manage," said Adalyn, preparing the saddle for the black animal, "and these are the finest horses we have. My father's men will be furious when they discover they are missing."

"So you mean that we aren't allowed to take them?" asked Hans.

"Tell me you're joking," said Avik, closing his eyes and shaking his head, pained by the remark.

"They are reluctant to allow me beyond my bedroom door," said Adalyn, a little less brash. "I have never had an unsupervised ride."

"Well maybe we should take some less significant horses, some that wouldn't be missed so much," suggested Hans, "just to be safe."

"The way I see it, if you are going to do something that you shouldn't, you had better make it worthwhile," said Adalyn, tying the last of her current bundle of supplies together. "Now, Lancen, will you help me with this saddle? This one is yours."

Lancen located a saddle blanket and stepped toward the beast. Kicking its feet, the animal shied away. Lancen had never worked with horses much. His knowledge of the ins and outs of making them comfortable was minimal. The truth was he would be afraid too if strangers were straddling him for an adventure that he had never signed up for.

"The storm is making them nervous," said Adalyn, "and Shera does not know you. She is my father's favorite horse and was always a timid one. Be sure to stand in front of her so she can see you. You have to gain her trust."

Lancen did so. The mare tensed and neighed.

"Do not worry, Shera," said Adalyn, "he is a friend. Try holding out your hand, Lancen, palm forward, but do not touch her."

As he did there was another deafening roll of thunder, causing the horse to move backward in fright. Lancen recoiled in fear of it rearing.

"Be confident, and talk her down," said Adalyn. "Tell her everything will be alright."

Lancen straightened up and looked into the animal's eyes. "It will be alright," he said stepping closer. "It is only a storm. It can't hurt you. Just calm down so we can get out of here."

The longer he held out his hand the less threatening he must have seemed. The black steed eventually gave in and moved forward to touch its head to his palm. The sense of calm and trust that came over it was empowering. Lancen felt an instant connection with the animal that he had rarely experienced before.

"There you go," he said, stroking her nose. In no time he and Adalyn were able to get it saddled and loaded. Hans and Avik had already mounted and were ready to go.

"*HEY!*" yelled a deep voiced man from the large open doors of the stable's entrance. Hairs immediately stood up on the back of Lancen's neck. Not only had they been caught, but he recognized the voice.

"Get behind me," Lancen whispered to Adalyn. Worry was evident in her expression. Pulling his iron sword from its sheath, Lancen stepped slowly out of the stall and into the center aisle. With new-found courage he stood assertive and faced their guests.

In his sight was the large, ugly leader of the Legion brigade he had met on the mountain. The man with the gold tooth stood before him drenched from head to toe along with four other legionnaires.

"You?" the man shouted in surprise, pointing his finger in recognition. Drawing his blade, he spat an order, "Stand down, boy! Hand over the princess!"

Adalyn hid herself behind Lancen and placed her hands softly at his waist. Hans and Avik remained atop their roans, frozen in trepidation.

"I am not his to give," called Adalyn, keeping her voice level. "I have my own free will and am here according to it! You will do nothing of it, Captain!"

Lancen stared down his rival with madness in his eyes. Goldtooth was a captain in the Legion and personally acquainted with the princess, but to Lancen, he was nothing more than a murderous sleaze. The captain getting between him and destiny just once was a time too many.

"You do not want to be around this boy," said Goldtooth gravely. "Trust me, Adalyn. He is a murderer and a danger to the kingdom. What would your father have to say?"

Lancen felt the princess stiffen behind him. Was it possible that she believed Goldtooth's accusation? Would she now take Lancen for a criminal? The part that scared him the most was that the truth would soon be uncovered. In some ways, Lancen *was* scum, but he was trying to make amends. He was determined to.

"He's lying, Adalyn," he told her calmly, "get on the horse."

The girl reluctantly did as she was told. Lancen squeezed the leather handle of his blade until his knuckles were white, anger coursing violently through him like the run-off in the city gutters. With a trembling jaw, he stepped slowly forward.

"Lancen, we need to go," said Hans nervously, not taking his eyes off Goldtooth. "It isn't worth dying for. Back off!"

"This man killed my dog," was all Lancen managed to say. Hatred had broken through all stays and flooded his being. The thought of revenge overwhelmed all others. It was now his opportunity to seize the moment, but just as emotion commanded him to attack, his vision darkened until all was shadow. After a brief moment he saw the image of a woman, outstanding from the blackness all around her. Decorated from head to toe in jewels, she looked to her feet. Her face was carved to perfection. Flowing white hair drifted over her shoulders and fell like drapes to the floor. She lifted her head and gazed directly at Lancen, seeming to look deeper than in the eyes alone, to penetrate something much more hidden. The woman uttered a single word, and it cut like a dagger into his soul—RUN!

Lancen's vision returned as fast as it had departed, and he stumbled backward at the sudden immersion into reality. Adrenaline pumping, he watched as the soldiers began running toward him. In an instant, before he even realized what he was doing, he had sheathed his blade and jumped onto Shera behind Adalyn. Kicking its sides, he narrowly avoided the reach of a blade as the animal turned and bolted out through the back door of the stable. Time seemed to alternate radically between fast and slow motion, the world involuntarily spinning around him. Looking back, he saw Hans and Avik right on his tail.

In full control and yet none at all, Lancen rallied the black steed to the eastern gates and tore through them, finding himself on the road to Transiric. Slowly his blood began to settle, and he gradually regained full control and consciousness. Adalyn's wet hair bounced lightly under his chin, still carrying its floral savor. Her body was warm against his. The dreamlike aspect of the contact nearly stunned him.

The four riders had traversed several miles beyond the walls of the city. The storm had settled slightly, and the sound of hooves beating the road competed with the abrasive wind hitting their faces.

"Lancen, how far are we going tonight?" yelled Hans from some distance. "We are going to kill the horses! *Lancen*!"

Lancen kept his gaze forward, repeatedly kicking the sides of his steed. He was still catching up to reality. He didn't know how far they had come or how much further they could go. For how long had they been riding?

"To the river!" he answered after some time.

What had happened to him? Had fear taken over? Or was it anger? He could remember his actions but seemed to have had little control over them. There was something very unearthly about what had stolen him from conscience. It was a force greater than any he had ever encountered, and there was no way for him to explain it. All he knew was that he had been told to run, and that was precisely what he did.

CHAPTER 10

The weather had lightened. While the moons gleamed brightly from above, clouds were fleeing the sky. Running gently through the Grasslands, the wide river rushed softly nearby. The ground was wet, and the sweet smell of rain filled the air.

The company of four had managed to find a flat area just off the bank of the river and nearly a mile north of the road. Sheltered from its view, they felt reasonably secure from Goldtooth and any other pursuer of the night. Hans sat near the fire while Avik wandered about looking for anything dry enough to burn. Lancen stood by the horses, attempting to clear his mind, a task most difficult with Adalyn only a few feet away. He viewed his mare and ran a hand down her nose. It was truly a magnificent animal. Black from head to toe, it stared back at him with reddish eyes that evoked a sense of comradery.

"What did you say her name was?" Lancen asked the princess, looking for an excuse to break the silence.

Adalyn held a look of fulfillment as she paid kind attention to the other two horses. She answered, "That's Shera."

"Shera, that's right," repeated Lancen, "no doubt named after the divine Noshera?"

"You said it," replied Adalyn, excited at the subject for conversation. "My father named her. He had an infatuation with the gods. He always had so many questions."

Lancen ran a hand down the side of the horse's face and contemplated. "Well Shera is a beautiful name for a beautiful horse," he said, "but I would think that after the outlaw of worship, the Duke of Calderon would change the name of his horse."

"The catch is we never worshipped. My family had more of an interest in the gods than an actual belief in them. My father and the king were often at odds anyway. He has a thousand laws; there's no need to strictly adhere to all of them, right? My father figures we give up enough in this kingdom as it is. So things like Shera, symbols of beauty, are important to hang on to. But it would be nice, you know, to believe in something powerful that truly cares for us, don't you think?"

"Sure, it would be nice," Lancen answered, "but there is no use pretending they're real. I know you are here now with me. I know my enemies follow us, but there is no reason to believe in people who are looking down on us from the sky…or whatever they do."

"Yes, I'm just saying that it would be nice to believe," said Adalyn as she made her way to Lancen's side. "I know it was only a savage tradition, but it seems like faith can carry a strength that non-believers will never know. If there is nothing beyond our world, then how sad of an existence are we living in?"

"A sad one indeed," said Lancen. His nerves were apparent as the proximity between himself and the princess was reduced.

A silence briefly fell between them, and Lancen's mind wandered to the blackout that he had experienced in the stables. Could it be that the vision was divine intervention? Had the woman he had seen been Noshera? That was an impossible assumption! How could a divine being communicate with him? If Noshera did exist, then experience showed that she would rather see him dead, unless there was a far greater heartache in store for his future and thus reason for the gods to continue his life.

Pushing the headache of a thought from his mind, he tried to recall anything else that he needed to do for the night. The fact that they had left without a fourth horse for Adalyn loomed a potential threat. Food would have to be rationed and supplies shared.

"I am sorry again that we had to leave before we could pack

your horse," he mentioned to Adalyn, ending the long drum of silence. "You can use my bedroll for tonight."

"What will you sleep on?" she asked sincerely.

"Not sure I'll be sleeping much. Someone ought to keep a watch anyway."

He had napped on the dirt the night before, why not again? Besides, what he had said about having too much on his mind was true. At any rate, he would now be able to collect his thoughts and form a decent plan. He still didn't know how quickly their pace must be to reach Obuthahn by the specified deadline, or most of all, how he would be able to proceed to the Native camp while his friends still thought that the intention was to rob them. How much longer could he hide his true objective?

"Well thank you, Lancen. That is very kind," Adalyn stated with a cute smile. "Do you mind if I go wait by the fire? I am freezing!"

Lancen laughed and nodded. "You don't need my permission! I'll join you in a minute."

Later that night, the four young Nobles sat around the campfire, swapping stories to lighten the mood. The events of the day were overwhelming to put it mildly. It would seem that there were some situations in life that only friends could make easier.

"I really want to see a troll," Avik exclaimed with a dreaming expression. He had always been the adventurous one. It sometimes seemed that there was no physical danger in the world that he wouldn't be willing to face-off with.

"Well there are plenty of them to be found in the Ashlands," replied Adalyn. "It is said that the Natives will throw prisoners into the grottos where trolls nest. Not even bones will come back to the surface."

"And what do you mean you have always wanted to see a troll?" Hans asked wittily. "Have you never looked in a mirror?"

Lancen and Adalyn were unable to hold back a good laugh.

Avik looked at them coldly.

"Do not be asking for my help then when an ash troll walks into camp tonight! Then I will be the one to giggle," he said expressionless.

"I would be crying!" Adalyn supposed between laughs. "It would be an amazing site because the *ash trolls* usually stay in the *Ashlands*!"

"Yeah, you dunce, the trolls don't come out this far," teased Hans. "Why do you think we have never seen one?"

Adalyn laughed, but the exact emotion driving her laughter was difficult to put a finger on. Was it amusement or fear?

"I do not expect it is the trolls we should be worried about, though," she pointed out. "It is the savages that scare me. They have no morality whatsoever and little value for human life. Some of the things they do are completely atrocious! Do we really need to go to the Ashlands? Why can't we just run to Rendonhall or something?"

"Well that would be because pretty boy over there feels inclined to make himself the savage king!" Hans answered humorously.

"Very funny," responded Lancen with heavy sarcasm, "but it isn't about that at all. If I could avoid them completely, I would. Like I've already said, sure, the victor of the Hero's Trial may have a kingly influence, but it is only a means to an end."

"And what about the savages?" Adalyn inquired nervously. "I have heard of many traditions other than the Hero's Trial. They sacrifice innocent people blindly to their gods and then delve into dark magic to empower the corpses — necromancy! They feed on flesh and do all sorts of black rituals! Are you sure it is safe for us to go there?"

Lancen laughed out loud and ran a hand down his face before blurting, "After all you just said? Of course it isn't safe! But higher risk provides for a greater reward. If it was safe, it wouldn't be an adventure, but I do doubt that they will be hostile. Etnah told me that it was imperative I be there."

"Hold on, did you say Etnah?" Adalyn asked with a brow raised and a dropping jaw.

Lancen was confused, responding simply, "Yes, why?"

"Etnah was the name of our servant," said Adalyn. "He worked in our court for years. I suspected it may have been him you were speaking of at the church, but I could hardly fathom it! He and my father were the closest of friends. Etnah was freed the night the messenger came from Oritha. It was maybe a week ago."

Lancen was speechless. Etnah had been a member of the duke's court? If he had still been there only a week ago, then he must have left that very night to find Lancen's cabin! Could it be possible that the messenger from Oritha had something to do with it? Lancen had so many questions brewing for his next meeting with the ash elf.

"This is crazy!" Lancen stated in astonishment. "What was the message?"

Suddenly Adalyn's expression hardened, and she looked to her feet, her typical response to an overwhelming situation. "I don't know," she answered. "My father never allowed me to be involved in matters like that. He always kicked me out when he had duke's business, but he and Etnah were very close. I'm sure it had something to do with why he sought you out."

"Your father was really friends with this animal?" Hans butt in.

"I wouldn't call him that," she answered. "He practically raised me these last couple of years. According to my father, Etnah is the greatest savage in Serondhel."

"Yet you still call him savage," Lancen pointed out.

"I suppose it is a habit," said Adalyn. "Everything I have ever read about the Natives has been resolute on making them the enemy. Most of them consist of nothing but treachery."

"Do you believe your books?" Lancen questioned. "I sometimes wonder what they actually do to be treated so poorly."

"How about when they kill our people on the roads," Hans suggested darkly. "If they would just stay in their camps, we would leave them alone! There is no reason for them to ravage our fields or murder our merchants and then cut them up to use bones as jewelry. They deserve to be hated."

"Perhaps with a little more freedom they wouldn't be inclined to do such things," said Lancen.

"I think you're getting tired, friend," said Hans. "Remember who the enemy is."

"I am well aware of the enemy," stated Lancen. "I'm not trying to defend them. I just question things at times."

"You know, I've been wondering. Why was the Legion after you in the stables?"

"I don't know," said Lancen, "I don't want to talk about it."

"Well I do," said Hans.

"Well I don't!" shouted Lancen.

The group was silent a moment. Hans and Lancen could both feel tensions rising. Fighting would achieve nothing. There was still a long journey ahead.

"Many consider my mother to be a savage," mentioned Avik after some time, "but she is the sweetest person I have ever known. She always helped me feel proud of who I am. I'm going to miss her while we're away."

"Really?" Lancen asked with a smirk. "Well maybe we should have brought momma along with us?"

Avik laughed and kicked dirt toward Lancen. "Shut up!"

"Yeah, shut up!" Hans repeated. "It's my job to make the jokes, and besides, the Shaharans have never been the problem. They at least keep to themselves on the desert shores. It is the elves that are savages."

"And yet it is not the elves we should be afraid of right now," said Lancen. "It is the Legion."

Hans went quiet. The evidence of his concern shown plainly on his face. All four of them were aware of the danger they had found themselves in. The Legion had caught them stealing horses from the castle! Goldtooth knew that Adalyn was with them, and there was never a greater danger than a duke's guard chasing a princess.

After a long while of silence Hans retired to bed and was shortly followed by Avik. Lancen and Adalyn moved beside one another and were intrigued by the random dashing motions of the flame. Though they were both exhausted, their minds were much too active to rest. On a whim they had decided to embark on an expedition that would potentially change their lives forever. The calm skies and the crackling fire provided comfort that they knew may not be available in the future.

"Thank you, by the way," said Adalyn softly, "for allowing me to come with you. I don't think you realize how grateful I am."

"Believe me, it is an honor. I wanted you to join us from the moment I saw you at the chapel, but with you being who *you* are, I just didn't want to risk anything. I am glad you are with us," Lancen responded openly. Looking to Adalyn, his heart raced at the smile he received.

Adalyn paused a moment and stared into the fire. She gazed with captivation and appeared to be deep in thought. After a few moments, she asked, "Have you ever felt like you were worthless?"

Lancen was surprised by the question, but he refused to let her know it. He nodded and chuckled, "More than I care to admit. I have spent the last year of my life just hiding. I've been afraid to face the consequences of a previous life. So, I just shut it out. The Hero's Trial is giving me something to work towards. Before it..."

"I'm glad I am not alone," Adalyn agreed. "Sometimes it just seems like every day of my life is spent in meaningless patterns, you know, like existence doesn't matter. It reminds me of the old song, 'Life as a Slave.'"

Lancen scrunched his brow. "What song?"

"It is so famous!" Adalyn said in a shock, bordering offended. "You have never heard it?"

Lancen shook his head, seeing a brightening in Adalyn's countenance. There was only one thing he would want at this moment. "Can you sing it for me?" he asked.

Adalyn blushed and shook her head. "I have never sung in front of anyone, Lancen. I can't."

"Sing it for me!" Lancen insisted. "You're the one who brought it up!"

Adalyn smiled and again looked to her feet. "Fine, but I am not any good so just pay attention to the words."

As she began, Lancen immediately knew that there was no reason to be bashful. Though she sang softly, not once did she lose pitch or balance, as if there wasn't already enough to like about her. Lancen joyfully listened, taking in every syllable.

> I pray, I strive, and I work to survive
> I wait for the day when I'll feel alive
> I'll rage, I'll struggle, 'til the battle is won
> My eternal progression will never be done
> Although I am plagued with failure and sorrow
> I get through the days by awaiting tomorrow
> I better my future through faith and direction
> And fight through the hours of endless succession

Watching her closely, Lancen was entranced by her blue eyes and long lashes, and as he focused, he did find a connection to the words that she had sung.

"You aren't half-bad," he noted.

Adalyn had no words. Her cheeks were red as roses.

"And I agree with the lyric," Lancen continued. "It is like there is no point in waking up if today will be no more significant than yesterday."

The princess smiled and looked at Lancen kindly. It seemed as if she had inched closer to him, or was it he that had moved toward her?

"Exactly," she said. "I have always wanted more purpose. I am so tired of being surrounded by stone walls."

"I am too," said Lancen, "figuratively speaking. Ever since my foster mother died, I have this burning in my heart that I can't seem to extinguish."

"How long ago did she die?"

Lancen strained at the memory. "Long enough for me to learn how to live without her, but recently enough to still be bitter."

"I am sorry. I lost my mother too. Not to the blade or sickness but gone all the same. She went back to the homeland three months ago. I doubt I will ever see her again."

"Why did she leave?" Lancen asked.

"It was because of my father. She insisted that he was far too caught up in 'dreams of peace.' She said that he paid too little attention to the world around him, and too much on the fantasies he created. She said he was putting us all in danger, that the king would execute our royal family."

Adalyn stopped and took a breath, fighting emotion that was sweeping in. She held out her hand to show him a thin silver ring around her pinky finger. In its center was a small, rounded ruby. "This was her ring. One day I woke up and found it on my night table. She was gone. I miss her, Lancen."

"And you are right to. I know that pain well, and it will never go away, but eventually I have learned to deal with it. At least you know your mother is out there somewhere. At least there is a chance you may meet her again."

"That is much easier to say than to believe," said Adalyn. "If she had asked, I would have gone with her, but now I wouldn't even know where to look."

"But perhaps one day you can try."

Flashes of orange and yellow cast a flickering glow on Adalyn's face. Her expression was dismal. "I doubt it. At the rate things are going, soon no one will be allowed to leave the peninsula. It is quite the odyssey to the homeland and Scharric increasingly tries to make us all his slaves."

"Well if there is ever a way for me to help you, I promise to do everything in my power," Lancen swore, but as he saw tears forming in the girl's eyes, and with the ache growing in his own heart, he knew that he needed to change the subject. "Well this is depressing enough to kill a jester!"

Adalyn laughed. "I agree. I'm sorry, but it has been weighing heavy on my mind lately."

"I don't mind," said Lancen. He loved connecting with the princess on such a matter. He could feel them growing closer. One of his biggest dreams was beginning to come true, and he couldn't appreciate it more.

"You look really nice in that dress by the way," he declared lightheartedly.

Immediately his throat tightened. Had he gone insane? Oh gods, she would think he was an idiot! His breath left him as the words hung in the air.

Rather than cringe and scoot away, Adalyn beamed and ran a hand through her silky blonde hair. "Well thank you, Lancen. You're sweet. I had to put it on to move around the castle without raising too many questions. I know it isn't the best clothing for an adventure."

Lancen released his breath. The relief that spread over him was like cold water on a burn.

"I am really glad you came with us," he said through a calmed breath. "If it wasn't for you, we never would have made it to Obuthahn in time. At first, I was reluctant to have you, but now if you tried to leave us, I wouldn't allow it!"

Adalyn wore an uncontrollable smile and shook her head. There were only inches between her and Lancen. "I don't mean to be strange, but I have felt you were different since the first time I saw you," she said, looking up to meet his gaze. "Thank you, truly, for everything."

Lancen leaned in even closer, magnetized by her bottomless eyes. He could hardly believe this reality he was lucky enough to be placed in. For so long he had dreamed of simply speaking to the princess, and now he could feel the warmth of her breath, the luring draw of her vulnerability. He watched her lips, appearing soft and perfect.

"Hey Adalyn, I found something for you to wear tonight," said Hans suddenly from behind them.

Immediately the two pulled away from one another. Lancen quickly began prodding the fire while Adalyn jumped to her feet to meet the approaching Hans.

"I figured sleeping in a dress wouldn't be the most comfortable."

"Oh, thank you," Adalyn responded, awkwardly accepting the clothing.

"I also have something for you tomorrow," said Hans, clueless to the electric moment that had just transpired.

"Night Wolf-slayer!" he said slugging Lancen on the arm and returning into the darkness.

Lancen looked at once to Adalyn, but after a brief connection she averted her gaze.

"I think it is about time that I call it a night. Are you sure it's alright that I use your bedroll?" she asked.

"Absolutely, I really wouldn't be able to sleep anyway."

"Okay then, goodnight Lancen, and thank you again."

"Goodnight, Adalyn, and if the divines are out there, may they bless your dreams," he said kindly, *and divines curse yours, Hans!*

CHAPTER 11

T he next several days seemed to fly by for Lancen. Growing closer to the princess was wonderful, even if there hadn't been more 'luring' moments between them. For now, Adalyn was either good at harnessing her feelings, or she didn't like him as much as he had hoped. It was stupid, and he hated being so concerned with love while there was so much else to worry about. Regardless, he was content to be reunited with his friends, and for the first time in what seemed like forever, he had begun to look forward to each new day. Though they had traversed miles on end, he felt that he had more energy than ever before.

It had been a fortnight since Etnah had shown up at his mountain home, and the Hero's Trial had snuck up on him far too quickly. The group had journeyed across an incredible distance of long, rolling Grasslands, filled with near endless acres of harvested fields and roaming cattle. They had climbed the beautiful central mountains and crossed through miles and miles of the burnt forest. The Ashlands must have been getting close, but Lancen couldn't help worrying that they would miss the trial and have come all this way for nothing.

Yet amidst the stress of time, one comforting thought remained with him. It had been nearly two weeks since they had left Calderon and Goldtooth had never caught up with them. Lancen could picture the ugly captain and his band of legionnaires stomping in a fury. He saw them spitting and cursing, wandering toward Transiric in disgrace.

Looking around, the current scenery was dull to say the least.

This was the farthest any of the young Nobles had ever been from the Grasslands, and their eyes were opened quickly. Trees were either dead or dying, knee-high brown grass seeming to exist solely for the purpose of hiding the gray dirt beneath. Occasionally an atling would spook and they would watch as it hopped away, but aside from very infrequent moments, the world was incessantly still. The more things around them calmed, the more nervous Lancen became that they would never reach Obuthahn.

The chillness of autumn did not exist in this region. A dry and unnerving warmth caused the young Nobles to shed their coats, and a light smell of sulfur rode along with the comfortable heated breeze. They must have been getting close to the Ashlands, but the shadows were growing long.

"Are you sure we're not lost?" Hans asked at the back of the group. For the last several hours, he had ridden with his head down and bobbing, his eyes wide as if he was going through the most mind-numbing venture of his life.

Lancen pulled on the reigns, bringing Shera to a stop. Adalyn awoke from a soft sleep in front of him.

"We're going the right way," Lancen answered, placing a hand on Adalyn's arm, "but I think we may want to stop for the night. We'll leave early in the morning before dawn and reach Obuthahn just in time."

"I'm glad you are so sure," Hans replied with some annoyance, "because if we don't, we will run out of food. We are almost out now. We only brought supplies for three, remember?"

"Yes, I remember," said Lancen, "but we are going the right way. If it takes us another day, then you can finish up the last of my portion."

"Aren't you as hungry as the rest of us?" Avik asked atop his own mount.

Lancen had to shake his head at the irony. If only they knew how starved he really was! He had been hungry ever since the bite of the death hound. As much as he denied it, he could tell that this was something more than meager portions. It was a hunger that no bread could satisfy, and what worried him most was that he knew why, and it wasn't going to get better.

With a steady stride Keira headed back toward her yurt on the northern side of camp. She and her friends had just finished rounding up a herd of olchers, cow-like creatures that had long beaks and small blind eyes. As she walked, she rolled in her hand a dowelled bracelet that Engle had given her. He was always so kind to her. He was the best man in the camp, and she liked him. She liked him more than she could ever explain, but she somehow knew that it wasn't love. Her heart never raced when she saw him. The fire within her stomach never danced or fluttered as the legends often told. Yet, considering all things, she knew that she should count herself lucky.

As her mind wandered and continued to roll without stopping, so did her feet, past the central amphitheater, across the shallow river, and along a crude, hardened path toward the outskirts of Obuthahn. As she grew near to her home, she could begin to make out the soft sounds of a tuparah. The melodic high-tone of the flute-like instrument spoke a familiar importance to her heart. Where had she heard this tune before? Beginning to hum along, the words of an old song began to slide into her mind. With deep interest, she began to sing them as they came.

> There once was a man
> Along a desert and stream
> But the cloak of the devil
> Was a simple regime

Humming along, she retrieved a brush from a bag at her side and began to run it through her worked and tangled hair. It was a beautiful brush with a handle of atling bone and bristles made of the stiff hair from an olcher's back. It had been given to her by her mother. It was the one thing that Keira had managed to take with her from Shaharum.

His heart was turned cold
As the story was told

She still couldn't place where the song had come from, but it brought memories of her childhood. She remembered playing in the river as a young girl with dark clouds swiftly rolling in overhead. People were yelling at her to get inside. It was the first ash storm she had experienced. She remembered being so afraid.

And the hope of the man
Was that he could go home
But the rocks and the shadows
Are where he will roam

As the melody continued and Keira approached her yurt, the brush fell from her grasp. The song had been sung to her during that storm. It had been sung to her during many storms and calmed her each time. She now recalled who it was that had offered it!

Several yards ahead, sitting on the steps of her home, was a thin black figure. Tears filled her eyes as she beheld the elf that she had missed for so long.

"Etnah!" she cried, dashing to embrace the person who had raised her.

Tears rolled freely down Etnah's face as he wrapped his arms around the young woman. He was unable to find any words requisite for their reunion.

Keira buried her head against his chest. "What happened to you?" she asked, hiding no emotion. "Everyone thought you were dead. That is what the warriors reported! Things have been so hard without you!"

It had been two long years since the elf had last set foot in

Obuthahn. "I was taken," said Etnah soberly, "but I'm back now, and that is what matters."

Keira tried to catch her breath. She had come to accept the thought of him being gone. She had found peace in believing he had joined with the roots of the earth to bring light and color to all the living. In her mind Etnah had been dining with Noshera and the gods, to bring about peace and freedom for the Natives. It was so difficult to fathom that he had never left this world!

"Look at you," said Etnah, stepping back to gaze at her with loving eyes. "You've grown into a beautiful young lady."

"Where have you been?" Keira asked.

Etnah squinted his eyes and forced a smile. "I was in Calderon among the Nobles," he answered, "but do not worry. I was treated fair enough."

"By the tyrant?" Keira asked in surprise. "But how? How did you end up there? How did you escape?"

"All questions will be answered in time, young one. Just know that it was never my will to leave. I was taken as a slave — though I use the term loosely — and that is enough for the time being. Let us simply enjoy our reunion. And tell me, what have I missed in the last couple of years?"

CHAPTER 12

L ancen had just finished tying up the horses when he heard a loud cry. It sounded like the howl of a wolf, but much more human. At first, he thought he had imagined it, but then there was another, a sound so hostile that it immediately produced a sense of danger. The noises grew until they were all around camp and growing closer. Turning about Lancen knew that there was no time to run. As quickly as possible he collected the three iron swords and sprinted to the center of camp where Avik had been digging a firepit. Lancen handed him a blade and tossed another to an incoming Hans. Adalyn rushed to Lancen's side as he searched frantically in all directions. There were gray trees everywhere, with nothing at all visible beyond their branches.

As the shouts and hollers closed in, they began to sound more and more peculiar. They came in definite words, but of no tongue familiar to the Nobles. They evoked a feeling of threat and madness with each syllable. Could these be the Natives, come to sacrifice Lancen and his friends to Athleon? With his sword held tightly, Lancen vowed not to go down without a fight.

It took only a moment before the beings creating the aggressive cries were in sight. About a dozen half-naked Natives poured into visibility through the trees and in a blur rushed into the clearing to surround the Nobles. Among them was one Shaharan and several different breeds of elf, most toting spears or spiked clubs. Some of them were old and strong, others thin and perhaps even younger than Lancen.

Each race was peculiar and distinct. The ash elves were mostly naked above the waist besides an occasional leather pauldron or bracer. They wore loin cloths with leather chaps, and their boots were molded and formed from what Lancen assumed was bone meal. The bog elves sported feathers in their braided hair, and the Darkwood elves, short and blonde, wore fur trousers and tall leather boots. All of them collectively seemed to carry either anger or caution on their faces.

Lancen eyed one ash elf in particular, a young-looking Native with ruby earrings and a red tattoo on the side of his face. He had combed black hair on one side of his head while the other remained completely bald. The elf watched Lancen with suspicion but did not seem hateful.

"We mean no harm," Lancen said calmly, eyeing the tip of a spear mere inches from his face. Adalyn cringed and attempted to hide herself behind Lancen's back.

The Natives continued to inch their way in.

"Anos yetah gra'ak!" the Shaharan among the Natives shrieked. He growled and bared teeth like a dog prepared to bite. A certain animal quality existed in not only him, but all of the strange warriors.

The Ashlanders were guarded and ready to attack at any moment, but Lancen, Hans, and Avik stood firm. If there was any fear inside of them, they weren't about to show it. Adalyn on the other hand, recoiled in terror. With his free hand, Lancen gave hers a confident squeeze. He wanted to tell her that everything was going to be alright, that he had things under control, and once again they would soon be sitting peacefully around a campfire to swap stories and watch the flame. But for now, the squeeze would have to do.

"We are not familiar with the ways of the Natives," said Lancen, trying to keep his voice steady, "and if we have broken any of your customs by camping here, we will ask your forgiveness. We come in peace."

Lancen eyed them with confidence, avoiding judgment and

taking time to look at each of them individually. He also held his sword strongly, prepared to pounce at any movement. How was he going to get out of this one? He was unsure of what to share with the strangers, but he needed to do something. Why not speak the truth for once?

"We are travelling to Obuthahn to participate in the Hero's Trial," he stated forcefully.

At once the Natives shouted and cursed. Looking one to another, they threw up their arms and prodded the air with outrage.

"Mov notei tahk lay parnuum!" the Shaharan cried. He was one of the younger in the crowd, but very tall and broad, not dissimilar to Avik. He couldn't have been older than nineteen.

Lancen looked at Avik in desperation. "Do you understand any of this?"

Avik remained peeled on the other Shaharan, braced for a fight. "Seriously?" he retorted. "You know I don't. My mother was no savage."

Lancen addressed the Natives carefully. He hadn't come all this way just to be ambushed and killed on the eve of the trial.

"We mean no harm," he repeated, focusing on the ash elf with the red tattoo — the most reasonable looking of the lot. "If you are of Obuthahn, then we know that you understand the tongue of the Nobles."

The black-skinned elf spat and looked at Lancen with disgust. "Aye, we speak your pathetic tongue, but how does the tyrant expect to join in the Hero's Trial?"

"I was invited by one of your own," Lancen stated plainly. He may have underestimated the empathy of this particular elf.

"No tyrant can have that honor!" the elf shot back amidst growls.

"You must die for such a notion!" the Shaharan snarled.

The ash elf lowered his spear and turned to his vocal companion. "No!" he shouted. "We will not kill them here, Engle.

We will take them to the chief. If he deems worthy, then they will leave the Ashlands with their lives. If not, then you have my word that I will slit their throats myself."

Adalyn gasped as the Shaharan named Engle lowered his club and walked over to the ash elf. Hans and Avik remained ready for the worst, prepared to battle at any moment. Lancen debated on striking while the attention of the elves was divided, but three against twelve?

After a brief conversation in the Native language, Engle again addressed the Nobles. "Very well, it is not my wish, but you will come to our leader. Then we'll kill you."

"Then your leader will see that we come with no ill intentions," said Lancen.

Following a very swift internal debate, he let his blade fall to the dirt. He had dreamed of adventure for his entire life, but as of now he longed for nothing but the warmth of his fireplace and the safety of his mountain home. Turning to his friends he motioned for them to lower their weapons.

"Is Obuthahn far?"

"It's just over the hill and across the valley. Come, try anything and our mercy will expire," the ash elf commanded.

"What about our horses?" Adalyn asked in concern.

"They will be brought to Obuthahn," spoke the ash elf. "They belong to us now."

The strange warriors prodded at Lancen and his friends, pushing them forward and into the trees. The shadows of the hour were numerous and eerie. Everything in this land seemed to be dark and depressed, even its native people. After a short trek uphill and through the dying forest, they reached the line of wood and were greeted by the red of dusk.

When the Nobles had adjusted to the contrast of the open space, their eyes widened as they beheld the great valley of dust and ash. Truly it was a land that had to be seen in order to capture the full vesture of its barren nature. A thin but long river ran from small blackened mountains in the north to as far as the eye could see southward. Flatlands and jagged rocks mingled throughout the basin. Jutting plateaus were frequent and awe inspiring, and in the distance to the west, the gigantic Ash Mountains loomed fearless and daunting.

Between the mountains and the Nobles rested a large collection of cloth tents and primitive wooden yurts. In total, there were hundreds, if not thousands gathered together tightly in groups of five or six around community firepits and wells. Torches were being lit sporadically and magnified the civilization in the darkening world. So this was Obuthahn.

It wasn't until they were prodded again that the Nobles' state of awe was reduced. Passing by many boulders and burnt logs, they walked on. As numerous as the rocks across the land were the many bones of different shapes and sizes. Lancen noted that some were atling, some probably troll, and some were unmistakably human. In the air was a light and bitter smell of decay. There was not a Noble in the world that would live surrounded by these conditions. Perhaps there was more truth to the term 'savage' than even the most prejudiced people believed.

After an unnerving walk across the valley, the group finally approached the edges of camp. Found there was a careful and unpleasant reception. Natives of every shape and color left their shacks to greet the incoming party, casting nervous glares in the direction of the outlanders. Many spat at the Nobles' feet and cursed them in the Native tongue. The inevitable aura of hatred and judgment bit at Lancen's skin, but he and his friends had expected as much. It was nothing they hadn't been prepared for.

As Lancen viewed the primitive Ashlanders, an odd feeling of embarrassment came over him. Who was he to walk into their camp, with swords and horses? The elves and Shaharans of Obuthahn were debased beyond measure, oblivious to the many common luxuries of the Nobles. Most were dressed sparsely in the same tattered cloth that completed their shelters. Few wore fur and jewelry of stone. A good number of the healthiest looking males sported various light armors, but overall, the sunken eyes and countenances, mixed with the disapproving expressions ate at Lancen's heart. He felt as if parts of their souls had died along with their deteriorating mortal form. To the Natives, even the poorest Noble was an aristocrat. Surely the divines had forsaken them.

Citizens of the kingdom of Oritha never went without a meal. They threw away what they couldn't finish. Their water was clean. Their clothes were expensive. As much as the Legion taxed them and for every one freedom King Scharric stole from their lives, they took for granted a thousand luxuries.

The final straw for Lancen's sympathy was worn on the face of a young child, no more than five or six. It was a small boy, black-skinned and dismal. Every bone of his body was visible through thin and dirt covered skin. As hungry as Lancen thought he was himself, he knew that this innocent child had suffered far more than he. There was little hope on the boy's face, only pain was evident.

As they walked it became clear that there were no classes of people in Obuthahn. Every member of the clan shared the same struggle. Each humble shack was roughly the size of Lancen's cabin, but four, five, or even six Natives were seen filing out through each door. The oppression was apparent, and with every step Lancen took, he felt deeper for their pain. He and they had a common enemy.

Once at the town's center, a sizable crowd had gathered to watch the friction. A hooded ash elf exited one of the larger wooden structures in the vicinity. It was a tall elf in a stained black robe that grazed the ground with each step. His red eyes dimly glowed in the late dusk, and with a white ring in his nose and heavy black eyebrows, the Native looked upon Lancen and his friends with concern.

"Eltou! Tahk Lai? Mov no kok meltai? What have you to do with these tyrant?" the robed elf exclaimed toward the young ash elf leading the Native warriors.

"Master Shekii," Eltou greeted with a bow, "we found this pack of scum in the burnt forest. We desire to bring them before my father for judgment."

"Denied," replied Shekii bluntly. "Chief Shikobin can't be bothered with such ridiculous matters. He is with Lady Nihwiah preparing for the trial."

Eltou gripped his spear and pointed to Lancen. "I understand, but this pale one claims to have been invited to join in the events."

Lancen wanted to explain himself, the reason behind their coming to Obuthahn. He started, "It's true. I was told—"

"You speak when spoken to, outsider!" Shekii charged angrily. Lancen jumped back in surprise, startled by the sudden fury.

"What claim have you on these tyrant?" the same elf asked Eltou, much more calmly.

"None, besides what they say of the trial," Eltou admitted.

"Then send them back to where they came from! Don't allow them to pollute our air any longer! We can't be burdened with such notions!"

Just then Shekii and Eltou went silent. The crowd of Natives hushed and moved away from the Nobles. A tall and energetic elf approached the group with his head tilted sharply to the side— Etnah. Lancen noticed a young woman with him, a Shaharan, with light brown hair and smooth tan skin. She was dressed in an old blue shirt and hide trousers. She looked directly at Lancen and glared. Clearly, she as the others carried a strong bias against the Nobles.

"I called the pale boy here," Etnah announced, entering their midst.

There were several gasps from the audience as Shekii himself seemed taken aback. "Chief Etnah?" he exclaimed. "We thought you to be dead!"

Etnah nodded and turned in a circle to view all the spectators, waving at some and giving odd looks to others. Finally, his gaze rested on Adalyn, and his eyes narrowed. "Well," he said with divided attention, "I am not dead."

Everyone was silent as Lancen's jaw slowly dropped. How many more surprises was he in for? Etnah was a former chief of Obuthahn! Of all people, Etnah? If that was true, then how had he ended up in the courts of Calderon?

"And though I am honored to be called Chief, that title no longer belongs to me," stated Etnah to an astonished multitude. "Shikobin leads this clan now. I am aware of his position and abilities. He shall not be removed."

"It has been years," said Shekii in bewilderment, "so what is it that you desire?"

"I only wish to rejoin the ranks in the council," said Etnah, looking to Lancen. "For as we are all aware it takes a councilman to recruit a subject of trial."

Chatter broke out amongst the watchful Natives. Engle and the Shaharan girl turned angrily to one another, discussing the outrage of such a possibility. Lancen looked to Adalyn. Her eyes were filled with fearful tears. She looked longingly at him for comfort. All he managed to do in return was mouth the words, "It will be okay."

"I fear that this situation has grown far beyond my ability to judge," Shekii noted with heavy breaths. He pushed up the sleeves of his cloak and wiped his brow. "I will call for Shikobin."

As Shekii left to consult the chief, civility departed with him. Natives spat and shouted at Etnah and the foreigners, being contained only by a few of the initial crew of warriors. Cursing and disgust filled the air. The young Shaharan girl shook her head at Etnah in revulsion.

The former chief nodded in understanding and turned to the four Nobles. "Lancen, I am glad you made it safely," he said, patting the young man on the arm, "but it was not wise to bring guests. The duke's daughter? That was especially foolish."

"I understand," Lancen responded, "but I never could have made it here without her, or my friends."

"Even so I fear what will become of them. You, I can vouch for!" Etnah smiled and nodded to the others. "And oh Adalyn, how are you, my lady?"

Adalyn let out a short laugh to hide her nerves. "I'm okay for now," she answered. "My father will never find out I'm here."

"I certainly hope not," Etnah replied, "for both our sakes. Roland was my friend, but I fear to see the wrong end of his wrath."

The elf forced a smile and extended his hand to Hans and Avik, who both shook it reluctantly. "I am Etnah by the way."

"That would be Hans and Avik," Lancen introduced. "They're not a problem. They are loyal and upright."

"Ah, good," said Etnah, "but I am not worried about their uprightness, bird. I am worried about what will happen to their corpses after they are forced to the altar."

Hans laughed obnoxiously. "Wait a second! Our corpses? Well you're quite high and mighty aren't you *Chief*, friend of the duke?" he slithered in confidently.

Etnah looked at the boy with an unshaken glance. "Aye, and you're quite the troll hunter aren't you *Halfling*?"

The others couldn't help but smile. Hans rolled his eyes and pretended to be distracted by the rioting Natives, but as the brief moment of humor dissolved, the angry Ashlanders did become unnerving. The hatred at face value was severe. Though the four Nobles in particular had never done anything wrong to the deprived people, the Natives produced a bitterness all the same. It seemed like an age before Shekii returned to sight, calling for order and the people's attention.

"Shikobin calls you and the boy to Nihwiah's yurt," Shekii told Etnah carefully. "Tread lightly my friend. The news of your arrival, much less the boy's, was ill-received. You will find little understanding in the chief and vatisus."

Etnah accepted the news and motioned for Lancen to follow him away from the crowd and beyond several battered shelters. Lancen gave Adalyn a reassuring glance before agreeing. As he moved past the spiteful Natives, he tried not to let their hatred penetrate his heart. They were ignorant of truth, just like the Nobles. If the common citizen of the kingdom knew what kind of poverty the Natives were in, things would change. Lancen just needed to survive long enough to exploit that information.

Nerves bit at him as he stayed as near as possible to Etnah's back. At once it hit him how tired and stressed he was. He longed to fall into his bed, put his feet toward the fire, and allow Rune to lick his fingers. Unfortunately, the privilege of comfort was dead, and so was Rune. At this point Lancen would be grateful for any opportunity to rest again.

Before he had prepared mentally, he and the elf neared the largest wooden yurt of Obuthahn. It was circular and elevated several feet, standing atop thin wooden supports. Several banners of different colors hung from its outer walls, and a thatched roof rested like a hat atop them. A plain sheet of red cloth hung in the doorway. Before they ascended the steps, Etnah stopped and placed a finger on Lancen's chest.

"You are about to meet the vatisus, the most revered member of Obuthahn," the elf explained softly. "It is customary to touch three fingers of your right hand to your forehead and then extend them towards her in greeting. It is a symbol of respect and can be used towards all women as a sign of affection, or in this case honor. Understand?"

Lancen nodded and watched the red cloth door with determination. He had made it to Obuthahn. He had reconnected with Etnah. Winning the approval of two clan leaders should be no trouble, right?

Etnah trotted up the steps and pulled aside the veil. "Alright then. After you, boy."

CHAPTER 13

L ancen stepped into the one room yurt with caution and surveyed his surroundings. Dark cloth draped over the walls, bearing crude images of trolls and elves. Hanging from the roof were many bones and unique artifacts, along with glass bottles of strange liquids and powders. In the center of the structure a ring of fire produced green and indigo flames, casting dark smoke through a small hole in the roof. A curious and sweet smell filled Lancen's nostrils.

Across the room, the vatisus and chief stood discussing one with another. In the dim green light, their ash elven features were very dark and shadowed, causing them to nearly disappear into the cloth drapery. However, it was no question that they were a spectacle. Nihwiah's skin was the darkest of blacks. Her hair was pulled back behind her tall elven ears and fell in a bundle below her waist, nearing the floor. She was clothed in a decorated robe of a variety of colors, and several beaded necklaces dangled from her neck to her naval.

Shikobin looked equally exotic in a bleached white breastplate that seemed to be alive. Electric veins ran up and down like lightning on its surface. He was tall and thin with massive defined muscles. His head was bald except for a single strip running across the center of his cranium. A long and rugged goatee extended beneath his mouth and chin.

Lancen took a deep breath, and immediately the smoky air clogged his throat and forced him to cough. As he tried to subdue the reaction, a sudden chill came over him.

"Do not worry young one. It is only the smoke of dehydrated charro shell," consoled Nihwiah half-heartedly. Her voice was low and raspy. Her eyes emanated sheer wisdom, piercing and red in the dark room.

Once he had gotten a hold of himself Lancen bowed and saluted her as instructed. *What the hell is a charro?* He thought to himself.

Etnah also bowed to degrading stares near equal to those Lancen received. Shikobin could not take his eyes off the former chief. Baring teeth, the two stood in rigidity. Lancen noticed that beneath Shikobin's hostile eyes were red tattooed lines, looking like rudimentary nails extending from his eyelids to mid-cheeks.

"Etnah, it's certainly a surprise to see you here," Shikobin barked, walking toward the entering duo. "Most in this clan assumed you were dead, but do not tell me that in these two short years you have forgotten our traditions and joined forces with the tyrant."

Etnah lapped his tongue and refused to blink. "Shikobin, it has been far too long my old friend," he said stepping to the chief and putting a hand on his shoulder, a customary way for Natives to greet a brother. "I hope you know that I would never betray Obuthahn, nor undermine its authority. I would never stab a brother in the back!"

The tension between the two seemed as thick as the smoke.

Sensing this, Nihwiah stepped between them. "Now is not the time to dwell on past sins when so many are evident in the present. Etnah, why do you pour poison into the wine, an outsider among the chosen people? You know it has been spoken for generations that Obah-a-Tou must be of Native birth!"

Etnah tore a smirk glare from Shikobin and addressed the vatisus with respect. "My lady, I do not question the divinations of past wisdom, but I cannot favor that wisdom over the prophecy itself."

"But do you realize what you have done here?" Nihwiah asked in all seriousness. She clasped her long-nailed hands together to keep them from shaking. "You have invited a tyrant to our holiest event of the year! The gods will not take kindly to such allowance! Even on your head, the atonement may not be attained!"

"He is not here to hurt us," reasoned Etnah. "He only comes to be tested against the prophecy."

"He has come to destroy us!" Nihwiah shrieked with worried eyes and a trembling mouth.

"If it is an explanation you desire, then I can provide," replied Etnah calmly.

"Em nol mahkte," said Nihwiah, "then please, do it quickly."

Etnah grabbed Lancen by the arm and pulled him to his side. "Come here, boy," the elf demanded impatiently. "Tell them about your parents."

Lancen hesitated for a moment, trying to make eye contact with Nihwiah. "I can't. I have never met them."

Nihwiah stared reluctantly to Lancen's feet, her attention gained. Her features were hardened, but there was a very certain beauty about her.

Shikobin grit his teeth and rolled his eyes.

"This means nothing!" he shouted. "There are thousands of orphans in Serondhel, many in our very clan!"

Etnah patiently accepted the outburst. "Yes, I would agree had I not been told about the boy's birthday. Tell them, bird. Tell them what you told me."

"I recently turned seventeen," Lancen stated, sensing Shikobin's utter hatred. "I celebrate from the night I was dropped off at the orphanage."

"Your birthday was two weeks ago, was it not? Do you remember there being but one moon on that night?" Etnah asked.

Memories flashed back into Lancen's mind — the smoke of his burning home, the crude commotion of the legionnaires, the sword in Rune's side. Lancen cringed and fought back anxiety. The night had been dark, cold, and lonely.

Looking up, he now met Nihwiah's gaze. She watched his eyes

carefully, eager to hear his response. He answered, completely ignorant of why these questions mattered. "Come to think of it there has always been one moon on those nights."

"Interesting! Orphaned in infancy on the one moon night?" Etnah added rhetorically.

"There is no need to recite prophecy here!" Shikobin blurted. "This proves nothing!"

"Boy, tell them why you are pale, why your eyes are gray."

Lancen's heart jumped. Did Etnah expect him to admit to skolism? Yes, his appearance had changed. Yes, since the night of the death hounds he had carried an unshakable hunger, but he *was not* a skole! He didn't respond.

"Speak when prompted, child, or face the flame." Nihwiah said, more to teach than to criticize.

Etnah waved a hand and clicked his tongue. "No, I will not condemn his silence. For some it is a gift. But tell me, Lancen, what attacked you that night at your cabin?"

Death hounds, Lancen thought, but he wasn't yet prepared to deal with it. The truth would be known in time, and until then Lancen would claim to be healthy, unscathed by darkness.

"They were just wolves, large and vicious wolves."

Etnah nodded mockingly toward Shikobin. "The wolf's dark cry shall spark anew?"

Shikobin shook his head in wrath. "No! Obah-a-Tou cannot be a tyrant! This is an outrage! This boy should be put to death for even setting foot in Obuthahn, and you, Etnah, should be ashamed to carry our blood!"

"I should be ashamed?" Etnah repeated, pounding a fist against his chest. "You do not have a shadow of right to dictate where shame will fall!"

"*SILENCE!*" Nihwiah cried, holding an open hand toward the heavens. "We are here to decide the fate of this pale tyrant, not to dwell on past disputes! Be calm, Shikobin, for I do not believe this is our champion. I trust fully in those that came before us and will not be so quick to turn against their prophecies. However, Etnah provides evidence that is difficult to ignore."

"My lady," began Shikobin, "you cannot trust pleading words from a lying mouth! If we test a tyrant in the Hero's Trial, then we shall be burned for blasphemy!"

"My mind is not yet made, Chief," assured Nihwiah, "I must first test the boy's integrity. For Etnah I have trusted for years. Though he is back from the dead, his words still carry heavy value in my heart. His notions are absurd, but Yehawa has granted me a belief in his honor."

"Perhaps you misread Yehawa's message," the chief pleaded, "and the tyrant is not capable of integrity. We should bind him to a tree and allow the storm to decide his fate!"

"Do not question the spirituality of your vatisus!" Nihwiah fired. Turning slowly to Lancen, she continued, "Pale one, understand that you are an unwelcomed guest here in Obuthahn. Even by the minute chance you did compete and succeed in tomorrow's trial, no one, and especially not I, would accept you as champion! You are interfering in our most highly revered tradition. Should we show mercy we will bring damnation upon our clan! Shikobin is justified in demanding your life."

Lancen stood beside Etnah, trembling. What was he doing? Why had he come to Obuthahn? He should have convinced his friends to join him on some other venture, one that did not involve so much hate. Lancen had come all this way to Obuthahn for nothing but a brutal death. Why had he not kissed the princess on their journey?

"My lady, we must not be closed minded," defended Etnah. "If we will but test him in the trial, then we can rest easy knowing that we did what was necessary in the face of opposition. The Nobles have hurt us far too long for us to throw any chance of vengeance by the wayside."

"We must test him in the trial?" Nihwiah questioned. "And risk losing every ounce of loyalty our people offer us?"

"It is a gamble, I admit, but our people would not be so quick to turn on a vatisus."

"Perhaps not. I have but one question for the boy," said Nihwiah, her piercing eyes burning through Lancen's defenses. "Do you believe that you are Obah-a-Tou?"

Lancen was at a loss. Etnah had not said anything about Obah-a-Tou. He mentioned briefly that Lancen could save the Natives, but nothing of this specific title. Perhaps this was what it meant to 'fit the profile.'

Fighting for words, Lancen let the response, "I don't know of Obah-a-Tou," slip past his tongue.

Immediately Nihwiah groaned in disgust. Shikobin gnashed his teeth and placed a hand on the axe tied to his waist. Etnah stepped in front of Lancen and held up a calming palm.

"I failed to relate that to the boy," Etnah reasoned. "The fault is mine."

Lancen bit his lip, specifically remembering Etnah telling him, *'Now is not the time for you to know sacred details.'*

"Then allow me to educate him," Nihwiah said forcefully. "Obah-a-Tou is the prophesied savior of our people. I imagine it is simply a title for our champion, but let me assure you, child, you are not Obah-a-Tou, nor will you ever be him! You are not worthy to utter his name! He is the hero of prophecy. You shall die on the morrow! I agree with Shikobin, we must settle this as our ancestors. There is a storm brooding. Obah-a-Tou lives in the dust and breathes the ash. You shall be killed by the winds!"

Lancen breathed heavily. His instincts told him to run, flee the yurt and make a break for the burnt forest. It had been a mistake coming here.

"Have you ever been in an ash storm?" Shikobin asked, amused by the distress on Lancen's face.

Lancen shook his head in the negative.

"They are known to tear the Nobles' flesh clean off the bone," the chief explained with a smile. "The dust darkens the sun and the air is so thick you cannot breathe. If you are not sheltered when the storm turns fierce, then you will die! And if by some chance you do not, you will have been torn to shreds. You will attempt to call on the gods for mercy, but will not be able, for your lungs will be filled with ash!"

Lancen's eyes widened. He didn't need an ash storm to take his breath, he couldn't breathe now!

"We give you the opportunity to forfeit the trial and leave our presence immediately. You will be unharmed. Your supplies will be returned to you, but you must leave at once. You have caused enough trouble as it is," Nihwiah offered with a tense stare.

Instantly Lancen wanted to say yes. Everything within him told him to take the offer and leave tonight with his life. He could save Adalyn and continue to grow closer to her. The thought of it brought warmth to his chest. Maybe he didn't need revenge. Romance could calm his troubled soul.

Still, something in the depths of his being would not allow him to quit. He couldn't leave Obuthahn. He had come all this way to find purpose. If he left without achieving anything, then he had only failed himself once again. That he couldn't allow.

Finding a courage deep within, Lancen replied with boldness, "I know little of your customs and even less of your prophecy, but the winds do not scare me. I desire to join in the Hero's Trial. I recognize how absurd it is considering the hatred between our peoples, but if I am your champion, then I will fight for you. Allow me to join in the trial. If I succeed, then you will at least consider me as your champion. If I fail, then you may deal with me as the tyrant."

Etnah raised his eyebrows and looked nervously to Lancen. "That was unwise," he whispered.

Nihwiah turned around and looked into the fire, her long robe swaying. Wafting the charro smoke toward her face, she breathed deeply and released a long sigh. For several moments she looked through the hole in the roof to watch the emerging stars.

"What say you, my lady?" Shikobin inquired, lacking patience. "Shall I take him beyond the camp and leave him for the storm?"

Nihwiah turned her gaze solemnly to the chief, shaking her head to his dismay. "No," she replied, looking to Lancen once more, "no, we will not kill you this night, but perhaps the storm will tomorrow. I will grant your request, child, and may the divines have mercy on my soul. You will compete as a subject in the Hero's Trial. Now be gone! Shikobin and I have much to discuss. If you are wise, you will ignore my acceptance and depart into the night."

Lancen had many questions but was glad to depart from this judgmental scene. He wanted to know exactly what the prophecy entailed. What was Obah-a-Tou supposed to do? How would it contribute to avenging Rune and Sidna? Why wouldn't Etnah tell him the blasting details? And what was going to happen to Adalyn and his friends?

Just as Lancen was about to speak his thanks, Etnah turned him around and walked him to the door. "Divines bless you," the elf mentioned to the chief and vatisus on their way out.

As soon as they were far enough away from the yurt, Lancen turned to the elf perturbed. "Why didn't you tell me about Obah-a-Tou?" he demanded. "I want to hear the prophecy, the whole prophecy!"

Etnah stopped in his tracks and clicking his tongue, turned patiently to the young man. "Would you like to hear my honest response, bird, cut where it would?"

Lancen gave an impatient signal to proceed.

"I did not tell you," Etnah began, "and I *do not* tell you because to this day, to this very moment, I do not believe you are the one. My suspicions are too strong to discard, but that does not give me an excuse to betray my heritage. When I discovered who you were, I could not allow my prejudice to get in the way of the Natives' liberation. I had enough discussions with Roland to recognize the good both our peoples can offer, but I revere our traditions, Lancen."

Lancen groaned to release frustration. There was so much tension and stress building up inside of him, fighting a desperate battle against his composure. The elf had just brought to light more questions that strained his mind.

"So why did you not tell me you were a servant in the castle?" Lancen asked. "And how did you find out who I was, where I lived? Was it the messenger from Oritha?"

"I did not tell you, because it was irrelevant," Etnah responded. "Do not be so curious, friend. Everything will be determined tomorrow. If you are a victor of trial, then there will be no more secrets. You will have my trust, but for now you must be patient."

Lancen shook his head. "I don't want to be patient."

"Life is not always sunshine and rainbows, as I'm sure you are well-aware. Why don't we continue walking, make sure your friends' heads still rest on their shoulders?"

Lancen threw up his arms and began moving again in the late dusk. As they neared where they had left the others, the sounds of jeering filled their ears.

"Curses be upon you for even breathing our sacred air!" a furious Native screamed.

The voice of Hans retaliated quickly, "I'll stop breathing when you do, muck-skin!"

Etnah looked to Lancen in amusement. "That one makes friends easily, no?"

As the two rounded the corner they were met by tormenting Ashlanders. Several more guardsmen had found their way to the clan center to hold back the mobbing crowd, but still the efforts were met with great resistance. Adalyn, Hans, and Avik stood tightly in a circle, surrounded by the same warriors that had escorted them to camp. In a small clearing at the head of the angry crowd, the Shaharan girl Lancen had before noticed paced back and forth, shouting fierce and damning words.

"You are a disgrace to Shaharum!" she cried, pointing furiously to Avik. Her voice was smooth even in anger. "None of you should live to see the dawn!"

"Keira! *ENOUGH!*" Etnah commanded, running to the girl's side. "All of you, *ENOUGH!* There is nothing to be gained here. Our visitors will not dwell with us long, do not worry!"

Keira looked to her guardian with an open mouth, demanding an explanation.

"Keira, go to your yurt and prepare it," Etnah ordered. "It is not my wish, but the outsiders will be staying with us tonight. We have no other options."

Keira stared back at him in astonishment. "You're not serious!" she howled. "How do you even suggest it? Clearly two years with the tyrant has destroyed your judgment!"

"My exquisite girl, it will only be for tonight. Do not worry."

"How can you even say that?" she heatedly questioned with tear-filled eyes. "Just get out of my sight! I wish you were still dead!"

At that the girl flipped about and pushed through the agitated crowd. Once free she took off running. Etnah watched in duress.

"Go to her yurt. It is the northernmost along the river, a little distance from the main camp. It is not a good idea to tarry here," he told Lancen. Looking the boy dead in the eyes, he nodded and patted him on the arm. "You'll be okay."

And with that Etnah tore through the mess of Natives and chased after his beloved Shaharan.

CHAPTER 14

As night had fallen in its fullness, Lancen and his friends gathered inside of Keira's wooden yurt around a small fire. It was much like Nihwiah's abode but lacked the numerous oddities and was about half the size. Two Native spearman stood at the bottom of the steps beyond the door, fending off the occasional extremist out for blood. The hate experienced earlier had been everything the Nobles were expecting and more. The feud between their peoples was fierce, and it took seeing the condition of the other side to truly understand why. The Natives were more savage than expected, and the Nobles were more of a tyrant than Lancen had ever before believed.

He closed his eyes and rested his head against the wall. He couldn't imagine winning the respect of the Natives. He had come all this way, putting his friends in great danger, and would have nothing to show for it. He was starving and tired. The Legion was after him, and very likely on a direct order from Oritha. How that had come to be Lancen didn't have the slightest clue, but it couldn't be a good omen. What had he ever been thinking? A Noble being a champion of the Natives was preposterous, even if they did share a common enemy. This time he felt as though he had bit off more than he could chew.

"So how are we going to do it?" Hans requested softly enough for the guards not to hear.

"How are we going to do what?" Lancen asked, eyelids closed and heavy.

"You know," Hans insisted, "gain access to their treasury. Did you learn anything from the chief?"

Lancen opened his eyes and sat up straight. He had forgotten that his friends thought they had come here to rob the place.

"Um, no, he didn't say anything," Lancen answered. "I think we should wait until after the trial. Remember that if I succeed, there will be a reward, and it is only after the trial that Etnah will provide more jewels. The Natives will respect us then."

"They will?" Avik asked in surprise. "That is interesting, because an hour ago they seemed intent on cutting our skins off."

Adalyn was silent and stared into the fire. Lancen could see that there was still fright in her eyes, but her emotion was now empty and hopeless. Lancen didn't know how to help her, but he wanted to more than anything. He didn't know what she thought of him, whether she liked him as he liked her, but if he could just keep her safe, then maybe she would in the future. He needed to be strong for her.

"I feel like we should act tonight," whispered Hans, his expression lighting up. "As you said, if Etnah can get a hold of those emeralds, then the savages must have stores of riches. We can find their treasure and steal back our horses before the demented creatures kill us. If we leave on horseback, there will be no way for them to catch us."

"I may have been misguided in believing there are treasuries," Lancen admitted, trying to speak in a way to keep his friends calm. "I didn't know Etnah came from the castle. He may have gotten the jewels there. Do you really believe these people, in their rags, are sitting on stores of riches? We must wait until after the trial, and I don't believe the Natives will kill us."

"I remember one specifically saying he wanted to wear my scalp as a loin cloth," Avik said loudly.

Adalyn cringed. "Please spare the details, Avik. I want those words out of my mind!" she cried, holding her hands over her ears.

"She's right," said Lancen. "We do not need to speak that way. Their threats were empty. The Natives only act that way because they are oppressed."

"You mean the savages," corrected Hans. "I haven't heard you say that word once since you sought us out in Calderon, but it is what they are, Lancen! They are savages. It is what they have always been. It is what they will always be! Are you so blinded by the prospect of power that you cannot see it?"

Lancen lowered his brow. It was true that he had refrained from using the term. Ever since his first conversation with Etnah, he realized that the Natives were at least somewhat justified in their behavior toward the Nobles. The ceremonies and sacrifices were another story, but for some reason when he looked at these people, Lancen saw the same pain on their faces that he himself carried. He was no better than they.

"I am not blinded," Lancen said in response. "If anything, I am the only one that can see clearly, Native or Noble. There are few differences between us and them. We both desire love and freedom. The Natives haven't seen either in the last fifty years. We took their land and left them with a broken culture. It was never their fault! It is the Legion that is savage!"

At once the room turned to a silence so abrupt it sent chills straight through Lancen's bones. Hans, Avik, and Adalyn all looked at him in disbelief. Lancen's face turned red as he lost his breath in humiliation. So the truth was out.

"What are you saying?" Avik asked, with hurt already beginning to show on his face. "Is this about Sidna?"

Lancen looked back at his friend anxiously. He didn't know how to answer that question. For their entire lives Hans and Avik had dreamed of serving in the King's Legion, fighting off the savage armies, and defending their nation. For Lancen to hold the Legion as an enemy meant that he was betraying everything his friends had ever believed. He was struck by a crashing wave of guilt. They now knew his real heart.

"It is more than just Sidna, much more," said Lancen avoiding eye contact. "Remember the captain that showed up in the stables? He came to my home on the mountain. He was sent to kill me. I was off checking traps when they arrived and burned my cabin to the ground. When I came back, they killed Rune. I fought them and barely escaped with my life."

"You should have told us," Hans stated, clearly holding in a storm of anger.

"I couldn't," Lancen said solemnly. "I missed you two so much. I wasn't going to bring you into this, but the legionnaires at the gate stole all those emeralds. I had nowhere else to turn. I have wanted to be honest, but at the cost of losing our friendship?"

"Why were they after you?" Avik questioned. He appeared nervous and fatigued. Several days of black stubble darkened his cheeks.

Lancen shook his head, holding in guilt. He couldn't give them an honest answer. He couldn't tell them the truth about Sidna. "I have no idea."

"It was the messenger from Oritha," said Adalyn, a fire being lit inside her head. "It all makes sense now. The courier must have brought a writ for your execution. That is why Etnah went straight to you. My father gave him a jump on the Legion!"

Lancen lost his breath. Could that be true? Had the messenger carried an order for his death? There was nothing he could have done to warrant such blatant actions from the king. Did Scharric himself know of the prophecy, and feel threatened by Lancen's potential among the Natives? It was the only explanation that made sense. Lancen felt like a window was opened in his mind, casting light on all things hidden in shadow.

"Why would the king order your execution?" Hans asked, not connecting the dots.

"Don't you see?" Adalyn answered before Lancen could respond. "There is weight to the savage prophecy! King Scharric does not want the Natives to have hope. Etnah travelled to your cabin to warn you! This is no coincidence. It is fate that has brought us here!"

Before anyone could respond, an angry Keira burst into the

yurt, followed by a reluctant Etnah.

Walking directly to Lancen, the Shaharan girl spoke harshly, "I have waited my entire life to be a subject of trial, and I will not allow you to ruin that occasion. You will die tomorrow, even if I have to slit your throat myself! I cannot refuse your stay in my home, but I will never accept you as a guest!"

Lancen didn't know what to say. He looked to Etnah for answers. The older ash elf looked weary and only nodded his head, being of no help.

Searching for a polite response, Lancen replied, "I don't mean to go against any traditions, but after all I have learned, I need to know for myself who I really am."

"I can answer that!" Keira scoffed. "You are the dirt beneath the rocks. You are scum, the brutal tyrant! Do you have any idea what you are meddling with here?"

"I have been told enough to know what I am getting into," Lancen answered calmly.

"False!" Keira cried. Her hair hung over the soft features of her face. Tears rolled freely down her dirt smeared cheeks. "You have no idea! Not only is the Hero's Trial too dangerous for your prissy blood, but you are desecrating a sacred tradition! You'll offend the gods and bring damnation to everyone you care about!"

Lancen noticed his friends watching tensely. He tried to be patient, but a fire was sparking inside of him. Why did the Natives so blindly despise him?

"I do not fear offending the gods!" Lancen said boldly. "They have been against me for some time now — and I can handle the trial."

"It does not matter what the precise task is, you will not survive it!" Keira warned madly, her expression was a cross between ferocious and disheartened. "Many have completed the trial, but none were the prophesied hero. Now you prance into our camp, into my home, boasting that you are Obah-a-Tou!"

"I am not boasting anything!" shouted Lancen, losing his nerve.

"That is enough, Keira," Etnah chimed in smoothly.

The girl paid Etnah little mind. She was fuming and desperate. "Pray to the divines that my people do not dismember you and your girlfriend limb by limb and feed you to the trolls!"

Lancen immediately rose to his feet with clenched fists. She had now crossed the line! He retaliated, "And you pray that the Legion does not come for us and spray your peoples' blood across the ash!"

"*THAT'S IT!*" Etnah screamed suddenly, separating the two. "No more! I've had it with this racist slander!"

Keira looked to her elder with disgust. "You may be able to sleep under the same roof as these creatures, but I cannot!" she shouted, gathering a blanket and cushion. "I'll be just north by the river. Only come if you have convinced them to leave!" And on that note the young Shaharan stormed out of the yurt and into the night.

Etnah put a hand to his face and rubbed his temple. The stress was evident in the bags under his eyes and the heavy lines around his mouth. "I suggest you all get some sleep," he mentioned. "Tomorrow will not be a happy day."

As Etnah turned once more to chase his loved one, Lancen remained standing, a cumbersome anger stealing his self-control. What was he even here for? He had escaped the Legion and was hundreds of miles from their grasp. What did he owe to the Natives? Nothing! He couldn't stand their ignorance! No glory or wealth was worth this ridicule. Vengeance on Goldtooth was nothing but a dream. It only existed in the imaginations of the night.

He could really use Sidna in this moment. His entire life she had always been there to calm him down and help him through his struggles. Now when he needed her most, the memory of her brought nothing but more pain. If only he believed in the divines as she did, perhaps he could find solace. As it was, however, he did not believe. Therefore, he could lean on nothing but his own strength.

"After tomorrow we will get as far away from this place as possible," Lancen stated, staring angrily out the open doorway.

"We?" Hans responded, rising to his feet. "'We' no longer exist. An enemy of the Legion is an enemy of mine."

Hans rose to his feet and gathered a few random supplies from those the Natives had allowed them to use. "I'm going back to Calderon. Avik, Princess, you are welcome to join me." Hans breathed heavy and strapped the items to his back. He stood before Lancen with a spiteful expression. Spitting at his feet, the livid young noble tore away his glare and left the abode, never looking back.

CHAPTER 15

After the departure of Hans, the remaining three Nobles sat in a silent shock. Adalyn and Avik remained seated, both appearing conflicted. Lancen watched them with uneasiness, waiting for one of them to follow their friend into the night, but they never did. Instead they sat nervously, staring blindly into the fire and refusing to pull their gaze to any other focus. The longer they stayed, the more apparent it became that they were not going to leave. Lancen had their loyalty for now, whether he deserved it or not.

After several minutes of brutal silence, Avik moved away from the fire and to his bed roll without saying a word. Adalyn finally looked at Lancen, giving a fearful but assuring nod before finding her own bed. Left alone to the soft crackling of the flame, loneliness welled inside him once more. It felt as if every force in the universe was pinned against him. His king hated him, his friends hated him, and the people he had journeyed hundreds of miles to fight for hated him. He felt like there was nowhere lower for him to fall. Following only a glimmer of hope, he had now lost everything.

He could hardly believe Hans was gone. For two weeks he had managed to reconnect with his best friends, and now one of them was completely repulsed. The pain of losing Hans in this manner was strikingly similar to watching Rune die. The loss of a friend left a vacancy in the soul that only time would fill. He just hoped that the prominence of its sting would diminish quickly.

Lancen was exhausted physically and emotionally. His hunger should have been the least of his worries, and yet it ached inside of him, continually coming back to his mind. He feared what he was growing into. Etnah had said, *'I believe you are becoming a skole, but are not one yet.'* What did that entail? How vile were these skoles, if they truly existed? And how much time until the beast would overtake him? Above all his many fears, he did not want to become a monster.

Perhaps his best option was to disappear. He thought of going deep into the mountains to set up a new homestead. He could purchase a new dog and set up a system of traps as he had before. Unintentionally he had led his friends into great risk, but he couldn't allow them to get hurt. He was going to protect Adalyn, even if it meant protecting her from himself.

But as the thoughts became more prominent, he had to discard them. He had left his friends before and wasn't about to do it again. Leaving now, he would have accomplished nothing. No matter what he turned into, skole or not, he was never going to allow himself to give up. Even if he lost every last thing there was to fight for, he would raise his sword nonetheless.

Eventually, Lancen tried to sleep but remained awake for hours too deep in thought to rest. The sleepless nights were adding up, but he was completely helpless to prevent them. After a long while he crawled out of his bed, looking for peace. Stretching his back, he wandered through the door of the yurt. The night was incredibly calm and the air outside cool, though still much warmer than the western region. The guards that had been protecting the abode were several yards away, pacing quietly with lit torches. Lancen was surprised to find Etnah sitting on the bottom step in front of him, smoking and looking up at the stars.

"Couldn't sleep eh, Lancen?" the elf asked without even turning his head.

"Not even close," said Lancen soberly. "You couldn't either?"

Etnah bowed his head and smiled. "Not even close. Have a seat," he said, motioning to the empty space beside him. He was smoking a peculiar looking pipe. It, to no surprise, appeared to be crafted of bone, with a short white stem and a diamond shaped bowl.

"It is a beautiful night," Lancen mentioned as he accepted the invitation and lowered himself to a seat at the Native's side. Looking to the sky, he took in the endless abyss of heavenly lights. He loved the stars, particularly on cloudless nights such as this. They represented perplexity and simplicity, emanating in their deepest forms.

"Aye, it is the calm before the storm. So what is keeping you up?" Etnah asked before taking a long drag of smoke.

"Too many things to count," Lancen responded honestly, "but if I had to name one, Kiera was right. I have no idea what I've gotten myself into. I've endangered myself and my friends, and I fear it will be for nothing."

"Aye," said Etnah simply. "You are a bird remember. You fly where you need to go whether the winds are strong or not. You are in a foreign land among a foreign people. You're not supposed to feel comfortable. Don't strain yourself."

Lancen shook his head and smiled. Etnah was something else. "I suppose you're right," he agreed, feeling somewhat eased. "So, what has been keeping you from sleep?"

"Oh, Keira partly," said Etnah, "and you partly. As you can imagine, you and your friends are not the only ones in danger. I really put myself on a dangling limb bringing you here. The only difference between my danger and yours is that I am not afraid."

Lancen narrowed his gaze and argued, "I am not afraid! I am just overwhelmed. My home has been destroyed, your people hate my existence, and my best friend just abandoned me."

"Wait, which friend?"

"Hans."

"Was that the short one?"

Lancen nodded.

"Hmmph!" grunted Etnah. He wriggled his jaw and pursed his lips. "I rather liked him."

Lancen laughed. Perhaps Etnah was the one person in the world that could see things from his point of view, and not completely despise a foreign person on no basis. For some reason, that similarity had Lancen slightly worried.

"My Keira would disagree though. I don't think she cared for him," said Etnah.

"Yeah, she doesn't care much for me either," mentioned Lancen. "What is your relation to her anyway?"

"I raised her," the elf answered. "I've been her guardian ever since she was a small child. Even as chief, I would always put her first. Now she can't even look at me."

"How did you end up with her?"

"I was leading a group of men to Shaharum during the Lurid War. Her parents must have died in the skirmish, and I found Keira, wailing in a burning home."

"I believe my parents were also killed in the war. I can think of no other explanation."

Etnah was silent a moment.

"Me either. Here," he said, handing Lancen the curious bone pipe.

Putting the end in his mouth, Lancen inhaled. He coughed as the thick smoke rolled down his throat. The taste was sweet like honey. Etnah smirked lightly.

"It's better hot," said the elf taking the pipe back. Holding it suspiciously, Etnah placed his free hand palm-up beneath its bowl and concentrated. Suddenly waves of heat emerged from his fingertips with a red glow. Lancen could feel the warmth from where he sat.

"How did you do that?" Lancen required in amazement.

"Have you never seen magic before?"

Lancen's jaw lowered. "Magic? I have heard of it in stories, but never believed it was real!"

"It amazes me how little they teach your people, but unfortunately magic is a dying art even among Natives."

"Can anyone use magic?" Lancen asked, his curiosity peaked.

"There is some magic that anyone can use, yes, and some that can only be called by those chosen," Etnah taught. "Care to give it a try?"

Lancen nodded and took the pipe. "What do I do?"

Etnah smiled and rolled his neck before proceeding. "Magic itself exists in many forms. It lives in a reality parallel to our own, in a community waiting to be roused. All we must do is find the appropriate keys to summon it. You must dig within yourself where no other emotions lie and drive the heat to your fingers."

Lancen placed his hand beneath the bowl of the pipe as Etnah had done. Closing his eyes, he battered through a crowded mind. He had a mob of complaints and stresses that were difficult to set aside. Depending on his instincts, he blocked out the pain as he often had before, trying to stop new thoughts as they entered his mind. Just as he felt his head was clear, he pictured Adalyn's face, smiling in the sunlight as they ate breakfast, preparing for the day's journey. As hard as Lancen tried, he couldn't force her image from his mind. Concentrating on the pipe, he tried to release his thoughts and heat his hand, but nothing happened. Pain he could discard but love he could not.

"Perhaps tonight isn't the best time for me to start," Lancen admitted, removing his hand. "There is far too much on my mind."

"Well one day you may have greater worries, and depend on magic to get you through," said Etnah taking back the pipe.

"Maybe you can just teach me about it for now, and I can practice later," said Lancen. "What are some of the keys you will need?"

"Often it is a clear mind, as you so obviously failed to attain. Though sometimes it is a certain word or phrase. Sometimes you will need a key substance. Other times you may require a combination. I can't tell you why this is."

"Can magic be used as a weapon?"

"Rarely," Etnah answered, "but yes, it is possible. I have been able to use it in conflict on occasion, but typically one is not able to draw power for the reason of death."

"Any clue as to why that is?"

"I have my suspicions, but the truth I do not know. My belief is that the realm of magic belongs to the divines. We are only granted permission to use it. Noshera, goddess of love, Athleon, god of strength, and Yehawa god of guidance: these divines will scarcely allow permission to use it in violence. However, I have heard tale of elves tapping into a different source, the fourth and fallen divine."

"Droth," said Lancen.

"You know of him?"

"Yes, I know that he betrayed the divines."

"Then be careful with the use of his name! You never know who is watching. We in the Native realm refer to him as the antethei. I would urge you to do the same. What else do you know?"

"He stood for a millennium in corruption and chaos. Eventually Athleon battled him, and killed him, according to the stories."

Etnah threw his head back and laughed. "Killed? That is hard to believe! Though Athleon did fight him. The fallen lord was defeated and cast out, forsaken by the three. His powers were removed from him, although his influence can still be found in the dark reaches of evil."

"Dro—the antethei isn't gone?" Lancen asked.

"No, he's around somewhere, lurking in the shadows, cursing all forms of life because he is lower than them all. Or at least that is what we are taught. We do not speak of him, nor of his mountain in the East."

"His mountain?"

"Are you deaf?" Etnah responded quickly. "I just said we do not speak of it, but for your sake I will answer. Yes, we named the mountain that erupted and created the Ashlands after him, but take this for what it's worth, Lancen, Droth is the devil himself. Do not become too curious. It is the divines you should focus on."

Lancen thought it best not to respond. Looking to the sky, he again wondered at the numberless stars. The two moons shone brightly, both at different lunar stages. Could there be something greater out there, influencing all who walked the land? Lancen just couldn't accept magic as sufficient proof.

"Lancen, what will you do if you are our champion?" Etnah inquired sincerely.

Lancen contemplated. There was yet another question he didn't know the answer to. He had several options. He could take the two bags of emeralds Etnah promised and disappear. He could find refuge in the mountains, or perhaps passage on a ship to the homeland. Out of reach and out of mind seemed the best option, but his heart wouldn't allow it. As much as he desperately wanted to abandon the racist Natives, he knew that he ought to stay. It would be the fight for what was right, to end the tyranny and oppression caused by the Legion. And for the love of Noshera, he did vow to kill the bastard Goldtooth.

"It is difficult to say for sure," he finally told the elf. "It all rides on the back of what happens tomorrow, but I am curious as to how I fit into the prophecy. If the Legion is after me, then it must be for a reason. I don't love your people Etnah, not yet, but pity them I do. If I will fight anyone in the end, it will be the king."

Etnah placed the pipe on the step to his side and ran a hand over his shaven head. "I suspect what challenge Shikobin will present tomorrow," he said with a serious glance. "I was the subject of trial many years myself, a long time ago. Some even suspected I was Obah-a-Tou after I had finally finished as a victor, but there was one trial that I could never complete. I served as chief many years and the times I presented this myself were not few. No one has ever finished it. Many have died."

"What would you tell someone that is willing to listen?" Lancen asked hopefully. He had been waiting for something like this, anything that would help prepare him for the events on the morrow.

Etnah sat in thought a moment and clicked his tongue in his own signature way. Finally, he reached into the hide satchel at his waist and removed a small glass vial. Washing around within was maybe a mouthful of dark blue liquid. The elf placed it in Lancen's palm.

"This is an extract of warlew jelly. It clears the lungs, providing means for them to separate air from liquid. In other words, it temporarily allows you to breathe under water. This is all I will give you. If somehow you are our hero, you will know when to use it."

Lancen viewed the potion suspiciously, having no idea when or why he would need it. "How long will the effects last?" he asked.

"It is difficult to tell," said Etnah. "Perhaps a few minutes, maybe more, maybe less."

"Well that's comforting."

CHAPTER 16

The following morning Lancen stood amongst the other subjects in a small tent pitched in the middle of what the Natives called 'the pit.' Earlier, Etnah had fitted him with Native bone greaves and boots while Avik had loaned him some oversized leather armor. He wore little else besides some minimal necessities in a small pack. Bearing no weapon other than the old iron sword provided by Adalyn and his own rusty dagger, he felt ill prepared to face an enemy. He missed his bow and arrows and did not feel at ease doing anything dangerous without them. Though he had often dreamed of it, the young Noble could not have felt less comfortable dressing up for battle.

He was standing in a dark shelter with a very hostile Keira at his side. Other angry faces in the room were Engle, Yantik (a Darkwood elf paling in comparison), and a focused Eltou. Shikobin and Nihwiah stood directly behind Lancen, breathing hot air on his neck. The quarters were so small that each person stood shoulder to shoulder, only adding to the tension. A chanting crowd hollered outside in the amphitheater, barely audible over a brutal wind. Whether or not the ash and dust would rise, it was clear that a storm was coming.

Lancen worried about his friends. Etnah had taken them under his charge. As of that morning Avik seemed to be holding up fine, but Adalyn's nerves were abundant. Lancen hoped she was okay and longed for an opportunity to console her.

Yantik quickly stole his attention. Leaning forward the Darkwood elf locked his eyes on Lancen and aggressively motioned across his throat. Lancen sneered and nodded as the cheering outside abruptly went silent. He wasn't afraid of a tiny pale elf.

"Clan brothers and sisters, I take great honor in welcoming you to the Hero's Trial!" a familiar voice called just beyond the cloth wall. Lancen recognized it as Shekii of the tribal council. "Year after year we have held the trial to test the valor of our finest young warriors. We determine the brave and establish our future leaders, with a prayer that we will one day find our true savior, Obah-a-Tou!

"For years we have waited under the repressing hand of the tyrant, but the great day of our liberation is near! Brothers and sisters, are you prepared to meet the subjects of trial?"

Once again, the crowd released a blaring noise. Lancen held his breath and braced himself. His palms were sweating, legs shaky.

"First, I am honored to announce Engle, son of Nokivi!" Shekii yelled. The Shaharan boy nodded and skipped through the tent door, throwing his arms into the air. The audience roared.

"Yantik, son of Yantaka!" The small elf looked at Lancen and spit at his face before exiting the shelter to a positive applaud. With a glare of annoyance, Lancen wiped wet drops from his forehead and cheeks.

"Now for our newest and youngest contestant. She was orphaned at a very young age and taken in by our former chief, Etnah. At fifteen years old she is now strong and beautiful. Keira, daughter of Etnah!" Shekii's enthusiasm was short lived as the multitude fell silent. Keira took a deep breath and looked to Lancen with hate-filled eyes. To no sound other than the howling storm, she left the tent in disgrace.

Shekii immediately demanded applause, producing a less than meaningful response. Lancen stared at the dirt beneath him. Her mere association with Etnah had been enough to cause disproof among her people. The former chief had only respected the prophecy enough to lay his opinions aside and produce a Noble to compete. Lancen felt an odd compassion for this girl who had done nothing but mock him.

In order to keep the crowd happy, Shekii called for the next subject. "Next is the strongest subject of trial today. He is proven in heroic acts of bravery and intuition. I give you Eltou, son of Shikobin!"

Again, the crowd exploded in delight. The amount of noise that could be created by just a few hundred people was astonishing. The Natives in the amphitheater released their excitement in a hopeful jubilation. Soon they began chanting the young elf's name, and Eltou smiled lightly as he looked to his feet, pausing for dramatic effect. After a moment he leisurely stepped out of the tent. As he did, another wave of cheers erupted.

Taking several minutes for the cries to die down, Shekii reluctantly attempted to continue. Lancen feared what would happen. Was it really necessary to announce him like the others?

"Now I must present our final participant," said Shekii quietly, getting lost in the winds. "He is here only due to striking similarities to the fulfillment of prophecy. I give you Lancen of Calderon."

In an instant the cheers turned cynical. One curse after another proceeded from what seemed like every mouth. Lancen stared courageously at the cloth door in front of him. With no delay he forced his feet to move, one boot after the other. In a near daze, he parted the veil and stepped into the sunlight. At once the wind nearly blew him over. It, combined with the monstrous jeers, sucked at his life-force. With heavy black clouds in the sky, he knew the ash storm was not far away. The confidence and bravery that he had worked so hard to solidify began to melt in rapid pace.

As he walked to where the subjects stood, he searched the crowd diligently for his friends. Face after hateful face watched him in bitterness. Natives of every age, shape, and color filled the seats of the outdoor theater. Finally, as he reached the other contestants, he spotted Adalyn watching him with tear stained cheeks. Her eyes were swollen and red, her hair a mess. Avik stood strong and watched confidently, for a moment meeting Lancen's eyes. Then there was Etnah who looked to the sky with an open mouth and snapped his fingers repeatedly beside his ear.

Lancen narrowed his gaze and resisted a laugh. What on earth was Etnah doing?

Guards on the skirts of the audience attempted to calm the most violent spectators. In the pit, council members waved their hands to quiet them, but the harsh rebuking would not cease. Lancen fought the desire to run, the desire to curse, the desire to cry. It was not easy to stand calmly by while others threw spiteful words that cut like razors. *They aren't savages,* he tried convincing himself. *They are oppressed. They aren't savages.*

"Clansfolk, enough!" Shekii ordered to no avail. "There will be time for judgment, but it is not yet!" The taunts continued.

"*SILENCE!*" a voice screeched from the front of the tent. Nihwiah stepped through the cloth and into view, shortly followed by Shikobin. "*SILENCE!*"

Straightaway the jeering died-down before it utterly ceased. The Natives were immediately compliant to their revered leader, never varying from her wise commands.

"Do not fear, but pray silently that he is not our champion!" Nihwiah called.

Shikobin's enchanted armor sparked as he walked to the front of the pit and called loudly, "Clan brothers and sisters, think of this not as a condemnation to our traditions, but only as a temporary blight! For this year's trial is one of history and one of proving. In the past, many have perished in the pursuit of this challenge. None have completed it."

Lancen's heart raced. Etnah's prediction was correct, and now he had a giant advantage. He had strung the breathing potion next to the key around his neck and reached up to clench it tightly. The Natives waited in pure anticipation. Every eye was glued to Shikobin. Every breath was short, every ear poised to receive the instruction.

"This year," announced Shikobin, "the subjects will travel to Nahabuk's Cavern!"

The Natives exploded into a barrage of hushed whispers. A justified shock resided on various elven faces, including those of the other subjects.

"As we know," Shikobin continued, "Nahabuk was a valiant hero of times long before the 'Noble' tyrant overwhelmed our lands. The valley in which we now stand was once great and prosperous. It is said that Nahabuk was a valiant chief and one of the first of clan Obuthahn. Our river has taken his name and, of course, so has the cavern in which he fought his final battle. In a last and brilliant conflict against the attacking coastal elves, Nahabuk fought off thousands, but was finally slain. It has been reported and verified by numerous witnesses in the following centuries that the crown from his very head still lies deep within the cavern today. Our subjects will be required to retrieve this item of legend and return it to camp Obuthahn."

Shikobin nodded and backed out of the focal point of the crowd. Shekii stepped up and into prominence in nearly as much shock as the rest of his kinsmen.

"The trial for Nahabuk's crown is certainly one of history," the councilman stated, getting a hold of himself. "Many great warriors have fallen in attempts to claim the sacred artifact. Some were even thought to be Obah-a-Tou. Inside the Nahabuk caverns are dangers unknown. There are ferocious creatures such as charros and trolls, but many more that have never been named. Anyone who tarries too long in its tunnels are sure to reach a violent end."

Turning to the subjects, Shekii explained the guidelines of the challenge. "As we know, there is no limit of time in the trial. There may be more than one victor if you wish to band together, but that is not always wise. We require you to bring back the artifact. You may keep anything else you may find, though it is not recommended. Dark forces are at work within the walls of that cave. You do not know what evil may possess the items inside. Subjects, are you ready?"

Lancen nodded but was surprised at the animated response of the others. Keira howled and shook her head rapidly. Eltou threw his head back and released a war cry to the heavens. The others growled and pounded their chests.

"May the divines watch over you," Shekii said, suddenly shooting fire from his palms toward the sky. "Depart!"

CHAPTER 17

Before another word was spoken, the Native subjects took off with the wind at their backs. Lancen looked briefly to Avik and Adalyn before departing. He didn't want to leave them. They were all he had left! But tapping into every ounce of motivation he contained, he forced himself to turn away and chase after the distancing competitors. He burned with emotion as he pushed himself to catch up. He wanted to believe that he wasn't leaving his friends forever, but a painful doubt tried to convince him otherwise.

The longer Lancen ran, the quicker he gained on the other subjects. They had rushed through the numberless blur of shacks and now moved speedily across a barren plain. As he moved, Lancen could feel the sharp stinging of sand attack his neck. Dust rose from the earth and clouded like fog in the air. With the wind behind them, it was clear that the storm would soon catch up. How far was the cavern, and more importantly, could they make it in time?

As the group ran southward, they stayed within close proximity to the river. It amazed Lancen how far the others could run without missing a step. With visibility worsening, Lancen seemed to trip over every random rock or jutting root that came before him. Fatigue seemed to set in early, and dirt was inhaled with every breath. With each step, more and more dust burned his eyes. His throat seemed to be closing by the second. How long until the storm would rip his flesh?

Struggling to continue, Lancen began to lose pace behind the others. It did not take long for them to disappear into the wall of gray ash before him. As they did, a panic quickly entered his being. He couldn't breathe, he couldn't see, and the increasing winds threw debris that scratched his skin. After what seemed like an hour of running aimlessly forward, he began slowing down, but as he did, he managed to spot the silhouette of Eltou on the opposite side of the river.

Turning in relief, but in choking desperation Lancen immediately splashed into the mucky water and moved toward the other side. The current was strong, and as he sunk to his knees it was difficult to keep his balance. When he had neared halfway across the river, he could make out the gaping mouth of a cavern, just off the shore. Ominous skeletons hung beside dead torches on its outer walls. Lancen had lost his breath, but he only needed to make it to the mouth. If he could do that, he would escape the reaper's touch.

As he neared the western bank, and about waist deep in the swift current, Lancen felt the warm pinch of a dagger entering the flesh of his right shoulder. At first there was no pain, only a surprising realization that he had just been stabbed. Before he could process what was happening, two small arms where placed around his neck, and in a solitary moment of distraction he was pulled under the filthy running water. Fully submerged, he gasped for air and took in a big gulp of grimy river. The unexpected liquid shot up his nose and caused an immediate burn in his temple. He was in a very bad position, tumbling downriver and with little way to wriggle himself free, but he needed to fight back.

In a rush of strength, Lancen burst upward out of the water with the creature clinging tightly to his neck. Judging by the weight and size, he finally processed that his attacker was Yantik, the Darkwood elf. Groping at his throat, Lancen tried to break free. A great pressure blocked his airway, and his body screamed for breath. With surprising force, the small elf dragged him back beneath the water's surface.

Pressure in his head built as Lancen fought back up. Desperate, he threw an elbow sharply into Yantik's side and finally freed himself from the harsh cling. Spinning about, he threw a fist mindlessly. Yantik dodged with great agility and countered, landing a fierce strike into the Noble's throat. Again, Lancen gasped for air, but no relief came. After a solid shove, he lost his footing and crashed further downstream. When he again gained balance, he angrily unsheathed his iron blade. Lunging forward, he slashed at the elf, cutting deeply into Yantik's hip. The elf stumbled and fell, and as he struggled to keep his head above the surface, Lancen struck him fiercely in the temple with the butt of his sword. Unconscious, the elf floated swiftly away down the intensifying river.

For a moment Lancen stood still, the mucky water pushing at his side. Trying to catch his breath, he proceeded to the bank of the river and pushed himself over an edge and onto dry land. The storm roared and cast sand like a thousand needles. Soaked in water, his pack was heavy and uncomfortable, pulling roughly on his wounded shoulder. Fighting past the discomfort, Lancen pushed north against the wind. With a hand over his face, he tried to save his eyes from a miserable burn. There was no longer a possibility of getting air, so he held his breath.

Finally, after a brutal struggle, Lancen made it to the mouth of the cave and stumbled inside. Crashing down to his stomach, he inhaled deeply and coughed up muck and ash. In anguish he reached over his shoulder and laid hold of the stone-carved knife still embedded in his flesh. Grimacing, he pulled it free and tossed it aside. Rolling to his back, he looked out to the devastating world. As he did, a strange confidence entered his being, one that he expected would this time stay. With a smile forming on his face, he began to laugh uncontrollably. For a brief moment he felt utterly invincible. He was a survivor, the Legion could not kill him with their soldiers, Yantik could not kill him with his dagger, and the gods could not kill him with their storm.

The fact that the Darkwood elf had attacked him was of no surprise, but *how* he had, jumping on his back in a blind and bitter setting, was. Lancen knew the elf should have killed him, and yet because of the strength of will and arm, he lived. He was finally in a position to accomplish something great. Yes, people detested him, but for now he could handle it. If he could only prove himself, they would surely change their minds. The Natives hated Lancen for his skin color, the Legion hated Lancen for what he meant to the Natives, and Hans hated Lancen for what the Natives meant to him, but he wasn't going to give up. Though everything that walked was out to get him, he would not falter.

When he had finally caught his breath, Lancen recognized the great ache in his upper arm. Painfully, he sat up and removed Avik's leather armor to find his tunic soaked in blood. Ripping off a mucky sleeve, he wrapped his throbbing shoulder tightly. If history were to repeat itself, he knew that he would heal swiftly. It was the bite of the hound that saved him, and the bite of the hound that would kill him.

Sliding the oversized armor back over his head, he tried moving his right arm gingerly. An instant pain shot from the top down to his fingers.

Flesh is weak, Lancen thought as he sucked in another deep breath of the ashless cavern air and rose to his feet. Facing the depths, he saw nothing but blackness. He was going to find the crown of Nahabuk and be the victor of trial. What happened beyond that was more uncertain. With a look of persistence and purpose, he wasted no time, and as the wind howled loudly behind him, he slowly moved forward and into utter darkness.

CHAPTER 18

The cavern of Nahabuk was dark, not like a starlit dimness that one expects from the night, but it was a blackness so heavy that it could be felt. On seldom occasion, small protrusions in the roof or walls would shed in a crack of light, but rather than help Lancen see, they only created an eerie whistle, reminding him of the self-destructing world outside. The air of the tunnels was thick and misty, hosting a chill breeze that left him shivering. Which way had the others gone? And how had they ever seen well enough to get there? Lancen simply felt along the rock wall, cursing himself for not packing anything to burn.

As he made slow progress deeper into the cove, a faint scent triggered his senses. It was strange and yet familiar. The further he walked, the sweeter the smell became. It was pungent and clear.

What the hell is that? Lancen thought.

Then it clicked. *'What the hell is a charro?'*

As soon as the thought came, a barrage of slime flew out of nowhere and splashed onto Lancen's neck. It was a grimy substance that wouldn't wipe off. Through the suffocating darkness a soft green glow began to lighten just beneath his chin, and an itchy burn began to fester. The discharge, whatever it was, produced a cold gleam, causing him to see perhaps a foot or so into the blackness.

In an instant Lancen recognized a moving thing only a few steps in front of him. It was a creature of some sort, large as a horse, and skilled at maneuvering through shadow. There were moments when a green glow could be seen from what looked to be the monster's back, and then in a flash it would disappear. Whether it was dangerous or not, Lancen couldn't tell, but he felt uneasy enough to draw his blade.

Before he was prepared, a spear-like leg hurled toward his head, narrowly missing and causing a spark on the wall behind him. In the blur he saw six long legs, and made out some sort of snappers, long bug-like extrusions extending from the creature's head. They were sharp like blades and clapped swiftly at him, barely missing his face. Then, as fast as it had appeared, the monster retreated back into darkness.

Standing firm, Lancen tried to keep his cool and prepare for the next strike. The charro moved back and forth between shadows irregularly, making it difficult to follow. Out of nowhere, a lightning-quick leg shot at him again. At once he dove out of the way and landed roughly on the rocky floor. Rolling in anticipation, he narrowly avoided the stabs of several legs pounding into the earth beside him, shaking the ground and kicking dust. Stepping over him, the creature reared up on its back four legs, and through a small orifice below its pinchers, spewed another round of the burning slime, hitting the side of Lancen's face.

Pushing quickly to his feet, Lancen leaped backward as the beetle-ish monster snapped its deadly pinchers. The Noble had little time to think as the beast tore after him. He spun about rashly and swung his sword, sparking it off a shell harder than iron. As his heartbeat quickened, just as when the Legion attacked his home, his reflexes and abilities sharpened. He began to predict every movement of his attacker, dodging strike after strike. In a blur, he lunged to the right and battered himself against the stone wall. As the monster turned, he dove beneath it, clutching his sword with both hands. Once more the charro reared up, and as it did, Lancen cast the blade through the spewing orifice and into a soft underbelly.

When he pulled his weapon free, an immediate downpour of greenish slime burst from the mortal wound, landing all over him.

Promptly, he rolled out of the way as the creature tremored and crashed to the ground. It screamed a piercing cry and desperately scurried its legs, only to die a moment later. The charro was defeated.

Rising to his feet, Lancen spit on the glowing shell of the beast's back.

"Pest," he said audibly as he stretched and moved with aching pains. His skin burned where the discharge had hit him, but now his body was warm and senses sharp. Lancen had won again, and as he noticed the body of the charro illuminating the space around it, he had an idea.

Pulling out his dagger, he lowered himself beside the creature and focused on one of its glowing legs. Its shell was too hard to be cut, but at the joints there was vulnerability. After several minutes of sawing, Lancen raised a severed leg to the air. The light it produced was dull, but it was enough. *Take that, darkness.*

Leaving the charro carcass behind, he moved on deeper into the grotto. With his newfound tool, he was able to find a path that weaved between rocks and down a series of shafts. As he moved, he pondered how time had seemed to slow whenever his adrenaline pumped. Although the legends described skoles as vicious flesh-eaters, perhaps, just maybe, they were not so. Lancen hoped above all that he could be an exception, that when the final transformation kicked in, he would still have his mind and his heart. Maybe becoming a skole wasn't such a bad thing.

After perhaps an hour of walking, Lancen exited a tunnel and lurched as he nearly stepped over the edge of a cliff. At once he noticed a bright light below him, perhaps an entire mile away, across a broad valley — a torch burning through the darkness. It was coming from a small tunnel, just beyond a disturbed pool of water. There was no mistaking that it belonged to the other subjects.

It was a comforting notion to have located them, but he knew that they would not feel the same. Personally, Lancen would have liked to join forces with the other subjects, and perhaps it could have happened in another world, but not in Serondhel. Lancen had a better chance of gaining the allegiance of a charro. As he watched their orange firelight slowly diminish, his plan was to follow them, and when the time was right, he would make himself known.

It did not take long before he had found a narrow path down the cliffside and started after the others. As he moved, he kept one eye peeled for Nahabuk's crown. If there had truly been multiple sightings, then his chances of spotting it were good, and because of Etnah's gift, he knew that he would find it somewhere near a body of water. Perhaps it would be by the pool through which the Natives had just passed, or perhaps he would need to wander much deeper into the abyss.

Before Lancen had made it even halfway down the cliffside, a roar sounded in the passage behind him. It was loud and deep, far from human. It sounded like the storm outside but as if it had been condensed and reformed into a monster's body. Whatever had made the noise was big, and it was heading in Lancen's direction.

Blood rushed as the Noble quickened his pace to reach the valley below. Skipping over occasional crevices, he moved as fast as possible toward the tunnel by the pool. With his heart pounding rapidly, he felt a darkness encompassing him yet again. Disturbing noises sounded behind him, and he dared not look back. He couldn't tell if he was being chased, and he didn't want to know. He just needed to get to the tunnel and follow the others. But as he ran, a not so distant sound of a whimper reached his ears. At first, he thought it might be a wounded animal, but as he kept running, the noise grew louder amidst the chaos. Finally, right before he entered the pool, the breeze carried a muffled but unmistakable word — *help*.

Stopping in his tracks, Lancen thought about the plea. It was human in sound, but subtle. His first reaction was to keep going. It must have been one of the other subjects, injured and abandoned, but he couldn't tell which. Whoever it was kept a steady moan and was clearly in pain. Lancen grit his teeth, debating on a course of action. If it were he lying broken in the dark, the Natives wouldn't have given him a second thought. They would be pleased at his suffering. Part of him wanted to feel the same in return. If he were to judge strictly from those he had met in Obuthahn, he would have no choice but to view the Natives as savage, and if he responded to common sense, he would have kept walking, especially with dangers so evidently near, but he couldn't. If Sidna were here, she would never allow him to turn his back on a wounded soul. It was her incessant sense of morality that would never let him walk away. He needed to help.

"*Ragh!*" Lancen barked, knowing what he was going to do. As much as he wanted to enact the opposite, he knew that he must stray from the path and rush toward the sound. Climbing over boulders and leaping across gaps, he followed the whine to its source. The sense of darkness, coupled with angry rumblings of approaching monsters, cut Lancen's breath. Luckily, after travelling only a short distance, he found the source of the whimper beneath a jutting rock, hidden in shadow. Stepping slowly toward it, he could make out the shape of a large-bodied young man lying in the dirt. It was Engle.

"Who's there?" the Shaharan mumbled. His head was down, facing the opposite direction. "Eltou, I told you to get out of here! It's not safe!"

Lancen wasn't sure why, but at the site of the Native, he chose not to approach, ducking behind a nearby rock and out of view. The image of the fallen subject had jolted him. Engle was clenching his neck which bled profusely. His fear had been plain, a pool of crimson soaking his shirt. After a moment, he heard Engle roll over, but harsh and worried breathing confirmed the Native's blindness.

"Who's there?" Engle asked, terrified. "If it's one of you monsters, just finish me off! I'm not afraid of death!"

Lancen crouched low, still deciding not to speak. A frightening scent came to his nose, one that was sweet and desirable—Engle's blood. He knew it was the wolf inside of him, the darkness he now carried, forcing him to crave such a substance. He somehow knew that only a taste would silence the hunger that worsened inside of him. There was so much blood.

"Who's there? *Just kill me!*"

With a struggle, Lancen shook his head and growled. It was the wolf, not he, who had been thinking such wicked designs. He would not allow it to overtake him. He would never result to drinking someone's blood or eating their flesh! He could care less how hungry he became! Refusing the inner beast, he moved from behind his cover and finally responded, "It's Lancen."

At once Engle clenched shut his eyes and grit his teeth. "Oh gods! Not you!" he shot through pained breaths. "Just leave me be. I'm as good as dead anyway."

Lancen forced himself to not walk away. He had no reason to help a savage that hated him. He had no reason to help savages period! Even if he was to become the champion of Obuthahn, there was little they could do to ease his pain or lift his burdens. If he decided to run from them following his return to camp, he would never have to deal with the Natives again. He didn't need them! But somehow, even after all that had happened, he knew the better question was: did they need him? Engle certainly did.

Frustrated, Lancen clenched his fists and asked, "So you want me to leave you for the trolls?"

Engle hooted and opened his eyes. "Trolls? You think trolls did this to me? No, trolls kill their prey, not leave them to bleed."

"Was it a charro?"

Engle laughed obnoxiously. "I kill charros in my sleep. No, whatever this was will kill you. It will kill Eltou, it will kill Keira, and I can only pray that it will come back and finish me off."

Lancen faced Engle again nervously. "What are you talking about?"

"I don't know what they are, but they were fast and strong. They were the most powerful things I've ever seen, but it was so dark." Engle shuddered.

"Where are they?" Lancen asked, looking around.

"They are everywhere, nowhere. You can't see them coming! Just go you filthy tyrant!" shouted Engle.

Lancen played with the thought. Why would he want to help someone so miserable? *AGH!* But he couldn't just walk away! He had already made the decision to stay. Monstrous roars and howls resounded through the valley. If Lancen left, Engle would be dead within minutes.

"I'm going to get you out of here," he said gloomily, "and then I'm going to find that crown."

"No, I don't want your pity!" Engle responded bitterly. "The only thing you can do for me is leave!"

"*Engle! I am trying to help you!*" Lancen seethed. How could this be happening? He was trying to save a life, and still it was prejudice that ruled all! "Listen, I could give a rat's tail about you! I don't care if you live or die, but I'm never going to get what I want unless I help your people! You are making that very difficult!"

"What could *you* possibly want?"

"I want the Legion to bleed!" Lancen yelled loudly enough for any monster nearby to hear.

Engle snorted.

"You're crazy, son of Calderon," he said, grimacing. "I'd rather die than accept help from you!"

Swearing, Lancen unsheathed his sword and held the blade to Engle's throat. With demented howls all around him, he gave one last effort. "This is it Engle, are you ready to die? I'll spare you the suspense!"

Softness dwelt in the Native's eyes. He was far too broken to fight. Tears slowly formed and rolled down his cheeks. The thought of death began to tear his composure, "Okay, okay, just get me out of here."

Immediately Lancen sheathed his sword, tied the charro appendage to his belt, and grabbed Engle's arms, pulling them over his shoulders. Holding the Native's wrists tightly, Lancen half-carried and half-dragged the giant Shaharan. He felt as though he had a bear on his back as he maneuvered steadily toward the cliff-side. The warm blood from Engle's neck dripped onto the side of his face. An inner battle ensued in Lancen to refrain from licking it up.

As he neared the cliffside path to the upper passages, he noticed a chill come over them. He felt they were the target of prying eyes. Hairs stood up on his neck as he struggled onward. The air seemed to be growing colder. Clouds of mist were formed with every breath as a feeling of evil surrounded them. He needed to go faster. Could this be caused by the monsters that had attacked Engle?

It seemed like an age before the light of the cliff's entrance came into view. Though the storm still raged outside, night had clearly fallen. Violent forces of sand and debris blew destructively in the wind. As they moved through the mouth, Engle began slipping in and out of consciousness, just enough to wriggle and twitch, making Lancen's job that much harder. Finally, as they neared what he deemed the safest distance between the raging storm and demonic darkness, he crawled from beneath the weight of the Shaharan and laid him down gently against a large stone.

His back ached greatly, but the relief of setting down the bear was monumental. Tearing off the other sleeve of his tunic, he wrapped Engle's wounds to the best of his abilities. With the cataclysmic storm still thrashing, Lancen knew that he would not be able to return the Native to Obuthahn. They were both stuck here, and as long as they were, Lancen wasn't going to give up on the trial. Without wasting any time and leaving Engle with nothing but a small amount of water, he endeavored back into horrific darkness.

With every step, he felt motion all around him. As he paced himself through the series of rocks and tunnels, eerie hisses seemed to flow from both ahead and behind. Quickening his pace, he reached the cliffside and hurried down its path. At the bottom he took off at a run. Something was clearly following him now, and it was closer than ever. It provoked an emptiness that seemed to pull at his life-force. He had felt this darkness only once before, when the death hounds had attacked him on the mountain. He couldn't let them catch him!

As he sprinted across the cave floor, he could hear rocks kicking up behind him. To his left and right nasty growls grew louder. Evil was closing in, but he was almost to the tunnel! He kept his head down, watching his feet move back and forth in a blur. The misery around him was consuming.

"Leave me alone!" Lancen called at full pace. "I'm already gone! There is nothing to gain!"

Finally reaching the pool, he jumped into it without a second thought and pushed across. It was deeper than it appeared, coming up above the waist. As it agitated and moved all around him, he could not mistake that something else had entered the water. Freezing like a criminal at a city wall, he reached to the hilt of his sword. The tunnel was only a few steps ahead of him, with nothing but death and shadow behind, but he could go no further. They had caught him. Turning his body to face the enemy, he gazed upon a horror that no nightmare could have ever prepared him for.

In the terrifying darkness of the underground pool stood several man-like creatures in wispy black cloaks. Their faces were covered in shadow causing only razor-sharp teeth and demonic white eyes to gleam through the blackness. Lancen counted five hunched-over monsters, all hooded, and all moving slowly toward him.

At the sound of a scratch, Lancen looked up to see another climbing straight down the rock face above the tunnel. Reaching out to grab fixed holds with bony hands, its sunken face was focused on Lancen. He had to wonder what type of hell these things had come from. Were these skoles? Was this what Lancen would become?

He clenched his sword with all his strength, standing strong as the beasts closed in. Malice frothed from their glowing eyes. They were going to kill him. Engle had been the lucky one. It was easy to see why the Native had been so afraid. These things hadn't hardly made a sound and moved much too quickly for Lancen to evade. They simply produced darkness, and instilled fear in their prey.

The skoles began to scream fiercely and run toward him. Hunger mingling with hatred magnified the devil in their movements. Lancen did not brace himself to be torn apart. He would only go down after they had tasted his sword. This was the end. So much for prophecy!

But just as all hope seemed to be lost, a blinding light appeared above the tip of his blade. It flashed like the bursting of a sun. Stumbling backward, Lancen had to shield his eyes. The monsters shrieked and chaotically spun about, fleeing the vicinity in an earsplitting rage. As he watched them leave through squinted eyes, Lancen's vision faded to darkness, his sense of control abandoning him. Everything turned black, but after only a moment a brightness appeared. His eyes focused, and he saw the woman, the same being that had visited him in the stables. Her white gown flowed gracefully around her body. Her light skin was fair, white as snow. Like before, she was staring at the ground, but again she looked up. Her eyes were bluer than the clearest sky at noonday, and endless as the ocean. Lancen felt warm as she watched him. He longed for her to speak, allowing him to absorb some minuscule quantity of her magnificence. But before she did, his sight clouded. All feeling was gone with comprehension. Everything departed into black.

CHAPTER 19

Sub-conscience illuminated the stillness of Lancen's mind. Projected images of past and present jumped to and fro. He saw the skoles. He saw Adalyn, and Sidna.

The compilation of scattered memory departed and culminated into a single and familiar image of the Master emerging from the dust. The being, clothed in a golden robe with intricate detail, stepped forward, this time through the door and into the subsequent room. The floor was vented several feet over boiling water. Steam clouded the space. The Master reached up and began to remove his hood…

Lancen shot out of the pool and gasped for air. Shivering, he spat out a mouthful of water and awkwardly stumbled to the dry land under the tunnel. In a shock and disoriented, he clasped the hilt of his sword. It was several seconds before he was able to gather himself.

Slowly, he turned to look at the darkness behind him. In his mind he could still see the evil of the skoles, the starvation in their eyes. Their faces haunted him, the thought of their cloaks and movements causing a shiver. It had been the most terrifying experience of his life. If the light had not appeared, he would have surely died.

Just as in the duke's stable, the mysterious woman had seized him. Could it be that these possessions had something to do with the prophecy? Who was this woman in his dream? Noshera? It was unlikely, but nothing else seemed to make sense. Were the divines real?

While Lancen stood in contemplation, he wondered about his friends. Adalyn and Avik had now spent over a day alone in Obuthahn. They were in one of the most dangerous places for a Noble to be. Sure, Lancen had a few unhinged monsters going for his own neck, but there were hundreds of heathen Natives that wanted to kill Adalyn and Avik. They could be starved, beaten, or lying on an altar. Had Lancen been so intent on glory or revenge that he had forgotten to pay attention to those closest to him? If anything happened to them, it would most definitely be his fault.

He wondered if Adalyn was thinking about him at this very moment also, worried about the danger that he may or may not be in. If only their imaginations could connect, even for a moment, then they could provide comfort one for the other. His mind wandered back to the first night of their venture, when he had sat alone with her by the fire. He should have kissed her in that moment. He should have kissed her, for he feared that he may not get another chance.

Keeping his thoughts on Adalyn, Lancen turned into the tunnel darkness and pushed on. It was only then that he realized how dull the glow of the charro leg had become. Still tied to his belt, the appendage did little to light his path, and after only a short few minutes, it disappeared entirely. He was again consumed by a suffocating blackness.

Removing the leg, Lancen threw it against the wall and buried his face in his hands. It was all he could do to avoid an encroaching panic. The darkness ate at him, feeding on his fears and doubts. How was he supposed to find his way out now? Let alone the crown!

He longed to go back to his friends. If he found his way out of the cave, he could make it back to camp easily enough. He would get his reward from Etnah and could leave with his friends to begin their next adventure. It was all he wanted, but exactly what he couldn't do.

His entire life had progressed void of anything significant. Running from Calderon after Sidna's death had been the worst decision of his life, and leaving his mine was worthless if he were to retreat before finding any modicum of success. He could not turn his back on this gift that he had received. If he was ever going to amount to anything, he was going to find this crown. This was his chance to do something important, and he wasn't going quit.

Taking a deep breath, Lancen reached out both hands and inched toward the nearest rock. Feeling along the walls, he began to move gradually forward. He stumbled, fell, and hit his head on low hanging rocks, but slowly, he progressed through the shafts. Eventually, after several blind hours, fluorescent blue mushrooms began to grow from the stone before his eyes. A beautiful blue light began to brighten his path, and at the same time soothe his troubled heart.

Periodically he would stop to rest, but after taking a breath and checking the wound in his shoulder (which was already beginning to close), he would continue on. It was impossible for him to gauge how long he had been walking, but he was simply grateful he hadn't run into any more monsters. Finally, after what could have been a week, a day, or perhaps only a few hours, Lancen began to hear voices echoing through the tunnels. Releasing a sigh of relief, he knew now that he was heading in the right direction. The more he walked, the louder the voices became. Eventually it was clear that they belonged to Eltou and Keira.

"He had to have told you something," said Eltou. "He is practically your father."

"He didn't tell me anything," Keira answered. "He was far too focused on that damned tyrant!"

"And where is the tyrant?"

"Hopefully bleeding somewhere in the dark!" Keira jabbed.

"Like Engle?" Eltou asked.

There was a brief silence.

"Look, Keira, if those creatures find us again, then we're both dead. If Lancen is alive, then we're one man stronger. Admit it, we could use his help about now."

"If Yantik had just killed him like we planned, then we wouldn't be having this discussion," said Keira. "Lancen is not Obah-a-Tou!"

"But if he is Obah-a-Tou, he could save us both, sand-walker!"

Lancen chose to remain in shadow as he approached the gaping room where the Natives argued. The two had set up a number of torches along the walls. Both were covered in dirt and sweat, Eltou with a bloody bandage around his arm and Keira with eyes like it had been weeks since the last time she slept. They stood before three wooden levers, erected from a square stone platform, beyond which, a ten-foot wall extended upward to a ledge, leading to a narrow tunnel that was blocked by a suspended iron gate. Rocks piled several feet from top to bottom on either side of a center aisle, while the ceiling loomed high overhead with many long stalactites reaching down like teeth to bite them.

Eltou stood patiently while Keira paced back and forth beside the corpse of a fallen troll. Angrily she threw her spear into its motionless body. Clutching her head tightly and pulling at her hair she asked, "So which lever do we pull? Before those things come and rip us apart!"

"I don't know! Do I look like I've been here before?" Eltou shouted in frustration. "All I can tell is that it's important we get it right the first time. These rocks didn't pile on the walls for no reason. If we pull the wrong lever, we'll be crushed."

"I can see that!" Keira responded smugly. "How do we know which one? Do we do two at a time? The trolls could figure this out before we will."

"Yeah, well let's just hope that Lancen finds us before they do."

Keira drew a rough bone dagger from her pant leg and pointed it at Eltou's throat. "The tyrant boy is not our champion!"

Eltou took a step closer to the blade. "Well I believe that he is. Why would Etnah put his neck on the line otherwise? I don't know how, but my father would never have allowed him to compete if he did not match the prophecy to the letter!

"What? Are you going to stab me? If we pull the wrong lever, we're dead. So unless you have any bright ideas, stop pissing on the only hope I have left! If Lancen is our champion, then not only will he save us from this cave, but he will save us from the true tyrant."

Keira stared angrily at the ash elf, her dagger now touching his throat. "Say it one more time."

Eltou did not back down. "Lancen of Calderon is Obah-a-Tou!"

Suddenly there was a loud rumble from the tunnels behind Lancen. Instinctively he flipped around to the sound of a definite roar.

"Another troll!" Eltou stated before hearing more than a few subsequent cries. Short of breath he corrected, "Several more trolls."

As the beasts raged closer, Lancen leapt from the shadows and into the large chamber. Before the Natives could greet him, four enraged monsters rushed in at his back. In a burst of wild fury, the head of the pack threw a giant palm into Lancen's side, launching him several yards across the cavern floor. Tumbling to a stop, he clenched his blade and pushed himself up, shaken.

Screaming, the creatures grouped tightly together, and with each standing nearly twice the height of a full-grown man, they loomed over the Natives like hairy gray mountains. With long and massive arms, the creatures pounded the floor and shook the earth. Rows of shark-like teeth lined the insides of their mouths as spit and muck flew toward their opponents. In an impulsive dash, Keira jumped to pull her spear from the dead troll's body. The monsters dispersed, one diving for the girl, the others charging Eltou. Narrowly avoiding death, Keira ran up the rubble lining the walls and jumped onto the ledge before the iron gate. Eltou dodged several strikes and lifted a torch from its position on the wall. Waving it swiftly, he stood brave against fierce growls. The trolls stopped in their tracks and recoiled at the flame.

They feared fire! At once Lancen ran to the nearest torch and pulled it free.

"No!" cried Eltou. "Get to the gate, Lancen, *NOW!*"

But Lancen held his position, moving forward to help wave off the trolls. The monsters grunted and stepped toward Eltou, only to jump back at the torch yet again. Keira howled from the ledge and threw her spear, sticking the rearmost beast in the chest. Crying, it pounded the ground before it ripped the weapon free.

"Lancen, *GO!*" Eltou demanded.

Lancen kept inching forward waving his torch. "No, you can't kill them by yourself!"

"We can't kill them with the three of us!" Eltou shot back. Cursing, he suddenly turned and threw his torch, his only way of fending off the beasts, at Lancen, barely missing him. "*GO!*"

Keira watched in agony as Lancen turned away and climbed to the mouth of the tunnel beside her. At once the trolls pounced toward Eltou. Taking several strong blows from massive clawed hands, the ash elf hit the floor and tried to roll out of the way. The fist of a monster broke his arm. The sheer weight of another crushed his leg. Pulling himself along the ground, he reached the square rock platform and stretched out toward the middle lever. Just as the monsters went for the kill, his fingers wrapped around the wooden switch, and he pulled it down.

Instantly a single large stalactite fell from the ceiling, followed by another and another, until dozens upon dozens dropped to crush Eltou and the demented trolls with him.

"*NO!*" Keira cried as the rocks continued to fall, creating dust as thick as the storm outside. And then after only a horrible moment, everything was still. The soft crackle of Lancen's torch was met by the utter darkness of the once well-lit chamber. Rocks piled all the way up to the ledge. Eltou was buried beneath ten feet of crude stone. In total shock and distress, Keira dropped to her knees and reached out to the spot where her friend had just been very much alive.

CHAPTER 20

As the dust began to settle Keira lowered her head and wept. Emotion that was long overdue had finally boiled to the surface. As her world overturned, Lancen watched solemnly. Eltou had just saved both their lives, but in the process forfeited his own. To Keira he was a close friend. To Lancen, he was the first person to truly believe in him. A Native had just saved his life. A Native had just insisted that Lancen was the champion. The black and white world he had always pictured now began to show signs of gray. Was it possible that the Nobles and Natives could grow to accept one another?

A startling screech suddenly sounded behind the two survivors. The iron gate began to creak and moan, rising steadily. With their way back to the entrance now blocked by a thousand stones, their only option was to go through the gate. Lancen turned to move on, but Keira remained still, oblivious to anything around her.

"Keira," said Lancen softly, "we need to go before the gate falls. We don't know how long it will stay up."

Keira didn't respond, remaining consumed by her grief. How could Lancen expect her to move? He understood the shock and anguish that coursed through her. Only time could bring reason back to her mind.

Taking no chances, Lancen acted swiftly. Grabbing Keira's arm, he lifted her to her feet and pulled her to the other side of the gate. It seemed she had no energy to resist as Lancen released her and debated on a course of action. Should he go on alone, and leave the girl to her sorrow? Or should he try to help?

Benefits to leaving her were numerous. Of all the Natives Lancen had met, she lived up to the name savage more than any. If Lancen continued alone, then he would have no contempt or argument follow. He could search for the crown by himself. Looking around water sources, and using Etnah's potion, he would surely find it and return to Obuthahn to claim his prize.

On the other hand, Keira had no supplies and no fire. Physically and emotionally she was defeated. As Lancen watched her cry the most genuinely devastated tears he had ever seen, he had a hard time not feeling sorry for her, but what if their positions were flipped? Would Keira stay and help if his friend had just died?

No, she hates me, he kept thinking. *Don't give in. She won't change.*

Finally, without saying a word, he decided. He was leaving without her.

Turning away, Lancen walked slowly through the tunnel to the sound of nothing but a cracking torch, leaving Keira in utter darkness. He fought the urge to turn around and kept his gaze forward. The only Native he owed anything to was Eltou, and he was dead. It was about time that he made his shoulder colder than theirs. Keira didn't need his help. She was a tough girl.

But after only a few minutes, Lancen stopped in his tracks. An unwelcome morality prevented him from taking another step. He tried to deny it, but underneath it all, he knew that he needed to help Keira. He needed to turn around and coach her through the pain as best he could, but he wasn't happy about it. Hanging his head, he fought the urge that was taking over.

She hates me. She cannot change. Don't waste your time.

But it was hopeless. He couldn't just leave her, and as he retraced his steps, it seemed that the forces of heartlessness and empathy were battling over his conscience. With a variety of emotions, he punched the wall as he walked, struggling to figure out if compassion was a strength or a weakness.

When he reached Keira, he saw that the gate had shut. She was still sitting in the exact spot he had left her, with her knees to her chin. If Lancen hadn't forced her through the gate, she could have still been on the other side, trapped forever in the chamber with Eltou. Reluctantly, Lancen lowered himself to her side. He opened his mouth to speak, but no words passed his teeth. This girl hated him, and he wasn't particularly fond of her. How was he supposed to be a source of aid?

He sat beside her in silence for some time as her tears continued to fall like stars onto the stone floor. Of all the people in the peninsula, Lancen knew death as well as any. Laying his torch down beside him, he leaned his head back against the stone wall and looked up to where the torchlight disappeared into darkness. He had fought off a savage Darkwood elf, killed a charro, carried a giant of a Shaharan up a winding path for over an hour, and yet consoling this miserable girl was the most difficult challenge of all.

"Keira," he finally said for starters, having no idea what was going to come out of his mouth next.

Immediately the girl turned away her head, refusing to acknowledge him. Lancen reached out and put a hand on her knee. She flinched at the touch.

"Keira," he repeated. "Listen, I know that you hate me. I know that you wish I had died several times over, but sitting here is not going to bring him back."

Keira cast him an angry glare, hurt worn plainly in her eyes. Her once pulled back hair now hung in straggles over her face. Moisture soaked her cheeks. Clearly the pain was consuming her.

For quite some time she didn't respond, but only stared at Lancen in resentment. Eventually she threw his hand off her knee and grit her teeth, forcing a reply, "You have no idea. This type of heartache cannot be felt by your kind."

Lancen bit his lip and shook his head. "That could not be further from the truth. I know exactly what you are going through."

"Did three of your friends just die?" Keira scoffed. "Did your long-lost parent show up out of nowhere as an enemy? The only thing we have in common is that we are both left to die in the company of an enemy!"

Lancen smiled and restrained from a smug reply. He already regretted coming back for her. "First of all," he answered, "*you* left Engle to die. I was the one that risked my life to save him, and as far as I know Yantik is still alive too. He may have failed to kill me, but then again maybe it was me that failed to kill him.

"And as for Etnah, you don't know how lucky you are to have him back. I would do anything to see my mother again!"

"Don't tell me of matters you know nothing about! You don't understand the pain."

"Do not speak to me of pain! You know nothing about me," said Lancen, tensing up.

Keira pursed her lips and looked to the ceiling, as if to call upon Yehawa for a way to respond. "I know enough," she said simply. "I know that you have never missed a meal. I know that you've always had clothes on your back. You've never paid a heavy tax. You grew up with a silver spoon, knife, and fork!"

"I have worked for everything I ever had. You don't know me, and you don't know my people! If you savages gave us the smallest ounce of respect, perhaps we wouldn't be so bad. What do you see in us that is so evil?"

"You took our lands. You forced us to these god-forsaken camps. You took everything!"

"You scarcely used the land, and never for the benefit of a nation!"

"Perhaps, but we never tried to control the water. We never destroyed forests or mountains with quarried stone. You think you can dig up the earth as if it is yours to alter freely. You spit on the land we have always cherished. Does that answer your questions, prying tyrant?"

Annoyed, Lancen chuckled, grabbed the torch, and rose to his feet. "You know what, you can rot in here for all I care. I'm finding that crown and getting out of here."

Immediately Keira jumped to her feet. "Have you not disgraced our traditions enough?"

"Me disgrace them?" Lancen asked. "What about you? You had Yantik try to kill me. You left Engle for dead. You know, for a long time I was thinking the Nobles were all wrong about you, but the longer I've been here, the more savage you appear. At least I tried to help Engle, not that he wanted it."

"Why did you help him?"

"Why *didn't* you?"

Keira blinked away more tears. "You wouldn't understand."

"Not if you don't give me a chance. This whole time I have wanted to be wrong about your people! I wanted to believe that you weren't savages, but you have only reaffirmed everything I've ever learned."

"Do you want to know why we left him?" Keira asked. "Because it is our way. The dream of our freedom is all that keeps us going. So throughout our childhood we are taught to complete the trial at all costs. When Obah-a-Tou comes everything will change for us. It is hope that drives us to revere the prophecy more than life itself."

Lancen sighed and moved his hand that had somehow found its way around his sword. "I can respect hope, but you're right, I don't understand it."

"Yes, well I'm losing sight of it myself," admitted Keira. "In my life I have never had anything. I'm an orphan, raised by the busiest elf in the tribe. I finally get selected for the trial and a tyrant comes to destroy everything."

"We are more alike than you think," said Lancen roughly, trying earnestly to soften her heart as well as his own. "I was raised in an orphanage. I have since lost my foster mother, my home, my dog, and a friend. I know loss and oppression as much as you do."

"Everything is ruined," said Keira. "If you truly know this pain, then how am I supposed to carry on, after I've lost everything?"

"There is no answer," said Lancen, "but moving on is just

something you do. Time moves forward and it is our choice whether or not to move with it. If we stand still, then the pain will never lessen."

Keira nodded and Lancen watched her anger slowly fade. A glimmer of acceptance shone in her eyes. "Is that why you are still here?"

Shaking his head with a heavy heart, Lancen knew she was right. He couldn't give up, because if he did, then every struggle of the past, every aching memory, would creep right back to his mind. This trial was all he had left. The thought of a future with his friends and revenge on the Legion were the only things that could keep him going forward. To quit meant abandoning the only brightness of future his mind could still conceive.

"You are exactly right. I will never stand still."

"Because of pride."

"No," Lancen responded softly, seeing more clearly than he had in weeks, "it's because of hope."

"So it appears," said Keira putting her hands on her hips. "Well if nothing more, you've talked me into getting out of this cave. I had best get looking for the crown."

"We should look together," Lancen suggested. "Four eyes are sharper than two."

Keira wiped away trails of tears from her cheeks and laughed. "This does not change who you are, but you do have a bigger heart than I once thought. I'll give in to your madness."

"There is only one way left to go," said Lancen. "Let's find that crown and get out of this pit."

CHAPTER 21

For the next several hours Lancen and Keira walked through darkness in search of the crown. The deeper they went, the more refined the tunnels became, until the walls were sheer and the ground was covered in polished rocks. Eventually they wandered into a room that had clearly been used ages ago as a dining hall. Ancient cloth banners hung over tables and chairs that were covered in cobwebs. Mysterious tools and utensils were scattered across the floor among dusty brown bones. Wooden fragments and old pots still rested on the tables, as if a meal had only just begun before a battle ensued.

"This place is amazing," stated Lancen.

"It shows what we are capable of when we have freedom," responded Keira, finding herself a torch on one of the tables. "It is not the Natives' fault we fell from this."

As the two continued on, they wandered through bedrooms, kitchens, and studies, searching every nook and corner for the crown. The two looked in silence, refusing to acknowledge the other. In every room they found bones, but in no room did they find what they were looking for. After several hours of searching in vain, Lancen tried to move past his feelings and spark conversation.

"So, what was it like to grow up in Obuthahn?" he asked as they walked side by side down a particularly long corridor.

"Why do you ask?" Keira questioned with suspicion.

"Because you come from a different world," said Lancen. "We are taught to hate you, and you are taught to hate us. I don't understand."

Keira ran a finger along the wall and looked ahead, contemplating an answer. "Do you know what we eat when we can't find game or roots?" she asked after a moment. "Absolutely nothing. We chew on old hide, make tasteless stews. We truly starve. Does that answer your question?"

Lancen didn't know how to respond. It was true that he had never known that kind of destitution, even as the poorest of Nobles. As much as they despised him, he had to admit the Natives had it bad. They were abused and had every right to view his people as tyrants.

"Well if it makes any difference, I'm not like the rest of them," he mentioned.

"What makes you the exception?"

Lancen had never thought about it, but after a moment he guessed the answer. "I am not afraid," he said. "I do not fear Scharric or his laws. I do not respect the Legion. My whole life I have viewed your people a certain way, but I am open to change."

"Well maybe what I know about the Nobles is misguided as well. I can see this with you. You're not what they told me a Noble would be like."

Lancen noticed his cheeks get warm and shook his head in surprise. Did Keira just make him blush? She despised him, and he could hardly stand her. He had to believe it was nothing but odd coincidence. They were enemies. As much as they might want it to be different, nothing could be said or done to change that.

"You would think that with so many reported 'sightings' we would have found the crown by now," Keira said with some frustration, changing the subject.

Lancen reached up and put a hand over his chest where the warlew potion rested. Should he tell her that they should be looking for a water source? How much could he trust her? After Yantik's attempt at his life, who knew what this Shaharan girl might do if she found out that he carried such an advantage.

"You ready to give up?" Lancen asked fairly.

"Not a chance," she said as they reached the end of the corridor and turned into a kingly bedroom, "because we may have just found Nahabuk's quarters."

It isn't going to be here, Lancen thought, but when he saw the hopeful look on Keira's face, he decided to follow her regardless. Similar to Nihwiah's yurt, this room had many strange objects hanging from the ceiling by fraying old strings. Along the walls were primitive relief carvings and shelves upon shelves of ancient scrolls. The rocky floor was decorated in red and gold cloth, complementing the covers of a giant bed in the center of the chamber.

Keira walked straight to the wall, grabbed one of the scrolls, and blew off the dust. She examined it with intrigue.

"What does it say?" Lancen asked.

"I don't know," said Keira. "I can't read, but I believe this is some form of old dwarvish."

"Nahabuk knew the dwarves?"

"Yes," answered Keira quickly, "it was during the final migration. Nahabuk aligned himself with them to defeat the coastal elves. I wonder what these say."

"Well I know nothing about them, so that would rule me out," said Lancen turning away.

"Yeah, but take a look at this," said Keira grabbing his shoulder. "Is that blood?"

Lancen chuckled and looked at the scroll. Leaning in, he noticed numerous dark stains across the paper. Pulling out another scroll, he saw quickly that it too contained the same type of blemish.

"Could be," he said, "or maybe the dwarves have shaky hands, drip ink all over the place. Should we take some of these with us? Maybe someone in Obuthahn can read it."

"I doubt it," said Keira. "I'm not even sure Nihwiah could. Besides, these are not our concern."

"But what if they hold information on the prophecy? That

would concern us."

"Perhaps we can mention them to the council when we get back to camp, but until then we need to focus on finding the crown." Keira returned the scroll to its shelf. She stepped to the foot of the bed and opened a crude wooden chest. Lancen shook his head. *You aren't going to find it here,* he thought. Laughing to himself, he continued to inspect the mysterious writings. It all looked like scribbles, dashes and dots.

"Do you want to help me or are you just an annoying shadow?" Keira jested.

"We've been looking for hours," said Lancen. "I think we need to go deeper into the cave."

"We will look for hours more — days if we must. Go and check the nightstand."

Lancen set the scroll down and bowed toward the Shaharan. "Yes, ma 'dam."

Shaking his head, he walked over to the antique lamp stand beside the bed and pulled out a drawer monotonously. As he took a seat, he began to sort through the container. Beneath several layers of stiffly pressed cloth, a slight gleam caught his eye. In the corner of the near-empty box was a finely-minted silver necklace. Embedded in the pendant was a fingernail sized dark green stone that sparkled in the soft torchlight. Checking that Keira was not watching, he picked up the treasure and dropped it into his pack. A gladness entered him as he thought about giving it to Adalyn.

"Hold on, I think I found something," said Keira, losing her breath. "Come look at this."

Lancen swore to himself as he approached Keira's side. Had she found the crown?

His excitement was cut short as he peeked in to see what she was exclaiming about. At the bottom of the empty chest was a ringed handle only a few inches in length. It was smoothly crafted but appeared of little value. It seemed illogical to place a metal handle on the inside of a container.

"Pull it," said Lancen. "It must be some sort of switch."

Keira rested her thin fingers around the odd device and pulled upward. Instantly there was a loud racket of two giant stones scraping against one another. At once the stone wall to their left broke apart and slowly moved inward, opening a way into a secret tunnel. Lancen felt as though he had jumped in an icy lake as a frigid breeze rolled out from the shaft's darkness. The whistle of an outer-worldly wind sounded as it had near the mouth of the cave. What had they just stumbled upon?

Keira stood up straight and rolled her neck. Pointing her torch toward the new passage, she smiled with confidence. "I think we should go that way."

CHAPTER 22

That first dark tunnel was short and soon opened up into a lengthy chamber with high ceilings. Again, the majestic neon blue of the cavern mushrooms lightened the occasion. The walls shined glass-like as water trickled down to the floor. Perhaps they were nearing a lake of some sort. Perhaps the crown would soon be discovered, but as time came and went, so did Lancen's motivation. In every way he was tired of searching. He was tired of walking through this endless underground abyss, he was tired of ignoring sleep and hunger, and he was especially tired of Keira's arrogant silence.

She walked by his side but scarcely looked at him. Pretending he didn't exist, she would mumble insults under her breath. She tried to hide her anger, and sometimes her remorse. She acted tough like there was nothing to phase her, but Lancen noticed everything. He had to admit that she was a strong girl and very determined. He wanted to know where those qualities had come from but couldn't find the right words to ask. It seemed like there was nothing he could say to her. She was from a different world.

Eventually the two wandered into a broad tunnel that appeared to be Nahabuk's private training facility. Along the walls were numerous racks of iron weapons and dead torches. Across tables and shelves were several metal darts, spurs, and bows. Standing erect were a number of crude dummies, and at the far end of the chamber against the back wall was a large burlap sack filled with straw, displaying a painted target.

Lancen approached the nearest table and picked up a short

wooden bow. He pointed it to the sky and pulled back the string. "Do you shoot?" he asked mid-pull.

Keira seemed a bit uneasy with the question. "I have been going out with the hunters for several years," she said, "but no one really taught me how. I've gotten pretty good on my own."

"Why don't you show me?" suggested Lancen, pointing down range toward the straw-filled bag. It rested maybe two stone throws from where they stood. The target consisted of a red bull's-eye, surrounded by a thick white ring and a smaller blue ring on the outside.

Keira seemed to think on it a moment before responding.

"We don't have time," she determined. "We should keep looking."

"What do you mean we don't have time?" Lancen exclaimed. "All we *do* have is time. We don't even know if there is a second way out of here."

"You're right," said Keira, "but what I do know is that the crown is here, and we haven't found it yet."

"Well if that is true, then it will still be here after we shoot a few arrows," said Lancen shaking his head. "We've been going at it for gods know how long! All I ask is for a little break. You have to be as tired as I am!"

"Are you really going to be this childish? Because we can split up."

"Oh come on," pestered Lancen. "Tell you what, we will both shoot a single arrow. If yours lands closest to the bull's-eye, we will keep searching, and I won't say another word. If I win, then we will stay here and shoot a few more."

Keira rolled her eyes and lifted the bow from her back. "Well if it will get you to shut up..." Reaching into the quiver on her belt, she retrieved an arrow and nocked it immediately.

"Now that's more like it!" said Lancen. "You first."

Keira took a deep breath and raised her weapon. Holding it in the air, she steadied herself and took some time to adjust her aim.

Her brow scrunched as she focused and pulled back the string. After releasing the chord, the arrow flew shakily through the air and slid into the blue ring.

Lancen smiled and clapped slowly. "Not bad for a girl."

Keira looked at him with an irritated glare. "What do you mean 'for a girl'?"

"I mean that girls cannot shoot arrows as good as men," he laughed.

"Ugh!" Keira scowled and looked away. "And you're a man? I ought to cut you where you stand, fair-skin."

"Okay," said Lancen with confidence. He reached out for the quiver at her waist. "May I?"

Sighing, Keira turned her hips so that he could reach an arrow. In one rapid motion Lancen tossed one up, notched it, pulled back the chord, and launched the projectile toward the target. In the blink of an eye the tipped bone arrow had pounded into the straw-filled bag. Bull's-eye.

Keira grumbled and shrugged her shoulders. "How did you do that?"

"Well you see, I'm a man," Lancen joked with a smug grin.

Keira dropped her head and rubbed her eyes. "You're a man like a fawn is an atling!"

Lancen laughed. She was quick! He added, "I have also had lots and lots of practice."

"Could you maybe teach me?"

Lancen was somewhat surprised by her request. "I don't know, you *have* said a lot of terrible things to me so — "

"Fine," said Keira quickly, cutting him off, "let's keep searching."

"I'm kidding," said Lancen in earnest. "Raise your bow; I'm serious."

"No, let's just move on."

"Keira, you said that no one had taken the time to teach you, but I am taking the time now! Raise your bow."

The girl looked back at him oddly, his ability to listen seeming to catch her off-guard. Without further prodding she did as he said.

"Okay, good." said Lancen. "Now spread your feet slightly and point your shoulders toward the target."

Keira rolled her eyes but followed his directions.

"Alright, now place the arrow and be sure to breathe throughout. Lower your stance a bit. It is better to be prepared to move, in case the game spooks. Go ahead and shoot."

The girl readied her bow and released the arrow as instructed. The shaft landed in the blue.

"This is yetah gra'ak," she said in frustration.

"That is because of your form," Lancen answered. "You look as though you've never shot a bow in your life. String an arrow and raise it again."

Keira listened reluctantly.

"Okay, raise your arm and turn out your elbow. Try again."

She released the arrow and missed the target completely, breaking the missile against the stone wall. She abruptly dropped her arms and looked again to Lancen. He was surprised when she began to laugh.

"That was terrible!" she said.

"Hey, you are right about something for once!" joked Lancen with a smile. "For one, you let your elbow turn back in, and for two, your breathing is really short. You need to control it. Here, I'll be of more help this time."

Lancen set down his own bow and stepped behind Keira as she readied another arrow.

"Raise the bow."

As she did, he placed a hand under her left arm and another under the opposite elbow. Moving them into position, he couldn't help but notice how warm her skin was.

"Now hold them just like that," he said, releasing her left arm and placing his hand on her hip. "Stance down, feet apart. Now breathe in slowly…and breathe out."

As she did, unprompted he noticed the heat of her body so close to his, the softness of her hair brushing his neck.

"And release."

The arrow sprung from the bow and seemed to fly in slow motion through the air and into the center of the target. Bull's-eye.

Immediately Keira spun around to look at Lancen, her hair casting a fragrance of sage as she turned. With her face only inches from his, he looked into her eyes and felt in his heart a deep and pleasant burning that he had never before experienced. For the first time he noticed how beautiful she was, perhaps the most beautiful person he had ever seen. The thought of it scared him.

Breathing heavily, Keira's smile faded and as she promptly stepped back, Lancen awakened to reality. He wasn't expecting anything like that to happen. Nothing could have prepared him for it. Adalyn was the only girl for him. He would never want a Native, he wouldn't! Keira was disgusting, vile, and rude. Lancen's jaw lowered as he realized how ridiculous the moment was. He couldn't feel something like that for a Native!

Still looking at him with widened eyes and an open mouth, Keira seemed just as surprised as he was. Confused, and with slight hesitation, she turned away and walked to the target to retrieve her arrows. Lancen watched as she refastened her bow to her back. He couldn't understand what he had felt in that moment, but it was magnetic, and though the image of Adalyn remained prominent in the back of his mind, something within him wanted to feel it again.

He knew Keira had felt it too, but she had shaken it off better than him. Fixing her hair, she asked, "Should we get back to the search?"

Lancen stared at her blankly and stumbled over his words. He couldn't think of anything to say after what had just happened.

"We haven't been this way," said Keira, completely discarding the moment, "come on."

CHAPTER 23

I n the next corridor, Lancen and Keira strolled through darkness pretending that nothing had happened between them. An enduring silence once again accompanied their search. Over the next several minutes, neither of them said a word, as if the moment a sound passed their tongue, the other person would cut it out. Whatever had transpired was not supposed to happen. Keira was stuck in her ways and hated Nobles. Lancen liked Adalyn. He wanted the princess and *no one* else. The awkward air between them was well-deserved and was received loud and clear.

As the tunnels weaved like a maze, the whistle of the outside wind grew stronger. If Lancen had allowed hope to enter him again, he would have believed that they were nearing an exit. At this point that was all he wanted, whether he found Nahabuk's crown or not was secondary. Removing himself from the presence of Keira would be reward enough. She was dangerous in more ways than one. Her silence was excruciating. She was unpredictable, turning from ferocious, to dismal, to candid in only a moment. But worst of all, the beauty she possessed was a weapon, destroying Lancen's judgement. If he fell for this girl, there would be no explaining himself. There could be no future between them.

Finally, he could take the silence no more. Digging within himself, he searched for something, anything at all, to say to her. "You know," he began, "you could be a really good hunter with some more practice."

"I am already a good hunter," she answered.

"Oh really?" doubted Lancen. "You're the main meat-bringer to your tribe, eh?"

Keira scoffed. "Who is the main does not matter. I have helped my tribe."

"So you are not the main, maybe second or third?"

"Our hunters work in teams."

"Ah, I think I'm sensing a lack of confidence," Lancen jested. "That's the first sign of a bad hunter."

Keira stopped in her tracks briefly and exhaled in bewilderment. "How did I get stuck in here with you?"

"I'm asking myself the same question."

Keira ran a hand down her face and let the humor of it enfold her. "Okay, I need practice."

"And I think with practice, you have a lot of potential."

"How did you learn?"

"Well I worked at a lumber mill for years and my friends and I would compete. We spent as much time as possible just pretending to fight," said Lancen, reminiscing.

"I've done plenty of that, and you're still a much better shot than me."

"Oh, just give it time. My friends aren't as good as me either," Lancen joked.

"You are so arrogant," Keira grumbled.

"You think *I'm* arrogant?" asked Lancen laughing. "Have you met my friend Hans?"

"Yeah, that one is a tyrant. Be a real shame if someone fed him some charro discharge."

The smile began to fade from Lancen's face. As much as he loved to joke about Hans, he couldn't change the fact that his friend had left him that night in Obuthahn. He wished he could have done something to prevent it.

"Well Hans may have bad jokes, but he is a good man," Lancen defended.

Keira disagreed, unaware that Hans had ever left. "Hans is the perfect representation of hatred toward the Natives. You may not be all evil, Lancen, but I refuse to call your people noble."

"I'm not asking you to."

"That also means you are not Obah-a-Tou, Lancen. The hero must have the blood of the old. He must be a Native!"

"So I've been told," Lancen stated, "but I can't completely agree when I have never even heard the full prophecy."

"It doesn't matter. You shouldn't hear it, because whether you act on it or not, you are still the tyrant."

"Okay," said Lancen, annoyance creeping in like an assassin preparing to strike.

"I mean you worked at a *lumber mill*! Your people insist on destroying the land just like they destroyed my people."

"Keira," said Lancen sternly, losing his cool, "I get the point."

Keira recognized Lancen's irritation and went silent once again. Lancen bit his tongue and tried to avoid a growing anger. Something about being spat on like that irked him beyond reason. This girl was relentless in her bias! But it wasn't just her, it was the entire Native population. Lancen couldn't fully believe there would even be a prophesied hero, but the more he was rebuked for simply testing it, the more he wanted to prove everyone wrong and forever silence their prejudice.

"I have an honest question for you," he mentioned fairly after some time. The two moved slowly down a steady gradient and through an icy stream.

"Then I will give you an honest answer," Keira replied, still pretending to search each crack and shadow, though the faith of finding anything had all but diminished from her eyes.

Lancen contemplated quickly, searching for the perfect words. "Okay, when Obah-a-Tou comes, how do you believe he will free the Natives? My people are a thousand times stronger than yours."

"He will be a Native," Keira repeated, "and he will find a way."

"Do you expect the Nobles will just bow-down without a fight?"

"Everything will fall into place."

"Don't you think it would be easier for a *Noble* to produce a rebellion strong enough to overthrow the Legion?"

"I don't know how it will be done, but the champion will be a Native."

"I'm not sure you understand the power of the Nobles," said Lancen harshly. "Yes, your lands were taken, and your people are mistreated, but is it not 'noble' that the king has kept you alive the last thirteen years?"

"No, it is cruel! We are no longer a complete people. We are as fragments of a memory, but the divines have kept us alive because this land belongs to us. We are the heirs of Serondhel."

"There are no divines," said Lancen with surety. If there were, he would have found the crown by now.

"Regardless, the Nobles will be defeated," Keira stated strongly.

"The Nobles are impenetrable! They are only growing stronger. Do you know how devastating another war would be? Your people would never survive it! How could your champion be a Native? I'm not saying the prophecy is wrong, but perhaps the interpretation is."

"I believe in the interpretations of past and present vatises. I am willing to devote my life to them," Keira testified, eyes beginning to well up in frustration.

"You have too much faith in what those 'inspired' people say," accused Lancen. "Simply wanting will get you nowhere without action!"

"Why do you think we hold the trial? Is that not action?"

"No!" said Lancen louder than he expected to. "It is complacency."

Keira was at a loss for words. She looked at him with fresh tears rolling down her cheeks. "I'm done," she said simply. "Just stop talking."

Lancen felt a brief moment of satisfaction. She had no defenses when he attacked the Native traditions. That was payback for calling him a tyrant. At least he had won the argument. He had been patient for so long, but this girl was incessant in pissing him off.

Keira stopped walking and sat down on a rock. Lancen watched grudgingly as she lost control of her composure. Dropping her torch, she buried her face in her hands. Looking beyond lonely and heartbroken, tears began to fall yet again.

"What?" asked Lancen without an ounce of sympathy. "Why are you crying?"

Pulling at her hair, she answered between sobs, "Everything is so wrong! With Etnah, with my friends dropping one by one, it's all horrible! My first trial was supposed to be glorious, but it has been terrible in every way!"

"I'm sorry," said Lancen without feeling. "Maybe it was deserved."

Luckily Keira appeared to not hear him. "Everyone is dead! Engle is dead! I saw what happened to him! Why can't he be here instead of you? I give up! Forget the crown, I just want to go home."

CHAPTER 24

L ancen had difficulty rolling his eyes, but he got the job done. He had already let his guard down for this girl, and one time was enough. There was true strength in the motto 'never make the same mistake twice.' Keira didn't deserve consolation. She was a savage in every sense of the word.

As he waited angrily beside the devastated girl, the sound of rushing wind in the distance reached his ears. It was subtle, but certain. It wasn't the same soft whistle they had been hearing for hours, but it was the full sound of a larger opening. It was the sound of freedom—freedom from Keira, freedom from this cave, and eventually freedom from the prophecy. It looked as though Keira would be granted her wish to go home sooner than she anticipated.

"Do you hear that?" Lancen asked.

Keira shook her head solemnly.

"Follow me."

Lancen swiftly lifted the girl from her seat and led her toward the sound. After winding through various passages, they stepped onto a narrow bridge over a deep chasm. Water leaked through the cracks in the walls and trickled into an endless darkness below. The sound of wind was growing louder. They were finally getting out of this place!

Once across the bridge and into the next chamber, the two adventurers waded through a shallow pool. A small opening to the outside world, about an arm's length in diameter, was visible in the roof above them. It was daytime, and the storm continued to rage as powerfully as ever. Dust fell mildly from the sky to the calm water below. Once through the pool and back onto dry ground, the roof seemed to droop lower and lower, the walls becoming more and more narrow. Then, only a short distance in front of them, when the storm was almost deafening, a small wooden door stood like a hero in the darkness.

"Thank the divines!" Keira exclaimed, running toward the barrier. Pushing as strongly as she could, the door flung open, nearly being ripped off its hinges by the wind. Sharp sand blew like a sheer wall on the outside. Ash entered the cavern and nearly choked Lancen in seconds. Reluctantly the two were forced to battle together in pulling the door shut.

When it finally latched heavy dust began to settle, and Lancen coughed through a clouded throat. Keira dropped to her knees in disappointment and laid back against the door. She proceeded to cry from absolute exhaustion, stress, heartache, and whatever other emotion it was that continued to overpower her pride. Lancen nearly cried himself, just knowing they had found the exit. This had been the most brutal journey of his young life.

When Keira had gained control of herself, they made their way back to the pool and sat beside it, several feet away from one another.

We just have to wait out the storm, Lancen reminded himself, *then we are both free.*

He removed his pack and laid his head against the hard stone behind him. The end was in sight.

Before long adrenaline wore off, and the two subjects began to feel the piercing cold of the underground breeze. Their torches had burned out, forcing Lancen to fold his arms and hug his knees for warmth. Looking to the roof, he saw that there was still daylight, but the storm remained at full force. When would it ever end? He could tell that Keira was just as cold as he was, shivering on the opposite wall.

Forget her, he thought. *Soon I will be back in camp, and Adalyn will warm me up. Ha'taat to that, savages!*

Blowing on his fingers, Lancen tried to keep them warm. He had experienced cold far worse than this on the mountain, not long after Sidna's death. This cave was nothing. He was far more concerned about the coldness that existed in his own heart. Before the Hero's Trial he had become increasingly tolerant and empathetic toward the Natives. He had truly enjoyed feeling an acceptance that he had never touched before, but after all the abuse he had taken from the other subjects, that mindset had completely reversed. He didn't like feeling this way, but he was also rational. The Natives were beyond saving.

Just then, the soft voice of Keira penetrated the stillness of the cavern. Mist flew from her mouth as she said his name, "Lancen."

He acknowledged her existence.

"I just wanted to say," she began through chattering teeth, "that I'm sorry."

Lancen laughed. She was sorry? She had hated him from the moment he stepped foot in Obuthahn, and now she was sorry?

"What do you have to be sorry about?" he asked. "And why should I forgive you?"

"I'm not asking you to," she replied. "You came to my camp with utmost respect. Though ignorant, you would never have strayed from that respect if I hadn't been so hostile. I'm sorry."

Lancen's frustration slowly softened. He didn't want to forgive her. Not because she had been a constant pest to him, but because he had said numerous cruel things back to her. If anyone should be apologizing, it was him. Accepting her admission of guilt would be stating fault of his own, and yet, unwillingly, his embargo against her was disengaging. Forgiveness began to tip-toe its way back into his heart. There was no waver in her tone. Keira had meant every word that she had said.

Finally, he responded in humility, "I'm sorry too. I shouldn't have been so quick to anger. I didn't mean the things that I said."

"Yes, you did," corrected Keira. "The reason your words cut so deeply is because they are true. The Natives stand no chance against the Nobles."

Lancen hung his head and sighed. "Don't say that. Eventually there will be peace in this land, and all who walk it will be considered equals."

"You are a dreamer, Lancen, but you and I are on peaceful ground now. I want no more quarrel."

Lancen nodded in agreement. Hatred and bigotry had reached their limits. They brought nothing but conflict to anyone within their realm of influence.

"I never should have come on this trial," Keira said. "They only selected me because I am an orphan. I have never proven myself as a warrior."

"I disagree," said Lancen. "You have proven yourself to me."

"Have I?"

"Yes, you have fought valiantly. Who else could continue forward through all of the adversity that you have faced?"

"I ran while you and the others fought," she answered dismally. "You are a true warrior, but not me."

"It depends on how you define a 'true warrior.' I have never met anyone braver than you."

"See, you are kind to me when I give you the chance," Keira admitted. She was shaking, frozen, with her knees pulled up tightly against her chest. Her hair hung over her face and her eyes were wide and solemn.

"I fear things will never be the same," she mentioned. "I don't know where to turn anymore."

"But you are strong," said Lancen. "You will get through it. The world is always most beautiful after the storm."

Keira gazed at the pool, exhaling into a wispy white. "I have always leaned on Engle when there was no one else. I am supposed to marry him."

"You don't have a choice?"

"No, but it's not because of tradition or religion. You know that elves cannot interbreed with men, right?"

"I guess I never thought about it."

Keira sighed. "Well they can't, and Shaharans are a race of man. There is no getting around that. Engle is the only other Shaharan my age in the clan. It was destined from the beginning."

"That doesn't seem fair," admitted Lancen. "Do you love him?"

"Yes," she answered quickly, "but not in any romantic way. I think of him more as a brother. I hate to admit it, but the thought of him being dead, along with all the sorrow, comes a small amount of hope."

Lancen shook in the cold and nodded his head, not knowing what else to say.

"I don't know why I'm telling you all this," said Keira.

"Don't stop," said Lancen. "Sometimes it is better to listen. When you speak you can only say things you already know. One must listen to discover something new. My foster mother taught me that."

"You have some strange sayings, Lancen. Sometimes I don't have the slightest clue what you mean," Keira laughed. After a short pause she said quietly, "You are lucky to have had such a special woman in your life. As long as I can remember I have been nothing but the chief's daughter. I am a Shaharan among elves. Etnah always loved me, but he was far too busy. I have never had someone to teach me the lessons you were taught."

Lancen looked at the floor in reflection. "I was lucky," he agreed, "but she is dead now, and there is no way to bring her back."

"I'm sorry," said Keira. "How did she die?"

Lancen shuddered at the question. It seemed like that was the story everyone wanted to know. Why could he not escape it? It followed him like a shadow, fading during the brightest moments of day, but growing as soon as the sun began to descend. He decided to answer her to the best of his ability.

"Her name was Sidna," he began. "She worshipped the divines her entire life, one of the few who did after the war, but…" Lancen trailed off. He had spent so much time avoiding the subject. Memory flooded back to his mind, bringing again all the pain, all the guilt of that day.

"But what?" Keira asked.

Lancen tried to come up with the words. The full truth he just couldn't seem to speak aloud. He could never let it out. "When Scharric outlawed the worship of the three divines, Sidna refused to give them up. She was killed because of that belief. She revered the divines more than life itself, and now I'm lost without her."

"I guess you are as acquainted with grief as I am."

Lancen nodded his head and held back emotion. "Maybe we aren't so different after all."

"Maybe not," Keira agreed. "You know I never knew my real parents. They died in the war when I was a young child. The only memory I have of them is something my father used to say to me: *'You can make more difference than the sun.'"*

"That's beautiful. At least the memory you do have is a good one."

"Any memory of yours?"

"Not a one," said Lancen. "I was placed on the step of the foster home when I was a baby. I have no idea who left me there."

Keira sighed in amazement. "Orphaned in infancy."

The girl shook her head and looked through the roof to the menacing storm. Her lips were blue and trembled, her whole body shook. Lancen contemplated on how he could help her. After a moment of awkward realization, he held out his arms and motioned for Keira to move closer. "Come over here."

She looked at him with raised eyebrows. "What are you talking about?"

"Come here," he said again with a smile. "I'm freezing, you are shivering. Why don't we try and solve this for the both of us? Come here."

"Oh gods, you're serious?" Keira asked in a shock.

Lancen shrugged his shoulders with a grin now frozen to his face. Reluctantly Keira inched her way toward him. Soon she had settled up against his torso, and he began rubbing her bare arms in an attempt to warm them up. Once again he smelled the sage in her hair as she rested her head against his chest. Wrapping his arms around her, there was a long moment of silence between them. It wasn't uncomfortable, just relieving. Finally, Lancen felt that his body was warming up. He felt a contentment that was much more needed than he realized.

After quite a while Keira breathed deeply. She hesitated to speak but eventually asked, "You had to have known my people would not receive you. Why did you still come to Obuthahn?"

Lancen debated on how he should answer. He could tell her it was for the prophecy, that it was for wealth, or he could even tell her it was for revenge. All these answers could effectively describe why he had come, and best of all, each of them were true. For once he could be completely honest on a subject that had haunted him for weeks.

"I wasn't going to come, but something about this felt different. It wasn't often that an ash elf showed up on my porch, you know? And still, I had made up my mind not to go, but then my choice was made for me. Everything that I had was taken by the King's Legion."

"I had no idea," said Keira.

"I guess that is partly why I am trying to respect your people. I know how terrible the Nobles can be under Scharric. They have taken everything I care about."

"They've taken much from me also," Keira related, clicking her tongue much like Etnah often did, "but when I really look at it, they are not entirely to blame. The Nobles killed my parents, yes, but it wasn't until I was older that I learned it was the council of Obuthahn that betrayed Shaharum to the tyrant. Etnah didn't like it, but the chief can say little when the council and vatisus are in agreement. The Natives are far from perfect."

"I know it means a lot for you to say that," said Lancen. His eyes were heavy. He was at ease for the first time in days and had no one to thank but Keira. An uninvited desire to raise her spirits had slowly encompassed him. "Here is another strange saying for you: there was never a river run that did not also bear rocks."

Keira nodded her head. "You are wise, Lancen."

After a short pause she stated quietly, "You know I have never felt like this before."

"What do you mean?" Lancen asked. "Are you still cold?"

Keira shook her head and laughed. "No, I mean I have never felt this comfortable, this safe. I have never felt like I feel right now."

A burn started in Lancen's chest, the same burn that he had felt earlier in the training hall. There was something inside of him that he couldn't explain for Keira. There was a connection between them that hadn't been placed at will. It was a feeling he never would have expected to have for her, but also one that he never wanted to lose.

What it all meant he didn't know. He missed Adalyn, and still felt a deep attachment to her, but there was also something within him making room for Keira. He knew that he couldn't have both, but he could sense that a battle would soon be raging over who would stay in his heart.

He shook his head quietly. *No. Only Adalyn.*

"I guess it wouldn't be so bad if you were our hero," said Keira finally, breathing deeply and nestling against his shoulder.

Sighing, Lancen relented, *or Keira.* Situating his arms snugly around her, he leaned back and closed his eyes.

CHAPTER 25

Several hours later Lancen's eyes slowly opened. He had no memory of drifting off but was not surprised in the least that it had happened. He hadn't slept much at all in the last few weeks, and the fatigue had been building like a cancer. His body must have finally reached its limit, but unfortunately his sleep was now behind him. The moment the current began to flow in his mind there was no stopping it. He was fully awake.

Around him everything was calm. Keira was curled up and sleeping soundly against his shoulder. In the stillness, he noticed that the storm had finally ceased. Soft light from the two moons poured in over the pool near Lancen's feet. His attention was taken abruptly as he spotted a vague shimmer just below the water's surface. *By Noshera, what is that?* he thought in excitement.

Immediately, he moved from beneath Keira and placed his pack under her head. She sighed and shifted but didn't wake. Attempting to remain calm, Lancen crawled to the edge of the pool and stuck his head out over the water. Wherever the moonlight touched, the ground that had once been solid evaporated to reveal an expanse of dark water beneath. Visible beyond the hole that the light had created was the subtle shine of a weathered golden crown.

Lancen's heart seemed to jump in his chest, tossing him to his feet. Brain moving fast as lightning, he struggled to hold in his excitement. He didn't want to wake Keira, not yet. Clenching his fists, he fought to keep his breathing steady. By some miracle, after passing through the depths of hell, he had managed to find the crown!

The artifact rested in plain sight perhaps a body length below the hole in the floor. Without another moment's hesitation, Lancen stripped down to his trousers and eased into the icy water. At first step it chilled him to the core, but the more he lowered himself the easier it became. Taking one deep breath, he ducked under the surface and pulled himself through the moonlit space.

At once he discovered that the crown was not nearly as close as it appeared. It rested half-buried in mud at least thirty feet below the original pool floor. It didn't take long for Lancen to recall the warlew jelly around his neck. There was no mistaking that this was exactly what Etnah had foreseen.

Re-emerging, Lancen caught his breath and reached for the bottle. Sitting with his feet through the vacant hole, he twisted free the cork.

"Here goes nothing," he whispered, toasting to the moons. Kicking back the potion, he downed the liquid in one gulp and tossed the bottle aside. The taste was bad but bearable, much like lukewarm tomato juice. Taking another deep breath, he counted to three. He didn't know when the substance would kick in, but he couldn't stand the thought of waiting for confirmation. He smoothly dove back beneath the surface and pulled himself downward. Not willing to test his breathing just yet, he kept his mouth shut tightly.

Swimming downward, the crown seemed to only grow farther away. The deeper he swam, the greater the pressure that built in his head. It felt like he was being crushed, like a dozen men were surrounding him and pushing at his skull, and as he passed what appeared to be the halfway point, he was running out of breath.

It was now or never. He couldn't go much longer. He had to test the potion. Even at this point, a swim back to the surface would be a challenge without it. Reluctantly he opened his mouth and breathed in with a silent terror. Instantly his mouth filled with water, but miraculously none made it past his throat. Air filled his lungs and he exhaled, pushing it back through the water in a barrage of bubbles. It worked.

Astonished, Lancen swam more diligently, and the artifact slowly grew closer. Taking deep breaths, he remembered specifically that Etnah never told him how long the potion would last. It could be minutes, or seconds, but he had to be ready to hold his breath at any moment.

Finally, as the pressure in his body was nearly unbearable, seeming to stab him with a thousand needles, Lancen touched the floor of the underground lake. Reaching down, he gently placed his hands around the crown, which sparkled slightly beneath the layer of mold and filth atop it. He pulled upward, but it was slick and didn't budge. Realigning his position, he squatted over the treasure and lifted with all his might. Steadily the crown gave but was suctioned back down. Abruptly Lancen released his hold and flailed in frustration, screaming thousands of bubbles through the freezing water. Grabbing the item once more, he put every ounce of muster he contained into pulling it free. Finally, to his great relief, the suction eased, and he raised it from the mud. But as it emerged, a half-deteriorated skeleton slipped through the muck beneath it. The crown slid smoothly off of its skull and was finally free.

Lancen lurched back in shock at the image. Could these be the remains of Nahabuk himself? The bones were withered and molded, a fine steel and bone axe still grasped tightly in its weathered hand. Lancen laughed and grabbed the corpse's bony fingers, pulling them back. Taking hold of the weapon, he held it under his arm and shook the skeletal hand. *Thank you Nahabuk, my friend,* he thought as he shot quickly upward toward the surface.

He pulled himself skyward as rapidly as possible. Though the deep lake was very dark, made lighter only by the moonlight, Lancen remained easily focused on the hole in the pool's floor. And then, as if in a nightmare, he watched as the light slowly darkened. A hope killing shadow began to roll over the opening.

Kicking with new fury, Lancen battled upward. The gap was closing steadily, but he was nearly there. He stretched for the last remnant of light, but just as his hand reached the opening, the ground had fully reappeared. He was trapped.

Attempting to scream, he pushed against the hardened earth. It wouldn't budge but was as solid as the stone of the cavern walls. Violently he scratched and scraped where the hole had been. How could this be happening? Curses rolled through his mind like rocks down a mountainside.

His luck went from bad to horrendous when he took his next breath. Without warning, a large gulp of water flew down his throat, nearly choking him. Regurgitating, he struggled and sucked in more water before he closed his mouth tightly. His mind screamed *don't panic,* but his body wasn't about to listen. Desperately he threw Nahabuk's axe against the stone above with all his strength. The weapon found a crack and stuck into the earth. Tearing it free, Lancen kicked and swung rashly. Water shot up his nose and down his throat with a terrible burn. The ground was not moving!

Lancen's vision darkened. His head felt light, his muscles tightening. The panic consuming him departed in a wave of hopelessness. All his strength was expended, but just as all faith seemed lost, the earth above him separated slightly. A glowing and fuzzy hand moved down and into view. In a last stage effort, Lancen reached out and grasped it tightly. Steadily, he was lifted up and through the small opening toward the light, and then the hand was gone.

In astonishment, his head emerged above the surface. He brusquely gasped for air and spit up a substantial amount of water. Keira awoke from the very spot he had left her, jumping up and rushing to his side. Stumbling, he flopped onto the dry land and fought for every breath. If it wasn't Keira, who had saved him?

"No way!" howled Keira in amazement. Her voice cracked and a look of pure excitement spread across her face. "No way did you find it! You found the crown! You did it!"

Lancen laid the axe beside him and tossed the crown to the rocky floor at Keira's feet. Struggling to catch his breath, his vision slowly retreated from a reddish black and returned to normal. His stomach cramped, and his muscles ached, but he was alive.

Keira jumped up and down, hollering in exhilaration. Fists pumping, she cried, "*YES!*" In a flash she fell to Lancen's side and pressed her lips against his cheek.

His face felt hot. He knew that he was blushing but could do nothing to stop it. He laid out flat, too exhausted to move or say anything at all.

Ecstatic, Keira continued to dance and celebrate. "Whether you are Obah-a-Tou or not, you are my hero!" she exclaimed with an uncontrollable grin.

Again, she leaned over and kissed him, this time on the brow. Picking up the crown, she attempted to wipe off much of the mildew and placed it on her head. As soon as she released it, the item fell down over her eyes.

Not seeming to care, she did a little curtsy and stated happily, "Nomahkta ha'yak toe mah! And you can call me Queen Nahktu, ruler of the peninsula!"

Giggling, she stumbled and dropped herself beside Lancen.

"Well, my queen," he said between breaths, "that jewel is the product of me nearly dying about seventeen times the last few days."

"And yet you are still breathing?" Keira jested, trying her best to mimic the Noble accent.

"Yeah barely," answered Lancen.

"I would say that such bravery deserves a reward!"

"Just lying here for a while would be nice," Lancen said laughing, between several coughs.

"That we will do! But just wait until we get back to camp!"

Lancen smiled and closed his eyes. He didn't know what that would bring, but he couldn't wait to see the looks on the Native faces when he strolled into Obuthahn grasping the embodiment of victory in his very hands. Perhaps his luck was finally changing.

CHAPTER 26

The next morning came in haste. In all the excitement, Lancen and Keira had found it difficult to sleep. Instead they had talked on and on of the glory that would greet them when they returned to Obuthahn. For once their futures seemed bright, their outlooks were positive, and everything seemed to be as it should. When sunlight first crept into the dark cavern, the two readied their packs and approached the door to freedom.

"How are you so sure that they will accept me?" Lancen asked, strapping his new axe to his belt.

Assuring, Keira responded, "Let's be honest, if I can come to accept you, anyone can."

Lancen laughed and had to agree. "Okay, you make a good point, but I still can't be so sure."

"Every subject that has ever returned victorious was greeted as a hero, Lancen. You have nothing to worry about." The excitement of the night had clearly begun to wear off, and Keira was showing her nerves with every word.

Lancen closed his eyes and tried to think of a world where they didn't have to worry, or hurt, or mourn, but the place didn't exist, even in his imagination. "Maybe you're right, but none of those subjects were Nobles," he said, trying to keep the conversation away from Keira's losses.

"That doesn't matter," said Keira lightly.

"Did you forget that I am a Noble?"

Keira gave him a dirty look, clearly having much more faith in the Natives than he. "The point is that completing the Hero's Trial, especially this one, will be enough to change their opinion about you. They may not believe you are our champion, but you at least deserve to be tested!"

"But I am a Noble," Lancen repeated slowly.

"And you will be a friend of the clan. You will be adopted as a brother."

Lancen shook his head faithlessly. Until he saw it with his own eyes, it wasn't true.

"There is only one way to find out for sure," said Keira. "Are you ready?"

"Yes, we should go," he agreed anxiously.

The two exchanged looks, and together, pushed on the face of the wooden door. A moment later, the soft light of dawn encompassed them. The outside world had never looked so beautiful. Though Lancen had once thought the Ashlands to be ugly and gray, they now seemed like an incredible masterpiece, waiting to be painted and hung in the halls of kings.

Over the last few days, they had wandered far through the underground passages. They now stood at the base of the Ash Mountains, many miles south of the cavern entrance. They were facing west, and ahead of them they could only hear the faint rushing of the mucky river.

It would be a long walk back to camp, but the first item on their agenda was stopping by the cavern mouth. The last time Lancen had been there, he had left Engle in very poor condition. Keira was calm, but she couldn't hide her concern — and she was right to be worried. Lancen feared that they would find nothing but a lifeless Native, entering the beginning stages of decay. Lancen now wished he could have done more for the Shaharan, but the time to help had long since passed.

As they embarked on the journey back, few words were mixed between them. It was not as it was in the cave, not awkward or spiteful. This silence was much more understood. For quite a while

Lancen thought of a future with the Native people. Finding the crown planted in him a shadow of belief that he was indeed their champion. If that was the case, he could forge a new path for himself and the deprived. For him, it felt like the dawn, like the new day would bring on unmatched freedom and equality. His enemies would fall before him. Lancen of Calderon would finally make a difference in the world.

And as he thought about staying with the Natives, he was helpless to prevent the thoughts of leaving them from also crossing his mind. He had accomplished so much since leaving the mountain. He had made it to Calderon and reunited with his friends, if only for a while. He had gained the allegiance of Adalyn, the girl of his dreams. They had travelled across hundreds of miles to a hostile camp and survived. And now, he had completed successfully the very trial he had come to participate in. How much more could he gain?

In the cavern he had practically made up his mind to leave, but now with the crown of Nahabuk in his pack, he was forced to reevaluate. What if he was the hero? He couldn't just abandon that for fortune and leisure. The Legion had not yet felt his wrath, but they would. If he could work with the Natives of Obuthahn, just maybe, he would be able to gain the support of other tribes and mount an effective attack. For the first time, he began to see validity in the Native's cause. If everything worked out just right, there was a minute glimpse of hope that they could one day overthrow the Legion. Lancen would not pass on the opportunity to be a part of that, however small.

As for Keira, the silence was not so much in hope as it was in angst. A dear member of her community had fallen. Engle was a person that she had been destined to marry, and now they would likely find him dead. Her breathing was harsh and anxious. Lancen had no words to comfort her and didn't believe it was his place. After the entirety of pain and adversity that she had faced in this trial, it was clear that she was already stronger than him. To hold her composure after all that grief was astounding. However, what they would discover at the cavern entrance would bring out emotion regardless of her strength. There was plenty of empathy in Lancen's heart, but no solutions.

When he and Keira had reached the mouth several hours into the morning, they wandered in and searched the opening tunnels. The tension was sharp, and neither wanted to say a word. Lancen's heart beat rapidly in anticipation of what they would find. Slight guilt dwelt with him as he approached the spot. In retrospect, he knew that he should have stayed with the Shaharan. There was no way the bear could have survived those wounds.

When they reached the rock where Lancen had left the body, there was blood everywhere, plenty to prove his story true, but there was no sign of Engle or any indication whatsoever that the Shaharan had moved.

"This is where you left him?" asked Keira, looking at a bloodied rock.

"It is," said Lancen, and he knew it to be true. He could still smell the enticing nectar that was Engle's blood. "That blood is his."

"There is no sign of him returning to the depths, and no trail suggesting he walked out the front," stated Keira, "but he must have."

Lancen couldn't explain it. He knew that he had left the Native just beside where Keira now stood. Engle had been broken and dying. Unless he was devoured by some creature of the dark, there were no answers. With the monsters he had faced in the dark pool, it seemed the only logical solution. It was the skoles, but how could he tell that to Keira?

"My guess is that the bleeding stopped, and he headed back to camp," Lancen lied, trying to soothe Keira's encroaching panic. "Perhaps we will pick up a trail along the way."

Keira breathed deeply and shook her head. "No. He could be back in the depths. We have to look for him."

If Engle had gone deeper, searching for him was a lost cause. Lancen had to convince Keira to head back to camp, even if it meant stretching the truth. He paused, contemplating what to say before he spoke. "No, Keira, he told me that as soon as the storm lessened, he would head back to camp. I believe he made it."

Keira didn't speak, she just nodded and turned around, holding in tears. Lancen reached out to touch her shoulder, but she was already walking away. He felt for her, but nothing he could say would help. Engle would not be at camp.

Regardless, they pressed forward, wandering north along the river and across the barren fields of endless ash toward the Native camp. Everything was so peaceful that it amazed Lancen to think that a horrendous storm had raged so violently only a day before. The world seemed untouched.

Keeping an open eye, the two found no trace of Engle's movements, and Lancen knew they wouldn't. The Shaharan had gotten his wish, the monsters who had hurt him had come back to finish him off, leaving nothing behind.

Before they were ready, the small structures of Obuthahn became visible upon the horizon. Lancen still sensed an ill reception, but Keira would not agree. When they were only a few hundred yards away, Lancen posed the question, "Are you going to forgive Etnah for bringing me here?"

"Why do you ask?"

Honestly, it was because he was trying to get her mind off of death, but he gave her a different answer. "Because when someone is treated unfairly, it is usually kind to apologize," he said. "Or is that just a Noble thing?"

Keira raised her face to the sky and embraced the warmth of the sun. "It is not just a Noble thing," she sighed. "I know you're right. You're always right. I will forgive him."

"Good," said Lancen, "and I know that when we get back there will be nothing to keep you from hating me again. For the record, are we friends now?"

Smiling, Keira ran a hand down the side of Lancen's arm, sending a warmth to his heart. "I think that's reasonable."

As she spoke, elves began to file from their shacks, moving out to gawk at the incoming subjects. An excitement rose into the air like a mist and entered every being. Natives by the dozen began to gather for the heroes' return. Lancen saw Shikobin emerge from the crowd with an eager countenance. Nihwiah walked with grace close behind.

Lancen searched carefully for his friends. Before he could face the clan leaders, he needed to know they were safe. He couldn't stand the thought of anything happening to them. Soon his stresses were silenced, and Etnah stepped forth from the other spectators with Adalyn and Avik. Lancen saw the princess search for him with worried eyes. She looked beautiful, though ragged. Draped in Hans' old clothes, she was far departed from the exquisite nature of the castle. When she realized it was Lancen, she ran forward at once to greet him.

Before he could say a word, she threw her arms around him. In a split second she had bypassed all boundaries and pressed her lips against his. Nearly beating out of his chest, his heart pounded as it never had before. His body felt numb, and his cheeks flushed red. Her kiss was lush and full. Like a panther, the moment he had dreamed of for so long pounced on him out of nowhere. It should have been the most incredible experience of his life, and yet, with Keira standing so close to his side, he couldn't help but be embarrassed.

As Adalyn continued to embrace him, Lancen put his arms tightly around her. The princess had just kissed him! His mind struggled to catch up to reality. He wanted to enjoy this moment straight out of a dream, but with so many new thoughts and emotions coursing through his already crowded mind, it was difficult. Adalyn, *Princess Adalyn,* had just kissed him!

"We thought you were dead," she exclaimed. "I was so worried!"

She kissed him again, and this time he was prepared to kiss back.

Is this real? he thought, unable to figure out his heart. This was such a brilliant instant in the expanse of mediocrity that he called life, and somehow, in some small way, it was tainted. He felt wrong kissing her in front of Keira.

When they had finished, Lancen glanced to the Native girl who watched without expression. Though signs of anger or sadness were absent, he drew the disapproval from her eyes. How was this happening?

Once Adalyn released him, the crowd had gathered much closer, bringing intimidation with them. Shikobin and Nihwiah stood front and center, ready to address him. Lancen bowed, putting three fingers to his forehead and extending them as per custom. There were several snickers and mumblings in the audience. Apparently it was not an appropriate time to use the greeting.

"Where are the others?" Shikobin asked with obvious tension in his voice.

Lancen took a deep breath as the color drained from his face. He had forgotten that Shikobin was Eltou's father. How was he supposed to tell this man, a man that already hated him, that his son hadn't made it? There had been so much death, more than he could bear. He looked to Keira, but she turned away, assigning the answer to him.

"Where are they?" the chief repeated with force.

Lancen cleared his throat. "Well, Yantik —"

"Yantik is fine," Shikobin cut in. "A group of hunters found him on the riverbank south of the cavern. They gave him shelter and brought him here last night. He is wounded but will recover."

"What about Engle?" Keira asked earnestly.

"We've no word. Where is Eltou?" the chief asked directly.

Lancen looked to the ground, stuttering. "Engle was wounded badly. We had hoped —"

"And Eltou? *Where is my SON!*" Shikobin roared. He was in a sweat, stooping with open palms. His chest pounded up and down, his stare unbreakable.

Lancen paused to gather himself, and answered, "Eltou is a fallen hero."

"You *TYRANT!*" Shikobin screamed, stomping furiously toward the boy. Lancen clutched the hilt of Nahabuk's axe as the chief drew his own, but just before a fight ensued, Etnah grabbed the clan-leader and held him back.

"Think about what you're doing here, Chief!" Etnah demanded urgently.

Shikobin fought to throw him off. "Gra'ak mane votch! This does not involve you, *Chief!*"

"Nor does it involve the boy," reasoned Etnah. "Do not be so swift to place blame. He could be our champion, our savior!"

"Yet he lives while my son is dead! The tyrant did not even complete the trial!"

"I wouldn't be so quick to judgment," said Lancen calmly, raising an open hand in peaceful gesture.

"What do you mean, boy?" required Shikobin, relaxing slightly.

Lancen's blood raced, and chills consumed his body as he removed his pack and reached within. Pulling free Nahabuk's weathered crown, he watched as every jaw lowered in utter shock. The axe in Shikobin's grasp slipped past his fingers and dropped with a clank to the dirt. Nihwiah stepped forward with an expression of unhindered astonishment.

"It cannot be," she whispered. "The crown of Nahabuk! May I see it?"

Lancen extended the item toward her. Delicately, she ran a finger over its peaks and crevices.

Shekii stepped forward from the camouflage of spectators and opened his mouth to speak. "Clan brothers and sisters," he called with ever so slight reluctance, "Lancen and Keira have completed the Hero's Trial."

Not a sound was made in response, only a stillness so sheer it could cut glass. Nihwiah very carefully placed her fingers around the crown and pulled it tightly to her chest. In silence she turned and surveyed the many dumbfounded spectators. In sincere awe she looked to the sun, falling slowly in the sky.

"Tonight," she said quietly, barely stronger than a whisper, "the ceremony will proceed as tradition demands. We must celebrate this divine occasion. For the first time an outsider has been made the subject of trial and has succeeded where so many before him had failed. Both he and the sand-walker shall be rewarded justly for their victory. Let us all depart and prepare, for this night we feast."

The Natives remained still, not the faintest whisper or mumbling rising up among them. Lancen stood in as much bewilderment as his spectators. Confusion and amazement hung in the air like an odor.

Shikobin bent down and retrieved his weapon from the dirt. Refastening it to his waist, he looked to Lancen in a face of pure hatred. His jaw trembled while unharnessed pain and animosity dwelt in his eyes. Turning to the crowd, he raised his voice before all, "Clan friends, our vatisus has spoken. Depart from here! But do not fear. This boy *is not* our awaited champion!"

As the crowd slowly began to disperse, Nihwiah turned to Lancen and Keira.

"You two," she said with concern, "meet in my abode promptly."

Lancen nodded, and after a brief reunion with his friends, followed Shekii, Etnah, and the others of the tribal council toward Nihwiah's yurt.

CHAPTER 27

One by one, the council members filed into Nihwiah's circular abode, followed closely by Lancen and Keira. Once inside, Lancen looked over the faces of the councilmen. Most were unfamiliar and intimidating. Nihwiah, Etnah, and Shekii were the only people besides Keira that he recognized. Shikobin was missing.

In the center of the yurt, the vatisus reached into a hanging jar above her and pulled free a handful of dark colored powder. "Fekta mun," she said, gently dropping it into the firepit below. Immediately the powder combusted, and familiar indigo flames shot up to cast a heavy blue smoke.

Lancen nodded his head, intrigued by the magic, and looked to Nihwiah. She seemed to have gathered her composure since receiving the crown. She cleared her throat in a call to attention.

"We obviously have something on our hands that neither I nor any of my predecessors have ever dealt with. I will leave the outcome to discussion."

There was an encumbering moment of silence as Lancen looked around for someone to speak. This was the meeting that would decide his fate. The seven present members of the council, eight including Etnah, all seemed to contemplate quietly.

Eventually Etnah stepped forward to warm his hands at the flame, whistling a brief melody. With no waver of tone, he stated, "The boy completed the trial we thought to be impossible. He should be rewarded as victor and named clan-brother."

"That is disgraceful!" burst an unknown member of the council.

He had a fully shaven head with white war-paint covering his naked scalp. "The boy is an outlander and a false prophet. He should be condemned as such!"

Etnah threw back his head and laughed with strange amusement. "He provided by his own hands the crown of Nahabuk! He ought to be tested as Obah-a-Tou."

"Brother Etnah," began Shekii, "we all understand your involvement here, but we also understand the prophecy. The champion must carry Native blood, the blood of them that have come before, the blood of the old."

"We do not understand the prophecy," Etnah mused. "It says clearly that the champion will uncover the true. He will reveal and unveil. We can't pretend to know it all when the substance itself states that we do not."

"We must look at this logically, Etnah," said another member of the council. "How could a Noble ever reunite the clans? We can't do it ourselves and you expect that the enemy will be able to?"

"Perhaps not," said Etnah shrugging his shoulders, "but he deserves to be tested."

"Do you suppose that the people will accept him? No, they will be furious!" chimed in the paint-head.

"What would the other clans think if we sent them this news?" posed Shekii. "We would have another civil war on our hands!"

"Yet if he is our champion, I would not want to be the one that casts him by the wayside!" said Etnah lividly, going from calm to animated in a flash.

"Neither would I," agreed Nihwiah, her voice calming the council like the strings of a harp.

Just as respect and order began to return, Shikobin entered the abode, tearing through the thin fabric door in a rage. At once he announced his thoughts. "I can take it no longer! This boy is worthy of death! Or if he claims to be Obah-a-Tou, we should treat him as such and send him to Glencroft to take the harbors!"

"Boy, *do you* believe that you are Obah-a-Tou?" Shekii asked fairly.

"That question has no bearing," argued Etnah.

"Let him answer," Nihwiah ordered calmly.

Lancen struggled to find words. This was a question that continued to come back to him, like a lucky arrow or the flu. *You will be a friend of the clan,* Keira had said, *they will adopt you as a brother.* She couldn't have been more wrong. In this moment he just wanted to ask Etnah for the emeralds and be on his way.

"Well, boy?" Shekii demanded.

"I have no idea," Lancen said honestly. "*I do not know.*"

"Then death it is," growled Shikobin. "If he be a tyrant, then he deserves to have his blood sprayed across an altar. We shall give him to Athleon!"

"We will *NOT!*" shouted Etnah, temperament phased.

Shikobin stood firm, face to face with the former chief. "The land bears too many Native graves. It calls for more of the tyrant!"

"The land knows no difference between the blood of the Natives and the blood of the Nobles!" Etnah charged furiously. "You ought to know that better than most!"

Shikobin again reached for his axe.

"*ENOUGH!*" shrieked Nihwiah. "Both of you!"

Shikobin grunted and released the hold on his blade.

"Shikobin, depart from here!" commanded the vatisus. "Cool down. Gather your emotions. Sober minds are needed here. Mohn yad notohte."

Etnah held his glare as Shikobin angrily backed away. Looking at Lancen with a demented scowl, he stated in pure hatred, "This is not over," and exited the yurt.

Those left in the room were now quiet, the tension as sharp as knives. Lancen was shaken, but keeping his head up and jaw clenched, he looked directly at Nihwiah, awaiting her judgment.

"What will be done?" he asked in eagerness.

Nihwiah contemplated, closing her eyes and mumbling under her breath. Sighing, she proceeded to walk across the room to the far wall and pull a worn roll of paper from a small drawer. Beside it, she unveiled a smooth stone, about the height and width of a large book, and walked back to the center of the yurt. Engraved on the face of the stone, Lancen noticed many strange markings of an ancient language.

"Written on this tablet is the Prophecy of Serondhel," Nihwiah announced to the captivated room. "It was carved by the hands of the ancients themselves. Two stones exist. One is written in Dwarvish and resides in Entupathia. The other is written in the ancient language of Obuthia and exists here before your very eyes. I exhort you all to keep it secret. No one outside of this room must ever know.

"And this, Lancen, is for you," she said, handing him the roll of old paper. "That is a copy of the prophecy in the Noble tongue. Study it. Revere it. I would rather be infamous for testing a tyrant than infamous for denying Obah-a-Tou his rightful place. You will be compensated as victor and we will test you against the prophecy. So, if you are to save the Natives, you must first get permission from them who died trying. You must journey to Mozan-Garo and awaken the saints."

Lancen nodded in compliance, not sure what she meant, but knowing that this was not the time to ask questions. He thought he heard Keira sigh in relief beside him. For some reason it brought him a small amount of satisfaction, but she was wrong to be relieved. Lancen was about to be tested as the Natives' divine hero, their savior—their war-leader! He had gone to Obuthahn to find purpose, to find the filling for whatever void had taken residence in his soul, but his journey had now escalated to a level that he never could have prepared for. Perhaps he was Obah-a-Tou, or perhaps he had embarked on an adventure that he would never live to see the end of. If the divines were out there, and for all he knew maybe they were, he prayed that they would help him.

CHAPTER 28

That night Obuthahn lit up like never before. Drums pounded loudly as the Natives danced round about uniquely colored fires that had been lit all across the camp. Magically fluorescent objects were numerous, causing the entire settlement to glow a soft blue hue. Olchers and game were being roasted by the dozen, the Natives keeping no mind for the morrow, inevitably dooming themselves to even greater starvation. Perhaps the most incredible sight of all, however, was to be found in the central pit where a monstrous natural flame burned brightly. The orange fire shot thirty feet skyward above a mountain of dried bones and wood.

Lancen sat comfortably on a bench near the top of the amphitheater, viewing the spectacular burning. Joining him were Avik and Adalyn. He had just finished relating nearly everything that had happened to him during the trial. He spoke humbly, leaving out all the details of his conversations and experience with Keira. The world was not ready to hear that.

Now they sat in silence. Lancen read over and over the lines of the prophecy, trying to establish what it all meant. If he was the fulfillment, then only the first two stanzas were complete. Nihwiah had commissioned him to awaken the saints, whatever that meant, and everything else was completely uncertain.

"This is what I don't understand," said Adalyn after some time. Lancen had a hard time focusing on her words with the emerald necklace that hung around her neck in plain sight. It looked nice on her, sure, but he couldn't help imagining how the piece of jewelry would have looked on Keira. Why had he been so intent on giving it to Adalyn? Back in Calderon she had probably received hundreds of pieces of jewelry even more valuable than this. Keira had nothing.

"Lancen," said Adalyn snapping her fingers.

Lancen brushed off the thought and looked the girl in the eyes.

"Why would those heartless savages leave the Shaharan boy to rot?" she asked, apparently for the second time. "Surely anyone with a soul would have at least tried to help him."

"And what the hell is a charro?" asked Avik.

Lancen couldn't help but smile at his friend's remark, but he chose to answer Adalyn first. "It's because they were taught to value the prophecy more than life itself, and they were in great danger. You two haven't seen those monsters, and I pray you never have to."

"Do you really believe they were skoles? And they came back and finished him?" Avik questioned.

Lancen shrugged his shoulders. Not wanting to think of any other possibility.

"What did they look like anyway?"

Lancen shuddered as the memory came back to him. He shuddered again to think that he could possibly, though very slowly, be morphing into one of them.

"The best way I can describe them is evil." The image burnt into his mind like a candle burning paper. It started as a small black mark, slowly consuming everything visible. "I could see it in their eyes. It was pure hatred like I have never known, malice even. They were almost human, but much, much darker."

Adalyn recognized Lancen's anxiety and rubbed a hand across his back. Even with his inner debate, he was thankful to have the princess by his side.

"What about the trolls?" asked Avik. "Were they as big as in the stories?"

"You are obsessed with the trolls!" Adalyn laughed.

"It's a fair question," said Lancen. "Yes, they were probably every bit as big as you imagine. I nearly passed out at the sight!"

Avik chuckled, "Was it their teeth? I heard that no one has ever counted the exact number of teeth in their mouths."

"Rows and rows," confirmed Lancen.

"How quickly could they have ripped you apart?"

Before Lancen could respond, Adalyn waved her arms and cut in, "Okay, I draw the line there! As much as I love talking about terrifying creatures attacking my Lancen, I would feel much better if we changed the subject."

She proceeded to kiss Lancen on the cheek and wrap her arm around his.

"Really?" asked Avik, rolling his eyes. "Like I'm not even here?"

"I'm sorry, brother," said Lancen honestly, but his friend didn't buy it for a moment. Adalyn had just said *my Lancen*. He didn't know whether to love or hate that. Internally he couldn't stop debating between Adalyn and Keira. They were both beautiful. They could both make him happy. His relationship with Adalyn wouldn't be accepted in Calderon, and a relationship with Keira would never be accepted in Obuthahn. Yes, he had wanted Adalyn for much longer, but what did his heart say?

It was completely unexplainable, and made no sense whatsoever, but the answer was Keira.

Yet as Adalyn entwined her fingers with his, he relaxed and went along with it. How could he ever refuse her when she was all he had ever wanted?

Lancen nearly chuckled. With all that was going on around him, with every ounce of danger he had been doused in, this was what he was worried about? Love? However, looking back he remembered something that Sidna had once said to him. *'Physical pain can only be suffered until death, but love is eternal. A broken arm will mend in weeks, but a broken heart can scar the soul forever.'* So which was really more important?

"I think it may be time for you to start believing in the divines," said Adalyn, entranced by the leaping flames in the pit. "It seems they have helped you more than once recently."

"Oh, I am not so quick to credit them," Lancen replied.

"Why not?" asked Adalyn. "What else could explain the things that have happened to you, like the woman? The disappearing hand?"

"I don't know," said Lancen, "but there must be an explanation. I just wonder why if the divines are really there, they would help me of all people."

"Well if you are this champion of prophecy, then that would make you the king of the savages, right?" the princess asked honestly. "I believe that would make you a prime choice for divine intervention."

"Wait, I like that," Avik cut in. "Lancen, King of the Savages!"

Suddenly, Lancen noticed Keira walking along side of the amphitheater, coming toward them. She had brushed her hair and changed into a short-skirted light blue dress, carved bands and bracelets coloring her arms. She looked amazing.

"Stop calling them that," Lancen mentioned boldly. "It isn't their fault."

"Seriously, what is it with you lately?" asked Avik, turning as dismal as the rising moons. "I understand why Hans left. You aren't who you used to be."

Lancen hung his head as Keira grew closer. "I am the same person. My eyes have just been opened."

Keira was now directly behind the large Shaharan boy, waiting to speak.

"You have always thought they were savages! At the mill you would call them that more than we did!" Avik fought loudly.

Lancen groaned and ran a hand down his face in frustration. "Hans has really rubbed off on you. You never know when to shut your mouth."

Avik then noticed the Native girl standing behind him. Giving her an undeserved glare, he stepped back to allow her to speak to Lancen. She bit down on her lower lip, fists clenched tightly. Firelight brightened her face and sparked in her eyes. She had bathed and emanated the scent of sage he was so fond of. She was stunning.

"Lancen," she said solemnly, struggling to keep her voice level, "can I speak to you a moment?"

"Yes," he answered earnestly. "What is it?"

Keira glanced at Lancen's friends and clicked her tongue. "Maybe in private?" she asked, motioning away from the amphitheater.

"Absolutely, no problem," he said, releasing Adalyn's hand. Butterflies danced in his stomach. Was this a chance to follow his heart? Or was it just an opportunity to crush someone else's?

Keira turned and moved away from the pit with haste. Lancen promptly jumped up and followed her to a relatively private spot behind a small cloth yurt on the skirts of the clan center. She turned to face him but refused to look him in the eyes.

"What is it?" he asked.

Keira shook her head and looked everywhere but at Lancen. "I don't know," she responded emotionally.

"Really," said Lancen, "tell me."

"I don't know," she repeated. "I just…I felt something happen between us in the cave. I know you felt it too."

"I've been meaning to talk to you."

"Please, just save it," Keira answered bluntly. "I don't know what happened, or why it happened, or why it affected me so much, but I have never felt the fire for anyone."

"The fire?"

"Yes, the fire! It dances inside the belly when you are with someone you love."

"Then I felt it too," said Lancen honestly.

"The problem is, you already have someone you love."

"Keira, love is a strong word."

"There must only be one fire. You must choose either her or me," Keira stated directly. Vagueness did not exist in her character. She was as a river, moving toward her destination, rarely straying.

"Can we talk about this?" asked Lancen. "It isn't that simple."

"Make it that simple," said Keira. "Please, I must know."

"Keira, I can't choose so quickly! I feel something for you, I do! But I have cared for Adalyn for years."

"There," said the girl, "you choose Adalyn."

"Wait, that isn't what I meant."

"Lancen, let me speak, and then we can be done," Keira said, finally looking up and into his eyes. "What happened between us was real, but it wasn't supposed to happen. It can't happen again. You do not need me, and I would be ridiculed for ever wanting you. It would never be okay for us to repeat those feelings."

Lancen looked at her in astonishment. "Listen, I liked Adalyn long before I met you. What did you expect would happen when we returned to camp?"

"Please," repeated Keira. "The decision has been made."

"But Keira, I never expected to feel the way I did for you."

"Nor I you."

"Can you let me explain myself?"

"I do not need to hear what you have to say," she said strongly. "It would not change the fact that you are a Noble and I am a Native! I no longer believe that you are the tyrant. You may even be Obah-a-Tou, but we cannot be together."

Before Lancen could argue, Keira had turned and briskly walked away. He remained motionless where he stood, completely astounded. How was this happening? Why, whenever he had a chance for everything to go right, would it always collapse on him and leave him lonely, wanting only what he couldn't have?

Then again it was possible that Keira had just made this easier all around. She had made the decision for him. He would be with Adalyn, which was exactly what he always wanted. So why was he still not satisfied?

Chapter 29

D
ressed in a sleeveless scarlet gown, the vatisus looked as amazing as she ever had. Her body-length hair had been wound tightly and stacked high. Neon paint ran up and down her bare arms and across her face, causing her to glow like some outer-worldly creation. Lancen and Keira stood beside her within the tight quarters of the tent in the pit, awaiting the moment they could step outside and receive their rewards. An inimical Shikobin fumed in front of them, breathing heavily and mumbling curses.

Shekii had just finished announcing them outside when Nihwiah looked at Lancen with a neutrality that she hadn't shared since he set foot in Obuthahn. She bowed her head respectfully and turned to Shikobin to whisper counsel. The moment of truth had arrived. Lancen feared the scorning crowd that he had faced before the trial, but upon exiting the tent, he stepped into utter silence. The air felt quite different than it had before. There was no hostility this night, no jeers, only intrigue and suspense.

Torch lights and numerous neon objects lit the pit to an astonishing brightness. Keira's dress lit up magnificently beside the fluorescent figures. With her head held high, her hair blew like fire in the breeze. Lancen tried to meet her eye as they walked, but she averted her gaze.

The chief and vatisus followed the two victors to the center of the pit where the mountainous flame had receded to a tall pile of glowing embers. Etnah, Shekii, and the other members of the council waited for them silently.

Lancen surveyed the faces of the Natives spectating. They seemed eager and even a bit hopeful. It was possible that their hero had finally come, Noble or not. Faces that had been wrought with hatred only a few days before now held expressions of gratitude and confidence.

Lancen tried looking to Keira again to gauge her reaction, but she refused to acknowledge him. He then looked to Adalyn, who watched lovingly beside a disgruntled Avik. This was the hand that Lancen had been dealt. He needed to accept it.

"Clan brothers and sisters!" called Shekii. "Your heroes!"

Cheers enfolded, with an unmistakable anticipation blowing with the wind.

"As is our custom," continued Shekii, "these victors will be rewarded by the council. We will hear the words of our vatisus Nihwiah, our Chief Shikobin, and even the subjects themselves. Etnah."

Etnah stepped toward Lancen and Keira, holding up a large wooden platter, covered by a red cloth. Unveiling the prizes, he smiled and faced the crowd. They marveled and applauded. On display was a finely crafted bow made up of polished bone. It had a unique and extravagant shape, with several rounded stones embedded into its glossy frame. Next to the weapon was a marvelous diamond tiara. It was small and delicate, but beautifully crafted. And beside it were two fist sized pouches, filled with what Lancen knew to be shining flawless emeralds.

Where do the Natives find these riches? Lancen asked himself. First there were Etnah's emeralds, and now the tiara. The Natives had no mines or systems, so where did it all come from? Any given Noble would lust after things of this nature. Greed would envelope them, and Lancen fought to reject that exact tendency.

"To my angel, Keira," Etnah started, grabbing hold of the priceless tiara, "I present the circlet of Malhanwin, once belonging to a great vatisus of past Obuthahn."

Keira bowed and allowed Etnah to place the exquisite item on her crown. Raising her head proudly, she looked incredible and elegant.

"And to Lancen of Calderon, a young man who has proven to be a true hero," said Etnah boldly, "I present the Sacred Tare, bow of the divines."

The audience responded in amazement while Shikobin scoffed, appearing very unsettled. Lancen reached out and humbly accepted his prize. His hand fit perfectly around its smooth handle. The weapon was light, nearly weightless as he controlled it with skill and swiftly put it into an armed position. He awed at its perfect and impeccable craftsmanship.

Lancen showed Etnah a thankful gesture, and the elf nodded back in understanding, motioning toward the two pouches. Putting forth his hand, Lancen retrieved the treasures he had come all this way expecting. He had done it.

As Lancen tried to contain his excitement, Nihwiah stepped forward, appearing to glide over the dark earth in her long gown. She raised a scratchy voice, "My beloved friends and kin to this chosen clan, the heroes we have before us are admirable without question. They have achieved what so many before them could not. They are victors of trial and will be respected as warriors in this clan.

"Keira has shown impenetrable strength and magnificent composure through opposition that would break even the greatest among you. She has chosen a path of honor, a path of grit over beauty. The divines have blessed us with a true and resilient soul in her.

"As for Lancen of Calderon, he will hereby be known as clan-brother to Obuthahn. He has proven himself with unmatched ability and unshakable courage. Though he may yet be the tyrant— " Nihwiah seemed to choke on her words. Pausing to take a deep breath, she calmed herself and continued with conviction. "Brothers and sisters, my word is law. I cannot deny the evidence, and I will not be known as the one who rejected our champion!

Though Lancen may yet be the tyrant, he *will* be tested and tried as Obah-a-Tou!"

The crowd remained in a silent wonder. No whispers sounded. No movement could be seen. Every being accepted the spoken words.

"I bid you all goodnight. May the divines bless and watch over us all," Nihwiah concluded.

As she finished and retreated, Shikobin reluctantly moved forward. He looked angrily to Lancen and Keira, then back to the clan before speaking.

Roughly, he began, "As chief and leader of this clan, I have pull and direction in events of importance like the one before us this night. Going against the discretion of our 'beloved' vatisus, I state proudly that Lancen *is not* Obah-a-Tou, nor will he ever be our champion! If it were up to me, the tyrant boy would be put to death for his mere association, and complete desecration to our ways and our prophecy! May none of us forget that he is our enemy!"

Nihwiah began to argue, "Chief that is —"

"Allow me the courtesy of breath for my concerns!" Shikobin fired at the vatisus. The Natives gasped as he spoke to her in such a fashion. No one had ever dared disrespect a wise woman in that manner. *Her word was law.*

"My people of ash," the chief continued, pointing a heavy finger at Etnah, "do not let the views of a mad man and a traitor blind your judgment. We must not forget who the tyrant is! Let us not lose sight of our roots, the ancestors that have fought continually for our freedom from the oppressing hand of Lancen's leaders.

"*My own SON!*" he screamed. "Eltou, the best of us all, has paid the ultimate price for our cause. I will not suffer our ways to be utterly spat on in this manner! Lancen must be killed! There is no such thing as restraint when dealing with the tyrant!"

As Shikobin finished he walked over to Lancen and spit in his face. Those in attendance held a silence as never before. There was no chanting or cheers, but all were concerned and unsure how to act. The quiet flare instilled a slight mass of faith inside of Lancen. The forces were finally changing to his benefit. There was a general hope that could be sensed from the multitude. It seemed as though they had found a place in their hearts where they actually wanted him to be their champion. He felt that this was an opportunity to seize the moment. With Shikobin now finished, it was his turn to speak, and he grasped it with boldness.

Stepping forward, Lancen faced the crowd and wiped the chief's saliva from his face.

"I know I do not share your blood," he began, "but I do share your spirit, your pain, and even some of your bitterness. I am not one for public speaking, but I do feel the right to address you as equals. I share your hunger. I feel for the oppression that you have all been burdened with. Honestly, as I have told the council, I do not know if I am your champion, but I will fight using the best judgment I can. If I do end up being your hero, know that I am on your side. I desire peace in this land for those that I care about, and if I must be an advocate in bringing that peace to fruition, then so be it. I am here for you, all of you, and I don't know what else to say."

As he concluded, he held his head up bravely. He knew he was building the trust of these people. It was shone in their eyes. He was becoming a symbol that could give them strength. They had repeatedly been through hell, starved, abused, and murdered. More than anything they wanted freedom from the nightmare that was their lives, and so did Lancen from his. Nothing was more desirable than rest from the stresses that had plagued him ever since the death of Sidna. So much had changed in such a small amount of time, and nothing in the world was more desirable than peace from the horrible pain that surrounded him.

Etnah stepped forward, nodding to Keira, and addressed the audience, "I know that my words do not mean much, and I am speaking out of turn, so I will be brief, but I must voice that

Nihwiah is correct, and we must trust her words. This could be the time foretold by our ancestors. This could be the day that our true path toward freedom begins. There is — "

Suddenly, as the former chief spoke, a flaming arrow flew over the crowd and pounded into the ground near Etnah's feet. Before anyone could react, the sounds of heavy footsteps and squealing horses resonated through the amphitheater. Natives rose to their feet as commotion combusted all around them. Without a moment's notice, dozens of Legion soldiers entered the vicinity, swinging swords and yelling curses as they began to charge through the spectators. As the Natives scattered and sprinted in search of safety, chaos enfolded. Many drew their primitive weapons, only to be surrounded quickly and forced into submission. Several horsemen galloped on a line and leaped into the pit, throwing incinerating torches as they went.

Lancen searched desperately for his friends, and as he did, a horrific sight entered his vision. At the top of the amphitheater, amidst the flailing and helpless Natives, and before the background of a growing wall of orange flame, an old friend stepped forth with a king's issue blade drawn and ready. It was Hans.

Driving it from his mind, Lancen focused on one thing at a time. Finally, he spotted Avik and Adalyn being cornered by a number of legionnaires. At once he took off toward them, drawing Nahabuk's axe from his side, but before he made it even a few paces, a heavy lance struck him across the chest and knocked him flat to his back.

Screams and crying were everywhere. The helplessness and shock of calamity forced the disconnection from all thoughts of prophecy. Flames swelled up around what pieces of the clan remained. The soldiers easily subdued all resistance as Lancen grimaced breathless on his back, staring up at the smoke-filled sky.

Forcing himself again to his feet, he saw a furious Nihwiah screaming at the attackers.

"We had an agreement!" she cried. "At the end of the war it was promised that the main camps would not be touched!"

"But you have something that belongs to us, savage!" said a large man from atop his steed.

Lancen's blood curdled and his fists clenched. He prayed this would be the last time he heard that voice — Goldtooth.

Not far away, a struggling Adalyn was dragged into the pit and thrown before Nihwiah and the Legion captain. Anger swelled inside of Lancen. He couldn't handle seeing this. Everything in his demeanor heated. Time was second to fury.

"You brought them here!" Shikobin screamed at Lancen, fighting the grasp of multiple soldiers. "It is your fault that tyranny is upon us!"

The chief was struck strongly with the butt of a lance and pushed into the dirt. Guards bound his arms and roughly battered him from all sides. "Curse you Lancen of *CALDERON*!"

Practical sense ceased to exist as Lancen's blood finally reached its boiling point. Goldtooth turned to face him, but before he reacted, Lancen had leapt upward, stepping into the captain's stirrup. Violently the boy grabbed him by the breastplate and threw him from his mount to the hard ground below. No thoughts passed through Lancen's furious mind as he landed punch after punch into the larger man's face. Just as adrenaline had completely overwhelmed his true will, the boy received a powerful blow to the head, knocking him face first into the ash.

A sharp boot nailed his back as a swift club blasted across his cheek. Lancen could no longer move. His mind commanded his body to rise and fight, but he was quickly fading from consciousness.

Goldtooth struggled to his feet and gave Lancen a brutal kick in the thigh. After spitting a mouthful of blood, he looked over and acknowledged Adalyn. "Well it is good to see you too, princess. I hope you have had a nice vacation? You'll be coming with us."

Lancen's vision blurred. Darkness started as an outer ring and slowly filled in his view of the world. As comprehension left him, he saw Goldtooth turn to the soldiers nearby. Wiping blood from his chin, the captain uttered one brief command, "Kill the boy."

CHAPTER 30

Memory and intelligence were abruptly brought to light. Color flowed in brightly, gathering and dispersing. Power of an influence greater than himself pulled thoughts, wishes, and images from the furthest, most diverse corners of Lancen's mind. As quick as a dash of light, the picture of the Master painted itself before him. The incredible being rose from the dust, golden robe glimmering in a soft light. As before, he moved through the door and into the room of boiling water, each foot seeming to hover above the grated floor. He stood perfectly still, back straight, head down. Slowly he raised a bony hand to the hood that covered his face in shadow. Like the sun rising, darkness left his face as the veil was pulled back.

The eyes of the Master were closed, his face gaunt and pale. There was a bluish hue to his skin, and a dark shadow cast beneath his narrow and pointing nose. Suddenly the image jolted closer, the Master's closed eyes now in prominent focus. They were violet in shadow but trimmed in gold lining. In a blink, the lids lifted. The oddities beneath were entirely white, with the exception of small black pupils in their centers. He opened his mouth to speak, but then everything was engulfed in darkness…

Clouds filled the sky in a dark gray while quiet thunder rumbled in the distance. A light rain settled gently on Lancen's face as his eyes slowly opened. Immediately he felt an uncomfortable throb at the back of his head. His vision was weak and blurred, gradually gaining awareness. He felt a hard floor beneath him, as well as the bumps of rocks. He was in the back of a carriage moving steadily on a Noble road. He tried to move his aching arms, but they were tied behind him. Everything hurt, but the worst of it all was a gnawing pain in the pit of his stomach.

Struggling into consciousness, he willed himself to sit up and view the world around him. There was a chill in the air, hitting his face like a sheet of ice. He assumed it was late morning, seeing as the sun had not quite risen over the giant mountains to the east. Looking out across the landscape, he saw a vast body of water, Aduran's Lake, not far in the distance, which proved he must be in the southern Ashlands. Several days must have passed since his most recent memory. The last thing he could recall was Goldtooth speaking, ripping Adalyn from the grasp of freedom, and Hans, standing above the pit like an artist of death looking over his masterpiece. The Natives had been ransacked.

Yet they were not the only ones to be damaged. How long until Lancen's own story would be over? For some reason he couldn't explain, breath still entered and departed through his mouth. Light still reached his vision, but how soon until he would go down as the Noble who tried to save the savages? He supposed that he could have left behind a worse story. At least this way he had fought until the end, even if he had failed in every matter of importance.

It was minutes before Lancen noticed the large mound of torn cloth moving up and down beside him. His head hurt, but it did not take long to discover that the pile was a beaten and broken Avik. They were alone in the rear of the carriage among a tarped-over mass of supplies. There were two legionnaires sitting on the driver's bench ahead of them. One promptly looked back and laughed at Lancen's disgruntled figure.

"Would you look at that, Alec, the notorious infant is awake!" he hollered. The soldier beside him hailed with laughter.

"How was the sleep eh?" the man Alec asked hysterically.

Lancen opened his mouth, dry lips tearing at the motion. His throat was scratchy and swollen. "Where are you taking us?" he managed to choke out.

"Oi! Walt!" Alec yelled. "The criminal speaks, he does!"

"Ha! That he does, my friend! Do you want to answer him or should I?"

"Why don't you do the honors?" Alec spat.

Walt looked back to Lancen and flashed a rotting and cocky smile. "The destination is Riverock, my good sir!"

"You mean his *final destination* is Riverock!" Alec piped back.

"Yes, well if it had been up to me, we would have ended him back with the savages!"

"Well it is a good thing you aren't in charge! The captain says we will get ten times the bounty if the boy dies by the block."

Lancen cringed at the mention of the captain. Coughing through a tender throat, he forced a verbal response. "He should have brought me himself."

"Yes, well he had a lil' princess to attend to now didn't he?"

"Your captain is a coward," Lancen said darkly. "He should have killed me."

The two soldiers erupted into obnoxious laughter.

"What reward would that leave us?" Alec asked, snapping the reigns of the two horses pulling the wagon. "If we took you back to Calderon, Roland would gut you. If we killed you on the spot, Roland would gut us! Captain Earnst is smarter than that!"

Earnst. Lancen's face heated as pounding anger forced itself into his body. The fiend had a name. There was now a title for everything evil. The golden tooth was attached to a vessel of the most vile, immoral composition imaginable, and for the first time, Lancen knew that the name of that vessel was *Captain Earnst.*

His suffocating hatred blocked out all other words spoken by the legionnaires. The man had ruined his life. He had now taken everything that Lancen had, twice. Earnst, the man who had killed his dog, the man who had led an attack on Obuthahn, the man who had taken Adalyn, would surely suffer.

"I vow through any power of heaven or hell, Earnst will taste the steel of my blade," Lancen seethed aloud, closing his eyes in the overwhelming aspect of revenge.

Alec and Walt laughed from their bench. "Maybe in the next life!"

Adalyn rode her own horse, but Captain Earnst followed her like a tail, excessively watching her every move. The burnt forest was as solemn and gray as it had ever been, the cold rain on her hair matching the sorrow in her heart. There was another storm coming. There was always a storm coming. Every corner of the land had grown dark and cold. It hadn't always been that way.

Words could never describe how she missed Lancen! Ever since the catastrophe at the celebration, there had been a gruesome ache in her chest. Tears had seemed to flow uncontrollably. In fact, it was incredible how many her body could produce. It would seem that after so many, the well inside of her would dry up, but it never did. She grasped the silver necklace that rested above her heavy heart. The boy she loved was gone, and the life she had always dreamed of had been dropped from beneath her like the platform of a hanging.

Her father would never let her leave the castle again. He would probably never allow her to leave her quarters, forever to be a prisoner within the walls of her so-called home. She hoped her father would stay weeks in Oritha. She understood that he loved her, that all he wanted was to protect her, but she hated his every order, his every demand.

She hated the thought of returning to Calderon. She hated the thought of Lancen being dead. She hated Hans for betraying them, now riding like a champion only yards ahead of her. The one thing she desired was to go back to Obuthahn and help them recover after the Legion's cruel jab, but it was impossible. Any window for her to run would be quickly closed. Even if she did make it back, the Natives would not welcome her. She couldn't return there, but the thought of Calderon made her sick. Longing only for what she could never have, she just wanted Lancen. She wanted the comfort of someone who truly cared, who wanted her to achieve her dreams, but that person was off to be executed. Everything was so wrong!

"You are lucky we found you before the duke returned," Earnst announced from behind her. "Can you imagine how worried this will make him?"

More tears. It was impossible to prevent them. She had never felt so empty.

"What is it, Princess?" Earnst asked. "You have everything a person should ever want back at the castle. Why would you spend time with those heathens?"

Adalyn closed her heavy eyes and felt the wind nip her cheeks. Taking a deep breath, she tried to picture herself in some alternate world where things hadn't gone hopelessly and helplessly wrong.

CHAPTER 31

The carriage finally rolled to a stop. Lancen was shivering, huddled in a ball next to Avik. Most of the day had been filled with bitter wind and a moderate rain. Now, at last, it had seemed to subside, and though daylight never seemed to come, night had already fallen.

Lancen was freezing and hungry. The beast inside of him was growing stronger every day. He eyed the legionnaires and held off the dream of ripping them apart. He somehow knew that their blood could satisfy his gnawing ache, fill the emptiness inside, but that was a road he refused to travel. To even think of such things ate at his conscience.

Walt and Alec were vile. Drinking, spitting, and laughing were constant at all sorts of horrendous notions. After setting up a makeshift camp, the two tied up the horses, lit a fire, and threw Lancen and Avik roughly to the earth beneath the wagon. Walt helped tie up the prisoners' legs before heading over to the fire, but Alec decided to be a menace.

"King of the Savages, huh?" Alec spat, giving Lancen a quick slap in the face.

Lancen didn't reply but stared at the ground with bottling anger. The outline of Alec's blonde hair and dirty face was blurry in his peripheral vision, heating his blood.

"It is a better title than you will ever know," Avik coughed, face wincing from the pain speaking caused him.

Alec turned abruptly and struck Avik across the head. "What did you say to me?"

"I think you heard him," said Lancen coldly.

The soldier threw back his head and laughed at the cloudy night sky. "Are you even Nobles? Because you seem more like weak savage girls! Maybe I should teach you something about strength."

Alec grabbed Lancen's head and threw it against the wet ground, forcefully pressing it against the earth. The disgusting man howled like a drunken wolf. Lancen grit his teeth and tried desperately to free his rope-bound hands. Straining, he released a growl in the struggle.

"Look at him whimper!" Alec shouted. "You're not escaping a Legion knot!"

With his head smashed against dirt, Lancen's frustration was growing out of control. If there was ever a fault in him, it was anger. He forced words past his mud-covered lips, "What kind of Noble are you?"

Alec released him and cackled. "Soon, a rich one!"

The man continued to giggle like an idiot and poke at Lancen's face. He was clearly looking for a reaction, and Lancen had to force himself not to give one.

"You're pathetic," said Avik from a doubled over and pained position.

Alec stopped prodding at Lancen and looked at the Shaharan happily. "You boys can learn a thing or two from me, eh? I'm what, four or five years older than ye?"

Avik had death in his eyes as he stared at the soldier. Lancen was back looking at the ground, his face now cold and damp. Wet dirt clung to his mouth.

Alec continued, "I am a winner, boys. You are losers. I win *because* I'm a bad man. Keep that in mind for the next life, in the off chance that there is one."

The awful man tapped on both of the young Nobles' faces and finally stood. After spitting on them, Alec left his prisoners to the darkness. It wasn't long before the mouth-watering smell of bacon emanated from his fire.

Avik groaned painfully. His breathing was harsh and forced.

"Are you okay, brother?" asked Lancen. This was the first chance they were given to speak openly since leaving Obuthahn.

Avik slowly lifted his head and smiled at Lancen. Bruises covered his face. One eye was swollen shut.

Lancen smiled and nodded. "Point taken."

Avik laid his head back with a grunt. A few moments later he started laughing unexpectedly.

"What?" asked Lancen in confusion, not being able to stop a smile from forming on his own face.

Avik didn't say a word but just continued to laugh. There was no humor in their situation. The world around them was unforgiving and cruel. They had been betrayed, forsaking everything for a far-fetched goal that they failed to reach. By Noshera, the two were heading to their deaths! What was so funny?

Lancen opened his mouth to ask but couldn't force words through his own fit of laughter. It was contagious as a plague. Something about Avik's amusement in the face of certain doom was hysterical. Staring west across the dull black lake, tears formed in Lancen's eyes as Avik's snigger intensified. It was several minutes of nonsense before the two finally trailed off and settled down.

Avik rolled over to his back and gazed up to the sky. Sighing, he spoke his mind. "Hans really did us over."

Lancen leaned his head back against the wheel of the carriage and closed his eyes. "Yes he did."

Before he had even finished speaking, Avik groaned in pain. "They got me pretty deep, brother."

"Where?"

"The side, in the hip," the Shaharan said through straining so fierce the veins in his neck nearly seemed to burst. "I think it went all the way through."

Lancen clenched his eyes shut. The events around him were

shouting that this was the end. Everything that he had ever dreamed of accomplishing would never come to pass. All the struggles and pain he had been through would be for nothing if he could not find a way to break the bonds on his wrists. How was it possible to have a life so short and so sad from start to finish? It was like he and Avik were trying to catch up to a reality where they actually had a chance to begin with. Freedom and survival were now their only incentives, just like the Natives.

Tugging and pulling, he fought with all his might to loosen the ropes that held so tightly around his wrists. He wanted tears to come to his eyes and release some of the density in his heart, but he hadn't been able to cry since Sidna's death. Now when everything was pitted against him, when there was so much unknown about the fates of Adalyn and Keira, and yet near certainty of his own, he was deprived of even shedding tears.

The girl he had found a love for would despise him, thinking it was he that had brought the terror that came to Obuthahn just a few nights ago, and in many ways, it was his fault. He had brought Hans to the Native camp, and it was he that caused his friend to storm off and find Goldtooth's brigade. Inside, he knew that he should be angry with Hans, but he had only himself to blame.

Now Adalyn, the girl he had always wanted, was being held captive, probably hundreds of miles away. Who knew what consequences would lay in store for her when her father found out?

Lancen dropped his head and pulled his wrists with all his strength. He could hear Avik breathing painfully beside him. He didn't know what else to do. It was like he was back in the cave with the skoles, having nowhere to turn and no chance of escape. Sidna had always taught him to call upon the divines in times of great need, but in this moment, he couldn't fathom them helping. After Sidna's death he had poured his heart out over and over, but not an ounce of solace ever came. For over a year he had abandoned all faith in the gods, and yet, even with all his doubt, he could not deny that something had intervened in the duke's stables.

Something had saved him from the skoles and lifted him free of an eternity underwater with the remains of Nahabuk. Perhaps prayer was worth a shot.

Calmly, Lancen opened his eyes and looked up to the sky. The two moons were glowing through mist and clouds. Only a few stars were visible. Was there anyone out there? Speaking aloud, Lancen asked in desperation, "Divines, I expect you do not exist, but Noshera, Athleon, Yehawa, if you will just give me the power to break this binding, I will remember you."

Lancen sat in silence for some time, with nothing but a cool wind and the soft cracks of a fire to disturb the ultimate stillness of the night. His mind was empty, and he could hear each and every breath. Something unexplained had been looking out for him recently. If that something was the gods, then now was the time for them to show it.

Avik struggled to sit up beside him. Lancen looked at his friend's pale face, sweating and sunken. Medicine was over a day away. They both needed this prayer answered.

Gathering all his force, Lancen pulled and pulled, exhausting all of the strength he could muster. The rope was tight, digging into his skin. His face turned red as he exerted himself past the point of breathing. His right wrist seemed to pop out of place at the tension, and then, just as he was losing vigor, his hand slipped ever so slightly. His heart pounded as he continued to tug, finding a second wind. The bond slipped more and more, burning off his skin with every little bit of progress. His body was hot as his shoulders cramped, but he kept pulling, until finally the rope passed the knuckles and fell loosely to the dirt. Lancen was free.

Breathing heavily, he held up his hands to show Avik, his right hand raw and throbbing The Shaharan sighed and smiled, closing his eyes in an exhausted relief. Lancen had to bite his tongue to keep from shouting for joy. Had the divines just helped him? It was hard to say, but if they were out there, he was grateful. Bringing a clenched fist to his mouth, he kissed it and threw it toward the heavens in appreciation.

After the initial excitement had cooled, Lancen looked under the carriage to where Walt and Alec crouched clueless over a sizzling skillet of bacon. With their backs to the wagon, they laughed, taking turns throwing back bottles of mead and warming their hands over the flame. Lancen wanted to kill them, his instincts telling him to tear them limb from limb. If anyone deserved such an end, it was them, but as usual, an unwelcomed morality battled off the desire.

"Are you going to run?" Avik asked with raised eyebrows.

Lancen shook his head. "No. I'm not leaving you."

"Then what's your plan?"

Lancen gave his friend a serious look. "I don't have one."

Gesturing for Avik to stay silent, he rose slowly to view the contents of the wagon. He knew that his axe and bow were somewhere among the piles of supplies in the back. Walt and Alec had boasted for nearly an hour about the fine craftsmanship of *their* new weapons. If Lancen could only find the Sacred Tare, he could take out the guards from a distance. He was practiced with his hands, yes, but he had always been much better with a bow. The sad truth, however, was that there was no way for him to climb into the carriage and dig through mounds of junk without alerting Walt and Alec. He had to find another way.

Very slowly, and as silently as possible, Lancen moved toward the legionnaires like a wolf hunting its prey. He was empty handed, and his head still throbbed from the strike he had received in Obuthahn, but somehow his confidence was high. This was his chance. Carefully, he crept up on the two men, holding his breath and fighting for maximum stealth. Each step was slow as he fretted over every stick and rock. When he was finally just behind them, Alec turned his head to sneeze, and Lancen froze like a spooked deer. Just an arm's reach away, the soldier spit and wiped his nose, then to Lancen's great relief, turned back to the fire.

It was now or never. Without weighing the consequences,

Lancen swiftly dove over Alec's shoulder and reached into the fire, grabbing hold of the hot skillet on which the bacon fried. Before he felt the pain of scorching metal against his already wounded hand, he threw it forcefully against Alec's head. The man immediately fell to his back on the cold ground.

Walt swore loudly and jumped to his feet. A seething burn bit at Lancen's palm as he immediately dropped the pan and waved his hand in pain. Walt reached for his sword a few feet away, but before he could make a move, Lancen had jumped onto his back and forced him into a choke hold. Wriggling, the soldier fought to loosen the grip, but Lancen only pulled tighter.

Choking, Walt managed to squeeze one word through his closing esophagus, "*Savage!*"

After only a short struggle, he passed into an overwhelming unconsciousness.

Breathing heavily, Lancen dropped the soldier and stood over his victims in amazement. Laughing out loud, he threw another kiss to the moons. Avik half-coughed and half-shouted for joy from his seat near the carriage. They had cheated death yet again.

Lancen wiped sweat from his brow and ran to the wagon to search through the supplies.

"What are you looking for?" Avik asked from the ground.

"Two things," said Lancen, tossing miscellaneous utensils behind his head. "More rope to tie them up, and more bacon."

Avik chuckled, "You are a monster."

Lancen found some wrapped meat and dropped it over the side of the wagon. The parcel landed with a thud beside the Shaharan.

The boy then found some rope and jumped over the side himself. With a smile on his face he couldn't help but say it. "I'm a hungry monster."

CHAPTER 32

F armer Curtis stared at the bowl of stew on the table before him. It was the same thing every night. The same carrots, the spices, the potatoes — everything was the same. And chunks of mutton, now that was something that he had learned to hate with a fiery passion. The food was like runny mire before him, something he could picture a pig eating. Is that what he had become, just a higher breed of swine?

"What's the matter?" asked Renna. "You don't like my cooking?"

Oh, and her voice! Stinging and shrill, every syllable irked him. She was never satisfied, always griping, always moaning.

"It's fine, dear," Curtis forced with half a smile. "Just not hungry, that's all."

"Not hungry my fat rear!" She retaliated.

He admired her honesty.

"You haven't eaten all day, and I'm not sure you even touched your supper yesterday."

Curtis sighed, "It's the mutton, dear."

"What's wrong with the mutton?"

Curtis held his tongue and spoke carefully, "The mutton, I am so sick of mutton."

"Well then do something about it, *dear!*"

Of course, one would think that with him being a farmer that he would have something to eat besides mutton and bread, but if it was only that easy! Life never was. He had all the crops he could ask for in his mountainous farm. From corn to potatoes, name it, and he had it. What he lacked nowadays was meat. He used to have cows, olchers, horses, and birds, but now he had nothing but sheep, hundreds and hundreds of sheep. They roamed like brainless zombies across his many acres of land just north and east of Riverock.

Angrily, Curtis dipped a wooden spoon into his bowl of slop. He was an average man, average height, average width. He sported a conservative clipped do and a long blonde beard. He was average, so was a little bit of beef every once in a while really that much to ask for?

He moved the spoon through the stew. He couldn't do it, he just couldn't. It wasn't the slightest bit appetizing.

"If you don't like my stew, then maybe you should do the cooking from now on," Renna scolded like a snob.

"Maybe I will!" yelled Curtis. "I do everything else around here!"

Just as he finished the outburst, a shocking scream rattled the house. It was a screech like he had never heard. Shivers ran down his spine. It was without question one of his sheep that had made the racket.

Renna sat unphased, blowing on a spoonful of stew. Curtis looked at her with wide eyes.

"Well, go check it out," she said carelessly.

Curtis grit his teeth and shook his head. Pulling on his pants, he moaned and grumbled different profanities. Quickly sliding his feet into his boots, he grabbed a metal spoke near the fire and headed out into the night.

The woman was fiendish. Who was she to sit around while he worked all day, and then tell him to go out again after he had kicked off his boots? Much less when it was freezing outside!

He wandered in the direction of the scream. This was just his luck. Another dumb ewe had walked off a ledge or wedged its foot between sharp rocks. He just hoped the stupid thing wasn't dead. He remembered his father telling him, *A sheep dead is a drachma wasted*. Perhaps it was that attitude that had caused a flock to gang up and trample the man in his old age, but Curtis knew better than that. Sheep were stupid and did not even taste good.

Before he had walked long, a graphic image began to unfold in the brightening moonlight. A fat sheep laid in gore ahead of him, an old female, surrounded by tall grass and thick dying flowers. The thing was torn to shreds. As Curtis stepped closer, the scent of blood filled his nostrils. He passed by a severed leg, a bloody ear, and finally a ravished head.

Nearly vomiting, Curtis stood over the half-devoured body. What type of demented creature could have done this?

Just then he felt a rush of cold air. There was a darkness, full of evil and malice, clenching at his heart. Looking up, he lost his breath and counted eight hooded figures around him. Their white eyes gleamed like candles. Their teeth were sharp as knives, mouths dripping with blood. Curtis longed for one last bite of stew as the beings slowly closed in around him, but it was too late.

The foremost skole growled and hissed in the most eerie voice imaginable, "We begin with this one. The Master will be pleased. Then, to Riverock."

"We could try Riverock," Lancen mentioned as he finished preparing the horses for travel.

"Why would we go there?" Avik asked breathily from the driver's bench of the carriage. His skin had become even paler than the day prior. Drops of sweat gleamed on his brow. "Goldtooth could have sent a rider to inform them of our coming."

"I admit it is a gamble, but you need a doctor. Riverock will have one."

"We should go back to Obuthahn," Avik insisted.

"And be killed on sight?" Lancen reasoned. "I don't think so. They will blame us for what Hans did, for what Earnst did."

"They may be savages, but at this point we are more likely to be killed at a Noble settlement. Besides, they might understand.

You are now a victor of trial."

"And an enemy of the chief."

"So what of the prophecy? Do we discard it?" asked Avik as Lancen pulled a pot of boiling water off the fire.

"I don't know," said Lancen. Removing the lid, he spooned out a stringy green weed and popped it into his mouth. *Disgusting.*

"What is that?" Avik asked with an upturned nose.

Lancen spit the mush into his hand and climbed to the driver's seat. "It is pit karp from the Swamplands," he answered. He had found it in a satchel among the legionnaires' supplies. He recognized it by the smell.

Lancen lifted Avik's shirt and removed the wrapping. He then pressed the weed into the open wound just as he remembered Etnah doing. Avik grimaced but held still long enough for Lancen to wrap a new bandage.

"Where did you learn to be an alchemist?" Avik asked with a smirk.

"Where did you learn to fight?" Lancen shot back. "Because those soldiers really got the best of you."

Avik laughed before curling in pain. Lancen watched him worriedly and looked to the sky. The sun had already emerged from behind the Ash Mountains. If they hurried, it would be possible to reach Riverock before the next dawn, if Avik could even make it that long.

"I may have to lie down in the back," Avik mentioned, closing his eyes and trying to slow his breathing. "If we go to Riverock, do you have a plan, in case they think we're savage advocates?"

Lancen turned his head and looked-over Walt and Alec, tied and gagged in the carriage bed. They squirmed and eyed him with hatred. Lancen moved on from their faces and down to their armor. The Legion insignia struck a nerve. Alec was just his size.

"I do now."

CHAPTER 33

That evening Adalyn sat atop a large hillside to watch the sunset. She stared with empty eyes and a heavy heart as Earnst's men unloaded gear and set up camp. The sunset had been beautiful, many shades of the darkest reds to the lightest orange. Yet it might as well have been gray and dismal, for it did nothing to improve her broken countenance.

She never should have left the castle. Clearly, she was not strong enough to face adventure, nor the hardships they accompanied. At least for a while during her stint with Lancen and the others she had felt liberated. She had felt like the sky was the limit, always pondering where they would go next and what they would do, but Hans had ruined everything.

She couldn't bear the thought of him. He had approached her several times since leaving Obuthahn, but she would push him away. Forgiveness was not something he deserved. Not yet.

A high-pitched howl pulled her thoughts back into the present. She stood and looked across the burnt forest around her. The sound was unnerving and demanded her attention. What had caused it? The men continued to unpack and wind down until it sounded again, this time louder and with many others.

Captain Earnst stepped forward out of his tent, longsword in hand. "What's going on?" he hollered. "Who's keeping watch?"

In curiosity, Adalyn moved back toward the company of soldiers and tents. Finding her way to the animals, she hid behind Shera, her father's trusted mare. An odd feeling of darkness crept into her heart. The horses squirmed and kicked uneasily, sensing the same thing. There was something coming, quickly.

Adalyn ran to the center of camp as a soldier to the north screamed. Ferocious growls were heard and a moment later, dozens of large black hounds emerged from the surrounding woods, storming into the camp from all directions. The monsters were swift and as powerful as tigers, muscles rippling. Soldiers armed themselves, but many were too late as the beasts pounced and thrashed.

In a fury, Earnst fought off two attacking dogs, his sword gleaming like lightning as he cut them down in a blur. Adalyn froze in horror, watching a display of gore and panic around her. Unable to breathe, she shrunk and covered her eyes. She sat there hopeless, just waiting for one the creatures to rip her apart. Terrified, she screamed as someone grabbed her by the shoulder, but looking up, it was Captain Earnst. He yelled and pointed fiercely, "In my tent, *NOW*!"

She complied immediately and ran into the open-ended structure. Growling and cries resounded outside as metal clanked and flesh ripped. Adalyn backed into the corner and stood on top of Earnst's bed, looking for some way to defend herself. She saw a small dagger stuck into a table on her right, but before she could reach for the weapon, one of the monstrous hounds rounded the corner and halted at the tent's entrance. It had short, clipped hair and long, vicious teeth, too big to be a wolf. Adalyn fought the desire to scream as the beast lowered its head and stepped toward her, snarling.

In a rush, she leapt from the bed and overturned the table. The dog jumped at her, a claw ripping the sleeve of her blouse. In desperation she tugged at the dagger stuck in the wood. The monster growled and fought its way around. The knife pulled free just in time for Adalyn to slash at the hound's nose. It recoiled long enough for her to jump up and cut a hole into the fabric of the back wall. Dropping the blade, she ripped apart the opening and tumbled through. Jumping to her feet, and not looking back, she sprinted into the trees. The sounds of battle bounced through the woods as she ran for her life. With no idea where to go or what to do, she only knew that she must get as far away as possible.

Suddenly her foot caught a root and sent her plummeting down a large hillside. Rocks and sticks tore at her as she rolled. Hitting trees and dropping off ledges did nothing to stop her momentum, but abruptly the ground leveled, and she tumbled her way to a stop. Gathering her wits, she tried to push herself onto her knees. As she attempted to find her breath and brush off the shock, a low growl rumbled just feet in front of her. Raising her head, she looked into a hound's demonic white eyes. The beast seemed as large as a bear, crouching before her like a devil in the flesh. This was the end. Adalyn had nowhere else to run.

Before it attacked, heavy footsteps crunched behind her. She couldn't help but scream as a giant hand grabbed the back of her blouse and threw her onto the rear of a violet horse. She caught a glimpse of the being as it tied together her hands and feet. It was a dark figure, tall and thin. A heavy cloak shadowing all of its features, everything except the glint of its sharp skolic teeth.

The afternoon had transformed into evening as Lancen and Avik journeyed across the southern Ashlands. Dust began to fade into white rocks that jutted from the earth. They had just begun their ascent toward Riverock, the cliff-side village. It was a town built high into the face of the mountain, and a monument to the strength of the kingdom. During the Lurid War, it had played a pivotal role in the movement of troops and the defense against the coastal elves. As a fortified settlement in the only pass of the southern mountains, it stood as an impossible force for the Endwan's to conquer, and subsequently crippled the Natives' chance at victory. Now it was one of the most revered townships in the kingdom, a place of honor and pilgrimage. Lancen only hoped that the rumors of its nobility were true, for the time was soon coming when he would depend on it.

As they rode, their route began to rise before them, as the river to their west began to fall. It did not take long before the water was nearly a hundred feet below their rocky cliffside path. The night was beautiful, cloudless as the first stars blossomed near the moons.

Walt and Alec were fidgety prisoners but learned quickly that there was no escape from their bonds. Avik breathed heavily and spoke little, leaving Lancen alone to his grievous thoughts. At this point he spent little time worrying about things being different. He had learned long ago that it was impossible to change the past. No matter how dark or regrettable, no matter how bad he wanted it, change could not happen. There was no use for him to fret over the disaster of Obuthahn. Right when he had received a hint of acceptance and purpose, the Legion snatched it from him. All he could do now was press on.

The legionnaires' carriage had been filled with plenty of supplies, food and clothing, but little riches. Lancen's bow and axe were now strapped securely to his person, but the two bags of emeralds Etnah had presented him with were missing. So much for fame and fortune. He and Avik were now rogue travelers. They would be hunted by the Legion, knowing no plan and few places to run. Riverock was his only solution, and it was immediate. After Avik received the necessary aid, Lancen hadn't the slightest notion of a plan.

His mind wandered back to the question Avik had asked him just that morning. What of the prophecy? Should he simply discard it for nothing? Over the last few weeks he had truly come to believe that there was something to it, that some weight was pulling him this way and that in order to fulfill the Native premonition. Yet in an instant it had all collapsed around him, leaving him with little knowledge of what to do, save that which Nihwiah had instructed. He was to visit the tombs of Mozan-Garo and 'awaken the saints.' He had to ask himself if it was worth it. Could the prophecy still be real? Somehow, through all the blood, scorn, and defeat, some small amount of belief remained within him. It was the only direction he had left. With Keira and Adalyn out of his control, there were few things left to drive him. The prophecy was one of those remaining.

As he thought, a distant light sprouted up in the darkening world. At first, it looked like a campfire, but as Lancen drew closer he could feel that it was something more. Screams were carried on the wind, the fire grew, and an overwhelming feeling of darkness enclosed around the carriage. A foul mood was present, and Lancen's nerves rumbled like an incoming storm.

Every minute began to seem like hours as they pressed forward. The fire burning before them grew larger. Lancen knew in his heart that it was Riverock facing doom but refused to accept the thought. He should have been prepared for this. Evil seemed to follow him with every step. It was the retribution of hateful gods, picking him up just to knock him back down.

After what seemed like ages, voices were heard from the road ahead. There were many people, women and children, running toward him. As they neared, their agony was apparent. Blood and tears stained their cheeks. Dirt and grime engulfed their garments while crying and remorse floated in the air. An unnerving despair was present on every face.

"What's happening?" Lancen asked as the commoners began to pass them by.

Shock was evident in their eyes. Their ears seemed closed to language.

"What happened?" Lancen hollered more forcefully.

A short and round woman blinked away her blank stare and looked up to Lancen and Avik on the driver's bench. "They attacked. They burned everything."

"Who attacked?" Lancen quickly questioned.

The woman's face softened as the memory of horror reentered her mind. Tears strolled down her cheeks. Shaking her head over and over, she turned away.

Lancen's throat tightened as he hit the reigns. Smoke clouded the sky as he pushed onward. Ahead he could see a soft orange glow lighting the sky. Buildings seemed to emerge from the horizon, constructing themselves along the cliff-side, some overhanging the sheer face entirely, supported by numerous diagonal braces.

"What should we do?" he asked Avik nervously.

His Shaharan friend grimaced and raised his head, too weak to respond.

Lancen wanted to hide, but something told him that whatever darkness was awaiting ahead was there for him. He would not run from it. If these last few weeks had meant anything at all, he needed to find out who had done this.

As they approached the gaping city wall, he brought the wagon to a stop and jumped to the dirt below. With a consuming cold flowing through his body like blood, he pulled the bow from his back and readied an arrow. Hate and depression worked their way into conscience, forcing him to breathe heavy and bite his tongue. There was no mistaking this feeling, no mistaking its enormity. Skoles had attacked here. He was sure of it.

Stepping slowly, he made his way through the main gate and into the township. He glanced back once at Avik, sweaty and pale above the horses. If the Noble-Shaharan had any chance whatsoever at survival, it depended on Lancen. Lack of confidence tore at him as he walked. Riverock was in ruins.

The carnage surrounding him was staggering. There were bodies everywhere, lifeless and ragged. Buildings were enflamed and carriages in shambles. Were it not for the yells ahead, he would have thought the village was already dead and defeated. Unfortunately, he suspected that those very traits would not be absent long.

With bow in hand, he walked steadily, watching every shadow and ready to shoot at anything that moved. Bumps of fear riddled his skin as anticipation stole his breath. He was close.

As he approached the rear of a large hall, fighting and destruction began to make themselves more current. Armed guardsmen, farmers, and aristocrats alike ran to and fro chaotically. Wind rushed, and shadows danced as Lancen felt the presence of skoles. When he had passed the building and rounded the corner, any courage remaining in him faded. The same monsters that had gotten the best of him in the cavern, the same sadistic shades, rushed through the wind like an illusion in the night. Like ghosts, they appeared and departed, their black cloaks like smoke behind them. There were at least eight of them in total, with over twenty men trying to fend them off. Their movements were swift and powerful. Their hissing and shrieks bit at all nerves.

Out of fear Lancen released an arrow and missed one of the larger skoles as it tormented a group of three exhausted townsmen. The monster pulled away from its task and turned its head slowly to Lancen. Its face was malicious and gut wrenching, with anger passing over it in a wave. In fury it threw back its head and violently cried to the sky, "*OBAH-A-TOU!*"

As if on cue, all surrounding skoles threw off the men that fought them and pivoted to look at Lancen. Demented others began to emerge from the shadows and step toward him. They all moved slowly closer, coming around him just as in the cave. The one who Lancen had shot at was clearly a leader among them, being larger than the rest and adorned in more ornate attire.

For a moment the battle had stilled. Men struggled to their feet and watched the skoles close in around Lancen. He was running out of time, seemingly helpless and suffocated by the darkness.

Urgently he searched for a strategy, no matter how far-reaching or desperate he had to find something! He would not stand down.

Looking around his person he scanned a flaming pile of rubble beside him. Among the trash and burning wood he spotted the handle of a torch. Driven by horror, yet eerily focused, he reached into the mass and pulled free the object that could have only hung on the wall of a large tavern or hall. Dropping his bow, he pulled out the axe of Nahabuk with his opposite hand and glared into the evil white eyes of the skolic leader. Abruptly he charged and swung his axe forcefully toward the monster. The creature shrieked a chilling cry and shot out of the way before the weapon could find its mark.

The skolic leader spat some sort of curse in an ancient and fearsome language before swiping back angrily at the young Noble. Lancen leapt backwards quickly, but a second strike found its mark before he even knew what had happened. He felt a warm scratch shoot across his chest, and another braze his cheek.

As he stumbled backward, the men of Riverock began to jump into action, catching several of the skoles off guard. The leader, however, did not lessen his focus on Lancen. Again, it swung a strong hand at the boy, its nails deadly and long. Just before the blow landed, Lancen threw up the torch and blocked the attack. The item shattered on contact, shooting sparks all around. Spinning about, Lancen sliced at a second incoming skole and watched as it fell dead to the ground.

With no time for celebration he looked again to the skolic leader just in time to duck another deadly strike. In a burst of unharnessed strength, he cocked back his axe and forcefully threw it into the monster's neck. In a flash the head was severed and dropped like a stone to the ground. What remained of the skolic being fell to its knees, and then chest-down to the dirt.

It took a moment for Lancen to realize what he had just done. Reaching up, he wiped black spatter from his face. Two dead skoles laid in gore at his feet! The remaining monsters cringed and shrieked in terror. As fast as they could they pulled away from the surviving men to flee the vicinity, back into shadow and then north into the mountains.

The men of Riverock stood exhausted in the town square, turning their attention to Lancen, aweing at the young stranger. They watched him closely as he breathed heavily and tried to ignore the shock that fought to overpower him. With no control he bent over and retched onto the lifeless body of the skolic leader.

As he gathered himself, one man, dressed nicely in a sea green robe and a golden circlet stepped forward from the group of Nobles. Blood dripped like sweat down his arms and face. His brow was low, and expression concerned. Earnestness lived in his eyes, while his soft features and blood-stained beard evoked wisdom.

"Who are you?" the man asked Lancen without waver.

Lancen did not know what to say. Avik's life could very well depend on who he said he was. If he responded wrong, the Riverock guard could finish what Walt and Alec had started.

"I am just a boy," he answered.

The old man nodded but held his curious gaze. "Aye, just a boy. Just a boy that drew the attention of skoles, and then slew two of them before my very eyes. I am Bondor, counselor of the mountain region."

Lancen nodded in response. As he did, he noticed four large scratches across his torso, and that they had completely removed the Legion insignia from his armor. He felt the wetness of blood soak into his shirt.

"I applaud the courage you have exhibited this night. What is it that brought you to this grim occasion?" asked Bondor.

Lancen nodded and carefully thought over every word he would say. He responded slowly, "I am with the Legion. My companion and I were attacked by two traitors. I managed to capture them, but my friend was wounded badly. I came here for assistance."

"The Legion, eh?" said Bondor skeptically, never breaking his gaze on Lancen. "Next time arrive sooner. We have many wounded of our own to deal with, but seeing as you were the one to drive them off, we will see to your friend first. What is your name, sir? Our bards will want to know the name of the crimson warrior whom they will praise in song."

His initial instinct was to trust this man. He wanted to tell them his name, his mission, and his struggles, but there was no one in Serondhel that he could truly trust anymore. Hans had proven that. Among the Nobles he could not be Lancen of Calderon. "My name is Rune."

CHAPTER 34

L ancen paced to and fro across the walk of an old cliff-side balcony. Within an aging hearth just a few yards away, Glendic the physician prodded into the open wound of Avik's side. Lancen tried not to watch, biding his time until the doctor's analysis. The night was dark, and the wind frigid so high against the mountain. The scratches on his chest burned beneath their dressings but did little to distract him from the cold. He'd rather take on burning flesh and frozen wind than face the anxiety of the physician's workshop. At least he no longer had to stress over Walt and Alec, who were sitting very secure within the walls of a Riverock cell.

As Glendic suddenly appeared in the doorway, Lancen's heart jumped in his chest.

"In all honesty," said the doctor steadily, "I doubt there is anything I can do here."

Slowly, Lancen released a breath, and worry overtook him. "What do you mean?"

To his surprise, Glendic then smiled and laughed, wiping a tear from his eye. "No, son, I think you have the wrong idea! This is a dark night indeed, but in your friend's case, luck is with us."

"How?" Lancen asked, confused. He had watched Avik all the way from Aduran's Lake. He was there as his friend had fallen in and out of consciousness, turning more and more pale, losing all strength.

"Believe me, he wouldn't be here if not for you," said Glendic optimistically. "The Swampland weed that was placed into the wound seemed to fight the present infection with a poison of its own. Your friend was weakened by the method, yes, but overall, signs of recovery have made themselves apparent."

Lancen could barely believe the weight that was lifted from his shoulders, the ease of each breath leaving his chest. Avik was going to recover. "Thank you, sir. I don't know what to say."

Glendic smiled and placed a hand on the boy's shoulder. "No need to thank me. This was your doing. Now if you'll excuse me, I have an unnerving number of others who require my assistance."

The doctor patted Lancen's arm and turned toward the entrance of the hearth. Looking back, he gave him an enthusiastic nod. "There is someone here for you."

Confused, Lancen stepped into the hearth and looked to the entrance. A normal looking man stood with his arms behind his back. At the sight of Lancen, he bowed and waved toward the door.

"Sir Rune, Counselor Bondor requests that you join him for supper," he announced.

Lancen looked to Avik at once. The Shaharan was lying on a sheeted bed with a feather pillow. He was resting easily for the first time in days. There would be no harm in leaving his side for a short while.

Nodding to the villager, Lancen followed him out of the hearth and through the ravished structures of Riverock. As they marched past the battlefield where Lancen had slain the skole leader, horror found its way back into his mind. Several men were at work to clean the gore and wreckage, but to Lancen it was as if the battle was still raging. There was darkness in his heart that evoked a disturbing fear. He never again desired to face a skole.

Before long they had moved beyond the village square and approached what appeared to be the town hall, the largest building of the settlement. Inside the massive front doors was a spacious anteroom, adorned lavishly with the giant horns and heads of many strange animals. Counselor Bondor waited just inside, sitting patiently in an arabesque lounge chair. His cloak had been changed, and the blood washed from his face and beard. In the torchlight, Lancen could now see just how old the man was. Heavy lines covered his face and dark circles surrounded his eyes.

"Thank you for joining me, hero," stated Bondor as Lancen approached.

"It is an honor, sir," he replied politely.

"Yes it is," said Bondor, gingerly rising from his chair on a swollen knee. "Walk with me."

Lancen complied and followed the man through a heavy door and into a high ceiling corridor.

"Who are you, warrior?" the counselor asked, limping at Lancen's side.

The boy responded in context, "I am Rune of Transiric."

"No, I asked who you are," said Bondor gruffly. His face seemed light and kind, but he winced with every painful step.

Lancen eyed him with suspicion. "I am who I claim to be."

"No," repeated the counselor calmly, "I'm sorry but you are no legionnaire. I can see it in your eyes. If you do not wish to tell me who you are, then fine, but at least answer me this: Who is it that you're fighting for?"

Lancen stumbled for words. Bondor saw right through him, a dangerous reality indeed. Lancen could not admit to defiance, nor could he continue his cover of being a legionnaire. In this moment he trusted himself and his friends, no one else. He refused to say anything that would implicate guilt.

"Well boy, do you wish to answer me?" Bondor asked.

The man seemed trusting, but so had many others. Lancen had to be careful. In these times the slightest admission of treason to the wrong party and it would be his neck in the noose. Finally, he attempted to answer. "I don't mean to be elusive but no. I will admit that I am no soldier."

Bondor laughed, "Do not play coy with me, boy. You are an enemy to the king."

Lancen chose not to utter a word. He did not want to agree with the statement, but he also couldn't force himself to deny it.

"Your legionnaire prisoners are foul, but they are honest," stated the counselor. "Tell me your mission."

Lancen contemplated a way out. If he turned and ran, he could most likely juke the guards and lose them entirely on the city street. But how could he escape with Avik?

"Your silence tells me more than your words ever could," claimed Bondor. "Do not be so naïve as to think I am not familiar with the name Obah-a-Tou."

Chills coursed through Lancen as the two rounded a corner and stepped into the main hall. A massive dining table was front and center, decorated with a feast for kings.

How did Bondor know of Obah-a-Tou? *And why has he not arrested me?* Lancen thought.

"You're right. I am no ally of the Legion," he admitted darkly.

"It is not wise for a man to name an enemy without first knowing his allies," stated Bondor, taking his seat at the head of the table. "But you need not fear speaking ill of the Legion here. Riverock has long been a stepchild of the Noble realm."

"Do you not support the king?" Lancen asked, being motioned to take a seat adjacent to the counselor.

"Boy, I have killed far more men than I care to admit. I have watched villages burn and children scream, all on the orders of our 'noble' King Scharric. He is no friend of mine."

Bondor proceeded to uncover a platter of roasted pork and began to fill his plate. "Go ahead, eat."

Lancen looked at his empty plate and then to the feast before him. He was starving, but the items on the table did not appetize. He craved something more.

"Obah-a-Tou is not a name that I have heard in quite some time," explained Bondor, "but these days are dark indeed. I suppose it is no surprise that the moment of the Natives' hero has finally come. I will admit, I am surprised that you are not an elf."

Lancen lowered his brow, trying to discern Bondor's allegiance.

How could a Noble counselor not be loyal to the kingdom? It did not make sense, and Lancen was hesitant to say anything at all. "It is difficult to believe I am their hero," he said guardedly.

"When a monster as dark as those we faced this night looks to you and shouts Obah-a-Tou, I take it as a pretty sure sign."

"I was just at Obuthahn," Lancen disclosed, "but I led the Legion straight to them. Everyone will blame me. I cannot be their champion if they hate me."

"They are a deprived people, and when the poor are hungry, they will not hesitate to eat from a dirty hand," said Bondor, watching as Lancen slowly dished himself a meager portion of food. "After the war I attempted to repair my relations with the eastern elves. I even managed to establish a black trade that had been operational until only recently. No matter how you have offended them, reparations can be made."

"You traded with the Endwans?"

"Aye, but it was discovered by the king. In my heart I have never meant harm to the Natives, but I fear they may soon pay the price for my derision. It is for this cause that I will be so quick to comply with your request."

Lancen was confused. "I've made no request."

"There is a council being held in Oritha as we speak to discuss the obliteration of the Natives. Normally I attend such meetings, but this time I was not summoned. On behalf of the Natives, you will ask me for aid, and I will comply."

Lancen was taken aback. He was still waiting for the catch. Why would Bondor be so open with a complete stranger?

"Why do this? Why trust me?"

Bondor chuckled and raised a cup of wine to his lips. "My village has been ravished this night. Our supplies have taken a great toll, and many have died. Surely the king holds me in contempt, and it is only a matter of time before he sees to take my head. I have little to lose."

Throwing back the cup, the counselor drank its entire contents and then continued. "That being said, my men are loyal. They will do what I say and go where I send them. Allegiance is what I offer you.

"War is coming, hero. The Natives have prodded, and the Nobles have more than given it back. Fire and blood will rain from the sky, and no one will go untouched by darkness. Friends in times like these are hard to come by. I ask you now Obah-a-Tou: what is to be done?"

Lancen looked to his plate and breathed deeply. He was not ready for decisions like these. He was too young to have such great influence, and too indecisive. However, Obuthahn did come to his mind. The people there were in dire need. He thought of Keira, hurting and hungry after Goldtooth's attack. With Roland soon to learn of Adalyn's venture, the camp would be at risk. Perhaps now was an opportunity for Lancen to help them — really help them. He had not spent much time thinking about it, but Obuthahn was depending on him. If he sat by and did nothing, Keira, and everyone else in the clan, was sure to perish.

"Send your men to Obuthahn. They have little food and are in grave danger."

Bondor closed his eyes and nodded. "It will be done. The time is coming fast when Scharric will order the death of all Natives. There is no more avoiding conflict. It is now time to prepare for that which is inevitable. I have already sent a caravan to Rendonhall for supplies. Upon their return I will move my people to the Ashlands."

"They will not receive you," noted Lancen.

"They will have no choice," said Bondor confidently. "I command a company of soldiers with powerful arms and sharpened swords. There will be no resistance when I offer my aid."

"Well you have my thanks, but I have no way to repay you."

"I do not require gratitude. What I do need of you is strength. I know nothing about you, but I feel a light. Obah-a-Tou is not a title to be used carelessly. You have no idea how imperative your calling is."

Lancen struggled to find a response. This was all coming on so fast. He was not ready to be a war general or ruler. He could barely take care of himself, let alone a whole community — an entire nation.

"I'm not ready," he stated.

"War is not convenient, hero. It never has been. There will be inconceivable loss, and all will suffer, but it is up to us, people like you and I, to rise up and guide our realm of influence in an honorable direction. If that guidance requires our lives, then we must give them. Regardless of the expense, our courage could prove the freedom of millions. Do you promise to join me and fight this war?"

Lancen's heart pounded rapidly. The counselor's words were empowering and resonated within him. For too long he had been unable to make up his mind. Though his encounter with the Natives had been far from flawless, he now knew with surety that it was them he needed to protect. With no doubt, he still knew that he would never betray the Nobles, but to wage war with the Legion was not the same thing. Oppression and tyranny had to end, and Lancen would do all he could to make it happen.

"You have my word," the young Noble answered with conviction.

"Very well," said Bondor boldly. "Then I pray that our alliance will be long and rewarding. Now I ask you again. Perhaps this time you will answer. Who are you?"

Lancen looked up and into the old man's soft blue eyes. "I am Lancen of Calderon."

"Ah to an extent, but who were you born to be?"

Lancen nodded. "Obah-a-Tou."

CHAPTER 35

The next morning a gray haze hung in the sky. A red sun rose and sent bright waves onto the struggling world. Swirling fumes of smoke drifted skyward from the shattered homes of Riverock. High in the mountains, an icy breeze gave a subtle nip.

Lancen sat exhausted on the steps of a leveled cottage near the highest point of the cliff-side town. Before him was a vast and marvelous view of Serondhel. From his perch he could see leagues in all directions. To the south, green and brown grass stretched for miles on the opposite side of the river. To the north was a grand view of Aduran's Lake, beyond which were endless jutting hills of dark ash, blemished only by the winding river. To the west were several small mountains, embraced by giant boulders and stark pines. And on the horizon, he could make out an endless line of trees that he knew to be Darkwood Forest.

Where he sat there was an immediate atmosphere of defeat and mourning. Riverock had been torn apart. Many homes were lost, and many bodies burned, but there was something about this scenic view that filled Lancen with wonder. Through all of the horror and destruction of the night before, there was a silver lining to be found. Bondor had pledged his allegiance to Lancen and vowed to help fight for the Native cause. There was no underestimating the impact this would have, and Lancen couldn't have been more grateful for the direction it gave him.

Yet even with this new development, there still an immediate choice to be made. Should Lancen return with Bondor and his men to Obuthahn? Avik had told him earlier that morning to follow his heart, but that was easier said than done. If he did not return to Obuthahn, his only option was to follow the prophecy — 'Travel to Mozan-Garo and awaken the saints' as Nihwiah had put it. That would be a hard task to accomplish when he hadn't the slightest idea where to find such a place.

As he sat in contemplation, Lancen reached beneath his tunic and retrieved the key that still hung around his neck. Feeling heavy in his hand, it still gleamed a flawless gold. The small arrow on its side was carved to perfection. He didn't know why he had kept it, but something about it told him to hang on. It signified the start of his journey, of his destiny. He liked it. Grasping it tightly, he held the object close to his chest and focused on the breeze brushing across his face.

Nearly an hour later, when Lancen had almost set his mind on returning to Obuthahn, he was summoned to the village gate. Climbing up a wooden ladder to a post atop the wall, he met with one of the Riverock guard.

"What is it?" he asked.

"There are people here," said the guard evenly, "a Native elder and a teenage girl. They claim to be looking for you."

"Show me to them."

At once Lancen followed the guard down the wall to a spot directly atop the wooden gates. Below them, just outside the village, stood a tall Ashlander and a slim Shaharan girl. They pulled behind them a stout olcher toting bundles of supplies.

A smile formed on Lancen's face as he bent over the railing and called down. "Wasn't expecting this," he jested.

Etnah and Keira looked up to him at once. They wore heavy brown cloaks and grim expressions. The girl stared up only a moment before turning her gaze. Lancen was glad she was here, albeit surprised.

"We are glad to find you alive," said Etnah with a hint of relief.

"The manner in which you were taken from Obuthahn was one thing, but to hear of what happened here…astounding!"

Lancen motioned to the guard beside him. "Let them in," he ordered.

Without pause the boy moved back up the corridor and climbed down from the wall. Meeting the Natives at the gate, he greeted them with a lightened heart.

"I don't mean to come off that it's not good to see you," he admitted, "but why are you here?"

"Must you even ask? The prophecy calls us," Etnah responded. "We were planning to rescue you. To discover you in such good health is a great relief. The villagers mentioned horrible creatures. Could it be — ?"

"Skoles," Lancen finished for him. "There was little I could do."

"They said you drove them away," said Keira suddenly, looking to her feet. "They said the *legionnaire* drove them away, 'The Crimson Warrior.'"

Lancen chuckled and shook his head, *The Crimson Warrior*? He was grateful for Keira's concern. He had expected her to blame him for the attack on Obuthahn, or if nothing else, resent him greatly because of Adalyn. Yet there she stood, within the gate of Riverock.

 "I did only what I could," he said. "It wasn't much."

"They said you killed their leader," mused Etnah. "And he struck you?"

"Only grazed the surface."

"To slay a skole," Etnah gawked, "your blood is truly curious."

Lancen sighed and noted Etnah's remark. The elf remained the one person to know that Lancen was bitten by a death hound. Sure, little was known about skoles, but the legends spoke darkly of any victim to their bite. Soon Lancen would want to question the former chief more about the disease, but there seemed to be more pressing matters at hand.

"How is Obuthahn?" he asked sincerely. "I never meant to draw the Legion there."

Etnah looked to Keira, but she refused to answer.

"The camp was wounded, but not mortally," the elf stated solemnly. "The two of us do not blame you, but the chief, of course, and many others hold you responsible. Fortunately, few were killed in the attack and only a handful injured. The Legion was there for the dual purpose of finding Adalyn and serving you 'justice.' They did not mean harm to the clan as a whole, not yet."

Lancen hesitated to ask but couldn't resist. "How is Adalyn?"

"She is well on her way to Calderon by now, but fine, I imagine. Although I do not expect Duke Roland will take kindly to our sheltering her. Retribution is coming swiftly to the Ashlands."

"I imagine that is why 'the prophecy' called you here," assumed Lancen.

"Aye bird, we cannot abandon thoughts of destiny when you may be the only hope we have left," said Etnah. "We followed your trail as soon as the Legion departed. The reality is, we do need help, and we're clinging to our very last hold — the prophecy."

"Well you will be pleased to hear that Riverock has offered their aid. They will travel to Obuthahn within the week in our defense."

"Obuthahn will be hesitant, but that is joyous news. The people of the Ashlands would never turn down such kindness. Not when they require so much aid."

"Shikobin will not be happy."

"Shikobin is a traitor," grumbled Etnah. "He was bent on the camp fleeing to the lands north of Desolate…buffoon! To cross the mountains in this late season would be suicide. Fighting is the only option we have left, and we must do it with our champion, Obah-a-Tou, leading the way."

Lancen stood still, not knowing whether to feel honored or intimidated.

"Where do we start?" he asked.

"Luckily we have interpretation to help us in this first action. While Obuthahn prepares for battle, we must rush to the Swamplands."

"The prophecy?"

"Aye, Mozan-Garo. You must attempt to awaken the saints. I do not know how, and I do not know why. It will be the ultimate test to determine whether or not you truly are Obah-a-Tou. I have been to those tombs before, and I will lead you there."

"I imagine we must leave at once. Obuthahn does not have time for us to rest." Lancen said, thinking aloud. His heart beat quickly. His objectives were clear, and he would not face them alone. His allies were few, but he was grateful for them nonetheless.

"I will fetch Avik," he said. "We'll gather any supplies that Riverock can spare and depart immediately."

CHAPTER 36

Within an hour the group had found their way beneath the village gate and on the road toward Aduran's lake. They were clothed in warm hooded cloaks as countless flakes of snow began to fall all around them.

According to Etnah, the route to the Swamplands was too rough for any carriage to survive, and any animal they brought would have to be set loose once they reached Darkwood Forest. After a discussion with Bondor, they determined that Riverock's limited number of horses would be better used in aiding the soldiers as they marched to Obuthahn. So with nothing but their own bodies, and the skinny Ashland olcher, they were off.

Heavy packs were strapped to their backs and determined looks worn on each face. Avik sat atop the olcher's back, packed on with whatever supplies they could not carry. Though he was clearly recovering, and he hated the thought of being a burden, he did not yet have the strength to walk with the others.

Lancen had managed to gather their packs, bedding, and many perishables from a Riverock merchant whose shop remained mostly intact. He had offered Walt and Alec's legionnaire armor as payment, but the shopkeeper insisted on donating everything Lancen requested. *The Crimson Warrior* would never again be charged a drachma in Serondhel if she had her way. Lancen marveled at the prestige but did not feel worthy of it. In his mind he was no hero.

As they walked, conversation was obsolete. Lancen watched Keira, who maintained a brisk pace ahead of him. She had hardly said a word since arriving in Riverock, and Lancen could tell that she was trying to send a message. Without words she was telling him that she was heartbroken. She was pretending to be strong, but he saw through the façade. There was a resentment about her that Lancen wanted to silence, but it was easier said than done.

"How are you feeling?" Etnah asked Lancen, quietly enough so the others couldn't hear. This was the first discrete moment they had been allowed since the night before the trial.

Lancen knew what the elf implied. Skolism.

"I'm hungry," he said. "It never fades. I know what will satisfy it, but I would never."

"Good," said Etnah. "You must be strong. While I was in Obuthahn I managed to steal a word with the Vatisus. I told her everything, Lancen. I needed, or rather, *you* needed her wisdom."

Lancen stared at the trail ahead and kept walking. The air was bitter and frozen while snow began to pack beneath his boots. This was the conversation he had been waiting for.

"Is there a cure?" he asked.

"Not that she knows of," said the elf, "but we agreed that your transformation does not match that of legend. We came to the conclusion that as long as you do not feed, you will never sink fully into darkness."

"Feed?"

"Must you ask?" Etnah retorted. "It is your curse, and you know it better than I. If the hunger is not unbearable, then you must discard it as a notion of evil and focus on the tasks at hand."

"What if it becomes unbearable?"

"The day you decide that is the day it will beat you."

"Well it has not beaten me yet," said Lancen, determined.

"And I have faith in your will. Do not fret over that in which you have no control. When fate brings us back to Obuthahn, Nihwiah will look further into the matter. Until that day, this subject is dead. We will speak of it no further. Understood?"

"Yes."

"Very well, let us continue forward. We have a lot of ground to cover."

Etnah clicked his tongue loudly and quickened his step to catch up to Keira. Taking a deep breath, Lancen held pace behind them. He tried to review his thoughts, remember and contemplate their plan of action, but one recurring word resounded unstoppably in his mind: *Feed.*

It seemed an age had passed before the company reached the bottom of the cliff-side descent. As evening rolled in, the sky remained lit in a dim brownish hew. Snow continued to fall and intensify, covering the land all around them. When it was more than ankle deep, Lancen considered their course.

"Should we find shelter?" he called through the wind to Etnah.

The elf stopped and looked back. Snow clung to his hood and salted his dark face.

"We must reach the lake tonight," Etnah answered, "especially if it continues to snow."

The elf nodded his head awkwardly before turning east and trudging away from the road.

"Where are you going?" Lancen asked, concerned.

"Something odd is at play," said the elf. "Continue to the lake. I will catch up."

Confused, Lancen watched as Etnah disappeared into a thick curtain of heavy snow. Where was he going? Why now of all times? Pressing forward, he had no choice but to trust the eccentric elf. Was there a method to Etnah's madness?

"Why is he leaving?" Lancen called to Keira, hurrying forward to her side. The olcher and Avik remained close at their backs.

"Do not ask me," said Keira. "Perhaps he needed to relieve himself."

"Why would he depart in the middle of a storm?"

"Maybe we aren't alone," suggested Avik.

And that thought stuck with them throughout the night. The

weather remained brutal and cold for a time, but after walking another mile or so, the blizzard lightened and eventually stopped. The world grew still, and Aduran's lake became visible in the distance. Marching through the ocean of snow, few words were minced among the three warriors. Avik spoke briefly of times past, but conversation did not endure. Fear was too thick in the air. The weight of the world was on their shoulders, and their only guide and leader had vanished into the night. With the former chief gone, the others would look to Lancen for direction. Leadership was a concept that he would have to get used to, quickly. When it seemed like their legs could carry them no more, they had finally reached the shore.

"We should make camp," said Lancen through shivers. "But we'll need to set a watch."

"I'll go first," said Keira, heaving her pack onto the ground beside her.

"Should we build a fire?" asked Avik before carefully sliding off the olcher's back.

"I'm not sure that's a good idea," said Lancen, "but I suppose we can make a small one until Etnah's return."

"Then the snow," stated Avik dismally.

"Then the snow."

The three proceeded to unravel and form a makeshift camp in a clearing not far from the road. When they finally managed to light a fire, it did little to warm them, so they simply wrapped themselves in every blanket they could find and laid atop the ice.

Keira stared off and up the road with apparent anxiety on her face. Lancen wanted to talk to her, but she did not seem welcoming. He had too much else on his mind to dwell on her not speaking to him. He had Adalyn to think of anyway. Where was the Noble princess? And was she thinking of him?

Solemnly, he rested his head, speaking but few words to Avik before drifting into an uneasy sleep.

CHAPTER 37

I n the capital city of Oritha a council met to discuss the ultimate fate of the 'savage' Natives. Among very prestigious company, Duke Roland sat behind a massive stone table in the center of King Scharric's grand palace hall. Leaders from all corners of the peninsula were present. Among them was Duke Furlott of Rendonhall; General Surget, commander of the King's Legion; Captain Branagan, leader of the king's personal guard; and of course Scharric himself, ruler of Serondhel.

Other less notable figures in attendance were counselors from the various smaller regions. There was Sir Goodrum of Andoville; Sir Canondir of Rutledge; and even Sir Mendoff of Glencroft had journeyed over mountain, plain, and sea to join in the discussion.

The king sat in grandeur at the head of the table. Dark shadows hung below his heavy brow as he quietly listened to his subordinates' debate. Gleaming, a large golden crown rested low upon his head, nearly touching his bushy black eyebrows. Draped in robes of gold and scarlet, the liege had not uttered a single word in hours, only looked on, intimidating and wise in the late evening.

Just as unnerving was the king's captain. Branagan's head tilted forward as he watched whoever had the floor through a silent glare. The man never said a word himself, but Roland could see a depth and understanding in his eyes. The captain was not oblivious to anything that was being said, and though he seemed neutral, it would take but one order from Scharric for him to slay everyone in the room.

It was now the dead of night. For hours the group had pulled back and forth between attacking the Natives and holding their peace. Serondhel was on the brink of destruction, the likes of which had never before been seen. Attacks from the Natives had become 'too frequent,' and a final decision needed to be made. The consensus agreed that their nuisance had gone too far, and the leaders in attendance disputed between mercy and blood.

"Just three weeks ago warriors from Tomutah attacked one of our caravans on the road to Oritha," Canondir brought up heatedly. "Their annoyance has crossed the line!"

"And before that they blockaded the highway on our end," said Goodrum, a giant of a bald man with a salt and pepper goatee and a low booming voice. "I agree, end the trout skins!"

"I'm sorry, but I will not have it!" Roland cried. He had no choice but to defend the creatures of which he knew were not entirely savage. "They have just as much right to the land as we. If our end goal is peace, then let us work through diplomacy. Let us begin a trade! The Natives can obtain valuable resources."

"Trade with the Savages! Have you lost your mind?" fired General Surget. "Why don't we all throw darts with trolls while we're at it?"

"The evidence remains," added Goodrum, "those no-good bog rats can't seem to keep their slimy paws off my merchants!"

Roland clenched his fists under the table. The bigotry in the room was as unbearable as it was biased.

"They wouldn't touch your men if you would just stay east of the lake on *our* road!" he stated strongly. "The Natives are more peaceable than you think, but they are only as civilized as we allow them to be. We have never given them a choice between civility and barbarity."

General Surget scoffed and pounded the table, enraged. "You don't think they had a choice when they killed six of my best men in their mushroom fields? They are heartless animals and nothing more!"

"May I ask what the hell your men were doing in their

mushroom fields?" Roland howled.

"That's enough gentlemen," said King Scharric suddenly. His voice was calm, but instantly the men at the table bit their tongues, albeit continuing to glare one at another. Scharric leaned back in his lavish chair and with one finger began scratching his trimmed black beard. His eyes were sharp, but expression relaxed.

"I have come to a decision," he said, "and frankly, it is one that I have been waiting to make for quite some time. For years the Natives have prodded, performing their offensive rituals and killing every Noble they can lay their hands on. They live by mindless blasphemy. Their faith in the divines is disgusting. We are the champions of this land. If I can make myself clear: there is no higher power than us.

"My mind is set, and my decision is final. All the elves of Serondhel are to be destroyed. They have long been a blight to my land, and if they somehow desire peace, then perhaps they will find it in the afterlife, by the small chance that there is one. We start with Tomutah, shouldn't take more than a few hundred men. From there you shall await further instruction."

"Yes, Majesty," answered General Surget at once.

Roland could not fathom what he was hearing.

"My king," he pleaded, "I beg you to show a small amount of mercy."

"*I'LL SHOW MERCY WHEN THEY KEEP THEIR DISTANCE!*" Scharric roared.

Instantly the ruler's calm visage had morphed into a fierce burst of indignation. The wrath in his eyes was unquenchable, but as fast as it had come, the moment subsided, and his countenance was composed once more.

"My mind is made, friend," he said softly. "I will not be mocked."

"I understand, Majesty," Roland forced through a shaky breath.

As he spoke, one of Scharric's squires reluctantly stepped into the hall. The Noble leaders at the table all turned their attention to him.

Sweat shining on his brow, the young man stuttered, "I bring word from Calderon. I request Duke Roland's leave."

Roland raised an eyebrow as drastic thoughts came rushing to his head. Was there an uprising? Were the fields pillaged? Did the wineries shut down? The last thing he needed right now was another dispute to resolve. Perhaps the bog elves had finally betrayed Calderon, disproving everything that he had just been fighting for.

"What of Calderon?" Scharric asked impatiently.

"It is a personal matter for the duke, Majesty, regarding his daughter."

Roland stood from the table at once and turned to the king for permission. Annoyed, Scharric rolled his eyes and waved his hand, granting the request. Immediately, the duke followed the young squire out of the chamber and into the marble-walled corridor.

The boy looked up at him timidly. Stumbling over his words, he began, "S-s-sir, I am burdened to bring you grievous news. You must know—"

"Tell me steward," commanded Roland eagerly.

The young man looked to his hands and held up a rolled piece of parchment. "I would have you read it, sir, so you will know they are not my words."

Roland zealously snatched the parcel from the squire's hands. The boy nodded and backed away, as if to flee from a present danger.

With trembling fingers, Roland unrolled the document, and as calmly as he could, read its contents.

My Duke,

> *Dark fortune is upon us. The boy of the mountains, whom you had sent us to kill, yet lives. He escaped our grasp and went under our noses to the castle stables. There he robbed you of your three finest roans. It is with heavy heart that I also inform you that he has taken Adalyn. She was kidnapped and dragged beyond the city walls. An informant approached us with the news that she had been taken to the savage camp of Obuthahn. I and my men are to travel there in haste. I vow that we will do all in our power to bring her safely back to Calderon. I will not rest until I find her. May our swords be sharp when we bring justice to her captors.*

> *Captain Earnst*

In a blur, the parcel slowly fell from Roland's fingers. The walls began to close in, spinning absurdly around him. The ceiling seemed to drop, and the corridor tighten at every angle. He could feel his blood pulse beneath his eyes, clouding his vision. Every new breath seemed louder than the last as his view of the world turned a scarlet red.

Feeling as though he were hit by a crashing wave, he fell roughly to his knees. His shaking jaw clenched as he balled his hands into fists.

A failed order. Sympathy for the savages. He himself had caused this world to crumble around him. Adalyn was gone, taken to lands wild and foreign. Worry suffocated his heart. Rushing back to him was the vivid memory of the stormy night, the soaking courier from the capital, Etnah's request to warn the target. Roland, against all common action and brainless sense, allowed his slave to walk free. Now the necromancing heathens had his daughter.

Grasping for control, he willed himself back to his feet. Hunched over and groping at his knees, he tried not to heave. He couldn't believe that Adalyn was gone. He had been betrayed by a filthy savage. To think that he had just spent the entire evening fighting for those monsters! The Natives were nothing! Whether they harmed his daughter or not, he would see them dead!

And as for the boy of the mountains, he thought. *If our paths ever cross, I will rip out his heart with my bare hand!*

He had been given a solitary order from the king, and he had chosen to show mercy. Never again.

Blood pounding, malice engulfed him. Rising erect, he strode swiftly back to the doors of the grand hall. Throwing them open, he stepped forward in a fury. All members of the council looked to him at once while Scharric grit his teeth and demanded an explanation.

"Kill all the rotten savages," Roland seethed. "I would see every last one of them dead! I demand an immediate attack on Obuthahn in the Ashlands!"

King Scharric tilted his head back, chuckling darkly.

"That's more like it, Duke," he said smiling. "Your wish is my command."

CHAPTER 38

When morning came, Lancen brushed a layer of snow from his blankets and sat up to greet the morning chill. The world remained brutal and dark as the sun hid itself behind the mountains. Not far in the distance, Aduran's lake was disturbed only slightly, reflecting the daunting black peaks to the east. The road wound toward it, forking just before the water. To the north, it led up and through the Ashlands. To the west, it wandered beside the lake and through barren trees before veering south toward Darkwood. Avik shook a few feet away, vigorously attempting to renew the iced-over fire.

"No need for flame," Etnah mentioned, walking past the large Shaharan. "We should be off at once. You will not be cold once your body awakes."

Lancen rubbed his eyes and shook his head. He wasn't sure whether he was happy Etnah had returned or not. The elf was confusing and stressful, but it was clear that the good of his knowledge outweighed the bad of his unpredictability.

"Did you find what you were looking for?" asked Lancen through a dry throat.

"Aye, bird, we were not alone on the road, but whoever was watching did not attack in the night."

"Who follows us?"

Etnah smiled and clicked his tongue. "I don't know. Keep your guard up."

The elf laughed out loud and began to whistle, throwing packs on the olcher and helping Avik to its mount.

Lancen crawled from his bed and prepared for the day's walk. In order to maintain sanity, he decided to brush off Etnah's strange response. He looked for Keira and found her up, tossing her pack over her shoulders. He couldn't say why, but he was unable stop thinking about her. They had barely shared a moment, but it felt like the tide, every emotion that he thought was lost returned whenever he looked at her. 'The fire danced within his belly,' and he quietly hoped that it hadn't been doused within hers.

Somehow, Keira appeared determined and rested. Lancen on the other hand, was exhausted. His motivation was weak and his resolve bitter. Drastically his world had lifted and dropped, over and over in the past few weeks. He had fallen for Keira; she resented him. He was given Adalyn; she was taken. He was named a hero; his clan was ransacked. Now Obuthahn was doomed to annihilation, and Lancen felt like he was poking at the foot of a giant. Since leaving his mine, he had failed in every matter of importance. Why would this current task be any different?

"Just keep moving forward," he whispered. "Nothing is in your control, except deciding not to fail." *No matter what, I cannot give up.*

Lancen blew on his hands and rubbed them together. He had wanted to be in this position, a position to do something great, but now that he was here, he felt powerless. Everything was poised against him. He had found himself in the middle of a fight that he knew he couldn't win, but to stop now could mean the death of thousands. So he rolled up his bedding and laced his boots. Holding tight to his axe, he raised his pack and followed the others back to the road. He had to keep going.

As they reached the lake, the group veered left. Moving swiftly in the distance, but growing closer and closer, was the river. Above the water, they could see a small but finely constructed bridge. As they approached, the sun crept over the mountain and cast beautiful rays on the crossing. Its craftsmanship was intricate and precise. As Lancen reached its base, he noticed that even the stones of the floor were riddled with worn tales of ancient kings.

"Who built this?" Lancen asked. "Was it the Natives? It's far too old to be Noble."

"This is the work of dwarves," said Etnah casually.

"Dwarves!" repeated Avik. "I thought they were a myth, although many say that the dwarves were the ancients."

"Many may say that the dwarves are the ancients," said Etnah smartly, "but those that do are a shade darker than stupid. Dwarves are still in existence. The ancients are not."

Avik pressed the subject. "How do you know?"

"Because I have met them—the dwarves, not the ancients," Etnah proclaimed. "True, many dwarven cities have been abandoned in our land. There is a ruin just to our east, through the gap in the mountains, but the dwarves are not extinct."

"Can you tell us about them?" asked the Shaharan from atop the olcher.

Lancen shook his head. Avik was too curious.

"I suppose," said Etnah. "Much like the ancients, dwarven cities are built mostly underground. They are carved delicately beneath the earth, with massive halls and stores of riches. I'm afraid it was the warring elves that caused them to depart. Most migrated north, to lands unexplored, and unknown by Natives.

"But one settlement does remain active in the northern mountains. It lies deep in the range, far out of view of the Nobles, and far out of mind of the Natives. They call it Entupathia, 'city of gems' in the Noble tongue. It is an exquisite place and one that I would very much like to see again."

"Why have I never heard of this city?" asked Avik.

"Because they keep to themselves," said Keira.

At once she dropped her head and stared at her feet, as if she had forgotten that she was refusing to speak.

"What do you mean?" Avik persisted.

Keira kicked at the snow and scowled.

"They make for excellent warriors, stout and strong," she said. "I curse them for not fighting by our side in the Lurid War."

She proceeded to walk across the bridge without waiting for a response. The others followed promptly.

Avik turned to Lancen quietly. "What's wrong with her?"

"Nothing," Lancen defended. His friend wouldn't understand. Keira had been through hell, and the fact that she remained so strong was astounding.

Avik raised an eyebrow and turned once more to Etnah.

"So," he began, shaking off the moment, "what do you know of the ancients—if they truly weren't dwarves?"

"Very little," said Etnah with a sigh. "Their disappearance has been a mystery for the ages. I have seen for myself some of their structures. What they accomplished beneath the earth was absolutely astounding—*cities* of gold! They contain machinery and metal works as the Nobles have never dreamed. Massive halls are lit by witchcraft. The air is full and rich, even miles below the surface. Piled into every crevice is fortune unfathomable.

"But ancient ruins are perilous. Native gems are collected from dwarven cities, not the ancients' halls. Evil lurks within the aged walls, wielding dark magic. There are creatures, *crones,* that would give even the bravest warrior nightmares. Few that traverse deep into a ruin ever come out, and those that do are forever changed."

"Have you ever seen a crone?" Avik questioned.

"Aye, but I wish I hadn't. I believe even skoles seem tame and approachable in comparison. Never before or since have I met something so vicious and fearsome."

"I'd like to take one on," said Avik vainly.

Lancen rolled his eyes. "I pray you don't get the chance."

"As do I," agreed Etnah, "but speaking of darkness, I feel that the sun has chased away whatever was following us. I feel comfortable settling down for some breakfast."

CHAPTER 39

The group unwound just beyond the bridge and only a stone's throw from the lake. The snow had thinned around them, brown grass rising sporadically throughout the white.

"How far to Darkwood?" Lancen asked as he pulled a piece of bread from his pack.

"Three days at least," said Etnah. "Though I wish it were less."

Lancen nodded and stared at the food in his hands. Though in good condition, the morsel was far from appealing. The taste of food no longer satisfied. The hunger still grew, slow but certain. He wanted meat, and more, but would never give in to the darkness.

With his mouth open in disgust, Lancen lifted his gaze. His cheeks warmed as he noticed Keira watching him from a few feet away. She turned her head quickly, but the damage had been done. Lancen was now certain that the fire still burned.

Determination took over as Lancen moved to where she was sitting. Avik reclined for a nap, while Etnah wandered slowly away from the road. Frustrated, Keira tried to avoid him, turning away and eating her bread, but Lancen knew that he could fix this.

"I'm sorry," he said softly, "about everything, but at least talk to me."

"I do not want an explanation," Keira answered.

"Then I won't give you one," agreed Lancen. "I just need you to be on my side."

Keira blinked away an annoyed glare. "I am on your side, but it is out of duty. Do not expect friendship."

"Then why did you come for me? Why did you join Etnah?"

"My people need you. That is why I'm here. Nothing more."

Lancen struggled as nerves were rolling in. He had to speak his mind.

"I need something more, Keira. I can't get it out of my mind."

"You have chosen Adalyn," said the girl, allowing her bread to fall to the snow. "You can't reverse decisions like that."

"I never chose Adalyn."

"But you did!" said Keira strongly. "And I am foolish. I wish I had stayed with Engle in the cave. He was perfect for me, and I took it all for granted."

Lancen bit his tongue, avoiding a curse.

"I need you Keira," he repeated.

"Why do you need me?" she asked, looking up honestly and into his eyes for the first time since Obuthahn.

He knew that he did in fact need her but did not know how to articulate the words. He cared for her, he desired her, and he longed for her, but why?

"You opened my eyes," he said after some time. He would speak from the heart, and not wait for his brain to contort the emotion. "You represent everything that is good about the Natives. You have shown me how great your people can be when treated as equals. I'm obligated to fight, and you let me know that it is not for nothing."

"But you chose Adalyn," Keira repeated. The response seemed to trump all others.

"I haven't chosen," said Lancen seriously. "The world has dumped on us an insurmountable task. I don't want either of you to hurt for my sake, not when you deserve so much better than me."

Keira looked toward the lake, and the Ashlands spreading far and wide on its opposite bank. For a while she stared silently, the glossy shine of water reflecting in her amber eyes. It looked like a sunset, deep and beautiful. Eventually she turned back to Lancen, her expression earnest but softened.

"You are the best there is, and I forgive you."

Lancen didn't understand her logic. *The best there is?* She didn't know him. Although he had wanted forgiveness, for the attack, for Adalyn, he wasn't sure that he deserved it.

"And I ask you to forgive me," Keira continued. "I don't want to believe any longer that your part in my life is over. I forgive you, but things will have to be different now. They can never be as they were in the cavern."

"I'm not sure they ever could be," said Lancen dismally. "For now we must be focused on the task at hand, and I can't do that with the thought of you resenting me on my mind."

"I don't resent you. You may think you need me, but I *know* Obuthahn needs you. How could I resent our hero?"

"I have done nothing heroic."

"Ah, but you're *The Crimson Warrior*!" Keira jabbed with a lightened spirit.

Lancen shook his head and took a bite of bread. Nothing.

"Will you answer me something honestly?" Keira asked in earnest.

"If I can."

"Do you believe we can save Obuthahn?"

Lancen looked out across the lake and into the Ashlands on the horizon. The answer was no, but how could he tell her that? With the aid of Riverock perhaps there was hope, however small, but against the entire King's Legion?

"I don't see how it is possible," he answered sincerely, "but we have to believe there is hope. I have nothing to go back to. If destiny is real, then Obuthahn has something to do with mine."

Keira sighed. "What better cause is there to die for, right?"

Lancen agreed soberly.

"I want to believe there is hope," said Keira, "but what hope is there? We are grappling for the end of a rope that was never even there. The Nobles outnumber us a thousand to one! There is no hope. And what of destiny? What can we really do about it? Simply hoping will get you nowhere without action, remember?"

"I will follow Nihwiah's counsel and awaken the saints. I will unite the kingdoms of old. I will battle the tyrant and strike down the false gods."

"Don't tell me that you now believe in the prophecy."

"But you do," insisted Lancen. "I know you do! And I will not give up on it."

"We should try speaking to Duke Roland," said Etnah suddenly from behind them. He approached swiftly, with eagerness in his expression. "He will be furious without question," he continued, "but Roland is a reasonable man, and a very close friend. If he will listen to me, then perhaps we can avoid an attack altogether."

"And if he doesn't listen, he will kill you," said Keira, trepidation apparent.

"It is a hefty risk, but one that must be taken. If they come at us with their armies, we will be defeated. Calderon could be a powerful ally."

"What of Mozan-Garo?" Lancen asked. "Are we to just abandon it?"

"No, you must continue," said Etnah surely. "I will go to Calderon alone, if you allow it, Champion."

Lancen considered it carefully. His heart sank to think of Etnah departing again. He was their guide and captain, how were they supposed to find Mozan-Garo without him? But his point was critical. If the duke's mind could be changed, then the risk had to be taken. Etnah was the sole person that had any chance of changing this outcome. If he was successful, it could mean the life of every last Ashlander. This was Lancen's call, his way of contributing to the Native's welfare.

"I would have you go," he said to Keira's dismay. She sighed and bowed her head. Now that she knew Etnah was alive, the thought of losing him again must have been piercing.

Etnah nodded and placed a hand on her shoulder.

"I will take you as far as Darkwood Forest," he said, "but then I must be off. Duke Roland will be returning soon, and it is imperative that I meet him there. With Adalyn on my side, I would say that the odds of succeeding are strong."

Lancen approved and looked up at the elf with conviction. "We should get going."

For the rest of the day the company pressed on over hill and crevice. The snow began to fade and the air warm. The dull colors of the Ashlands departed, and browns and greens began to emerge. For a brief moment Keira stopped and looked toward her home in the north, as if to say a final goodbye to the land of her upbringing.

But they were pressed to continue, and as the day progressed, few words were spoken. The soft clops of the olcher's hooves were the only sounds in the quiet afternoon. As evening came, suspicion of followers resumed. Noises were made and darkness was felt. Trees seemed to close in about them, casting shadows in all directions. Rising slowly, the two moons cast a gloomy light on the weathered road.

Closing whatever gap there was for relief, clouds moved quickly into the sky. Before long rain began to fall softly, and then increase more and more until it was an absolute downpour. By the time they were ready to stop, the group was soaked from head to toe and freezing yet again, but this storm was only getting started.

CHAPTER 40

The night dragged on, and Lancen's friends were miserable. When it came time for his watch, it was all he could do to throw on his hood and wrap up in blankets. Though he hadn't slept a second, he was awake and alert. Sitting in the wretched cold, suspicious feelings met his acquaintance yet again. He felt that he was in the sharp view of prying eyes. The dark aura by itself was enough to assure that he and his friends were not alone on this road. It was only a matter of time before their followers made themselves known. Under his bedding Lancen gripped the hilt of his axe. When they came, he would be ready.

After a grueling night, the morning finally came. A dull shade of light painted the sky a heavy gray as rain continued to pound unmercifully. Beyond leaving camp, an extensive day of wet bodies and tired feet ensued. By midday the road steered south, and the company, for the first time in days, moved away from the lake.

As they journeyed, it was not long before the land roughened, and rocks began to protrude from the earth. For miles, the road descended in a straight line before them, escaping the grasp of high ground and retreating into a narrow gulley. The rocks beside the road were as sheer walls, varying from fifteen to twenty feet at their highest, and short forested plateaus rose beyond their crests. Occasionally there was a break in one of the walls where another sharp trench would run perpendicular for miles. Much like a roofless tunnel, the shallow canyons reminded Lancen of the chutes back at his mine. Only instead of rocks and clay, it was he and his friends that would be washed through its system.

"We are entering the Valley of Rohgast," Etnah announced. "It goes on for miles just like this. It is the last place we want to be during a storm such as this."

"Do we go around?" asked Lancen.

"That is not my decision to make," said Etnah. "Time is pressing, and I fear what is behind us, but following the road in these conditions is unwise."

"How long would it take to avoid the valley?"

"A week, maybe less if we move quickly."

"Can we afford that?" Lancen asked.

"Obuthahn does not have time for us to dawdle," said Keira, "but if we die in the cracks, we are of no use either."

"I think we should travel around," said Avik. The Shaharan leaned heavily against the olcher at his side, but for the first time in their journey, he was strong enough to spend some time on his feet.

"It is a valid option, bird," said Etnah. "Though time is of the essence, we cannot make foolish decisions."

"We should go around," agreed Keira.

Lancen remained silent only a moment. A small burn started in his chest. He knew they must continue without delay.

"No," he said. "What happens if we take this detour and Roland departs for Obuthahn before you can reach him? What happens if we don't awaken the saints before the Ashlands are wiped out? If we had time to waste, we would go around, but we do not!"

"If the slots flood, we will have no escape," said Etnah. "We will be dead in seconds."

"Once an entire army disappeared," said Keira. "*'When the Valley of Rohgast roars, rivers own the cracks.'* That is what they say, Lancen."

"You would rather add a week to our travels, a week that we cannot spare, than risk the *chance* that a flood may come?" Lancen asked in disbelief. A subtle anger snuck quietly into his heart.

"If the waters rise, we die," insisted Keira.

"If we do not hurry, everyone dies," said Lancen.

"It is too dangerous."

"You would not risk two days of danger? For every moment we waste, Obuthahn is one step closer to destruction. The lives of the thousand are more important than the lives of the four!"

"But if the four should perish, then so will the thousand," argued Keira.

"We're going forward!" demanded Lancen. "You can either join me or I will go alone!"

The group seemed taken aback at the comment. Lancen refused to step down. If they did not act quickly, Obuthahn would never make it. Though he didn't know what awakening the saints entailed, he was counting on it to provide direction, direction that was critical to the lives of every Native on the peninsula. He waited breathlessly for a response.

Finally, Etnah broke the silence, "The *champion* has spoken, and I will follow."

"As will I," said Avik.

Lancen looked to Keira. He could see that she was reluctant, even angry that the others had chosen his side. She shook her head and stared at the ground.

"It seems that I have no choice," she said in frustration.

"Then let's get moving."

The rest of the day was demanding and frigid. The road was an endless line before them, stretching on and on, descending until it eventually disappeared. Water fell in a rage from the heavens and gathered into pools between the cobbles. Walking near the left wall, Lancen ran his hand across the smooth surface. Only a body's length, away Keira did the same on the right. The gulley was narrow and barren, but moving was quick.

The group traveled well into the night before deciding to settle down. Though fatigue had beset them, the four had great trouble sleeping. They seemed to lay in their blankets for ages, listening to the deafening rain pound the canvas that stretched above their beds. A nightmarish and icy wind howled through the canyon, pushing several inches of cold water down the road like a stream. Propped up on rocks and boards to avoid the river, the small company laid uncomfortable for hours, just waiting for the sun to come up so they could resume their travel.

After quite some time it appeared that Etnah and Keira had finally managed to fall asleep, and Avik uttered a whisper to Lancen.

"This sucks."

Lancen sighed and laughed quietly.

"We will go at first light," he said. "We would go now, but I prefer not to walk blindly, and at least the others will get some sleep."

"I often wonder if this is worth it," said Avik.

"What do mean?"

Avik was quiet, and Lancen could tell that the Shaharan was choosing his words carefully. There was clear dismay in his voice when he continued, "I wonder if I should have gone with Hans that night. I owe nothing to the Natives, and now the Legion would never have me."

"I'm glad you're here," said Lancen, taking no offense. "I'm not sure I could do it without you."

"Why are we doing it at all?" Avik responded quickly. "Our entire lives we have talked about fighting the Natives, and now we are joining them. It doesn't make sense."

"But it does! The Natives have done nothing to deserve their pain. The Legion does nothing to deserve their prestige. I know why I'm fighting."

"This isn't how I expected it."

"Isn't how you expected what?"

"Adventure," said Avik. "This isn't exciting or rewarding. It is miserable."

"Success has never come before pain," said Lancen.

"Well for us it has never come."

Lancen breathed deeply and agreed. Truer words had never been spoken.

"If it is not for the divines, or the kingdom, or riches, then we are fighting for the Natives solely," said Avik, "and that feels like a betrayal."

"They should never have been the enemy."

"But they are heathens, Lancen. They aren't the same as you or I. I don't want to fight for them. I'm here to fight for you!"

"Then what are you worried about?"

"You love the savages," whispered Avik. "They are necromancers, animals. You've turned your back on everything we stood for."

"Maybe we weren't standing for the right things."

"Maybe not, but I don't see them as you do. You aren't who you used to be."

"How have I changed?"

"Well you're still duller than a butter knife, so that is the same," mused Avik. "And you're stubborn as a troll."

"At least I don't look like one," joked Lancen. There was something about a friend that allowed you to be completely serious and completely foolish at the exact same time. Avik was a great friend.

The Shaharan laughed and then grew serious.

"I remember the days when you called them savages, when you'd pretend the wood blocks you shot your arrows at were Native warriors."

Lancen sat up and looked at Keira and Etnah. Both appeared to be fast asleep.

"Perhaps this isn't the best time to talk about that."

Avik smirked softly, then sighed and continued, "I guess it's not all bad. You're stronger now, more determined, but you're also sad. I can see it in the way you walk, the way you eat your food. Sure, you've taken the Native world upon your shoulders, but you're forgetting to take care of yourself."

"There is a lot I have to think about. There are things I live with that I can never forgive myself for."

"Like Adalyn?"

"To name one, yes."

"At least she's safe," said Avik. "She's heading back to Calderon with Earnst. She will be miserable there, sure, but no harm will come to her. Me on the other hand…"

Lancen laughed, "Yeah, I'm horribly worried about you! You just survived a sword wound to the hip. If there is anyone that can't handle his own, it's you.

"And though Adalyn is safe," he continued dismally, "I worry that she will resent me."

"Resent you for what?" asked Avik. "You gave her freedom, if only for a while. That was all she ever wanted. If anything, she is longing to see you again, or mourning because she thinks you're dead."

Lancen thought about Adalyn in a small chamber of the castle, sitting in a comfortable chair and staring endlessly through a tiny window. In his mind she was beautiful, with the sun pouring in to brighten her face. His heart warmed at the thought. He had dwelt on this image over and over, hoping that one day he would be able to meet her. Now he had, and he cared deeply, but somehow he also cared for the girl sleeping only a foot away from him.

Keira was in mortal danger, a risk that she had chosen to take on his behalf. Like him, Keira had suffered through horrible trials, and fended off incredible pain. She knew oppression and hunger. She knew the wild and stood up for her own. She was intelligent and beautiful. Without ever making a list, Lancen knew that she checked every mark. The fire burned.

"I don't know what to do," he said aloud.

Avik chuckled. "But you're the only one who seems to know."

Lancen had a hard time believing that. "I make decisions but that doesn't mean they are wise. I have trouble listening to my heart."

Avik sighed. "Sometimes the heart is quiet for a reason, because fate is not ready for a decision to be made. Do you remember that girl I met in the market?"

Lancen smiled. "How could I forget? But I don't see how that relates."

"I was buying a shawl for my mother when —"

"When the most stunning girl in Calderon approached the merchant. She said, 'I'm looking for a tall decanter.' And you leaned in and said, 'How about a caramel-brown warrior?'"

"That isn't what I said," said Avik punching Lancen in the arm. Keira shifted and grumbled something incoherent.

"I know the story, Avik," said Lancen trying to keep his tone soft.

"For one, I said something like, 'this merchant wouldn't have any, but I know of one not far from here.' Then I asked if I could show her there."

"How did that work for you?"

"Not well," admitted Avik with a chuckle, "but what I never told you is that when I returned the next day with a flower, she was so grateful that she gave me a kiss."

"That never happened," said Lancen amused. To laugh for a change brought an unmatched therapy to an otherwise urgent situation.

"Okay, it didn't. I did return with a flower, but I never saw her again, but that's not my point."

"I'm failing to see it then."

"My point," said Avik only slightly annoyed, "is that fate may be real, but it is not dictated by desire. Events in our lives lead us to certain ends, but often neither the end nor the journey was what we expected."

Lancen nodded in the dark. "I guess you have a point. Avik, *The Philosopher*!"

"That's it, I'm done talking."

He jested, but Lancen knew very well that Avik made a good argument, and he tried to internalize the message. Perhaps he would never have to choose between Adalyn and Keira. If fate was real, then everything would sort itself out one way or another. On the other hand, fate had never brought him peace before. Why would it start now?

He didn't know if he would ever solve this dilemma but did not want to dwell on it anymore tonight. There were much bigger problems at hand.

"See you in the morning, Avik. Try to get some sleep."

"*Try* is the word."

CHAPTER 41

The morning arose with vehemence. The wind built to charge through the slot canyon relentlessly, pushing against the backs of Lancen and his friends. Its mere roar was so deafening that every mildly uttered word was lost in the air. There was no silence in the rain and no solace on the road. Several hours into the morning, Lancen's feet were horribly sore. Blisters had developed and long since rubbed raw. With every step he winced, and the pack on his back felt as heavy as the olcher walking beside him. When Avik could walk, Keira and Etnah took turns riding. Lancen in his pride refused the relief.

It seemed like the road would never end. Below them it extended and extended, disappearing entirely before hope could be found in the view. Water built up around their ankles, rushing quickly and reminding Lancen of the river in the Ashlands. With his pack weighing down, he imagined Yantik clinging again to his back, the sting of the knife in his shoulder returning to memory. Back in that moment Lancen had willed himself to fight. He had powered through the pain and forces against him to survive, and he planned on doing the same here. He was stronger than his body made him believe.

Suddenly Avik yelled something unintelligible, and Lancen looked to him in confusion. Raising his arms, he motioned for the half-Noble to speak louder.

"Do you hear that?" Avik cried at full volume, barely audible over the storm.

"What?" asked Lancen. "Hear what?"

But before Avik could answer, a clear horse's neigh reached Lancen's ears. A feeling of darkness entered his heart. Behind and above them, chanting and yelling was prevalent.

"Run!" cried Etnah. "We do not know who follows us!"

That instant, three figures on horseback rode up to the edge of the crevice. Lancen pulled the bow from his side as his company began to run. The horsemen appeared tall and daunting above the road, pushing their steeds to keep pace beside the group below. Hooded and clothed in tan and brown robes, the three continued to yell in a foreign tongue frightening to Lancen and Avik.

"Tolta moray! Toto bawah!" the lead horseman cried. He was larger than his companions and wore cherry red boots.

Suddenly, Etnah stopped and looked up to the strangers. "Yetah mora!"

"Boto leya! Gra'ak toto bawah!" hollered Red-boots.

Lancen and the others stopped and looked back to Etnah anxiously. What was the elf doing? The communication continued back and forth for a few phrases before Etnah fearfully pointed up the canyon from whence they came.

Lancen followed the motion and looked up the road. In the distance, a roar he had thought to be thunder revealed its true nature. A deadly wall of water rushed monstrously downhill toward them, like a stampede taking no heed to what lay before it. It approached as an avalanche with incredible speed, devouring all in its path.

Red-boots leapt from his mount and pointed to the raging monster. "You must climb! Every crack of Rohgast will be filled!"

Cursing and yelling, the four below scrambled and clawed at the sheer rock face. Lancen looked over every area within sight. There were no holds, no way up. Spooked, the olcher bucked and took off down the road in a sprint. With no time to chase after it, the group decided to let it, and the bulk of their supplies, run away futilely.

As the menacing wall of water barreled toward them, Red-boots fumbled threw his luggage above. Retrieving a rope, he tied one end to his horse and threw the other down in furious pace. Keira grabbed it first and began to climb, made difficult by her heavy pack. With help from below and above, she struggled to scale the fifteen-foot face but eventually made it, collapsing next to Red-boots, breathless.

Etnah motioned for Lancen to go next, and with no time to argue, he reluctantly listened. Pulling himself up the rope, he could see why Keira had struggled. What should have been an easy climb was impeded by the weight on his back. Avik stood below him, helping to lift him to the top. Stepping on to the Shaharan's shoulders, he managed to grab the edge and lift himself over its face.

Avik was next, who climbed in similar fashion, but as he reached the top, the wall of water crashing nearer and nearer spooked the working horse and sent it running. Lancen's friend hung on desperately as he was dragged along the wall. Lancen dropped his pack and sprinted after him, diving and catching Avik's arm just as he lost grip on the fleeing rope. The Shaharan struggled to climb onto flat land, cuts and scrapes from the trip along the wall covering his arms and face.

With the horse and rope out of reach, and the deafening waves nearly on him, Etnah searched frantically for another way up. Letting his pack fall to the ground, he attempted to step off the wall and leap for Red-boots' outstretched arm, but it was to no avail. At the last second, he grabbed his leather pack again, emptied its contents and ran up the wall, heaving the bag as he went. With nothing but his fingertips, Red-boots caught one of its straps and lifted the elf to safe ground, just as the thunderous river plowed below his feet.

Safely at the top, Lancen's company and the strangers all breathed heavily, squandering in shock. Keira rushed to Etnah and threw her arms around him, relieved and exhausted.

Shaking off the suspense, Lancen observed the strangers.

Though he had never seen one in person, he could tell by their looks that they were Endwans. Being tall, with high cheek bones and deep eyes, they were similar to ash elves, only with light skin instead of black. All three wore short dark beards. Of the two still on horseback, one stared down his nose with piercing eyes, the other was bent over and sickly.

"My name is Motl," said Red-boots loudly, so all could hear him over the rain. He stood a little shorter than Etnah and nearly as broad as Avik. "Come."

The Endwan motioned for the group to follow, leading them to the relative shelter of a nearby pine. The tree was massive, large enough for even the horses to walk beneath its branches.

"We have been following your company since Riverock," Motl claimed once the entire group had joined him.

"Why did you follow us?" Lancen asked as his companions caught their breath.

"Not even a thank you?" replied Motl sarcastically. "Why wouldn't we follow a group such as yours? One Noble, two Shaharans, and an ash elf! Who wouldn't be curious?"

"Two Nobles," said Avik coldly, water dripping down his face.

Motl smiled and nodded to the young warrior. "We set out with a large company, headed to Riverock. Bondor told us about your quest, and we wanted to investigate."

Lancen narrowed his eyes. "Why were you in Riverock?"

"Where are the rest of your men?" chimed in Avik.

Motl's expression hardened. "We were raided by Nobles from Rendonhall a few weeks back. They burned our crops and stole some women. We were making our way to Riverock to ask for help in retaliating. Bondor has long been a silent ally.

"As for our men, we set out in a party of thirty-five elves. We are all that remain."

Motl looked up to his companions who dropped their heads solemnly. The pain was too clear on their faces for this to be a lie.

"What happened?"

"We stopped to camp one night, high in the mountains, when we were ambushed by horrible creatures. They wore dark hoods. Their eyes gleamed like devils."

"Skoles," Lancen said with a heavy breath.

"So we feared, but did not believe until we found Riverock had been attacked by the same creatures."

"Why did you not reveal yourselves sooner?"

"We needed to affirm Bondor's judgement, and now that we have, we wish to help."

Lancen looked at Motl skeptically. Another new face to trust. What was the risk this time? What was the benefit? The Endwan *had* just saved their lives.

"Why should we trust you?" he asked honestly.

"If there is any prayer for the Natives freedom, it lies with you. Yes, your blood was a concern, but I learned long ago through the people of Riverock that Nobles are capable of decency. I will not yet admit that you are our champion, but I will not turn my back on the chance."

Motl stopped and pointed to the two mounted horses, and then the third that trotted in circles out in the rain, still dragging the loose rope. "We have supplies for twenty-five warriors. I do believe you just lost most of yours. Would you accept our aid?"

Lancen looked to Etnah who immediately gave a nod of approval. Keira and Avik also gave motions of acceptance. It seemed he had no choice but to allow it.

"We would be grateful for your help," Lancen said. "I'm not sure what Bondor told you, but our quest takes us through Darkwood Forest to the tombs of Mozan-Garo. My name is Lancen. This is Avik, Etnah, and Keira."

"Pleasure," consented Motl, proceeding to announce his own companions. "This is Ret," he said, pointing to his sickly friend, "and Lena," introducing the other. "It will be an honor to join with true heroes of Serondhel."

CHAPTER 42

The company moved slowly for what was left of the day. All the ravines and slots of the valley had turned into swift moving rivers, and though the rain was finally fading, travel remained grueling and uncomfortable. With the road buried beneath fifteen feet of deadly water, they trudged through muck and rocks. Some relief did come as Lancen and his friends were able to remove their packs and tie them to the duns, but the soreness of their feet remained in every step. It was evening before the rain ceased once and for all, and the surviving earth was left beaten and flooded.

When they eventually stopped for the night, not a one of them had avoided exhaustion. Ret was helped down from his horse, appearing to be in far worse shape than even Avik. Though not injured like they, Keira joined them in going straight to bed after a makeshift Atling dinner. Of course dry wood had been impossible to find, but Motl had managed to start a fire with the combination of Charro powder and the words 'fekta mun.'

As the night rolled on, long after the others were asleep, Lancen, Etnah, Motl, and Lena all remained awake and huddled around the fire.

"What takes you to Mozan-Garo?" Motl asked after some time.

"The prophecy. Did Bondor not tell you?" Lancen responded.

"No, he failed to explain that connection."

Etnah chuckled, extending his hands to the fire for warmth. "I know you are not ignorant of the tales of Mozan-Garo, Endwan."

"No I am not," agreed Motl, "and if you are referring to

Mendlot, you ought to know he is no tale."

"Who is Mendlot?" asked Lancen.

Motl peered over the fire to Lancen with a raised eyebrow. "You have never heard of Mendlot, the hero of the coast?"

"No, I haven't."

"He is no tale because his story has never been altered. He lived in a generation not far removed from us and probably in the same as this old man." Motl said pointing to Etnah. Lancen got a good laugh.

"He was the first general of Endwah in the Lurid War, orphaned as an infant and survivor of a wolf attack as a child. Everyone thought he was Obah-a-Tou, but when he journeyed to the Swamplands, paying respects in the ancient tomb of Mozan-Garo, he never came back. Most assumed he fled the peninsula. I on the other hand, know differently."

"What is it that you know?" prodded Etnah.

"I know that his body still lies deep within the tomb. It is shadowed in darkness and curses. I beheld it with my very eyes."

"So you know the way?" questioned Lancen.

"Yes, I know that road."

Lancen felt some relief, but there was another question weighing on his mind. After a few minutes of silence, he couldn't help but ask, "Why would Rendonhall attack Endwah?"

"Why would any Noble attack a Native?" posed Motl. "Why would a wolf attack a fawn? It wasn't the first time they have broken the truce. Their reasons are beyond me, but Duke Furlott is filth. He is vile and corrupt, perhaps even more than Scharric."

"What else has he done?"

"Does he need to have done more?" Motl shot back. Lancen noticed Lena shift in his seat. "If I still had my men, I would be closing in on Rendonhall as we speak."

"If you don't mind me asking," spoke Etnah, "how is it that of thirty-five men, the three of you were spared?"

Motl looked up from the fire to cast a frustrated glare. "I

avoided death by sheer chance. I was scouting ahead when I heard commotion back at our camp. A dozen or so skoles just *appeared* in the night. By the time I got back, it was already too late.

"Grimy creatures they are, skoles. They tore apart valiant men without mercy. Those who were able fought with vengeance, but the monsters were too strong. We managed to slay only a few before they finally departed."

"We?" asked Lena, astounded. "*We* were getting slaughtered. *You* were the only one to slay one, actually three if I recall correctly."

"Well regardless," said Motl, "most of us didn't make it. Ret was torn apart and lost an ungodly amount of blood. It is a miracle he still lives."

"Was he bitten?" questioned Etnah suspiciously. "You know he will rise as one of them?"

"We don't know, but nothing has happened yet," asserted Motl, "and if that moment ever comes, we will fall him, but I refuse to leave him for death's grasp."

"Fool! Have you not listened to legend?"

"I have and am very conscious of it. That is why a watch must be set, for inside the company and out."

"You think that will be enough?" asked Etnah. Lancen straightened up uncomfortably, nervous of his own blood and somewhat angry with Etnah's objection. "If only a dozen skoles can slay thirty-two men, and then move on to Riverock to slay a hundred more, what do you expect one will do to only a handful of us?"

"I can handle Ret," claimed Motl seriously. "He doesn't remember being bitten. Even if he was, it is not your concern."

"A skole in our midst? You had better believe it's my concern!"

"The moment his mind goes, that's it. Ret knows this."

"Etnah, if he wasn't bitten it's not a problem, right? And if he was, then as long as he doesn't feed, we have nothing to worry about," said Lancen in Ret's defense. He was the only one in the circle who truly knew the hunger. It was awful, but compared to the alternative, very possible to resist.

Etnah clicked his tongue and smiled, finding a strange amusement in the conversation. "Aye, but some can handle the temptation better than others."

"If he becomes a threat, we will know," said Motl, "but he won't become a threat."

"It doesn't work like that, coast dweller. The process of changing is too slow, and he will be well-aware of his condition. Why would he divulge self-damning information to you?"

"Because he is trustworthy."

"Trust means nothing," said Etnah briskly. "I am reminded of the old epic, 'Etimar's Battle.' Do you know it?"

"I do not," said Motl.

"Etimar was a prince with a thirst for blood, much like skoles. Eventually he was forced to choose between his betrothed and his lust. There is a piece of it that goes:

> The inner battle that I try to avoid
> Persists until I eventually bust.
> I want her so badly. I quake for a taste.
> Shun like a poison! A peek I won't take!
> It starts as a whisper, slowly fills to the brink.
> I scream to discard it. I hold back a shake.
> My mind is held captive with much on the line.
> I accept my death and give into her touch,
> Enter into the passion to behold the fake.

That is what I imagine the change into a skole would be like. Blood is something you need and crave, but once you finally have it, you are still left hungry."

"So Ret will be hungry, and even if he kills and feeds, the pain will not leave him?" Lancen asked.

"That is why skoles continue to kill."

What does this make me? Lancen thought. If the elf was so concerned about Ret, then what were Etnah's true thoughts about him? Who was Etnah to assume to know anything regarding how it felt, what it was like?

"We will not make this decision tonight," Lancen ordered. "If what you say is true, then I believe even if Ret becomes a skole, he still has time before the hunger is too strong."

"That type of leadership will be vital, Lancen," Motl stated.

"Or dangerous," added Etnah.

Lancen allowed the heat to recede from his head. Though he wanted to be angry with Etnah, he finally convinced himself that it wasn't necessary. The elf had said very little. Why did Lancen take offense?

"I imagine you are somewhat of a leader to Endwah," he said to Motl, trying to cool down and get his mind off the subject. "I can tell by the way you carry yourself."

"In a sense that is true," said Motl, looking into the flames. "Mostly I was a fisherman, or a warrior when I needed to be. I was called to the council only recently, but the chief as well as Endwah's entire council were killed by the skoles. Which would make me its last surviving member."

"You are the chief!" exclaimed Etnah in surprise.

"He has always been a chief," noted Lena. "Endwah turned to him for guidance long before he joined the council."

"It would seem that way," confirmed Motl.

"If you are the chief, then do you not feel it is important to return to your people?" asked Lancen.

"Do not make judgements in matters you do not understand," said Motl on the defensive. "I would like nothing more than to return to my clan, but how can I go back so empty handed, bearing nothing but the grief we carry?"

"What do you gain by following me?"

"If you are the champion, there is no better place for me to be."

"If I had a home," said Lancen steadily. "I feel like there is nothing that would keep me from going back to it."

"And I follow you to ensure that I have a home to go back to."

"As do I," said Etnah.

Lancen was blown away. Everyone was beginning to call him the hero, looking to him for answers, but he knew no more than they.

"Maybe I am the champion," he said, "but not a one of us knows what that entails. So I will unite the peninsula. I will defeat the tyrant. How is that to be done exactly?"

"If you are truly the champion, you just will," said Lena.

"I disagree!" said Lancen forcefully. "Do not abandon reason because you see a light at the end of the tunnel. Dangers still await us in the dark. What does it mean to be Obah-a-Tou?"

"It means freedom," said Motl, "for all the oppressed. Even if you are not the champion, I will fight by your side until proven otherwise."

"And what of the Nobles?" Lancen asked. "I do not question that tyranny must end, but how, in the end, do you expect to co-exist with the innocent among the Nobles?"

"Co-exist?" questioned Lena. "'The tyrant cries and becomes the prey.' The Nobles must perish."

"All of them?"

"Yes."

"How can you demand that an entire people be condemned for the sins of the few?" Lancen inquired. "Blame King Theroll. Blame King Scharric, but do not blindly judge all Nobles for events they never had say in!"

"They blindly judge us," defended Lena.

"Then you are just as guilty as they! If there is any tyrant, I know it is the King's Legion solely, not the Nobles as a whole. Those outside of his loyalty will not suffer. If I am to fight for the Natives, then that is my indisputable condition."

"Agreed," said Motl, putting a hand on Lena's shoulder. "Do not forget Riverock, friend."

Lena nodded silently. Lancen couldn't tell if the elf agreed or just did not want to argue any longer.

"There are many good Nobles," said Etnah. "If I manage to get Roland on our side, we may avoid immediate bloodshed. With Calderon's army we will stand a fighting chance against the Legion."

"And I absolutely hope you succeed," said Lancen, "but perhaps we should decide what to do in the event that you fail."

"It is hard to say, but hope is bleak," said Etnah. "The best move may be to follow Shikobin and exodus to the unknown lands."

"Exodus?" asked Motl. "But Serondhel belongs to the Natives. Perhaps one day we can share it in peace, but let us not forsake what is rightfully ours!"

"You would have us run?" asked Lancen.

"Aye, bird, fly to a new place."

Lancen shook his head. "No. The Natives cannot flee, especially from Obuthahn. You told me yourself that they wouldn't survive the journey north. They cannot go west, closer to the enemy. They cannot go south; they hardly have enough food as it is! They would not even make it to where we now sit."

"But how could they stay?" asked Etnah. "We can try to fight, but the duke commands thousands, the king hundreds of thousands! You saw what the Legion did to Obuthahn with just fifty men. Imagine fifty multiplied by fifty, multiplied by fifty more, with all of them on a quest for blood! Obuthahn would be devoured. It is not what I want. It is simply the truth."

"It remains," said Lancen, "if we cannot run, then we must fight. How many warriors are capable in Obuthahn?"

"You mean how many warriors will we sentence to death? This is a joke."

"Then make me laugh," said Lancen seriously.

"Perhaps three hundred elves, and that is if you can track down the hunting parties."

"How many remain in Endwah?"

"Maybe one hundred that can fight," said Motl.

"Riverock will provide maybe three hundred more," said Lancen. "What of Tomutah, or Maktakalah?"

"They would never fight on the same side of the spear," said Etnah.

"Then what about Maktakalah alone?"

"It is not even worth mentioning. The Darkwood elves live deep within the forest. The road is perilous, and they do not welcome strangers. In fact, they do not permit them whatsoever. You would be dead long before you arrive."

"Then Tomutah?"

"Perhaps two hundred. If they were willing to help us, which is far from reality."

"With the Legion's dagger to their throat, they will do anything. That would give us nine hundred men."

"Nine hundred against ten thousand," said Etnah woefully.

"That is all we have," said Lancen. "With nine hundred, perhaps we could fend off an attack."

"Yes, until the Nobles send a second wave."

"We must not lose faith," Motl mentioned.

"I am not losing faith," insisted Etnah. "I retain faith in consulting with Roland, but I am only being realistic."

"If you fail, we cannot run," said Lancen. "Motl, I would have you return to Endwah and convince them to make haste to Obuthahn, just in case."

"I would stay by your side, Lancen," requested Motl.

"I will go," offered Lena. "They will listen to me if I speak for Motl. Say the word."

"Do it," Lancen said with conviction. "The rest of us will visit Tomutah."

"If you must," said Etnah, "but I pray that you will not find blood there, there or any place in between."

All agreed with this statement. The four were exhausted, and though it was not spoken, they were afraid. Any hope for victory was faint, if it could be found at all. Yet they were hell bent on pressing forward, no matter what the outcome would be. For life or for death, they would fight on. For Serondhel, they were willing to die.

CHAPTER 43

The next morning came all too quickly. Lena had departed at first light, taking with him one of the horses and a very small amount of supplies. For the rest of them, the course was tedious and grueling. With time, the waters in the valley receded, and as the sun came out, the company rejoiced. Oddly, Lancen's joy did not entirely match his companions'. The warm heavenly rays seemed too hot, uncomfortable against his bare flesh. It was strange, and it frightened him. He did not want it to be skolism, and if it was, the others could never know. So he grit his teeth and continued forward, masking the discomfort as best he could.

By midday the waters in the slots had receded to the point where the group could climb down to the road. Lowering the horses would have been a challenge, but luck was on their side as they found a gradient along the wall to lead the animals down. As they moved on ahead, a quiet knowledge crept in on each of them. Time had played an interesting game, for the moment of Etnah's departure to Calderon was fast approaching.

Before he would leave, Lancen wanted to gain as much advice and information as possible. He had a well of questions, and Etnah was his pail for retrieval. He wanted to ask more about skolism, regardless of what they had discussed before, and when the end of the canyon was in sight, Lancen decided he could wait no longer.

"Can I speak to you a moment?" he asked the elf.

"This topic is dead," said Etnah coolly, seeming to read Lancen's mind, "remember?"

Lancen bit his lip and pressed the subject more.

"I just have a few questions," he whispered. "About Ret, about the sun, there is too much I need to know."

"Perhaps you do not need to know as much as you think you do. I would rather we enjoy the time we have left before I leave."

Lancen clenched his fists but submitted. "Okay, we will save it for our reunion."

"Aye."

Although slogging through several inches of water, travel on the road was much easier than progression above. Before hearts were prepared, the group beheld a fork in the road not far in the distance, as well as the end of the slots making up the valley. On one side, the road continued south, across a greenish field until it disappeared into Darkwood forest. The other route headed west and north, toward Transiric and eventually Calderon.

Keira stayed close by Etnah's side for the remainder of the distance. She knew better than any that the time was coming undeterred when he would be leaving them. Her face was sober and eyes were tired as they walked. Saying goodbye to him was the last thing she wanted to do. She had already lost him once.

But time could not be stopped, and the road refused to cease moving beneath their feet. As they reached the fork, Keira fell into her guardian's arms.

"For Obuthahn," she whispered.

"It will be alright," Etnah responded. "Stay with Lancen, and be strong, *for Obuthahn*."

After some time Etnah proceeded to say goodbye to the rest of the company. Approaching Avik, the elf extended a hand in courtesy.

"You are level-headed," said Etnah.

Avik nodded, waiting for more, but after a moment with no response, he shook Etnah's hand and smiled. "Thank you," he said awkwardly.

Turning away, Etnah met with Lancen last. Cocking his head,

the elf looked at the boy with confidence.

"Take care of Keira," he started. "Hard times will come, but if you stick to the prophecy, you will not falter. I would have gone with you to battle the antethei himself."

Turning to the company as a whole, Etnah looked over their tired and anxious faces. "The time has come swiftly, but I leave in necessity. Motl knows the way to Mozan-Garo and will be a faithful guide. Nothing I could say would change the pressure of our mission, so I will not attempt to do so. I exhort you all to stay true to the course, and never accept defeat, not even at your dying breath. Koto mei. Farewell my friends."

Lancen walked with the others across the open distance that followed the channels of Rohgast. It was a good feeling to be free of the narrow slots, but Etnah's departure had seemed to sober them all. That being said, Lancen felt much safer with the ability to see what was around him. Ahead, Darkwood Forest was massive and gloomy, its enormity exceeding even his wildest imaginations. From horizon to horizon the trees stretched, the endless line preceding an ocean of green.

After several hours had passed since Etnah's departure, the remaining group was quiet. Though confident and anxious, there was an unquestionable solemnity in their strides. Keira had pressed forward with her head held high. Lancen could see that she was trying to be strong, but she could not hide the sadness on her face. With Etnah gone it would fall to Lancen to protect her. He laughed at how easy a job that would be. Like himself, she didn't need someone else to protect her. She had gone plenty long without it already.

Walking over to her side, he wanted to say something that would ease her mind, something that would bring her hope and amusement. He wanted to say something perfect, but his thoughts would leave him before he could spit the words. A burning entered his being and stole his breath. It was time to speak, now or never.

He needed to make the most of this vulnerable moment.

"Hello." *Smooth.*

Keira turned her head with a raised eyebrow, the sadness already leaving her face. "Hello?"

"How are you?"

"How do you expect? My feet hurt, but I'm still walking as I have been for the last two weeks," she said with some amusement. *Check.*

"Well at least you look good while you're doing it," Lancen said confidently. It was time for a bit of transparency. He felt something for Keira, and to some level wanted her to know it.

Keira shook her head and responded. "Oh really?"

"Sure, I guess it's to be expected of a princess of Obuthahn."

Dimples formed on her face. "I'm not really sure how to respond to that."

"Your cheeks are turning red," said Lancen boldly.

"No they aren't," she defended. It was now apparent that she was trying not to smile.

Lancen joked, "You're really telling me something here."

Her lips tightened and eyes lit up.

"Next time don't be so forward," he added quickly.

And with that she lost her disguise. An uncontrollable grin spread across her face. With red and dimpled cheeks, she turned and slugged Lancen on the arm.

"What was that?" Lancen laughed.

"How do you joke when the world is so full of gloom?" she asked.

"Because Avik told me I couldn't get you to smile," Lancen lied.

"No I didn't," piped Avik from a few feet behind them.

Lancen looked back to his friend and received an interesting glare. *'What are you doing?'* the Shaharan mouthed.

Lancen didn't have the energy to stress over what Avik thought. He may never live to see Adalyn again, and if that was the case, he figured he might as well not spend his last few weeks ignoring what he felt for Keira.

She laughed in a muffled titter. Lancen smiled at her self-consciousness.

"I just think that the both of us can use all of the relief we can manage," he explained.

"That I can agree with," she said gladly, but her lightened spirits soon faded. "This is the first time I ever remember being outside of the Ashlands, and I'm here with two Nobles and two strangers."

"Do you miss it?"

"No I don't," she noted, "but I am afraid that I may never return. Under these conditions I only want the option of going back."

"I know what that's like," said Lancen, "but I have no home, so I must shut out the thought."

"I'm sorry."

"Don't be," said Lancen. "I'm right where I need to be. And you should know that you're not alone. Even though you walk with two Nobles and two strangers, I am here for you, and I'm not going anywhere."

With that statement in the air, Lancen stepped away to explain himself to Avik. He noticed Keira pull her hands to her heart as she processed what he had said. Walking behind her, Lancen could imagine the smile on her face, and suddenly, the thought of Etnah being gone did not seem so bad.

CHAPTER 44

The sun seemed to set early that day. The air was cool, but it was a massive improvement from the frigid conditions they had become accustomed to. The group continued forward for a time, but when they reached a flattened grassy area on the steady climb up to the forest, Lancen called the company to a halt.

"We will stop here for the night," he said. "Tonight, I'd like to celebrate our journey. We will risk a fire and set a watch, for tomorrow we enter the forest."

The company spread out and then returned with fuel for a fire. They pulled out a cooking plate and threw on well sized portions of meat. For the first time since leaving Riverock, as a whole they felt safe. There was no feeling of darkness this night, no suspicion of prying eyes. For at least in this moment, things seemed to be exactly as they should be.

A sense of accomplishment dwelt with them. Motl had been to Mozan-Garo before and was a capable guide. Lancen and Keira had repaired their relationship and Avik continued to heal with every passing day. Though still moving slowly, there was a certain enthusiasm in his movements. As the Shaharan sharpened the Legion sword he had taken from Walt, he seemed strong and alert. Even Ret was feeling better, walking around and participating with the others.

"It has been a long time since I have seen a night this clear," mentioned Motl, marveling up at the endless stars. "Rain used to be a pleasant change. Now it is the guest that stays long beyond its welcome."

"I wonder if it is uneasy feelings that bring the storms," said Keira thoughtfully.

"I don't think it works like that," laughed Lancen.

"Even so," said Avik, "the divines would be too mindful to throw salt on the wounded."

"The divines?" repeated Lancen in surprise. "Since when have you believed in the divines?"

Though he had seen things in his recent journey that were unexplainable, he still wasn't able to chock it up to the divines. The woman in his dream was strange. The light above his sword, the hand in the water, the ropes falling from his wrists: they were all peculiar, but to immediately credit the divines did not make sense. He couldn't do it.

"I'm not sure that I do believe," said Avik. "It just feels like I have been sensing their presence a lot more lately."

"Interesting," said Motl, "because I have felt their absence. We ourselves have pushed them from the peninsula. The Nobles haven't paid them heed since Scharric took the throne, and though the Natives keep their traditions, they lack honest faith. I have seen this change in the world with my own eyes."

"It can be hard to believe," said Keira reluctantly. "What have they done for us since the Lurid War?"

"Exactly my point," agreed Motl.

"Just because we have not seen or felt something," said Avik, "does not mean that it was never there. What about this prophecy? How could Lancen fulfill so much of it to the letter, if it was not established by something greater than us?"

"It may be a coincidence," said Lancen.

"We are far beyond coincidences, brother."

Keira sighed and agreed. "I do believe you fulfill the prophecy, which I suppose proves the divines are out there somewhere, but why do they never hear our cries?"

"It doesn't prove anything."

Motl laughed out loud and wiped a tear from the corner of his eye. "Well this is really something!"

"What is?"

"We are following a young man that we believe to be Obah-a-Tou, and not only does *he* not believe in the divines, but we ourselves are questioning their existence! It's quite funny really. The only one defending them is holding a Legion blade!"

"Who would have thought?" Lancen said with a smile. "You seem old enough, Motl, did you not fight in the Lurid War to protect the divines?"

"I did," said Motl, "and it very much was to protect our worship. I should not question what I have always believed. Then what would be left for me to stand for?

"I was around the age of you lot when King Therin disappeared and Scharric began to spit on our ways. Endwah was a great civilization then, even larger than Obuthahn at one point. We had cottages and villages all across the region. The king, in his *opulence*, sentenced all Natives to rot within one of the five clan capitals. All settlements outside of those capitals were to be burned, and any Native on the road without proper cause was to be killed. Needless to say, most of us did not accept those terms, but regardless of what we accepted, the Natives still lost. Now all that remains of Endwah dwindles hungry and weak on the eastern shores."

"It never recovered," added Ret, appearing pale and weak, but in good spirits. His eyes were sunken, and Lancen could practically see the hunger in them.

"We used to have thousands of horses," said Motl, "but after the Legion slaughtered them by the hundreds, and we were forced to eat them in winter, the number of our horses on the peninsula is now as few as the dwarves."

"He speaks of great gloom," said Ret, "but what he fails to tell you is how heroic a display he put on in the war. Motl single-handedly fought off armies in defense of Endwah. He saved my life on more occasions than I can count."

"Ret exaggerates," said Motl. "He always has. He was barely old enough to swing a sword by the time the war ended."

"I don't exaggerate. Some people just hide from the truth. Motl, by himself, saved my entire camp when I was a child. Do you want to tell them or should I?"

Motl shook his head. "You and I remember it differently."

"Then I'll tell them," said Ret, rubbing his hands together in excitement. "We were settled just outside of Rendonhall, which was just a small village then, rather than the great city it is today. Hundreds of Legion soldiers gathered between us and their fort. They knew we were there and were on their way to destroy us. We had no time to run, nowhere to go. They had taken hundreds of our horses, and Motl here decided to use that to our advantage. So as the Legion marched toward us, he snuck behind their backs and released every last animal! When they discovered him, he must've killed fifty, sixty Nobles! He saved everyone that day: myself, my parents, Lena, Ae—" Ret suddenly stopped midsentence. Motl scowled at him fiercely.

"Who else?" pressed Keira, curious.

Motl shook his head no, but Ret reluctantly finished. "Aeva."

"Who's Aeva?"

Ret avoided the question and tried to change the subject, but Motl stopped him.

"It's okay," said the older Endwan. He took a deep breath and looked in the fire, a very serious expression formed on his face. "She died in the war, very near to its end. We had arranged to be married."

The group was silent for a moment. No one knew quite how to respond. Motl did not require sympathy and did not initiate further discussion. It was a subject that perhaps should never have been pursued, but Lancen felt he could relate. As he rolled around a small rock in his hand, he thought deeply on the subject. Learning more about Motl could prove beneficial. As Chief of Endwah, this elf was exactly the type of friend he needed.

"I was very young when the war ended," said Lancen. "Of course I remember none of it, but its effects are felt by us all. I do not know who my parents were, but I am certain it was the war that tore them from me."

"Mine as well," said Keira.

"And mine remain slaves," said Ret.

Motl stared dismally into the fire, eyes jumping here and there with the dashing flames. "I know that I am not the only one who has suffered. I have seen more men die than I can count. I lost family and friends, but nothing can compare to the loss of Aeva. Legionnaires flooded out of Rendonhall in endless waves. She was captured and abused, long before they decided to kill her. Resentment cannot begin to describe the feelings of my heart. It is a cool but constant grudge, one that is urgently waiting to be satisfied, but likely never will be."

"Tell me if it's not my place," said Lancen, "but do you know who killed her?"

"I do," said Motl coldly, "but they will remain in my heart. I am afraid that if I let them out, the anger will fade, and when our paths cross, I want no amount of mercy to be possible. I will wait quietly, and eventually, I will sever their Noble heads."

"Why *Noble* heads?" asked Avik aggressively.

"I was being specific."

"The Nobles are not the problem," said Avik, getting worked up. "It is the king. Do not get that confused."

"Avik," said Lancen in warning, "he meant nothing by it."

Motl shifted in his chair and clenched his teeth. "I could care less the shape of their ears! The fact they are Nobles is an observation, not a crime."

Avik grabbed the hilt of the sharpened sword on his lap and squeezed it until his knuckles were white. Lancen looked at him anxiously. What had gotten into him?

To make matters worse, Ret posed the question: "What is the difference between the king and every other Noble?"

"What is the difference between a Native and a pile of dirt?" Avik shot back loudly.

"Well the Natives would never demean like that," said Keira loudly.

"You're all demeaning right now! But perhaps your Native brains are too small to know it."

"Avik, calm down man," stated Lancen. He didn't want to explode, but anger was also rising in his chest with every breath.

"My brain is Shaharan," said Keira, "and I know that at least half of yours is too. Look at you!"

"Stop it!" Lancen ordered, rising to his feet. Furiously, he kicked dirt into the fire and threw down the rock he had been playing with. "Why is it that only one can stand in the end? The Nobles took your lands and oppress your people. The Natives attack our roads and live in the past! *We are all flawed!* Our peoples may never live together, but in this company, we are one blood!"

The others quieted and fiddled their thumbs. As they cursed under their breaths, Lancen continued a bit more delicately.

"How can we expect to 'free' the peninsula, if we cannot even have respect for each other? Motl, Ret, Keira, I am a Noble. I'm sorry but that is not changing. It is simply what is. You have followed me this far. Judge by my actions, not my skin. I believe in change, but the change must be right. We cannot exchange the positions of Nobles and Natives. We must unite them. If we ignore that, then there is nothing to fight for! Can you accept that?"

"As you wish," said Motl lowly, in a mix of a growl and a whisper.

Avik nodded in frustration. Ret responded "Aye" while holding his glare on Avik. Keira stared at the dirt and agreed.

"You will watch your tongues in this fellowship," said Lancen. "As Motl said before, we are heroes of Serondhel, and I wish to live up to that. We are of *Serondhel*, not of the Nobles or the Natives solely.

"Let us not forget why we are here. I think we should all get some rest. Morning will come swiftly. Avik, you will take first watch."

CHAPTER 45

Lancen's eyes opened. He didn't know how long he had slept, but the night was still dark. New stars had entered the sky while the two moons had journeyed across its abyss. The wind blew gently, sending glowing embers through the air and above Lancen's bed. The fire had settled into a dark pile of coals and ash. A few feet away, Avik slept soundly, and above him was a pair of dimly shining eyes.

Lancen lurched to attention, stomach churning. *Eyes!* They remained still and focused on the sleeping company, silently being joined by a dozen others. Lancen rolled from beneath his bedding, watching the outlines of many small figures closing in around them.

Grabbing hold of Nahabuk's axe, Lancen shot to his feet. "Wake up!" he called.

His companions stirred, but in an instant twenty small hooded beings surrounded the camp. They were Darkwood elves, each holding a short bow with a sharp arrow fixed to fly at every one of the strangers. Dressed in many different furs and skins, the nocturnal halflings positioned themselves over and under one another in an effective ambush formation.

"What is a Noble doing at the foot of our realm?" spoke a fair skinned elf darkly. He had dagger eyes and a fearless visage.

"I am unsure what I am," said Lancen prudently. The statement was true for multiple reasons. Slowly his companions rose to their feet, guarded and fearful.

"Why do you approach the forest?" the elf asked. "Choose your words carefully."

Here Lancen stood again, in a position to confide in a stranger. Should he tell them of his quest, of the prophecy and Mozan-Garo?

"Our mission takes us to the Swamplands," he said, heart racing. Glancing quickly at Motl he looked for advice. The Endwan stared at him gravely, inferring that they couldn't be trusted.

Lancen cleared his throat and continued guardedly. He had to trust them. So far no one but Hans had given him reason to doubt. But he couldn't tell them everything. "Darkwood is the fastest route. We fight on behalf of Obah-a-Tou."

The elves flinched at his mention of their champion and moved in tighter around the outsiders. The elf spokesman spat at Lancen's feet.

"We should shoot you where you stand!" he hissed. "What proof have you of this?"

Before Lancen could speak, Keira stepped forward bravely. "He sent us himself," she said. "He is part of clan Obuthahn."

The elves looked around to one another skeptically, then seemed to lean in and pull their bowstrings tighter.

Lancen raised a hand quickly in defense. "I have proof!" he said. "Please, don't shoot!"

"Last chance, stranger."

Lancen hurried over to his possessions and fumbled around their supplies. In trepidation, his fingers laid hold around his bow.

Not knowing what he would say, Lancen lifted it and stepped back to the speaking elf. "This," he said, "is the Sacred Tare. It is the bow of the divines and is a holy relic of clan Obuthahn. It was Obah-a-Tou's reward for completing the Hero's Trial. We are on a quest to return it to him in the Swamplands."

The elf nodded and eased his bow to an unarmed position. Leaning over to the Native at his side, an older bearded elf, the two conversed for a moment in hushed tones. Lancen's company stayed silent, their anxiety apparent. Carefully looking aroundm Lancen saw the concern on their faces. If the elf made the order, they would all be dead.

Finally, the bearded one looked to Lancen with stern eyes. "My name is Kelta. The elf you've been speaking to is Yanlah. I will not say that I believe your story, but I do believe your intentions are clear. I would never trust a Noble, but we will lead you through the forest."

As Kelta spoke, the child-like elves lowered their weapons. Lancen's group released held breath. Suspense quietly subsided.

Lancen narrowed his brow. "We can travel alone. No need for you to bother."

Kelta chuckled. "We admire your bravery, but you would not survive a night. We were heading back that way regardless."

Lancen refused to take his eyes off of the elf leaders. Something did not feel right about them. "Thank you for your courtesy, but I insist—"

"Well I command!" said Kelta jubilantly, raising his arms and looking to his companions. "I would not have you walk to your deaths! Every Noble is either a killer or an idiot, and you don't look like a killer. We will see you through the forest. What are your names?"

Lancen smiled at the insult. He saw no harm in sharing their names. "I am Lancen of Calderon, my companions are Motl, Avik, Ret, and Keira. You have my word that we bring tidings of peace."

"Very good," said the elf with a smile. "You seem like a decent lot, and if your quest is true, then we wish only to help. That being said, we must depart into the forest at once."

"We cannot complete our rest first?"

"Oh no. These are dangerous times, and we are not safe here. There have been rumors of evil creatures appearing in these parts."

"Skoles," said Ret quietly, but just loud enough for the elf to hear.

"Aye, those are the rumors."

"Will it be safe in the trees?" Lancen asked.

Kelta smiled and looked to Yanlah. They began to turn without a response.

"We will be safe in the forest?" Lancen repeated seriously.

"There are darker creatures than skoles beneath the boughs of Darkwood," said Kelta walking away, "but stay with us, and perhaps you will not have to meet them. We must leave at once because it is not wise to travel when the darkness sleeps. In the forest, one must rest in the light and not so much as blink in the night. If you do, something *will* find you."

Lancen breathed deeply and consented. "As you say. We will gather our supplies and depart immediately."

The company was able to pack up in haste. Reluctantly, they sent their horses into the night and carried as much gear as possible upon their own backs. *'The path through the forest is too dangerous for gentle beasts,'* claimed the Darkwood elves, reaffirming what Etnah had told them days ago. Lancen, against Motl's discretion, chose to disclose to Kelta information regarding the coming attack on Obuthahn, and asked if Maktakalah could afford to send aid. The elf seemed to understand and promised to do all he could to gather help from his clan.

"The need is pressing," Lancen kept repeating.

As the comprised company of Nobles and Natives departed toward the tree line, very few words were spoken. Lancen walked with purpose, Motl with caution. Darkwood stood black and ominous before them, and as they neared, the air grew colder. One by one the elves began to file into the suffocating shadow of the woods.

As Lancen grew closer, he was able to distinguish just how thick the overgrown terrain truly was. The small path they followed led to the trees and then disappeared completely into a wall of blackness.

Keira stopped in her tracks and stared ahead, trepidation coursing over her. Lancen neared her side and placed a gentle hand on her shoulder. With widened eyes, she looked at him anxiously.

Glancing from the girl to the darkness, Lancen reached down and clasped his hand with hers, careful to interlock the fingers. Nervous, but together, the two of them stepped forward, and entered slowly into shadow.

CHAPTER 46

I f it hadn't been for the cavern of Nahabuk, Lancen would have thought he had just set foot into the darkest place he had ever walked. Avik and Motl marched just an arm's reach in front of him and he could hardly make out their figures. There was not a fragment of heavenly light that could break through the thickness of the forest roof, and the lack of visibility was unnerving.

As his group moved carefully and helpless, Darkwood elves filed skillfully around them from behind and ahead. The elf Yanlah walked beside Lancen, giving direction as they went.

"We apologize that we had to leave your camp so abruptly. It is not safe to sleep in the night. We must be on the move in darkness. The more time you spend in our realm, the more your eyes will open. There are not many night hours left. Just follow the person in front of you, and you will soon be able to complete your rest."

Lancen clenched his jaw and clung tightly to Keira's hand. No matter what he would go through in this forest, he was grateful that she would be by his side.

Travel in Darkwood was bumpy. Rocks and roots sprung out of the narrow road sporadically, never failing to trip one of the foreigners. Spider webs were so frequent that eventually Lancen stopped brushing them off. When it seemed like dawn would never come, light finally broke the heavily wooded roof. In the dimness of morning, true colors of the forest began to emerge. Overgrown greens of every shade covered the floor and crawled up trees, while mangled branches cast an array of chilling shadows. Faintly, the small elves began to whistle and chime amongst themselves.

As Yanlah broke away from Lancen to move ahead and talk to Kelta, Motl stepped back and whispered quietly, "I do not trust them. They are too quiet, or perhaps too casual. Something is off."

Avik looked back with a stern gaze, agreeing.

"You think that I trust them?" said Lancen softly. "Of course I don't, but unless you have a solution, do not remind me of the problem."

"It was not wise to tell them of Obuthahn's need," said Motl.

"Why not? What harm could they do? They understand our pain, and they may even help. If they are of Maktakalah —"

"They are not of Maktakalah."

Suddenly Yanlah reappeared in front of them, heading straight to Lancen. Motl immediately stepped away. The company had marched into a pocket where the trees were not so condensed, and the road was mostly clear. In places, the sky was visible in blue and gray above them. The area appeared to be a very common stop for the elves. Built crudely into every tree were several crow's nests and flat watch platforms, bones and feathers hanging below their planks. Different floors and bridges ran around and between the widest trees, and on the forest floor, a dozen stone circles were built waist high for holding fires. Altogether the fortified clearing seemed barbaric and unwelcoming.

"We will stop here for a few hours," said Yanlah. "Feel free to shut your eyes. This place is well secured."

As they proceeded to wind down, the elves found their various places along the ground and balconies. When Lancen's group began to unravel their bedding, Motl and Avik huddled in around Lancen to finish their discussion.

"What do you mean they're not of Maktakalah?" asked Lancen. "It is the law that they reside in the main camp."

"Noble law does not exist in this forest. Have you ever heard of the Legion patrolling Darkwood?" asked Motl.

"I've heard stories."

"Well that is all they were. The Nobles do not risk walking these roads, especially when Darkwood elves seem of no threat."

"Then why are they helping us?" asked Keira, butting in.

"Helping us?" repeated Motl. "Not in the least."

"What are they doing then?"

"Waiting for the right moment to pounce."

"The right moment would have been back where they found us," said Lancen.

"Lancen, this isn't courtesy," said Motl. "It is religion. These elves do not worship the same gods as you or I."

Lancen rolled his eyes. *Gods.*

"They're leading us into a trap," said Avik, "like cattle to the slaughterhouse."

"I understand that they can't be trusted," said Lancen, "but present me with an option. Does it look like they will allow us to leave? Do we even dare wander the forest without them?"

"Just be careful," said Motl. "I have been through this land long ago. These are not our friends. They will sacrifice us without a second's notice. When an opportunity comes, we must escape from them."

"Believe me, I agree with you," said Lancen, "but we must also look deeper into the situations we are placed in. If we are to succeed in this quest, risks have to be taken."

"I agree with Lancen," said Ret stepping in. The elf gave Lancen a supportive nod, but for some reason it was more unsettling than it was assuring. In that moment Lancen noticed how healthy the Endwan looked, walking without a limp and full of energy. Even Avik still hobbled.

"If we are to succeed, we cannot linger with these people!" said Motl.

"To succeed," said Lancen, tearing his gaze from Ret, "not just survive, but truly come out victorious, we must see things as they really are! They haven't killed us yet and Obuthahn needs their help. All I am saying is that nothing is as simple as it appears. So do not put blinders beside your eyes. That is a fool's task."

"I will follow you Lancen, but do not discard my words."

"And I do not!" said Lancen strongly. "We should save this topic for later and get some rest. We are not slipping away from *this* camp unseen, so let's take advantage and build our strength."

"We should set a watch."

"Avik, think you can handle it this time?"

The Shaharan grumbled and complied.

Lancen awoke to a nudge on the shoulder and sluggishly opened his eyes to see patches of soft blue sky. The frustration of interrupted sleep did not faze him. He had gotten well acquainted to life without it entirely. The weight of his mission, the pain of his past, and the danger of his present all did their part in bringing him swiftly to attention.

"It is your turn brother," said Avik kneeling beside him.

Lancen rubbed his eyes and looked up. "Get some rest. It probably won't be long before we are back on the road."

Avik agreed and straightaway retired to his own bed. Sitting up, Lancen surveyed the camp through misty breath. Short Darkwood elves crawled all across the clearing, patrolling in the trees above and warming their hands around the fires below. With bows and arrows ready to arm, they were well prepared for any attempted attack, or escape.

"How do you feel?" came Ret's voice softly through the silence.

Lancen was somewhat startled. "What?"

"How do you feel?"

Lancen looked at the Endwan, who sat up straight with tired eyes, huddled in blankets and skins.

"I feel fine. Why?"

"Because I feel hungry."

Hairs stood up on Lancen's neck. Ret *had* been bitten, and it was progressing. "I have some bread in my pack."

"That won't do," answered Ret. "You know what will. I see the way you look at your food."

Lancen began to notice the fairness of Ret's skin, the lightness of his hair and eyes, sunken sockets, concaved cheeks.

"I don't know what you're talking about."

"Really?"

"Yes." Lancen's heart began pumping. Did Ret know about his own skolism? Would he tell the others?

"I don't believe you."

"I don't know what you're thinking," said Lancen nervously, "but you're wrong."

"Do you miss the night?"

Lancen emerged from his blankets and rose to his feet at once. The air was chilling, but he longed to distance himself from this situation. He had to get away from Ret.

"I am on your side," said the elf in a low and steady voice. "I will follow you as I follow Motl."

Lancen nodded but wasn't comforted. Turning away, he walked to the nearest fireplace and began to warm his hands. Several Darkwood elves stood with him, most casting unpleasant glares. For a moment, their treatment reminded him of Obuthahn. It was blind hate.

He proceeded to stare into the flames, trying to get his mind off of Ret. If the elf knew that Lancen was a skole, it could bring about the ultimate end of this adventure. If the others found out, if *Keira* found out, he didn't know what he would do. Being a Noble was one thing, but if she discovered his skolism, there would be no penance.

After a while, when Lancen began to breathe a bit easier, Kelta, the Darkwood leader, stepped up to his side and stared deeply into the fire.

"Why do you and your companions stir during the time we have given you to sleep?" the elf asked politely.

"To speak openly," said Lancen, "my companions do not trust

you. We arranged to have one of us remain awake and keep eyes for trouble."

"What have we done to be unworthy of your trust?" asked Kelta. "We have forfeited precious days to escort you through our lands, a task your company could not have done without us."

"And we are grateful, but these are dangerous times. We must always be cautious."

"No matter. We will help you nonetheless. Your Noble blood bothers my men, but I see no problem. We all bleed the same."

Lancen didn't know how to respond to that statement. Bleed?

The bearded elf turned and pointed to a cart on the road. "As a token of our trust, we give freely of an exquisite resource. In that wagon there are several barrels full of the finest Dark-sap mead. Wake your friends and tell them to drink. It will keep them warm and awake. We never know when something will surprise."

Lancen graciously accepted and departed to do as he was told. When the others were awake and moving, he led them to the cart where he had been directed. The barrels were as large as an olcher's torso and made of heavy dark wood. With little hesitation Lancen retrieved his cup and placed it under the toggled wooden spout. Pulling the pin, he released a thick bronze-colored mead and filled his cup to the brim. His thoughts were clear. There was no doubt that the odds of this drink being poisoned were great, but just as great were the odds that he would be killed by the forest. So why delay?

In steady motion, he raised the cup to his lips and tilted back. It satisfied as it smoothly rolled down his throat, the thick nectar warming all the way to the core. The flavor was sweet with a hint of spice, and the result was instant. For the first time in weeks, Lancen began to feel awake and rested.

When it appeared that there were no negative consequences, Keira followed and drank quickly. Ret and Motl were more hesitant, but after observing the others light up, they chose to drink their share. Avik was more stubborn.

"It *is* safe," said Lancen. "You will feel better."

Avik didn't even reach for his cup. "I'm not accepting anything they offer me."

"But you need this more than any of us. You've had maybe an hour of sleep. You should take some."

"I have a choice," said the Shaharan calmly.

"It is very good," said Keira. "I feel full of energy, even after so much travel. If you don't drink, you'll be weary."

"I would rather be weary than poisoned."

CHAPTER 47

Y ou scare me."

Lancen looked at Keira suspiciously. Her face was smooth, aside from the tired bags beneath her eyes. Her lips showed no sign of a smile, but also no purse of anger.

"What are you talking about?" he asked curiously.

The girl was quiet as she thought over her words. The company had walked throughout the remainder of the day, and it was now dusk. Travel in the light had been far less disturbing than in the black of night. Few bushes ruffled or branches broke. Evil seemed to be sleeping, or in the least waiting. Yet even in the silence and comfort, the presence of enemies was not absent. The elves were not to be trusted, and paranoid, Lancen watched Ret's every move, waiting for growth and darkness.

"Can I be honest with you?" Keira asked.

"Always."

"You may not want to be bothered, but there is just something weighing on my mind."

"I'm listening."

"Well, you know Etnah was all I had growing up," she began. "I had the clan, and friends, but Etnah was the only one important. When he disappeared…the day he left on a hunt with members of the council, only one member returned."

"Shikobin?" Lancen guessed.

"Aye," said Keira with a slight pain in her eyes, "Shikobin told us that they were attacked by the Legion. He said that he had barely managed to escape himself, and the others were killed. That's no coincidence is it?"

Lancen tried to be sensitive to her emotions. "It is hard to say."

"That day I lost the one person I really loved, and it was all a lie. The person who consoled me, who led me to believe that I was alone, who I looked up to as chief, was nothing but scum and a liar."

Lancen simply looked forward and waited for her to continue, not wanting to speak until she had finished. They had more in common than he could have guessed, but it hurt him to think of Keira abused.

"After I lost Etnah, it seemed like the divines had abandoned me. I didn't believe in the prophecy, or in tradition. It was the only time that I ever felt completely lost, so I ran away.

"I nearly made it to Aduran's lake before I stopped. It wasn't long before someone found me, but in that time alone, I decided that I would never love anyone again. I was set to marry Engle, but I never let him close. Noshera, I miss him! But I never *needed* him, nor Eltou, nor anyone. Am I making sense?"

Lancen nodded with a subtle smile. "Go on."

"My point is that I have never let myself close to anyone since Etnah. You scare me Lancen, because I want to be close to you."

Lancen's chest warmed. He had a hard time with trust, but to be desired, and maybe even needed, for more than just the prophecy, sure felt good for a change. He wanted her confidence, and sought to be worthy of it, but somehow that was not as easy as it would seem. To completely offer himself to her would be to abandon Adalyn and everything he had grown up knowing. On the other hand, there was something special with Keira, something that he had never known he always wanted.

"Is it a danger to trust me?" he asked earnestly.

Keira thought briefly, watching her feet as she marched. "Yes."

Lancen hung his head. The reasoning was clear, but he still had to ask. "Why?"

"You are reckless, never on one side or the other," she said. "I don't know if you support the Nobles or even care about the Natives, and you do not believe in the divines. So yes, you are a danger to trust, but within my heart I know I want to."

Could Lancen even offer her trust? Was it something he was even willing to give himself? Given as difficult as it was to believe in his own morality, how could he ever put it out there for someone else to grasp? As badly as he wanted to say yes, he didn't know the answers.

But that did not stop his brain from rolling. He questioned who he was without Keira. An angry and unguided boy? And yet with her, he felt like a man with direction and purpose. If he did give himself to her, it would mean added responsibility, more pressure on his already burdened shoulders. She would become family, and he would have to look after her as his own. But wasn't that exactly what he desired?

Finally, he submitted. "I want you to trust me."

She gazed up at him with the hint of a smile, but before she could respond, they were interrupted by Yanlah and Kelta.

"It will be night soon," said Yanlah. "It would be wise for your company to drink more of the sap."

Lancen nodded. "I will tell them."

"Before you do," said Kelta, "we would have a word alone."

Lancen agreed, and after squeezing Keira's hand, he stepped away with the Darkwood leaders.

"The next few days will be grueling," said Kelta, casually scratching his light brown beard. "You may not be fit for the struggle."

"I am fit," Lancen replied.

"Perhaps," answered Kelta with a smile. After a moment, he changed the subject. "Where are you from, Noble?"

"Calderon."

"I have heard stories of Calderon! It is the giant city made of stone, 'Pinnacle of the Grasslands' some call it."

"I'd say it is a fitting name," said Lancen, waiting for the point.

"We have one real question for you Calderonian," said Kelta, skipping-over other formalities.

Lancen nodded to proceed, concerned at what they might ask.

"How does a Noble child become the leader of a band of Natives?"

It was a valid question, one that Lancen had been expecting. "Does this concern you?"

Kelta exchanged a brief glance with Yanlah, then looked to Lancen neutrally. "Makes no difference to me, but my men raise questions."

"I am a soldier of the Legion," Lancen lied. "My group follows me because I offer information and insurrection, among other valuable assets.

"Can I ask *you* a question?" he requested, trying to change the topic quickly.

"I'd say you have that right," said Kelta.

"Why help us? You could have let us travel the road alone, but instead we get an armed escort?"

"The forest is sacred," said Kelta. "It is not typically kind to strangers. The forest will decide who lives and dies, but without proper action by travelers, the choice is always death."

"For the foreigners?"

"For everyone."

Lancen watched the elves closely, he couldn't help but think they were hiding something.

Kelta must've noticed Lancen's suspicion and ended the conversation where it was. "You should drink more mead. We have a long night ahead of us."

And a long night it was. Though the mead was a delicious comfort, when the sun set, the monsters awoke. The trees were loud, perhaps angry with the strangers for passing through their home. They seemed to communicate amongst themselves and close in around the travelers in an attempt to suffocate. Branches snapped and trunks moaned on both sides of the road. Gloomy green lights were seen floating through the trees near the path, growing more and more numerous beside the company.

Eventually morning did come, and the wanderers retired to rest. With the Dark-sap mead wearing off, they all slept peacefully. A watch was still kept, but it seemed counterproductive at this point. The Natives of Darkwood had the upper hand. If an attack was to be made, there would be no stopping it, and they would all be better off rested.

Before any of them were prepared, they were back up and moving. Though they had only slept a couple of hours, the elves insisted on covering more ground. For a boost, everyone drank freely of the mead, except Avik, who continued to refuse.

The next week progressed with similar travel. After the redundancy nearly made Lancen lose count of the days, the terrain roughened. It climbed and dropped roughly. Trees seemed to grow larger and somehow even tighter together, only adding to the already extreme darkness. Cobwebs and moss became prevalent along the path. One late afternoon, the company had started up a steep and difficult climb along the endless road as the sun was about to set. Their day's travel had only begun.

When they had finally made it to a more flattened area, the sky was growing dark and Kelta called the group to rest. "Let us stop here for a while," he said. "We have an exhausting road ahead of us this night."

Most of the elves fell to the dirt below where they stood, a stark contrast from the immediate guard positions they normally took. Aching, Lancen slowly moved to a seat on the cold, moist ground. Avik could hardly take his seat. His side was causing him constant pain, and without the mead to help him fight, fatigue had struck him far worse than the others.

"Will you be able to make it through the night?" Lancen asked him.

"I can make it through anything," answered the Shaharan with arrogance. "Quitting is a decision, and I will not choose it."

As Avik spoke, Yanlah approached them carrying a large bowl full of Dark-sap mead.

"We will not rest long," said the elf. "There is no time for sleep. We must drink this and be back on our feet within the hour."

One by one the group filled their cups, even Avik, but the moment Yanlah turned his back, the Shaharan of Calderon dumped it to the dirt.

As the others drank, Keira shook her head. "You need it Avik! Take some."

"No," said Avik with a smug look. "But with the rest of our hour I'd like to get some sleep. I'll need all the rest I can get."

CHAPTER 48

Avik awoke to a blackness so thick he could taste it, and so dark he had to reach up and touch his eyes to confirm they had ever opened. He was disoriented and exhausted, but as consciousness steadily returned, he noticed his companions were lying next to him. For the first time in Darkwood, there were no elven torches as they rested, no whistling or chants. There was only the quiet and eerie rush of wind gliding between the trees. As Avik sat up, the observation was confirmed, Kelta and his band of elves had forsaken them.

Swearing, Avik felt his way over to where Lancen was laying and shook his friend's shoulder. "Get up," he said angrily. "They left us, just like we said they would."

Lancen did not budge.

Avik gave him a punch to the arm. "Wake up!"

Still, his friend did not respond. Avik leaned his head over Lancen's chest to confirm a heartbeat. Losing patience, the Shaharan raised his voice. "Lancen! Wake up, Native-loving dupe!"

Again, after no response, Avik moved to Keira and tried to shake her. She was definitely breathing, steady heartbeat, but no movement. Grumpily, he rose to his feet and stumbled over to Motl, giving the Endwan a somewhat fierce kick to the side. No answer.

Putting his hands on his face, Avik scratched down his cheeks in frustration. He knew that something like this would happen! How had the others been so blind as to not see it? Of course the

Dark-sap mead would be poisoned!

At least his friends were not dead. They all gave breath, signs of vitality positive. The only question now was when they would wake — assuming they would wake at all.

Avik froze mid-thought as there was a rustle in the thick of forage behind him. The sound continued only a moment before it lost itself again in the wind. Avik looked back and saw nothing. Standing like a spooked deer, he waited for more movement. Impatient and anxious, his teeth began to chatter. He needed to make a fire — now.

As quickly as possible, he scraped the forest floor for twigs and tinder. When he had pulled together a small amount, he noticed a glowing light appear out of the darkness through the nearby trees. It multiplied and grew into a dozen or so spots, moving steadily closer. In a panicked rush, Avik grabbed flint from his bag and the knife from his waist. He immediately began sparking it, but paired with moist tinder, the effort was tedious and unsuccessful. The lights grew ever closer, spreading out and circling around him. They all appeared the same light green.

In desperation, Avik lurched over to Motl and searched his person. Soon he found the small pouch containing the powder they had often used to start fires. Charro shell? Or something like that.

"Come on, light!" he shouted, throwing a pinch of the dust onto the sticks and tinder. Nothing happened.

"Ragh!" he groaned in annoyance. The lights were nearly on him, and he was helplessly blind. As he struggled, he knew that the fate of his own life, as well as the lives of his friends, hung in the balance of time and intuition.

What was the word the elves had used to start these fires? he thought madly. He had heard it many times: on the road with Etnah, with Motl, with the Darkwood elves. *What do I say? Fohta rum? No, Mokta rune? No, no, NO!* Finally, his breath cut short. He remembered.

"Fekta mun!" he called, throwing more powder at the twigs. Instantly, the pile blew up into flames of green and blue. As the light cut through the darkness, features of the world became visible. Waiting for him, just a few feet away on the opposite side of the fire, crouched a large and angry feline beast, growling softly but heated.

In shock, Avik jumped and fell backward. An evil and hungry face looked directly at him, lit up in flashes by the small fire. The creature was a monstrous cat, as big as a bear, and it hissed a threatening sneer. Fluorescent fangs, as long as his forearm, hung in a snarl below raised lips as short glowing horns sprouted from atop its head. Bright claws raked the dirt in an act of intimidation. Avik had heard of this creature before while training in the Legion. It was a saber.

Adrenaline pumping, the Shaharan of Calderon pushed himself to his feet, his gut shooting pain in the process. His wound had all but healed, yet still caused pain when he moved quickly. As he tried to hold his ground before the saber, he noticed other lights closing in all around him. If the beasts could sense fear, they would find none in him. Digging within himself, he took a confident step toward the visible cat and yelled a hostile cry.

The tiger was covered in black fur but had patches of neon that pricked up as it crouched to kill. Smoothly, the monster moved around the fire and carefully stepped over Ret's sleeping body, all the while never taking its eyes off of Avik. Delving deep into a well of predation, the cat released a powerful roar like the waters of Rohgast. Avik shuddered but stood his ground.

Suddenly, while he was focused on the visible cat, a second beast dove out of shadow to flatten him. Instinctively, Avik ducked and evaded, just in time to avoid being pinned down, but slow enough that he received a burning claw across his back. His body chilled as he fought nerves that were crawling in. In a rage of defense, he threw his dagger quickly at the first saber, which had swiftly leaped forward to attack. The beast flinched and cried viciously as the short iron blade pierced its breast.

With no time for rest, the second cat had turned to pounce

again. At the last possible second, Avik grabbed his pack from the ground and swung it with all his might at the monster, barely deflecting the blow. Finding his sword from the dirt, the boy turned and slashed the face of a third tiger as it leapt into the vicinity. The monster fell to the earth with a thud and lay still next to Keira.

Avik looked around sharply at the two surviving cats. Holding his blade erect, he tried to remember to breathe. In a moment, the dagger-wounded beast charged him and was swiftly cut down but was replaced by a fourth and a fifth saber. Screaming, Avik kicked the fire and shot burning embers toward the faces of the newcomers. He then turned and hacked at the second beast, missing narrowly. In a blur, a sixth tiger leapt into the circle of flickering light. Growling, the four surviving creatures circled around the lone Shaharan, stepping over the bodies of his companions. They all rumbled menacing growls as they kept their eyes glued to him with unwavering ferocity.

"Come at me!" barked Avik. "I've got all night."

The boy turned in circles, following the moving cats. The spark of the fight had helped to keep his mind focused on the beasts, and not on the pain in his side or his aching limbs.

Without warning, a giant paw swung from behind him. It felt as though a catapult had launched a rock into his back as the strike landed and sent him tumbling forward to the earth. In the pummel, he had lost hold of his sword, and before he could find it, another beast pounced to kill. Avik blindly reached to his side, and in an act of the gods, he found the hilt of his blade and threw it upward and into the diving animal. An incredible weight collapsed on him as the monster fell limp.

Screaming with passion, he wriggled and fought to free himself from beneath its massive corpse. Just as he had finally squeezed free, a dangerous paw clawed across the side of his head. He attempted to stand at once, but before he could he make it to his feet, another strong blow hit him across the torso, ripping his shirt and knocking him flat on his back.

He noticed blood running down his face as the three surviving sabers hissed and roared. He was tired, and his breathing was pained. His whole body felt broken and screamed to retreat, but he could not allow failure. He willed himself to stand, crawling up the side of a dead cat. Now weaponless and fatigued, he stood powerless, but knew in his heart that he was the only thing standing between the sabers and the certain death of his friends.

Intuitively, he reached for the pouch of charro shell on the ground beside him and grabbed a pinch. Just as the next of the three tigers crouched to pounce, he threw the dust toward it, crying "*Fekta mun!*"

The substance sparked in the air and cast a spurt of blue flame toward the cat.

In response, the beast hissed wildly and took a retreating leap backward.

"*Fekta mun!*" Avik screamed again, seemingly shooting fire from his fingertips toward the other cats. Crying again and again, he continued to throw more. The sabers grouped tighter and backed away from the Noble cautiously. Anger and intensity had left them. Trepidation was now alone within their eyes.

Reaching into the pouch, Avik grasped what remained of the dust. With a large handful of black shell, he wound up and threw it violently toward the monsters. "*FEKTA MUN!*"

A large ball of blue and green flame exploded from the dispersed particles. Screaming piercing and ungodly cries, the massive sabers shot backward. With large and final roars, they turned and launched back into the depths of shadow, becoming once more nothing but floating lights within the darkness of the forest.

The night was left silent except for the soft cracking of the small abused fire, as well the heavy breaths leaving Avik's mouth. The Shaharan hunched over the three dead monsters and his four sleeping companions. Wounds covered his body, but his heart pounded too rapidly for him to know it. His anxiety was still great, but eased. Danger had passed for the present.

With his thoughts wandering to the erupting dust, only one question lingered in his mind: *What the HELL is a charro?*

CHAPTER 49

Lancen's brain seemed to pulsate inside of his skull, growing larger and smaller rhythmically. He was groggy and disoriented. Chest pounding, it hurt to breathe. His eyes felt weighed down by an unbearable force, but a tired determination drew them open. Light flooded his view as broken rays of sunshine warmed his face. Memory flew back to his mind in waves. Sidna, Rune, his mission, his failures, it was all there.

"About time," Avik said gruffly, watching his friend struggle back into reality. The others were still asleep.

Lancen tried to talk, but the words caught in his throat. He swallowed and coughed to a terrible dryness. Staring at the branches above him, he dug a little deeper and managed to choke out a question. "What happened?"

Avik chuckled. "Your savage friends drugged you. Had I drank the mead, you and I wouldn't be talking."

"What?" Lancen asked, coming more to his senses. Stomach lurching, he sat up in an instant. Tumbling around in the dirt, he reached for his axe. The sight of the giant sabers was chilling, and Lancen gripped his weapon uneasily before he was certain they were dead.

"There were six of them by the way," said Avik, laughing at Lancen. "Don't worry, I chased off the other three."

With great concern, Lancen looked at once to Keira. When he saw her lying unscathed a breath of relief escaped him.

"Your girlfriend is just fine," said Avik sarcastically. "Everyone is fine. I was torn up a bit though. Thank you for noticing."

It was only then that Lancen looked-over his old friend, who sat unconcerned, whittling at the end of a large stick. His tunic was ripped open in several places and dried blood painted the side of his head and his entire torso a reddish black. Spread out across his body, gruesome claw marks added extra flavor to the already grisly image.

Bothered by the sight, Lancen reached into his pack for one of his blankets and placed it around the Shaharan's shoulders.

"Are you in pain?" he asked.

"Only if I stand up, lie down, or sit," answered Avik. "Other than that, I'm feeling great."

Lancen laughed and went again to his pack to retrieve his water skin. He was surprised to find it so full. After taking a small drink himself, he proceeded to help his friend clean and dress the horrid wounds.

"Let's hope you aren't too tired to travel today," said Lancen, pretending not to be impressed by Avik's heroism. "We're already pressing for lost time."

The Shaharan grimaced as dried blood was cleaned from his face, pulling at his scraggly beard. Laughing, he jabbed back at Lancen. "Let's hope the next time you're poisoned and helpless I am not too tired to save you."

Lancen smiled and continued to address the cuts and bruises. Motl began to stir a few feet away, grumbling and swearing. The Endwan leader soon sat up with a look of pure misery on his face.

"What are you whining about?" Avik asked as a cut reopened on his forehead, and a drop of blood rolled down his face.

Motl scowled and massaged his torso. "Noshera! I feel like I've been punched by a troll!"

Coughing to prevent a laugh, Avik remained silent, forcing Lancen's suspicion.

"Must've been the sabers," Avik mentioned dryly, scratching his head, seemingly in the one spot that wasn't wounded. "Are you alright?"

Motl's eyes widened humorously as he looked over the giant dead cats. "I'll be fine, probably a broken rib is all. I've dealt with worse. How did you—"

"Didn't think I had it in me?" interrupted Avik. "There were nine of them by the way."

"You told me six," Lancen laughed.

The Shaharan glared suspiciously and slowly looked up at his friend. "Well either way, I think we ought to get more of that charro shell."

Over the next hour, the rest of the fellowship arose and prepared for departure while there was still sunlight. Lancen, Ret, and Motl proceeded to saw the fangs, horns and claws from the bodies of the dead sabers, and sew them onto their clothing. The appendages still glowed a dim green, and the group figured that wearing them would help to fend off predators in the night.

Most of their food and supplies had gone untouched by the Darkwood elves, including their weapons and bedding. For some unexplained reason, additional amounts of bread and flour existed in their packs, and every one of their skins and canteens were filled to the brim.

As the company set off just before sunset, Lancen had to ask the group, "Why did they leave us with our weapons and supplies?"

Keira shrugged her shoulders.

Avik shook his head, hobbling along with the help of Ret. "So we can cut them down the next time we meet."

"They believe in divines of fate," said Motl assuredly, ignoring Avik's comment. "They left our outcome in the hands of the forest, and this time, the forest chose life."

"Yeah, the *forest* chose life," piped Avik smugly.

"It still surprises me that there are Natives who do not believe in the three divines," said Lancen, ignoring his friend with a smile.

"Well the number is very few, but there are some. Perhaps they began by believing in our gods, but over time they have twisted and morphed them to fit with their own carnal desires. I'd imagine that to take our weapons would be to deny us our proper fate, and that would be a transgression of law."

"They are corrupt," said Keira. "We should have known it from the beginning."

"We all felt uneasy," said Lancen, "but we were left with no choice. Sometimes there is only one path to follow, and it is not always pleasant."

"We all had a choice," said Motl, "and we'd be dead if Avik hadn't made his."

The company continued to walk, slower than before but steadily climbing and descending the steep and rugged terrain. After some time, when Lancen walked at the head of the group, Ret approached his side, Motl taking a turn in helping Avik.

Lancen was uneasy with the young Endwan so close to him. He knew that the Native was well beyond full recovery and on his way to skolism. Other than a few thick pink scars on his neck, there were few signs to show that he had been nearing death just a week or so earlier. As Ret marched near him, Lancen felt a strong darkness, and yet it was warm and familiar, as if Ret was his kin. There was no denying why. The elf had grown pale. Like Lancen, the sun was a minor irritant, and if anyone were to look closely, they would notice his teeth beginning to sharpen. Ret was a great threat, and in more ways than one.

Not only was the Endwan becoming a monster, with incredible and macabre temptations, but he was also the only one in the group that knew of Lancen's similar darkness. If Ret were to tell someone, it would be the end. There would be no more Obah-a-Tou, no freedom for the Natives, and no penalty for the Legion.

"I can sense who you really are," Ret whispered chillingly, quietly enough so that the others didn't hear. "Can you feel it also?"

Lancen closed his eyes and sighed. He wanted to avoid this conversation. "I don't know what you're talking about."

Ret laughed softly. "Don't play coy, Lancen."

Refusing to look at the Endwan, Lancen kept his eyes on the road ahead. He debated on addressing the situation head on. There were pros and cons to disclosure, but it seemed there was no way around it. "It is a curse."

"Is it?" asked Ret openly. "I am completely healed, and I have never felt so strong. How is that a curse?"

"Because we are hungry, and we grow hungrier every day. It can never be satisfied. We must always fight the desire."

"That is difficult to believe," said Ret, slightly frustrated. "We were made to hunt."

"But we will not," whispered Lancen strongly. "I refuse to drink the blood of anything."

"Yet it is blood that will sustain us! It is the strongest desire that has ever been placed in me! I know it's wrong, but it is all I can think about."

"You control your appetite. Do not allow it to control you."

"I feel like a new person," said Ret. "It is confusing, because feeding does not seem so wrong anymore."

Chills ran up Lancen's spine. Although he had been concerned about Ret for several days now, perhaps the situation was more dire than he realized. "Are you Ret? Or are you a creature with an instinct to feed?"

"Could it be by chance that we have been brought together, Son of Calderon?"

Lancen didn't respond. He did not want to indulge this discussion. Was it denial? Did he still refuse to accept what he was becoming? Whatever it was, he knew that he had to hang on to all of the goodness left in him. He needed to grasp it as if the force of a hurricane was coming to rip it away.

"I have had dreams," hissed Ret. "The Master is calling, Lancen. It isn't what I want, but it is what I am becoming. I do not want to waste this gift!"

At once Lancen's breath cut short. Somewhere in the depths of his mind, the image of the Master came forth. How he knew it was the Master was unsure, but it was engrained deep into his conscience. What horrible dark magic had been used to put it there?

"We don't need to heed his call," said Lancen. "We must stay on the true path. Skolism is evil, Ret. You should know that better than anyone. They killed many of your brothers."

"But you are my brother now!" said Ret darkly. "We cannot deny the Master. You and I must awake and go to him!"

"I will not allow lies to dictate my actions!" said Lancen somewhat aggressively. He had to look behind him to make sure the others were not suspicious.

"It does not feel like a lie," said Ret.

"No, it doesn't," Lancen agreed. He couldn't explain it, but there *was* a desire placed in him. He didn't know where the Master hid, but somehow, he knew that if he allowed them, his feet would take him there.

Ret stepped toward him and placed a hand on Lancen's shoulder. The Noble was tense and uncomfortable.

"I will be loyal to you, brother. I do believe that you are the champion, even though other forces pull at me. I want to feed. I want to accept who I am, but as long as I follow you, I will do all I can to fight it."

Lancen wanted to be comforted. He wanted to believe the Endwan and rest his mind, but the feeling of darkness that he had sensed in every encounter with skolism lingered within him now. Ret was changing, just as he, and it would take nothing short of heroic hearts to defeat their carnal yearnings.

Lancen tried to give Ret a confident look but did not feel it. All through the night, he thought over the subject, mind not knowing what to conclude. Ever since they had entered Darkwood, Lancen could not take his eye off of the skolic Endwan. Remaining close to Keira, he knew that he would protect her first and foremost. He was well-aware of his own repulsive cravings, but he hated the thought of someone else being so close to the people he cared about while battling the same enticements.

Eventually, when dawn began to overwhelm the dismal sky, Lancen ordered the group to stop and rest. Avik appeared ready to collapse at any moment, while everyone else was drastically in need of their own rest. Motl offered to take the first watch, and Lancen agreed, but quietly refused to sleep himself. His senses were fixed on Ret. Though Keira was near his side, he did not assume that she was safe from the skolic influence. Lancen would die before he let Ret hurt her.

He debated for a moment on whether to tell the others of Ret's progressing condition, but soon discarded the notion. Doing that would also expose himself as a monster. He had to question how the others did not already see it. The graying features, the sunken eyes, these were completely unnatural traits! Then again, skoles had not been around for centuries. How would anyone but Lancen and Ret recognize the signs of turning?

The Endwan had leaned against a large tree across the road from Lancen and Keira. He shut his eyes and seemed to slip quickly into a sound sleep, but Lancen couldn't be sure. He would not risk the Endwan going unwatched, though fatigue was attacking him. His eyelids were heavy, and his body was sore and tired. Sleep was fighting him and Ret did not stir.

Lancen unwillingly closed his eyes and nodded off, but quickly shook himself back to watch. He refused to fall asleep. The skole was a great danger, but exhaustion was winning the battle. Deprivation and hunger were constant enemies. Again his eyes shut for only a moment, then abruptly opened, and then closed…

CHAPTER 50

Clashing waves of alternate realities exploded and condensed. Phantasms of scattered light swirled, and for a brief moment Lancen could see the woman dressed in white. She stood silent, surrounded in black, with her eyes staring down. Abruptly, she faded and was overtaken by the image of the Master, his gray-blue skin, his eerie white eyes. The being was large and magnificent, coming to life in the steam filled room. Lancen saw the Master's mouth, lined in gold. His lips were dark, his teeth white and clean, dropping like daggers to his lower lip.

"Come, my son," he said coolly, in a smooth and low voice, "join me."

Lancen's heart burned. He wanted to obey the call, but the voice of the woman forced itself into thought.

"Run," she said.

But Lancen still viewed the Master. "Join me," he called again.

"Run." It was urgent.

The Master remained dominant. Lancen could scarcely breathe as the two forces clashed inside his mind.

"*RUN!*"

Lancen jerked awake. A light hand was resting on his shoulder. Reacting quickly, he reached to his leg and pulled a dagger from its sheath.

"Woah, Lancen!" cried Ret. "It's me!"

Lancen shot to his feet. A fearful rage was in his eyes. "Get back!" he growled, swinging the dagger viciously.

Ret lurched back, narrowly avoiding the swing.

"Lancen!" yelled Motl. "What's wrong with you?"

The boy paid no mind, but continued to aggressively draw closer to Ret, backing him into a tree.

"What's your problem?" Ret asked in confusion.

Lancen swore and pushed the dagger up against the elf's neck. "I will slit your throat right now!"

"Stop!" came a weaker voice. It was Keira. "Stop! What are you doing?"

Lancen stared at the dagger in his hand and held it tight against his enemy's skin. Breathing heavily, he glanced at Keira. Her expression was fearful and concerned, but it was not directed toward Ret. She was looking straight at him.

Promptly, Lancen lowered the blade and stepped backward in a slight daze. He searched for words but couldn't find them. What had just come over him? Ret leaned his head back against the tree, watching Lancen calmly.

"It is past midday," said the Endwan unphased. "We should get going."

The short blade fell from Lancen's palm and landed with a thud on the dirt. As he awakened to reality, there was an evil in his heart that he could not describe, one that was immovable. Why could only Ret bring it out?

The Noble looked over to Keira. She still watched him, brow narrowed in confusion. There was an awkward air around the entire company. No one wanted to speak, to address what had just happened.

"I'm sorry," said Lancen, turning back to Ret. "It must have been stress, or something."

Ret stared back with piercing eyes. The elf seemed to know more truth about Lancen's outburst than the others. He would assume that it was darkness, or the Master, or any number of the influences their disease carried.

A sudden punch in the arm made Lancen bite his tongue.

"You good brother?" asked Avik.

"I'm good."

"We should depart," said Motl. "I feel we are nearing the edge of Darkwood. The air is thick, and I can smell the bog. Its scent has never been so pleasant."

"I think we've all spent too much time in these trees," said Keira, approaching Lancen's side and resting a hand on his shoulder. He was grateful for her comfort.

Releasing a strained breath, Lancen pointed down the road. After giving Keira a one-armed hug, and a kiss on the head, he began to gather his things.

"One day you'll have to explain what that was all about," said Avik quietly.

"I don't trust him," said Lancen, throwing his pack over his shoulders.

"I wasn't talking about Ret," said Avik. "Why Keira?"

Lancen smirked and shook his head. He understood the confusion, but for Avik, he had a simple answer. "You know she's a fox."

Avik rolled his eyes and leisurely stepped away. "Eh, she's alright."

Hours later, daylight continued to pass between the leaves and branches above the road. As Lancen walked, he tried to avoid eye-contact with Ret. He had to let it go, wait for Ret to step out of line. It would happen soon. The skolic hunger would grow too strong, and the Master's call too tempting. It was only a matter of time, but until then, Lancen was powerless.

As he moved along the road, he watched the trees ahead until he passed them by, over and over on an endless line. Sobering thoughts poured through his mind, splashing this way and that without order. Why was Ret any different than he? Why could the elf not handle the hunger when he could? It was no guarantee that Ret would falter. Why was Lancen consumed in angst?

On occasion, he would look back to Ret. The elf was only a few years older than himself, and not much larger. His eyes were sunken and tired, while his mouth hung open, surrounded by a patchy black beard. Was he such a threat?

Lancen couldn't help but dwell on the look that Keira had given him earlier. There was a certain fear in her expression that ate at him like a wolf with its prey. Had Ret done anything wrong? Anything at all? Or was it Lancen that was dangerous? Was he the one that was a danger to Keira?

He didn't like the thought, but he knew that for now at least, he must cease to be so antagonistic toward his Endwan companion.

The longer they walked, the more the premonitions of the Swamplands became apparent. Lancen could smell its heavy and sour scent. The road climbed and narrowed. The trees thinned and air cooled. It seemed that they were nearly there, but when the tree-line broke, rather than beholding the dark valley of bogs, the group saw before them a long and deep chasm. Dirt walls ran parallel as far as the eye could see in both directions, overgrown in forest weeds on either side. The ravine was at least a hundred feet deep, and a crude bridge made of wooden planks and weathered rope led to the opposite side where the road continued. A muddy river appeared motionless and abysmal at the bottom of the crevice.

Looking back and forth, Lancen bit his lower lip nervously. Observing the suspended bridge more closely, he did not feel comfort. It was shoulder width at its greatest, and appeared weak, scarcely used. If it was ever crossed at all, it was by Darkwood elves, who were small and nimble, about half the size and weight of someone like Avik.

Motl seemed to be having the same thoughts, gazing side to side across the chasm. "This doesn't look safe," he mentioned. "What is your call Lancen?"

By sight alone, it did not seem trustworthy. Though it was only a stone's throw between them and the opposite ledge, if the bridge did not hold, the fall would result in certain death. Yet there were only five of them. Could it last just long enough for them to get across?

"What do you think?" Lancen asked Avik.

"I don't feel good about it, but by the gods, I want out of this forest!"

"It isn't worth the risk," said Ret, disagreeing. "I don't think we should cross."

"We don't have time for a detour," answered Lancen. Raising his arms, he pointed in either direction. "Is there an alternative?"

"I don't like it," repeated Motl.

"Keira?" prompted Lancen.

"We follow you," she answered.

"I assure you; we would be better off going around," said Ret. "That bridge isn't going to hold."

"Do you see another way?" asked Lancen, harsher than he had intended. What was it about Ret that brought this out of him?

"There isn't one," said Avik in agreement.

"We don't have time to waste for a detour," said Lancen. "We will cross here. One at a time."

Lancen continued to analyze the bridge. The ropes were thin and tattered, the planks cracked and worn. "Avik, you go first. If it holds up for you, the rest of us should be fine."

The Shaharan looked at Lancen, offended, but without statement stepped out onto the first suspended plank. Immediately one of the two support ropes frayed and tightened under his weight but held. Swearing, Avik took another step, and then another, longing for something to hold onto as the bridge bobbed and swayed beneath him.

Looking down, he marveled, "Word of advice: keep your head up!"

Once the Shaharan had made it safely across, Keira was next to go. The worn rope stressed, but not as severely as under Avik. Though the bridge swung beneath her, the Native girl made quick work of it with great balance.

Motl went next, the rope straining more and more with every step. The elf moved slowly, and held his arms out wide, trying to stay balanced. Leaping the last few feet, the Endwan clapped his hands on the other side, unscathed.

Lancen motioned for Ret to go next, but the elf refused. Shaking his head, Lancen moved forward himself and nervously stepped onto the hanging crossing. As with the others, the rope frayed with his first step, and twitched again and again with each subsequent.

Just as he began to feel like he would make it across, the plank beneath his foot cracked and gave way in a horrific instant. Immediately the bridge shifted, and Lancen tumbled over the side. Keira screamed as he reached out to clasp onto anything at all before he fell to his muddy grave. At the last possible second, his right hand found hold around one of the thin base ropes, and with nothing but his fingertips, he managed to hang on.

Incoherent screams sounded from both sides as Lancen strained to maintain his grip. Without warning, Ret stepped onto the bridge to help him, but the moment he did, both ropes shredded and split, one slightly before the other. In an instant, the planks fell from beneath him, and before they could react, both he and Lancen dropped downward.

With his stomach jumping to his chest, Lancen cried and reached out toward the Endwan with his free hand, holding tight to the rope with the other. He felt time separate from reality as they flew downward. Forcing himself to reach further, Lancen grabbed hold of Ret's wrist just before the rope pulled tight and sent them colliding into the opposite cliff-side.

By sheer chance, Lancen managed to hang on as they crashed into the moist dirt and foliage. Abruptly, a great weight tugged on his arms, not only causing his grip to slip, but it felt like he was being ripped in half. As they held against the wall, Lancen noticed a warm drop of liquid fall onto his face. With his teeth grit and breathing short, he looked up to see his arm mashed between the wall and a sharp plank. Before he felt the pain, he saw the skin open and torn, with blood running down his arm.

"Help me!" Ret cried anxiously from below him.

Groaning in pain, Lancen was too strained to breathe. Excruciating force tugged on both arms as he did all he could to simply hang on. Peering down to Ret, he saw that the elf was in even worse shape than himself. The Endwan's shoulder was deformed and stretched. It must have completely dislocated when they caught on the rope. Lancen's grip on the young man's wrist was the only thing preventing a fall to certain death.

"Help! I can't move my arm!" Ret howled viciously. There was a consuming fire in his whitening eyes, a monstrous snarl from his pointed teeth.

Lancen seemed to forget the pain in his own arms and immediately considered his opportunity. He did not prompt them, but thoughts rushed into his mind. There was no need to consult the others, no need to wait for Ret to give in to the darkness. Right now, he was in a position to be the judge — and the executioner.

"Dammit!" Ret screamed. "Help me!"

His face was gaunt and filled with anger. The Endwan was skolic, and there was no room for doubt. Only Lancen knew what that entailed, and he had worried about it since the moment he discovered that Ret had been bitten. Now the young man's life dangled helpless at the end of his fingertips. He had the choice to save or sentence, and a battle raged inside him over what he should do.

If he were to let go, his greatest present worry would be gone, dead a hundred feet below in the murky river. Keira would be safe, Lancen would not be revealed as skolic himself, or even worse, tempted to feed and join the Master. With Ret out of the picture, every part of his quest would be easier!

However, if he were to save the elf, there would be no blood on his hands. He would have an incredible ally, and a friend every bit as strong as himself. There would be someone near him that could understand and empathize over their arduous hunger. There would be no burden of conscience.

But in this moment, he could scarcely hear the morality inside of him, even though he knew that it was screaming for him to do the right thing.

"*LANCEN!*" Ret growled. "*SAVE M —* "

Lancen released his hold on the Endwan's wrist. In a slow and painful clarity, he watched his companion tumble and fall. In seconds, Ret had grown smaller and smaller before crashing into the muddy wall and being swallowed completely by the thick brown river. The water stirred only briefly, and then was still.

CHAPTER 51

I n a strange stupor, Lancen hung by his bloody arm, staring down to the grave of a former companion. His eyes remained wide, as if they were afraid to blink. What had he just done?

"*NO!*" Motl screamed from above. "Divines, *NO!*"

Lancen looked up the slats of the bridge as his grip around the rope began to slip. Through great pain in his shoulders, he swung his other arm to grab hold of the closest plank and slowly worked himself upward. When he reached the top, Avik helped him over the edge. At once he fell forward to his hands and knees, all the while mumbling, "I couldn't hang on."

Motl dropped to one knee and put his face in his hands.

"I'm sorry," Lancen kept repeating, the world spinning around him. He stared at his arms in the dirt, one covered in blood and the other bare. Had he just murdered someone?

Everyone was silent, shocked and horrified at what had just happened. Did Ret truly need to die? Lancen tried to steady his heart. With the significance of the quest at hand, difficult decisions had to be made. It was the undecided man that allowed honey to slip from the comb, and he had made a choice.

Avik and Keira went to Motl's side for consolation. As Lancen slowly sat up, he watched with a sour taste in his mouth and a sinking pit in his stomach. He wanted to puke. He wanted to believe that he had done the right thing, but now that the moment had passed, he felt sick.

"There was nothing you could do," said Avik genuinely, giving Lancen a solemn nod.

Lancen dropped his head, knowing that his friend was utterly wrong. Yet as the time lingered, he began to remember why he had let go. Ret was a skole, plain and simple. He was a danger. He wouldn't have been able to resist the call. So Lancen had done the right thing, hadn't he?

"*Hypocrite*," he whispered. Would he be able to resist the call himself?

"We should get going," mentioned Keira. "It's almost dark."

"I don't want to spend another minute in this place," added Avik.

"Give him some time," said Lancen. "He just — *we* just suffered a great loss. Allow us time to catch our breath."

Motl suddenly looked up and straight into Lancen's eyes. The elf's brow twitched as he seemed to dig deeper into what he was seeing. Lancen felt uncomfortable and averted his gaze.

"Obuthahn does not have the luxury of time," said Motl darkly. "The girl is right."

Pain was in the elf's eyes, even anger, but his resolve to carry on was unblemished.

"Are you sure?" asked Lancen.

Motl rose to his feet with a clenched jaw, again looking at Lancen with a hint of contempt. He responded aggressively, "Let's move, *Champion*."

The group walked quietly downhill along the rugged and unfamiliar path. Lancen wanted to speak, but he was too afraid that Motl was beginning to sense his darkness. He feared that the Endwan knew Ret's death was no accident. The word 'murderer' lingered in his mind, refusing to leave. The others had to have known what Ret was becoming! How could they not see it? Yet even after all that had happened, he could not bring himself to tell them. After Lancen had charged the elf with a dagger, who could believe that dropping him was an accident?

He felt that there were eyes on his back as he walked in the front of the group. He would have to be perfectly tempered for the foreseeable future to earn back Motl's trust. Lancen felt like the elf was watching him in the same manner that he had been watching Ret.

His inner struggle must have been evident as Keira grabbed his arm and stated, "The pain will pass."

Lancen hesitated. "What if Ret could still be here?"

"'What ifs' bring only harm," said Keira. "So stop thinking about it. It's not going to bring him back."

"I just…I could have done more."

"You should feel no guilt. You were barely hanging on, your arm pinned badly. No one could have done more," assured Keira.

"I think maybe I could have."

"Lancen do you remember what Eltou and I did during the trial?" asked Keira. "In the cavern of Nahabuk, I left the only person I should have loved bleeding, alone in the dark. Maybe you could have done more, maybe not, but I know with certainty that I could have done more for Engle. Guilt does no favors."

"That was different. I looked into his eyes. I watched him fall," Lancen could not hide the horror on his face. "I am no leader. How can I go on? Why am I here?"

"Time is moving forward Lancen, and it is your choice to move with it. You told me that, and it looks like you're still walking."

"I know," said Lancen, hating that she remembered his words enough to use them against him. "Thank you."

"Do not thank me," said Keira sharply. "Just get over the past."

"Do you smell that?" Avik interrupted from behind them.

"It's just the bog," said Lancen, but before he could say another word, his foot sunk into moist soil, and Avik began to move quickly past him.

"But it is much stronger now," said Avik in excitement.

Motl at once began to move more quickly with the Shaharan, surpassing Lancen and Keira.

"The Swamplands," said Lancen in sudden realization.

He and the girl began to move as swiftly as the others. A constant tunnel of trees was left behind them as they passed by dirt and timber on the overgrown road. The putrid smell continued to grow stronger with every step forward. Trees began to space apart, and a mist seemed to seethe up through the ground, bringing a cold moisture with it. Lancen could feel the dirt grow mucky beneath his feet. His heart beat rapidly as he approached the line of trees with the others.

Darkwood Forest was now officially behind them, and ahead was a broad and dark valley. Black soil was littered with mosses and shadowy grass. Distorted trees populated the landscape while pockets of muggy water weaved between the various foliage. Mushrooms were diverse and thick. Many were glowing a deep green tone, lighting the intense fog of the land in a gloomy hue. Webs and hanging weeds spread from tree to tree as the setting sun cast light down only to the top of the mist. There was sure darkness, but also hope in the sight of the dreary terrain. They had reached the Swamplands.

CHAPTER 52

A dalyn's eyes were dry. She promised herself that the last tear had been shed. No more. Though she grew increasingly terrified with every moment, the time for weakness was over. In the end, it was no one's fault but her own that she had ended up in this position. She regretted ever leaving the castle.

She hung, gagged over the shoulder of a large man, if it was even fitting to call him that. She had not seen the face of this one in particular but assumed it was like the others. They were gaunt and wrinkled, with white eyes and sharp teeth, nothing more than beasts.

Everything around her was dark. She didn't know whether it was night or day, or even if she was indoors or out. All she could tell was that the air was cold and musty here. Several skolic creatures moved all around her, known only by their evil auras and rushes of wind.

She knew that she was in danger. It was evident in every howl of the hounds, in every mumbling from a skole. As she was carried helpless and blind on the back of a monster, she couldn't help but wonder why she had ever left the city. There had been nothing for her in the world outside of its walls. There were no fairy tales or happy endings. Her father was right to keep her locked within the bounds of Calderon. There was no such thing as destiny.

It was true that for a while she had found the adventure she desired. She had seen danger and glory, and even felt love, but it was all over now. The journey had not been worth the price she was forced to pay.

A voice rose from the body beneath her, casting a chill over her entire being. "We couldn't have done it without you, girl. You're the key to a new world! It won't be long now."

Adalyn shuddered. The voice was low and raspy, spoken with a foreign, almost Native accent. She didn't respond to it. Why would she? She knew that the end was coming with the force of a ram. There would be no stopping it. She was powerless and had nothing to show for her sixteen pitiful years of life.

But as she thought, she felt the very slight weight of the emerald necklace around her neck. She longed for Obuthahn where she had received it, and for Lancen who had given it to her. Of course the odds told her that he was already dead, but she just couldn't allow herself to believe it. The only thing that kept her from completely giving up was the hope that he would still come for her. Deep down she wanted anyone to come for her, her father, Earnst, Hans, anyone! But the subtle truth that she refused to believe was that no one was coming. Lancen was gone, and now she was left alone in this nightmare—but he wasn't dead. Adalyn knew that he wasn't dead! She missed him too much. She loved him.

"WHERE IS SHE!" Duke Roland screamed, throwing his goblet across the castle hall. Captain Earnst stood before him with cuts and scrapes across his face.

"I don't know, sir," repeated the head of Calderon's castle guard. "We were ransacked at sundown. More than half of my men were killed. I have never seen anything like it. She could be anywhere."

It was nighttime in Calderon, and Roland had just arrived. They had served him dinner and presented him with his nightly clothing, as if nothing were awry.

Roland clenched his fist and bit at his knuckle, trying to control his anger. "But she is alive?"

Earnst looked back at him with cold eyes. "It is hard to say. We never found her body, but that doesn't mean —"

"Yes it does," said Roland sternly, putting his finger to the table between him and the commander. "Yes it does."

"As you say, sir."

Earnst kept his eye on Roland, annoyingly. The captain walked around the table and stopped just next to his leader. Lowering his voice, he suggested. "Send me to the northern mountains."

"You told me that the cursed boy was dead."

"And he is," said Earnst nervously, "but I know that he had something to do with this! There was only one other time that I have ever seen the darkness I encountered in those dogs' eyes, and it was in the eyes of the boy! I can't explain it, but I would recognize that evil anywhere."

"Earnst," said Roland, seething, "tell me the boy is dead."

"He is! He was executed in Riverock. I sent two of my best men. Lancen is lying dead in a pit, with his head in his arms."

"Why do I not believe you?" asked Roland, trying to contain the impossible storm that was raging within him. "I gave you one simple order, to kill a damned seventeen-year-old boy! How hard could it be?"

"I'm sorry, my lord. He is slippery, but if he still breathes, it will not be for long."

Roland closed his eyes, his jaw shaking. He needed to stay rational. He would never find his daughter otherwise.

"I would send you to the mountains tonight," he stated after a moment, "but the majority of your men are wounded or dead. It will take a few days to round up the entire city's Legion. When we do, you will take a hundred men, and you will find my daughter, or your own head will be in a pit."

"And what of Obuthahn? The chance is slim, but she could have been taken back there."

Roland pounded on the table in front of him, then began to pace back and forth, clenching and releasing his fists in rhythm. "They will get theirs as soon as I can put boots in the ash. Every last one of those soulless scum will pay."

"How many men will it take?"

Roland leaned over the table, looking at the map that rested on its surface. His eyes did not see lines or words. Everything was red. "We have ten thousand, perhaps, with several thousand more on their way from Oritha."

"That would leave the city with a minimal defense."

"We do not need a defense!" said Roland, sure of himself. "This is the Natives we are talking about."

"So what is your command?"

"We cannot wait for Oritha. They must meet us in the Ashlands. I need you to help prepare the men at once and tell them that I will lead the march myself. Once everyone is gathered, you will depart with the search party. If you do not find her, and she is not in Obuthahn…" Roland paused for a moment, breathing deeply. "Just pray that we find her."

Suddenly the doors of the hall were thrown open. Roland hollered and punched the nearby wall, enraged, all before throwing a framed painting from where it hung. He hated the interruptions of messengers. He did not need it! Every time they had brought him grievous news.

Turning slowly toward the incoming nuisance, he grit his teeth, nostrils flaring. As he saw who it was, his eyes widened. The storm within him was breaking loose.

Held by two guardsmen and led to the center of the hall, was a bound and beaten ash elf. Standing in his former home, the creature was none other than Roland's old servant, Etnah.

"This savage," said one of the guards, "told us that he used to work in your court. Says he knows the law but told us you would vouch for him."

Roland eyed the Native in utter amazement. The elf wore a concerned and betrayed expression, emotions not often found in the former slave.

"This," said Roland, eyes glued to Etnah, "used to be a servant, but any leniency he had departed with him upon his release. Anything he has to say is futile. No words can bring back my daughter."

"Neither will steel," said Etnah quietly.

Roland laughed. "You think you have the right to speak to me?"

"I can help you find her."

"Because you *DON'T!*" the duke cried.

"We can find her!" said Etnah raising his voice for only a moment. "But you must not attack my clan."

"You forfeited the right to negotiate the moment you saved that boy! Were it not for you, my daughter would still be here, and I would not be after your people for blood!"

"You don't need to do this Roland," said Etnah, keeping his tone level. "Vengeance solves nothing."

"It is called recompense. I will only give the Natives what they warrant."

"The Natives have done nothing wrong!"

"Who gave you the right?" asked Roland fiercely.

"If you allow me to explain," said Etnah. "That boy is central to the peaceful future you and I used to dream of. The time has come!"

"Will the boy bring Adalyn back to me?" Roland probed. "No! He merely stole her and left her to die in Obuthahn! There will be a peaceful future, Etnah, but the Natives will share no part of it."

"There will never be peace with Scharric. You know that. Your daughter was not stolen, and when you see her again, she will explain that. She was running from Calderon, not longing for it."

"How dare you approach me and speak such words!" said Roland fiercely. He noticed Earnst was holding the hilt of a blade at his waist. With one simple order, this Native's head could fall to the stone floor, but what fun was there in that? No, the satisfaction Roland required could not be obtained by such an impulsive measure. "Obuthahn will be leveled, and you will be killed, *savage!*"

Roland spit at the elf's feet. Etnah's eyes widened as he raised his head and looked down his nose to the duke. Roland had never spoken that way before, and the elf would never have expected it.

"You must not attack Obuthahn," repeated Etnah calmly, ignoring the curse. "You are interfering with powers greater than you or I."

Roland scoffed and turned away. Leaning down over the table, he raised one arm casually. "Take this scum to the dungeons. I don't have time for this."

"You will see before the end," Etnah mentioned quickly, before he was hit over the head and dragged off to a cold, dank cell.

CHAPTER 53

S ave me.' The words repeated in his head like the ripples of a pond. He couldn't seem to wipe the image of Ret staring up at him, with heated and desperate eyes, from his conscience. What made Lancen think that he was better suited to resist the call?

"Lancen," said Motl, cutting through the silence, "we should get moving. We're almost there."

"Are you sure we aren't lost?" Lancen asked, rising to his feet and trudging through muddy soil. The group had been walking for nearly two days through the dark and peculiar terrain. The shadows were growing eerily all around them, and the humidity left them all soaked, freezing, and uncomfortable. None of them wanted to spend more time than necessary in this stinky, miserable bog.

"We're not lost," said Motl. "I've been to Mozan-Garo before, don't worry."

Lancen rolled his eyes and tried to be patient. He wasn't worried. He was angry and starving. The others could never understand his pain or how he longed for the night. He regretted killing Ret, the one person who could actually relate. The young man didn't need to die, and if he were still alive, it would have solved so many problems. Lancen knew that he would have sided with the Endwan. Eventually, he would have chosen to feed, and perhaps that was exactly why he needed to let Ret fall.

"Are you okay?" asked Avik, seeming to read Lancen's mind, at least in part.

"You do look rather pale," added Motl slanderously.

Lancen clenched his jaw. "I'll be fine," he said. "It is just anxiety, lack of sleep and food. I'll be fine."

"How can you be sure?" asked Motl. "You haven't been the same since back at the bridge."

"I'm fine, alright?"

"I was only making sure."

"How about you watch your own back?" asked Lancen. "Mine is covered!"

He regretted the words immediately as they moved beyond his lips.

"Watch my back from what?" asked Motl sharply. "You?"

"That's not what I meant."

"Are you sure?" the Endwan drove on. "You've barely said a word for days."

"I've been upset," said Lancen.

"Clearly," said Motl. "It makes me suspicious."

"Of what?"

"Oh, you know what!"

"Do I?"

"What if Ret's death was no accident? Maybe you let go!"

Lancen swore and kicked the dirt. Catching his breath, he seethed, "I couldn't hang on. What more did you expect?"

"A little more endurance for the life of a friend! Why did you do it?"

"I didn't," said Lancen as Motl turned to him dauntingly. The Endwan was twice his size, but Lancen was ready.

"We were all there!" shouted the elf.

Lancen stared up at his guide, not wavering. "I did not let go!"

"The question is why, not if!"

Angrily, Lancen placed his hands on Motl and forcefully pushed him away. "Because Ret was a skole!" he exploded. "Is that what you wanted to hear? He told me he was slipping, that he wouldn't be able to control it!"

Motl bared his teeth and gripped his sword. Before retaliating, he turned away and began to march again along the small path they had been following.

If only Lancen could believe his own words. Of course, Ret had told him no such thing. In fact, the skolic Endwan had claimed the exact opposite.

"This is foolishness," said Keira. "Bickering does only harm."

Ignoring the voice of reason, Motl chimed from ahead. "I never should have followed you. You are no hero."

"Then why are you still here?" asked Lancen coldly, moving swiftly to catch up to the elf.

"Because I mistakenly took you for a good person."

"Stop it!" called Keira. "This helps nothing!"

This time her cry did not go completely unnoticed, though Lancen could scarcely distinguish his guilt from his anger. He wanted to lash out, to draw his axe from his waist and settle this in gore, but that wasn't him. Although he felt far from a good person, he was giving it all he had. He believed he was Obah-a-Tou, and he wanted to make decisions for the greater good, regardless of the mild pain it might also cause. This desire for blood was a separate influence entirely — a fiend.

"I'm sorry," Lancen forced, not feeling the words, but knowing they were right. "I wish I hadn't dropped him, okay? It's all I can think about, and I wish he was still with us."

"It is too late for wishes," said Motl, "but I should not be so quick to cast judgment. I will try harder to fight beside you, not against you."

"You are fighting beside me," said Lancen, cooling off. "All of you are. I couldn't be more grateful. But Ret...he had other motives. I can't tell you what they were, but I know they were there. I didn't let go, but I would have had reason to, right?"

"I don't require further explanation," said Motl. "Besides, we have arrived."

CHAPTER 54

The sight of Mozan-Garo was unpleasant and daunting. Through a thick and rancid mist, the structure stood, carved entirely into a jutting rock. Buried under shadow, a primal wooden door rested in its hollowed center, on either side of which two stone pillars carried dead torches and intricate designs. Lancen dreaded entering, for uninviting did not begin to describe the catacomb and its ominous vibe

Between the company and the structure was a wide pond full of thick, greenish muck. Dead stumps poked through the surface, covered in algae and thousands of tiny mushrooms, while black and gangly trees hung over the site like spider-legs ready to crawl. With strange shadows and restricted visibility, Lancen felt like he was in a peculiar and horrid dream.

"I never imagined that I would be standing before this vile tomb again," said Motl, staring fervently at the structure in the rock.

"What would force anyone to come here?" asked Avik softly, a concerned but determined look painted on his face.

"I spent but one night in those halls. The Nobles were swarming the bogs, and we had nowhere to run. Tomutah had just surrendered, and if the Legion had discovered us, we would have been killed or made slaves. The former was preferred, so we fled to this place."

"It was only one night?" asked Keira.

"Yes," said Motl, "but it was a night I will never forget. Though there are many graves in that tomb, it would seem that not all of its occupants favor death."

"What?" asked Lancen, disturbed.

"There is a reason why a century has passed since Mozan-Garo's last burial."

"It feels haunted. Why would anyone be buried here?" added Avik.

"It wasn't always like this. It was once beautiful, an organized catacomb for only the most valiant and wealthy Natives. But long since has it become a den of necromancy and darkness."

"And prophecy," muttered Lancen quietly. "We are part of this place."

"Or maybe death," Motl suggested coldly. "As was the case for Mendlot, the greatest Endwan to ever live."

"Aye," agreed Kiera, "death is written all over this scene."

"I survived a night in those halls, but I would suggest making this visit quicker. This is not a happy place."

"The places I go rarely are," said Lancen gravely. Drawing his axe, he waded at once into the repulsive water. "No sense in being afraid of the dark."

He continued forward without checking to see if the others had followed. In the pool, his feet sank deeper into suctioning filth with every step. Slithery creatures slimed past him, forcing chills, but Lancen continued forward. When he had finally reached the hole in the rock, he climbed out of the water and took a moment to view the ancient carvings on the pillars. Upon them were several separate stories of an elf warrior with a great sword. In the first image, the hero battled a giant demon, many fallen warriors surrounding. In another, the same warrior knelt before distinct scholars, beyond whom was a collection of men hovering above the ground. And in the final depiction, the hero sat in great power atop a glorious throne.

"Obah-a-Tou," said Motl, coming up from behind. "This place has long awaited his arrival."

"I am no elf," said Lancen with more shock than wit, "but I feel a connection to this place. I can't explain it."

Motl held a determined glare on the old wooden door. "After you," he said coolly. "Let us determine your legitimacy once and for all."

Lancen put his head down and grabbed the ancient stone handle. The barrier creaked as it opened, and instantly a chill breeze shot from the space. Taking a moment to prepare and light their torches, the group lingered with an anxious resolve. Through the open doorway they saw nothing but darkness. After struggling through Darkwood, as well as Nahabuk's cavern, the idea of utter blackness was far from a foreign concept. However, it remained dreaded and unnerving, at least for Lancen's companions. To him, it was only a mild complication.

When Keira and Avik had given their approval, the company stepped forward into the opening hall, saber appendages glowing in the blackness. The entry was a mere ten feet wide and only a stone's throw deep. Thin pillars lined the walls while rubble and dirt beleaguered the floor. Broken statues and shattered frames were strung along the skirts, and at the far end of the room, a narrow doorway loomed open and intimidating.

In the darkness, shadows sent forth a hellish vibe. Strange and eerie noises were soon made out to be distant and angry whispers.

"The dead refuse to sleep. I heard them the last time I walked these halls also," said Motl softly.

No one else dared utter a word as they lowered their heads and moved through the passage and into subsequent corridors. Lancen stepped carefully at the front of the group, torch in one hand, axe gripped tightly in the other. There was no mistaking the feeling of danger present in the darkness.

The following tunnels were constricted and narrow as they wound downward. Lancen had to wonder why they had burrowed so deep into the earth, as if the builders had worried the bodies would escape. Shrines and memoirs were frequent in recessions in the walls. Many caskets were open, with decaying mummies still clinging to the treasures they had held in life. Other graves were completely empty. A foul and rusty stench hung in the air as it was warmed by the torches. The farther they walked, the more numerous and large the corridors became.

As they wandered, the whispers grew louder. They remained incoherent, but they were sure. There was something other than Lancen and his friends alive in Mozan-Garo. He was certain of it.

"These corpses give me the chills," said Avik, startling the others at the sudden noise. It seemed as though they had been walking for hours without a single word. They had moved carefully, checking around every corner and listening desperately for changes in the whispers. The sound of Avik's voice sent shudders across the group.

For a moment, everyone remained quiet, refusing to respond. They waited intently for a repercussion to his speech, but none came. Finally, Lancen decided to reply.

"It is probably best that they don't hear us coming."

"Sure, but who are you referring to?" asked Avik nervously. "The saints?"

"I wouldn't be so quick to say that," said Motl quietly. "Seventeen years ago, when I wandered these halls, the darkness was just as thick, but I met no saints."

"Did you meet anything else?" asked Lancen. "It seems that would be fitting information for us to know."

"No," answered Motl, lip quivering, "but I didn't need to see them to know they were with us."

"You are talking about the dead? Come back to life?" asked Avik incredulously. "That's impossible."

"No, it is quite common," said Motl, to the Shaharan's dismay, "but they must first be tampered with by crooked mages or necromancers, who must sacrifice the living to raise the dead."

"Necromancers?" repeated Avik. "I can handle necromancers."

"Don't be naïve," said Motl. "They are real, and they are dangerous — very dangerous. The type of dark magic they tap into can only be obtained through an intimate relationship with Droth, the devil himself."

"Please don't say that name in such darkness," said Keira with a trembling voice. "I don't want to entice the evil around us."

"And why not say his name?" questioned Motl, raising his voice slightly. "Why live in fear of something that has little say over the world? When Droth was cast out, Athleon banished his power with him. People may find that hidden pool of evil, but they can only dip so much from it."

"Yet in that pool, they can easily ignite a power strong enough to destroy the four of us," argued Keira.

"She's right," said Lancen, biting his lip. "I hardly believe in the divines, but I do not feel comfortable talking about the antethei here."

Keira cringed.

"We don't have to," agreed Avik, carefully stepping over a skeletal arm, "but I agree with Motl that we should not fear him. If we were not harmed by necromancy in the Ashlands, I do not expect it here."

"What is that supposed to mean?" Keira heatedly pried.

"Nothing," said Avik, putting his hands up in innocence, "I'm just saying that we did not face necromancy in the Obuthahn, so I doubt we will face it anywhere."

"There is no necromancy in Obuthahn!" said Keira harshly, her breath becoming brash and less controlled.

Lancen turned to his companions and pointed his axe. "He didn't mean anything by it. Can we stay focused?"

Keira closed her eyes and whispered a curse, but calmed.

"It is only outcasts and rebels that seek the darkness," said Motl, trying to further alleviate the situation. "It matters not what race they were to begin with."

"Perhaps we should speak of brighter subjects," said Lancen, noticing a dull light coming from below a small wooden door ahead of them. "Like maybe that?"

At once the mood changed. Motl was especially captivated and moved quickly toward the door. "It is the saints!" he exclaimed in excitement. "They have risen!"

CHAPTER 55

When he opened the door, all whispers immediately fell silent. To his dismay, there were no spirits within, only a spacious chamber, lit sparsely by a few narrow slits in the towering ceiling.

Sighing in disappointment, the Endwan moved slowly forward to investigate the room with the others. Lancen noticed immediately that the decorations were far different than anything he had ever seen. A variety of elaborate and colorful fabric covered the walls, extending from the ceiling high above all the way to the cold stone floor. Painted murals hung by thin, nearly invisible wire at various heights and angles. In the center of the chamber, four extravagant statues stood in a circle, appearing wise and timeless in the gloomy light. Everything depicted Obah-a-Tou, and everything was ancient and untouched.

Lancen was captivated at first, marveling at the history and renditions of Obah-a-Tou. It felt as though he had stepped through a portal and out of time, to a world that existed long before the Natives and Nobles quarreled. And yet, as he studied each and every design, a disappointing thought began to overwhelm his curiosity. There were no doors into subsequent rooms, no tunnels or windows.

"This is a dead end," he said solemnly.

"It can't be," said Avik. "Did we miss a turn? There must have been a tunnel somewhere."

"No," said Motl. "This is the last chamber. This is where Mendlot's body lies."

The three younger companions were directed to the area where the statues stood. Between them, lying old and decaying on the floor, was a skeletal corpse, hands clenched around an old torch and a small stone hatchet.

"There must be something missing," said Keira shaking her head. "Nihwiah told us to come here. It was divined!"

Lancen continued to look around. There must be a trap door or hidden passage somewhere. This couldn't be the end.

"I don't see any spirits," said Avik grimly.

"Just keep looking," said Lancen. "We'll find something!"

Motl set his torch in a holster on the wall and folded his arms, staring dolefully at the body of Mendlot. "I thought we would find them here. I really did."

Lancen belted his axe and dropped his torch. This wasn't the end! He knew that the prophecy would continue. There was something missing. There had to be!

"I don't see anything," said Avik.

"Lancen," said Keira nervously, losing control of her emotion. "You are our hero. Call on them!"

Lancen looked at her and somberly shook his head. He couldn't. He had to think. There was something here, something familiar, but what was it?

"There were carvings," he said enthusiastically, lifting a finger as the thoughts came to him. "They were back outside, by the door. One of them pictured an elf, Obah-a-Tou, kneeling before, I believe four men. The room beyond was filled with hovering beings. Maybe it is a puzzle, one that Mendlot never figured out."

"Like the switches in the cavern?" asked Keira soberly.

The memory of the three levers propped on a stone base came back to him. Eltou, the son of Shikobin had chosen to pull a lever, regardless of the consequence. The gate had risen, and the roof caved in.

"Yes, like the cavern. There must be some sort of trap."

"There are strange holes in the floor," said Avik, who stood the closest to the statues.

"Could be some sort of poison gas," mentioned Motl. "I've heard of similar things in old tombs such as this. And look to Mendlot. There are no wounds on his corpse."

"Then we don't want to be wrong," said Lancen, moving over to the center ground between the statues.

"So what is the puzzle?" asked Keira. "Is there a lever? Perhaps we must do some sort of ritual."

Lancen shook his head. "No rituals."

Examining the statues more closely, he took note of each unique depiction. All four were crafted of fine stone, and each displayed the same elf warrior, presumably Obah-a-Tou, showing very different and distinct emotions. In the first, he was standing tall. A smile was on his face as he looked to the sky. He carried a sword, held erect, but not in threat.

The second was nearly a mirror image of the first, only on its person was a heavy cloak, with a large hood pulled up and over the forehead. Instead of a smile, the elf wore a more annoyed, or even angry, expression.

The third statue depicted a distraught hero. His face was buried in his hands as he bent over. There were slashes on his arms and torso, making him appear broken, both inside and out.

In the final piece, Obah-a-Tou placed a hand over his heart as he stared into the distance. A serious and contemplative expression worn on his face.

"Are these supposed to look like you?" Avik joked.

Lancen broke his concentration and laughed with the Shaharan. "They should have made me taller."

"I see the resemblance," said Keira smartly. "They do seem pretty arrogant."

Lancen tried to glare at her but couldn't break his smile.

"Perhaps they are facing the wrong way?" Avik asked, approaching the hooded statue and trying to turn it.

"I don't think so," said Lancen with a grin.

"This one is wearing a necklace," said Motl, referring to the smiling statue. "Looks like some rather high-class silver."

"There is one here as well," said Keira, investigating closer the contemplative hero. "It has a big face. The Native rune for love is scratched into it."

"There is a sun on this one."

Avik bent over the corpse of Mendlot and opened a satchel at its skeletal side. "There are two more here. On one there is a wolf, on the other...a depiction of the moons. What does it mean?"

"I think we need to place the correct pendant on the correct statue," said Lancen, taking the necklaces from Avik.

"These traps are fool proof," noted Motl. "Set off the trigger and we are dead."

"We aren't going to test something based on assumption, are we?" asked Keira concerned.

"Do we have another way?" Lancen responded. "What does your gut say Avik? You were right about the Dark-sap."

"I think we should try it. We didn't come all this way for nothing," said the Shaharan.

Lancen nodded and thought about the puzzle. He wanted to take on the challenge. But what if he got it wrong?

"Could you all wait by the door?" he asked. "I don't know how this gas works, but I'd feel better if you were farther away."

Reluctantly, the three listened and moved away from the statues but remained close enough for conversation.

"Where should I place them?"

"Only you will know the answer," said Motl after a moment. "This is a task for the champion."

Lancen stood still, weighing every possibility over and over. *Only you will know the answer.* Too much was at stake to get it wrong. He needed to consider everything. After a relatively long silence, he rolled the two pendants in his hand and looked up to his friends.

"It looks as if Mendlot got one of these correct," he said, trying to ignore the thought that the other placement had killed the warrior.

"It must be the love rune that is incorrect," said Avik. "The sun pendant would make no sense on the other statues."

"But love is manifest in his consideration," argued Keira. "Love is not always easy, it is a choice, and an exchange from one way of life to another."

"It could be either," said Motl. "Lancen must be the one to choose."

The Noble contemplated audibly, "There are four statues: glad, angry, broken, and thoughtful. There are four pendants: sun, moons, wolf, and love. So, which goes with which?"

Only you will know repeated in his mind uncontrollably. As he closed his eyes and contemplated, it all began to come together like the clouds forming a storm in the sky.

Without a word, Lancen walked to the smiling statue. Hesitating he held his arm out to the sun necklace. What if he was wrong? What if the poison could reach his friends by the door? What if this was the end of everything?

Reluctantly, his fingers found their way around the silver and pulled it free. Nothing. Moving steadily, he approached the hooded and angry statue.

"Think this through," said Avik, tensely. "Why would the sun pendant go there?"

"Trust me, brother," said Lancen, hiding his nerves. "I am thinking this through."

In the sun, Lancen felt overwhelmed. His skin burned, and he was uncomfortable. A hood allowed him to thrive under shadow. If it was true that *only he* would know the answer, then this was the only possible solution. Everything was on the line. This could be it, the final act of a hopeful adventurer. Carefully, he raised the necklace and slowly placed it over the statue's head. As he let go, he braced himself for the gas to be released, holding his breath in anticipation, but no poison came. He had made the correct choice.

Releasing a breath in pure relief, Lancen stared down at the two remaining pendants. He knew what he had to do. Going back to the smiling statue, he held up the necklace of the moons. In their soft light he felt free and comfortable. He could marvel at the stars and had become well acquainted with darkness. There was no other answer. It had to be correct. Slowly, but with less hesitation than the first, he raised the jewelry and eased it down to its rightful place. No consequence.

His friends waited in anticipation as they watched anxiously from the doorway. They couldn't connect the dots, but they didn't have to. Lancen approached the distraught statue and held the wolf pendant lightly in his hand. The beast inside of him was troubling and consumed him. He despised every thought of it. It had attacked him from multiple angles, never letting up, never giving time to rest. The sign of the wolf could mean nothing else, so Lancen placed it over the statue.

As if on cue, a loud drum was heard, and the solitary beat resonated throughout the high-ceiling chamber. At once there was a flash of light, and smoky figures began to swirl down from the roof. The whispers returned in full force as a glowing blue cast blinding glares to the group below. Matter began to materialize, out of the paintings, through the walls, and from thin air. It was wispy at first, moving downward, quickly spinning and inching toward Lancen. With a small gust of wind the fragments came together, and a single shape began to form. In a matter of seconds, a bright and cloudy personage appeared just above the ground in front of Lancen.

In awe, he dared not utter a word. The shape was womanly, clothed in an elegant and decorated gown. Only a slight blue pigment of color existed in her being. She was tall and marvelous, most likely an ash elf in her previous life.

Chills ran down Lancen's spine as she spoke, "Traveler, my name is Rendlah."

CHAPTER 56

T he glorious being stood, hovering above the stone like a hummingbird without wings. Lancen flinched at her greeting, confused and amazed. His friends watched from behind him, refusing to take their eyes off of the remarkable spectacle.

"We have been watching you for some time," the spirit spoke again, paying no heed to the company's amazement. "You are Obah-a-Tou, child. You are the one of prophecy, and should you choose to do so, you will battle the tyrant. Your destiny will be formed and fulfilled according to the decisions you make. Do not mistake the prophecy for certain fate. For it is not a guarantee of victory, but rather a map to where success might be found. Your path is very much your own, and failure is a resounding threat."

Lancen could feel his blood quicken as the full scope of his mission came down to him like lightning. Only a few weeks ago he had been no one, a recluse, a gold miner. Now the certain realization hit him that he was indeed the champion of the Natives. He was fulfilling the prophecy. He was Obah-a-Tou!

"Your journey is young, and you have come here seeking wisdom and counsel," said the great spirit, Rendlah. "Before it can be given, you must first listen to our stories, and understand why we have been chosen as the saints 'to guide and foretell on the path of destruction.' Do you accept our guidance? Do you accept your destiny as Obah-a-Tou?"

Lancen took a moment to reflect and consider. All doubt had been removed from him. He knew that he was the foretold hero, but even so, could he commit to a life that seemed so uncertain, full of danger and death? It would not be an easy mantle to take upon himself. The road would not be friendly, nor would it be short and gentle, but it would be grueling and perilous. A great burden would be placed upon his shoulders to lead, fight, and conquer for the rightful cause of Serondhel. It was not a light decision, but he knew that there could only be one answer.

"I accept."

"Then I shall begin by telling you my tale. In life, I was a daughter of Obuthia, a land that has long been engulfed by what you now know to be the Ashlands. I lived in a time and world far different than the one you have inherited, Champion. In my days, the prophecy was young, and the ancients had been gone for little more than a century. Yet we kept no records, and even so soon after their disappearance, we remembered nothing of their nature or culture. Their abandoned fortresses had scarcely seen enough time to gather dust, and we were completely ignorant that they had ever existed. Because of peace, abundance of crops, and great wealth, my people were proud and lived only for the moment, giving no heed for future generations.

"The sole thing we did retain from the ancients was the sacred stone, on which was written our divine prophecy. In those days we had no understanding of it. In Serondhel we were united as one, and the dwarves were as numerous across the peninsula as the blades of sward in the Grasslands. There were no such things as Nobles, nor Shaharans, nor any race outside of dwarven and elven. To this world was I born.

"Soon after my birth, my parents abandoned our civilization to journey to the lands north, along with many others. In my lifetime, dwarves and elves by the thousands took part in an exodus to the unknown lands of promise. I was left utterly alone, an orphan, and as such I became the very first 'subject' of prophecy. I was named queen and leader of Obuthia. Under my reign, we revered the prophecy, we created the Hero's Trial, and we kept relationships strong among the other races. Though I was widely regarded as Obah-a-Tou my entire life, in the end it was not so. The land needed no such hero at that time.

"Not long after my death, a war broke out amongst the gods. Athleon and Droth feuded without mercy, until finally the evil one was cast from the heavens. It was then that the great mountain erupted, and the bulk of my civilization perished in its wake. Lancen, the vesture of your life is much greater than was mine. My people were not prepared for the great flame, but you must be! You are not exempt from the perils that threaten life!

"The wisdom that I give you is simple. Do not mistakenly believe you are invincible. Though the prophecy is certain, you as its victor are not! A sharp stick would end you just like any other. Learn of the ancients. Follow the divines.

"I must now part again from this world, but I will not leave you empty handed. Upon your exit of Mozan-Garo you will find four fine steeds, to be used by you and your company. Goodbye, Champion, and good luck."

Before Lancen could even thank her, the light inside of Rendlah diminished. Smoothly yet abruptly, her form distorted and dispersed, and in an instant, she had withered down into nothing but smoke.

Lancen was taken aback, trying to process all that he had just been told. He longed for a way to record the wisdom he had received for future use, but before he was given any time to contemplate, the next of the spirits began to take form with rushing wind. When it emerged as a distinguished being, Lancen tried to take in every detail. This spirit was male, clothed in a heavy skirt. Leather straps and stone weapons rested colorless across his shirtless torso. In his pure white and glowing splendor, Lancen recognized the being as an Endwan.

"Champion," the being said, bowing kindly, "my name is Kohlmet. I hail from the eastern shores, from the land now known as Endwah. I was born unto the dawn of a great animosity between the different regions of Serondhel. By the time I was old enough to carry a sword, war had enveloped the land, and pride had brought civilization as I knew it very low.

"Early in my life, I was off hunting with my brother when a pack of wolves attacked us. I took off running and climbed the tallest tree I could find. My brother remained, and fought bravely, but in the end that was not enough. I stayed in the tree for hours before a party came looking for us. From that day forward I became a subject of prophecy.

"Many times in war I was ambushed, and every time I ran from the enemy. It seemed that they were never fast enough for me, but ultimately, my cowardice was also my demise.

"One day, our fortifications were completely overrun, and I took off toward Darkwood Forest. In my fright, I ran straight into an ambush of enemy wood elves, and my life of running had finally reached its end.

"I was not Obah-a-Tou. I had nowhere near the valor required. My entire life I saw nil but death and pain. I do not wish the same for you, Champion."

Suddenly Kohlmet reached down and into a realm that Lancen could not see, then came back up, holding a physical pair of extravagant brown boots.

"Though I do not suggest you run from your troubles, I present you with my famous boots. They are blessed by the divines and known abroad as the Boots of Kohlmet the Flyer. May they hasten your quest and lead you swiftly to victory."

Lancen accepted the gift and thanked the spirit humbly. In an instant, the light within Kohlmet faded and his form dissolved into the air. The next ghostly figure appeared as the others and stepped forward without a moment's hesitation. This being stood shorter than the two before him. Were it on the ground, it would rise only to Lancen's chin. He recognized it immediately as a bog elf.

"My name is Motloghas," he spoke immediately. "I was born in the region where we now stand, long after the beginning of the civil war. I fought proudly for my people, and before I was too stricken in years, I saw an end to the horrible conflict that had been raging for nearly three centuries. In the close of that regrettable era, I raised my people up from the dirt and united them to build the greatest city Serondhel has ever seen, Toltgaro.

"The city once stood not far from this very tomb. We were rich and covetous. We became too satisfied in our wealth and were cursed in our greed. My champion, I was not Obah-a-Tou, and because of my carelessness, Toltgaro was doomed to fall. I was prejudiced and morally weak. You must not fall into the same traps.

"I have nothing tangible to give you, but what I do have is the gift of foresight concerning my posterity. I pray you will accept my counsel concerning them. As they now stand, the bog elves are doomed to destruction in only a matter of days. The situation across the peninsula is more dire than you could have ever imagined. As we speak, thousands of Legion soldiers march to the Swamplands with the intent of killing every last Native. You must not allow this to happen! My people are resilient and could be a great ally in your righteous cause! They will listen to you, Champion. Their trust is my gift to you. Good luck."

Lancen's heart pounded as Motloghas vanished. An army was moving on Tomutah? And what of Obuthahn? This meant that all-out war no longer remained on the fringes. It had crept up and was the very present danger that Lancen had been dreading. It made him sick to his stomach. He was not ready for this, not so soon. Tomutah had but one option, and that was to flee at once to the Ashlands!

Lancen had no time to dwell on his fears as the next elf stepped forward. It was another bog elf, female and exotic. Her hair was braided in tight bundles and several beaded necklaces hung from her neck, resting over a flowing white gown. With no delay, she addressed him.

"I am Taylah of Toltgaro," she said sternly, staring down her nose in an unmistakably demeaning fashion. "I lived a fruitful life, the refreshing successor to a disappointing leader, Motloghas. In life I was given a sacred connection to the divines, and as tensions between my people and the Darkwood elves lingered, I provided visions of destiny to fend the creatures off. I was named the first vatisus of Toltgaro and provided many insights and soothsayings that have survived the long ages since my days upon the land. I was a powerful sorceress, unlike any other Serondhel has seen, but alas, my destiny was not to fulfill the sacred prophecy.

"As service to the apparent *champion*, I will call out words of power one last time. Allow me the touch of your axe!"

Lancen loosed his weapon at once and extended it toward the spirit. Placing a glowing hand upon its blade, she began to speak in a beautiful yet fearsome tongue, "Kektoloh ye mun forkteh. Nohl menloh heylun sancta! Nohl ghotlo mun. Nohl gholto fekt."

At once the axe sparked and quickly gleamed an enhanced luster. Lancen marveled at the beauty which overcame its once weathered blade. The handle smoothed distinctly beneath his palm as Taylah removed her hand and spoke a final remark.

"This weapon you carry is now forever sharp and shall hereby be known as *Securis*, blade of the reaper's touch! Always will it cut smooth, never to dull nor chip. Light will be its burden and strong will be its blows. This is my gift, and I take my leave."

At that Taylah faded as the others, whether into a foreign world or a vast abyss of nothingness was not known. As she departed, Lancen continued to appreciate the weapon in his hand. *Securis*. It felt much lighter, and he moved it through the air with ease and grace. Ancient symbols that had been covered in dirt and grime were now clear and marvelous. This, no longer Nahabuk's axe, but his own, was truly a blade fitting of the Champion of Serondhel.

As his eyes were still widened by the blessing, the next spirit addressed him. He had no idea how many there would be but had quickly become grateful for their wisdom and gifts. The new personage was short, nearly half the size of Lancen, but he spoke with heavy confidence and great diction.

"Greetings, Champion. The name I was known by in life was Malik. I was brought up in the darkness of the great forest, and over time, I became well acquainted with stealth and shadow. I was raised for a single purpose, as were many of my friends and kin, and that purpose was to destroy Toltgaro. In the end, after countless assaults, it was my leadership and arrow in the chest of the vatisus that provided us with an ultimate victory. It was strategy that won us the city, and ignorance that allowed us to burn it to ashes. Among my people, the bog elves were commonly known as the Tyrant, and before finally showing mercy, we scattered them to near extinction. To this day there remains a deep animosity between our peoples.

"Though I never believed that I was the prophesied hero, nor that my people would be its only benefactors, I was named Obah-a-Tou by my clan. The truth did not coincide with that decision. There was much blood that stained my hands, and at the end of all things, I will be held accountable.

"My hero, choose your friends wisely, but take even more heed when choosing your enemies. Never judge an event by first glance alone. Do not forget this counsel.

"My gift to you is to be used in silence. I present you with a bundle of Darkwood arrows. They are poisoned with a lethal concoction, devised from the darkest and most abominable creatures beneath Darkwood. The shafts were crafted to fly forever straight, and the heads sharpened to pierce like daggers. May these simple arrows fall your enemies before they are ever close enough to be of danger. I give you these, and bid you farewell."

In gratitude, Lancen accepted the gift and immediately dropped the arrows into his quiver. Of all the gifts he had been given, these might very well have been his favorite. His years of practicing at the mill had led him to love the art of shooting, and these arrows, combined with the masterful quality of the Sacred Tare, would make for the perfect pair.

Like clockwork, Malik departed, and the next guide twisted and contorted itself into life. When he appeared, Lancen's jaw slowly lowered. He was a tall ash elf, with a strikingly familiar appearance.

"Etnah?" Lancen asked, eyes deceiving him.

The spirit smiled and corrected, "That is a name that I know very well, for I was his grandfather and guardian. I have been very mindful of his steps as well as yours, and how they both relate in the scope of events yet to come, but time is a luxury that we do not have. I must deliver my message.

"My title is chief, and my name is Etmah-lee. I was born for the ash and became one of the first dwellers in the settlement known as Obuthahn. As a victor of trial, I became a respected warrior, and after years of dedication and labor, I was named chief of my clan. It seemed that the world was made just for me, to be enjoyed and cherished, but events would soon take place that neither I nor my people could have ever anticipated.

"It was a clear and crisp morning, just over fifty years ago when the messenger from Tomutah came to our village in urgency. He spoke damning words of a great foreign people landing on the southern shores. It was only a matter of weeks before a band of explorers and legionnaires stumbled upon Obuthahn. At the time, they bore gifts, and we thought it to be a glorious union. In return, we shared with them the only things we held dear: our knowledge of the prophecy and of the divines. The prophecy they discarded, but because their own beliefs were not dissimilar, they accepted our gods and began to worship much the same as we did.

"As you well know, peace did not survive between us. The 'Nobles' as they called themselves were expansionist and insatiable. As our villages were ravished and our ways desecrated, we soon discovered that the outlanders were no allies of ours. We began to view them as the Tyrant and consider them a fulfillment of prophecy. We were not willing to share the sacred lands we thought to be ours. To our great dismay, we fought them and started the terror of a war that would endure for the next thirty-five years. The truth is that we brought it upon ourselves. It was selfishness that spawned the Lurid War.

"I was not Obah-a-Tou, though I attempted to lead my people as such. I was racist, ignorant, and biased. These are traits that you must never develop if you wish to succeed. Regrettably, they have trickled down to taint my posterity in an ugly blemish, but you must not choose the popular side to fight for. For once you do, great tragedy will surely follow! You fight for Serondhel and all her people, deposed and otherwise. Is that clear?"

Lancen nodded with conviction. "I understand."

"Very well," said Etmah-lee. "I must soon depart, but there is one more subject I must address. I would ask a favor of you, Champion."

Lancen narrowed his brow. "What is it?"

"Your friend and guide is very dear to my heart. When you see Etnah again...*If* you see Etnah again, I would have you relay a message to him from the man who raised him. You must tell him that 'The dark wind blows. Dust has risen above the throat. If you breathe, it will know.' He will understand its meaning. Can you do this for me?"

"I will," said Lancen, repeating the saying in his mind. *The dark wind blows. Dust has risen above the throat. If you breathe, it will know.*

"Then I take my leave. Farewell, Obah-a-Tou."

As quick as he had appeared, Etmah-lee disintegrated into a condensed white vapor and left the mortal world forever. Lancen was not surprised to see another saint begin to form. He breathed deeply and held his head high. It seemed like there was no creature too fearsome and no mountain too high. Though his burden was great, his mission was now clear. He now knew exactly who he was. He had purpose, and a destiny to fight for! There would be no stopping him.

As he turned to greet the next apparition, the color immediately drained from his face. His mouth opened as he tried to speak, but no words would come. He couldn't believe what he was seeing. Hovering before him unmistakably, was the ghostly specter of a young ash elf. It was the son of Shikobin, cherished hunter and warrior of Obuthahn. It was Eltou.

CHAPTER 57

Lancen couldn't believe his eyes as the warrior who had saved his life in the cavern of Nahabuk stood before him from beyond the grave. Keira slowly wandered to stand by his side, tears rolling down her face. No thought or feeling in the world could describe what they were experiencing!

"Lancen, Keira," said the ash warrior, forming a very sensitive but subtle smile, "It is an honor to play this role in history and guide you in your quest for freedom, but as the others, though I wish it were not so, I cannot linger. I must only share my story and depart."

"I must thank you," said Keira soberly, wiping tears from her cheeks. "Allow us that."

"I can see it in your demeanors, and that is enough," said Eltou. "Though I joy to see you, there has never been a more somber occasion for us to meet. I must continue."

"As you will," said Lancen, looking up with unwavering interest.

There was something in Eltou's expression as he nodded slowly, eyes closing for a moment before he spoke. "As you know, I was born just eighteen years ago. My father, Shikobin, was a victor of trial and continues to lead the people of Obuthahn. In life, I was a skilled hunter and a cherished son. My existence however, had only a divine purpose. In the caverns of Nahabuk, I recognized your true nature, Lancen. I was the first to know and truly believe that you were the fulfillment of prophecy. In the end, I gave my own life to save yours, and it is because of that act that I stand before you today.

"I leave my story short, though there is more to tell, for I have been given the great burden of bringing horrible yet necessary truth to your attention. Time is of the ultimate importance, if there is any left at all.

"A terrible and ancient ritual is about to take place that has not been enacted for millennia. More than the conflict between the Natives and Nobles, this ritual would scar Serondhel forever, and send its righteous inhabitants into oblivion. This rite is a plot by the tyrant to destroy the heirs and exalt themselves! They required an artifact; they found it. They required a sacrifice, a living sacrifice of pure blood; they found it. Unlike the other saints, I bring you little wisdom and carry no gift of fortune, only knowledge. It is to my great dismay that I tell you the tyrant has chosen Adalyn, Princess of Calderon, as their sacrifice."

In an instant Lancen's heart seemed to stop beating in his chest. His eyes glazed as a pronounced horror was brought into focus. What had Eltou just said? Had he heard him correctly?

"What do you mean Adalyn is their sacrifice?" asked Lancen, still processing the words. "That doesn't make sense."

"I'm sorry, Lancen."

Every hair on Lancen's body stood on end as he thought about Adalyn being dragged to an altar. His eyes darted back and forth as he thought over what could have happened. Goldtooth had taken her from Obuthahn with fifty men. She should have been safe — unless Goldtooth was the tyrant? Or could it be that the tyrant was the Nobles as a whole, just as the Natives had always believed, and Goldtooth was a puppet?

"Where is she?" Lancen choked out, barely hearing the words that left his mouth.

"I do not know," explained Eltou grimly. "As saints we are given only what we are given. We cannot ask for more. We cannot ask for less. There is but one thing I can tell you: the answer is in the prophecy. She is in dire need Lancen, but hope is not lost! You will find her in these words:

> *Ancient saints shall awaken as signs*
> *To guide and foretell on the path of destruction*
> *By an arrow pierced in the heart of Divines*
> *The clues are restored which were bound by obstruction*

"I am sorry Lancen. I truly am, but this is all that I know to give you."

"It can't be," uttered Lancen in shock. "You must know more!"

"I'm sorry, but I am bound to depart. You must stop this ritual at all costs, but I have faith in you, my champion. Do not lose hope."

Immediately the final spirit began to diminish.

"No!" cried Lancen in a panic. "That can't be all you know!"

Lancen reached out to stop Eltou, but his hand only passed through the wispy figure as it dispersed.

"No, don't go! How do I find her, Eltou?" Lancen called desperately. "How do I find her!"

But it was too late. Eltou had vanished to an unreachable distance and would not return, leaving Lancen alone in a horrible and helpless nightmare. A furious silence had him heaving for air, fighting to hold onto sanity.

All he knew was that Adalyn was in peril danger.

He needed to find her.

Now!

Without breathing, he tied his axe to his belt and stumbled back to the door leading out of the room. Pushing past Avik and Motl, who tried to calm him, Lancen hurried blindly through the dark corridors of Mozan-Garo. Of the two, he had chosen Keira, or so he had thought. So why was everything inside of him now screaming for Adalyn! Ignoring all calls from his companions behind him, he rushed back up the numerous corridors to the tomb's primal entrance. Stumbling quickly beyond the wooden door, Lancen breathed-in the raunchy mist of the Swamplands. Paying no mind to the four beautiful horses just outside of the mucky pool, he felt the weight of the world on his shoulders, and it brought him to his knees.

How would he find her?

This was no longer a choice of love. Lancen had been perfectly content with Adalyn being carried safely back to Calderon. Unlike every other person he cared about, at least at the castle the princess was certain to be out of harm's way. Never had he expected that Goldtooth would betray the duke. All the other wisdom and prophecies of the saints would have to wait. This was personal now.

The only thing rolling through his mind was *find her, find her, find her,* but how? She could be anywhere in Serondhel, and he did not have the time to search in every corner.

Cringing, Lancen growled helplessly and leaned against the stone pillar that displayed the pictures of Obah-a-Tou. Why was this happening? Why, when he had been given only a glimpse of hope and courage, was it immediately taken away?

In humble desperation, he looked to the sky. The stars were innumerable, and the heavens were clear.

"What do I do?" he called to the divines. Waiting tensely, he stared upward, honestly hoping to receive an answer. How could he go on without one? If there was ever a time for the gods to prove themselves, it was now!

"Say something!" Lancen yelled, lip trembling. "Please!"

Dropping his head, Lancen noticed his friends walk out of the catacomb and step up behind him.

"This is a beautiful night," said Motl, "however terrible, but we do not have time to mourn."

"Give him a moment!" said Avik edgily. "A few minutes will make no difference!"

"A few minutes could make all the difference," Motl earnestly disagreed. "We must act now."

"But what are we supposed to do?" asked Lancen rolling his eyes. "Everything is against us."

"Sometimes we must act even in the face of uncertain consequences. We must create a plan and stick to it, never to waver. That is our option, Lancen, and you must be the one to lead us!"

Lancen closed his eyes and hung his head. Motl was right, but that didn't make the task any easier.

"Give me a moment to think," he said. "I know we must act quickly."

The truth was that he was overwhelmed. He had always known that this journey would not be easy, but he never could have envisioned the magnitude of anxiety and heartache that it had brought him. He wanted to crawl into a hole and disappear. He wanted to run and never stop, leaving his troubles behind him, but he knew that neither was an option. He could not afford to twiddle his thumbs while Adalyn's life was threatened, while Obuthahn and Tomutah dangled on the brink of extinction. His situation did not allow him to give up, as much as he wanted to.

With no control, tears began to feel heavy in his eyes and slowly broke free, rolling down his cheeks coldly, like the trickle on a cave wall. It forced him to consider the last time he had truly cried, the day that Sidna had died. He tried to stop them from falling, but he had no defense to prevent it. In a way it was calming, letting him know that he was still human, that some emotion still existed in him besides anger, but why could they not solve his problems?

He yearned for Sidna's help. He needed advice from a loving mother, the person who had taught him everything, but she would never return, and slowly but certainly the thought came to him: he didn't need her anymore.

Think, Lancen, think! he told himself. *You can do this yourself. You are a warrior, destined for greatness. You are Obah-a-Tou. Think!*

Now what did the prophecy say? 'Ancient saints shall awake as signs, to guide and foretell on the path of destruction' — that told him nothing. 'By an arrow pierced in the heart of divines, the clues are restored which were bound by obstruction.' An arrow pierced through the heart of divines. An arrow — *an arrow!*

It was the weight around his neck! As swiftly as he could, he pulled the key out from beneath his shirt. Defined clearly into its side was a thin arrow. At once he knew what he must do. He must return to his mountain home. Obviously there was more to his mine than just the small hollow where he had found the key. It was where he would find the heart of divines. It was where he would find Adalyn!

At once Lancen rose to his feet.

"I have a plan," he said, wiping the tears from his face. "I can't be sure, but I might know where she is."

"And what of the bog elves?" asked Motl.

"What of Obuthahn?" added Keira.

There were too many problems and a great lack of solutions. What was he supposed to do about the Natives in peril? He wished he could be in two places at once.

"We will have to part ways for a time."

"What is the plan?" asked Avik quickly.

"One of the saints said that Tomutah is doomed to destruction in a matter of days," said Lancen, "but I must go after Adalyn. Avik, I would have you and Motl go to the bog elves. You must convince them to flee for Obuthahn!"

"Are you insane?" asked Motl at once. "We cannot just walk into Tomutah and convince them to abandon all that they have! Of all the tribes, they are the least likely to join us!"

"If you tell them of me and of the saints you have just seen, they will listen," insisted Lancen.

"I want to stay by your side," said Avik anxiously. "I want to help save Adalyn!"

"And you will help to save us all by going to the bog elves. I know it doesn't make sense, but I need you to do as I say on this one. Serondhel needs you, friend, but Adalyn needs me."

"They will not accept us," said Motl. "We will likely be killed."

"Well if they do not join us then we will all die when the Legion attacks Obuthahn and we have no reinforcements," said Lancen harshly. "We don't have time for argument! Do as I say!"

Motl took a deep breath and looked at the boy uncertainly. "As you wish."

"Avik will you go?"

"If I must," the Shaharan answered.

"Keira, I have reason to believe that Adalyn was taken to my mine north of Calderon," said Lancen. "I would have you join me there."

He proceeded to show his companions the golden key and explain his conclusion.

"Lancen," started Keira, "I will gladly join you, but perhaps you should bring Avik, and I should go with Motl."

"I need your help," he answered.

"But why me, and not Avik?"

"Why not you?"

"Because I...because Avik should help the Noble, and I should help the Natives."

Lancen opened his mouth as he tried to understand her reasoning. Looking at her sincerely, he shook his head and stood his ground. "I need it to be you. I need your hope, your courage. Mine is not sufficient."

Looking Keira in the eyes, he could see how much care dwelt within them. He could see her true objection. She did not want to lose him to Adalyn as she had after the Hero's Trial, and he did not want to lose her. His heart swelled within him as he considered how much he truly cared for her.

"I cannot ask you to look at this from my perspective," he continued. "That is not a position in which I would put my worst enemy, but I know you will help me. Eltou told us that the Legion is on the brink of completing a terrible ritual! Whatever that entails, I know with all my being that it must be stopped, and I will need your help. If it is sometimes necessary to go to hell and back, it is best to make that journey with someone who gives you strength."

Lancen finished and waited in silence for her response.

"Of course I will join you," said Keira in a quiet but sure tone. "I would follow you anywhere."

Lancen gave her a solemn smile, relieved to have her on his side. Turning to face Motl and Avik, he was not ready to go on without them. But time was of the essence.

"We should be going at once," he said somberly, "but this is not the end. After we rescue Adalyn, we will ride to Obuthahn and await you there.

"We have been chosen to walk on a deadly road, but nevertheless we must fight the tyrant! We must be careful, and we must be sure, but most importantly, we must have courage! Serondhel is depending on us."

CHAPTER 58

L ancen pulled sharply on the reigns of his horse, coming to a stop. The animal shifted below him as he stiffly swung a leg over its back. His thighs were sore and chafed while the hair of the dun was soaked in sweat. He and Keira had ridden without a break since departing Mozan-Garo. Throughout the night they had traversed through shadow, and when morning came, they did not stop. Even after the many miles, Lancen did not want to rest, but the horses could go no further.

The constant worry for Adalyn's well-being attacked his conscience, and the stress seemed to hinder most rational thought. It would be days before they could reach his mountain home, and he feared that they lacked the time to manage a rescue. It was unthinkable that she could already be gone, but if by chance she wasn't where he had found the key, it was all over anyway. The tyrant would have won. With all the heartache in his life thus far, he couldn't help but expect the worst.

The scenery around him was discouraging. He had hoped to reach the Grasslands before taking a break, but the trees remained dark and thin. The ground was moist and putrid, its hideous nature reminding him of his mission, ugly and hopeless. Yet unlike the Swamplands, Lancen knew that he must emerge from the shadows. For the sake of his loved ones, he had no other choice.

"I don't want to wait long," he said, leading his dun to a shallow creek. "We must move as soon as the horses are rested."

Keira grimaced as she slid from her mount. "Do you expect to ride like this the entire way? I doubt the horses will endure."

"They must."

Keira rubbed her legs, then ran a hand down her face. Sighing, she relented, "I wish I could just go home, to make bread, and tea. I want to sleep in my own bed, a full night for once in forever."

"Well that isn't an option," replied Lancen coldly. He wasn't looking for conversation now. He was only after solutions.

"I know," said the girl dismally. With clear reluctance, she pulled the last piece of bread from her pack and fed it to her tired horse. Her eyes wandered down to her feet. She fully understood what she was giving up.

"If we hurry," said Lancen, trying to compute the time and miles ahead, "perhaps we can reach the northern mountains in four dawns or less."

"I don't think I can keep going today."

Lancen tied up his horse and stepped over to Keira. He looked-over her tired eyes, messy hair, and face of lost hope. What was he supposed to say? He wanted her to rest and feel peace, but it wasn't that simple.

Licking his lips, he realized that they did need a moment to breathe. Perhaps he needed it even more than she. "Are you alright?" he asked honestly.

She held her head high, but it was clearly a struggle. "I am not as strong as you, but even if you don't show it on the outside, I know you are hurting just as bad as me."

Lancen helped Keira over to a spot where they could sit. "I wish we had never been required to go through with this," he said, hanging his head. "I am miserable, and it is taking everything I have to carry on. If I just ignore the world, then its burden is easier to bear."

"Ignoring your troubles will not solve them," said Keira, emptying the last bit of water from her skin.

Lancen offered what was left in his.

"I'm so tired," he said, but the thought of Adalyn kept his eyes wide open.

"Aye. I wish that the prophecy had never involved me, even though I've spent my entire life wanting it to," Keira lamented.

"This is no different than ever before. We just have to carry on."

"How are we supposed to do that?"

"Push our problems down below the surface," said Lancen, tilting back his head.

"No," answered Keira, leaning closer to him. "Avoiding our problems has gotten us nowhere. You told me in the cave about your mother. Repressing that hasn't saved you from pain. It has prolonged it."

"Did you not repress the deaths of Engle or Eltou? What about when Etnah left?"

"I may have for a time, but eventually I accepted that they were gone. I found a way to move past it. You haven't Lancen. You abandoned your home, and I don't understand it. Why did you leave Calderon? There must have been reasons to stay."

"Of course there were," Lancen answered. "I had my friends, and family at the orphanage. I had the market, the games, and the mill. I didn't want to leave, but I had no choice."

"One day you will get it through your head that there is always a choice."

"Maybe there was, but I don't need to revisit my past when the present is so demanding."

"You clearly ignored my point, so at least answer the question," asserted Keira. "Why did you leave Calderon?"

Lancen looked at her with a disgruntled stare, but he lacked the energy for it to endure. He couldn't answer as the memories flowed into conscience, not while he could see Sidna's brown hair, or her warm smile calling to him. He remembered the nights that he was sick, and she stayed by his bedside until he was fast asleep, giving him everything he had needed. She read to him by the fire, taught him how to make rabbit stew — with extra carrots. Somehow it was all still clear in his mind.

He could still see the sun, falling below the mountainous wall behind her, and the dark armor glistening on the man who announced her writ. There was no waver in the hands that tightened her noose, no slack in the rope after it fell. All the while Duke Roland looked on from above, emotionless and cold.

"I never left Calderon," he eventually said, almost too softly for Keira to hear. "Who I once was died with Sidna. I was not alive in the mountains."

"How did she die?" asked Keira, moving in even closer. She now sat directly beside him, her arm warming his. "Tell me what drove you away."

Lancen started, but the words could not find their way to the surface. Turning his head, he began to sort through his pack, looking for bread. "We should be going."

"In the cave you told me to keep moving forward," said Keira, "that time would somehow erase the pain of the past. You said to keep moving forward, yet you continue to allow your own memories to hurt you! That is not progression! I don't know who you were before you arrived in Obuthahn, but you must quit avoiding whatever happened!"

"I can never go back to change things," said Lancen, lifting his hands in surrender. "So why should I tell you?"

"Because you can never be free of something that you're grasping so tightly!" Keira said, leaning forward and pulling moist grass from the dark soil. Slowly, she let it all drop back to the earth.

"You speak words of wisdom to me frequently, but now it is your turn to listen," she said. "The grass I pulled will die, but there is enough left over to live on, to fulfill its purpose. Lancen, history cannot be altered, and some things can never be forgotten. But we can move on. We don't have to run.

"I don't want to be here in the Swamplands, on a quest to save Adalyn. I want more than anything to just go home, but for some reason you can never go home. Tell me why."

"This conversation is over," said Lancen bluntly, tossing a

morsel of bread into the girl's lap.

"This conversation ends when you begin to heal! Lancen, I am afraid and tired, but you are burdened with more than just the task at hand."

Lancen sighed deeply and rubbed his eyes. She was impossible! How could he tell her when he wouldn't even allow himself to dwell on it?

Looking to the darkening sky, he pretended he could fly to the heavens and delve into a strength that he knew wasn't there. The first few stars were just becoming visible in the broad cosmos that separated the known world from eternal mystery. Should he tell her? He had held onto it for so long. Deep down, it was something that he had always wanted to get rid of but never could. What would she think of him?

"I told you once how she died. Do you remember?"

"Yes, I do."

Lancen thought over his words but had to stop. He would never say them if he contemplated. There was no sense in running anymore. He may not be alive much longer anyway, so on the off chance that disclosure could bring him peace, it was worth it.

"I will tell you the full story, but you must remember that it was you who required it of me. I will understand any reaction you may have."

"I'm listening, Lancen."

He noticed her amber eyes, magnified in the setting sun. There was deep care in them.

"Very well," he began, trying to control his breath. "It all began when King Scharric outlawed the worship of the divines. Sidna was such a faithful woman, and this new law had her distraught. She could not imagine a life without worship.

"There was a sacred relic, a small statuette of Lady Noshera, in the chapel we used to go to in Calderon. For some reason it meant everything to her, so I told her I would get it.

"One day, after I finished at the mill, I stopped by the chapel on my way home. I still had my bow and arrows strapped to my back from practicing. When I arrived, there was a legionnaire waiting inside, guarding the building. I asked him for the relic, but he refused, and refused, and refused."

Lancen stopped speaking, fighting an inner battle of emotion. This was the first time he had ever told someone. He hadn't even told Rune. How would she react? How would she respond to him?

"Don't stop," said Keira. "You can trust me."

Lancen continued to look into her eyes, finding strength in them. There was a lure there, something that drew him closer, giving him reason to tell her more.

"I tried to take the statue, but he didn't like that. We had a scuffle, and he beat me to the ground, punching me over and over. He grabbed the relic and ran toward the door, calling for another guard. I wasn't thinking clearly, so I sat up and sent an arrow through his arm, forcing him to drop it. As I tried to reach it, he drew his sword and sliced at my leg. When my fingers found the statue, I turned and hit the guard over the head, as hard as I could.

"He fell at once, and there was nothing I could do. He wasn't breathing. I-I killed him. He was dead, Keira.

"My leg was throbbing, and I was covered in blood. Most of it wasn't mine. I ran straight home. The moment Sidna saw me, she knew exactly what had happened. She screamed for me to leave, and in my shock and stupidity, I set down the statue and listened. Minutes later, the Legion broke down her door, and she claimed at once to be responsible for what I had done. She was hanged the next day.

"Though I do not allow my mind to visit this memory, not a day goes by that I do not feel guilt."

Keira sat a moment with widened eyes. He knew it was a lot to handle, but she did not run or fight him. She just sat, planning out the perfect response.

"It wasn't your fault," she finally said.

Lancen dropped his jaw in disbelief. "Wasn't my fault?" he

exclaimed. "Of course it was my fault!"

Keira squinted her eyes, still trying to work through all of the information. She seemed very concerned and sincere. It was obvious that she intended to help, not condemn.

"I cannot say that I understand that pain," she said, "not entirely. I can only imagine how awful it must feel, but you must forgive yourself before you can ever move on. You must compensate for the shame you have felt."

Lancen looked back to the sky with a smirk. "How am I supposed to do that?"

"Be our champion!" said Keira. "Protect your friends and devote your life to benefitting others."

Lancen stared solemnly to the ground, trying to find solace in her words. On his feet were the Boots of Kohlmet the Flyer. He was Obah-a-Tou. There was influence in his calling. It was true that the past could never be changed, but his future was less certain. Perhaps it would be possible for him to do enough good to outweigh any and every old affliction. Keira was right. The only way to do that was to be the champion.

"You are a hero, Lancen," she said. "One day you may be the greatest Serondhel has ever seen. It does not matter who you used to be! People change, and I assure you that no one will remember you for your sins!"

A very small but sincere smile began to form on Lancen's face as he looked up to the girl from the Ashlands. "Thank you."

Keira grabbed his hand and held it in hers. After all he had told her, she seemed to believe in him now more than ever. Why, he didn't know, but he was grateful. Remorse did not exist in him while he was with her. The things she could do to help him were unmatched. She was strong, intelligent, and kind—when she wanted to be. Lancen felt abundant relief around her, like the problems of the world were not too great to handle. Every time he looked at her, he remembered why he needed to free Serondhel. In that process he somehow knew that he would also free himself.

"Do you feel better?" she asked, looking into his eyes.

Lancen decided not to answer, but very slowly moved in closer. Keira did not recoil or tense, but waited, her breathing fast and excited. Lancen's heart began to beat rapidly, his blood quickening inside of him. A magnetism had surfaced between them, and he refused to fight it. He was being drawn towards her, and she toward him as adrenaline preceded an unmistakable mutual connection.

His breathing halted without control, and his senses were sharp as glass. Time and space seemed to evaporate into the cloud of a solitary moment, with no thought or act of conscience that could prevent his lips from meeting hers. As she kissed him, her mouth matched perfectly with his. With each move he made, she followed gracefully. Her cheeks warmed. His heart raced, and in the culmination of heightened emotion, they separated.

After pulling apart, Keira blushed and beamed a beautiful smile. Lancen could barely recall the last time he had seen it, but excitement and appreciation enveloped her expression. Watching her, he could sense the comfort, as well as the joy. It was several minutes before he realized the scope of what had just happened. *He had kissed a Native!* But he couldn't have cared less. The moment she proceeded to lay her head against his chest, he knew exactly why it had happened, and did not regret it.

"I feel better," he whispered with a laugh.

He could tell that Keira was smiling also, wrapped up in his arms.

"Things are not so bad," she said confidently. "Look on the bright side. At least you're not a skole."

CHAPTER 59

Hans stepped out of the barracks and pushed his way through the crowd. Thousands of soldiers had gathered in, confident and strong as they prepared for war. No more would their lives be limited to bandit raids and minor scuffles. The time had finally come to pursue a worthy cause, the eradication of all Natives. It was just his luck, a bunch of meatheads out for their fix. He shook off dust toward their naivety.

Hans had waited his entire life to silence the savages, to rid the peninsula of their filth, but somehow this day was not as glorious as he imagined. He wanted to be ecstatic, singing and hollering with the rest of the soldiers, but the excitement wouldn't come. As much as he tried to bottle it inside, the thoughts of Lancen and Avik remained in the front of his mind. Because of him, they had been captured in Obuthahn. Because of him, they were dead.

Duke Roland and Captain Earnst looked on from above, admiring how quickly the army was able to assemble. Hans awaited the order, trying to keep a neutral expression as he fastened his armor and approached the balcony overlooking the square. He craved a real fight with the scum of Obuthahn, but his stomach churned. How could he ever find joy now? How could he live with himself after all he had done?

He did not view the Natives as allies. How could he? His loyalty was with the Legion, and there was no changing that, but the thought of a life without Avik, and without Lancen, tore at him! He didn't know why he had let it get to him. It was their fault for siding with the enemy! It was them who had chosen the evil path, not him!

The savages never had a prayer to begin with. Regardless of what he and his friends could do, it would never be enough to stop the Nobles.

As he remained deep in thought, he noticed Earnst step forward and raise a hand in a call to attention. Now there was a man who was loyal, a man with honor and strength. Earnst wouldn't have given a second thought to turning over his friends. He would have done it at the first sign of corruption. That was who Hans needed to emulate.

Holding up a fist in tribute, Earnst called loudly to the legionnaires who now gave their attention. "The duke wishes to address us before we depart."

The captain abruptly stepped back and left the floor open for Roland. The duke thanked his second in command and approached the railing. Hans admired the leader's stature, his broad shoulders and ornate heavy armor. A serious scowl rested on his face, strong and ready to do whatever was necessary. Regardless of what he said, he held a commanding presence, radiating leadership.

"Men of the West!" called Roland loudly, speaking with force and articulation. "I breathe in, and feel the air, cold and crisp. Winter is nearly upon us, and though the day is young, there is no mistaking its magnitude. Victory is so close I can taste it. The time has come for all of us, male or female, young or old, to serve our kingdom and personally spill savage blood!"

The soldiers roared and threw up their arms in approval, prepared and anxious to go to battle.

"Not long ago," said Roland, "an elf from the Ashlands wandered into my court. He claimed that there could never be peace under Scharric's rule, and that the Natives and Nobles could learn to live as one. He begged me to not attack Obuthahn, but I begged to differ! There will be peace, when every last savage is wiped from this glorious nation!"

Hans took a moment to ponder. An elf from the Ashlands came

to Roland's court? He spoke of peace, and begged for mercy? It must have been Etnah! Hans knew without question, but even in the face of destruction, the elf could not have honestly believed that he could stop the Nobles!

"This is a great day!" continued the duke. "This day we set off to claim that which is ours! For too long we have been bothered by the prodding of those less capable. We are smarter, faster, and stronger than the Natives, yet they persist to insult and disgrace us year after year. For too long have we suffered them, but our prerogative has finally changed! The savages of the Ashlands have been a nuisance and a blight to my personal court. They've been pleading for an end, and we will give it to them. Piss off the dog, and it will bite! Rest and prepare, for soon the Nobles will be the sole possessors of this brilliant land. It is time to rise and fight. It is time to claim victory for our children, and we shall not fail!"

The noise made by those present was deafening. For them, and for all, this movement was monumental. It was finally time for the Legion to do something important, something to be remembered. It was time to finish what the Lurid War had started.

Hans did not cheer with the others. There was a coldness in his heart that he couldn't warm. Though he still wished to fight for the kingdom, he wanted to talk to Etnah first. He wanted to be sure that Avik and Lancen were dead, for if they weren't, he would once again question where his true loyalties stood.

Her wrists were bound tightly, rubbing the skin. An icy breeze tunneled through the halls of wherever she was. Adalyn did not know where she had been taken, but she sat on a cold stone floor, glossy and smooth. It appeared to be granite; a precious resource found only in the Ash Mountains. She couldn't tell where she was for sure, but the lands east of Obuthahn was her best guess.

The hall in which she now sat was unlike anything she had ever seen. It was phenomenal. Outside of her cage, the room was spacious, and the air was so clear that she felt like she was outside.

Giant pillars shot from great bases to a height so tall they disappeared into blackness. Works of gold and gems were prevalent in all directions. Strange metalworks moved, pumping and recessing at will, with the occasional release of steam into the filtered air. The space was lit by magic, and Adalyn had to question whether or not she was still alive, for the world in which she now sat was far different from the one she had always known.

A dozen evil men filed methodically all around her. They worked desperately, tinkering with strange machinery and speaking odd languages to receive reactions from the metal. When they spoke, it was in hushed tones, but a feeling of anticipation was very present. Where was she?

All of the men seemed to follow the same cloaked figure, the very one that had grabbed her on that last day with Earnst. With his face always cloaked in shadow, she had begun to call him 'Knave,' a person of dishonor. He was the worst of them, sitting near her before a wall of pumping engines. Several switches and dials were within his grasp, enabling strange lights and eerie noises. Beyond him was a large round pit, lined in silver and gold. What was within it, she did not know, but it seemed central to whatever the skoles were trying to accomplish.

The largest and ugliest of the monsters approached Knave's side. He had trimmed white hair and deep lines that covered his face. He had been going back and forth between the wall of switches and a shadowed hall out of sight. Adalyn's head hurt. It was all so foreign!

"Are all of the systems ready?" asked the large follower.

"No, Ventok," said Knave in a slow, raspy tone. "Not yet."

"I have double-checked all of the lines. We are ready. All systems are in place for the sacrifice," said Ventok.

"No," repeated Knave calmly. "The time must be perfect, and perhaps we will find the key yet."

"You said that we wouldn't need the key."

"And we shouldn't, but we have not yet reached the time for

taking risks. The Master would be disappointed. Besides, the sacrifice must not take place until the storm is upon us, otherwise it will continue whatever weather is current."

"Why does that matter?" asked Ventok arrogantly.

Knave turned to his subordinate, facing Adalyn. Nothing but his pale chin and razor teeth were visible. "We are skolic, imbecile. We thrive under shadow, and if the sun does not shine, then we can move as we please."

"How long until the next storm?"

Knave laughed sadistically and turned back to studying the panel before him.

"Three days at most," said the demented leader. "Three days."

Adalyn gulped and pulled at the bands around her wrists and ankles. She did not have much time.

Roland focused on the scar that ran across the eye and cheek of Captain Earnst. The man was giving him a detailed report, but Roland could care less. Revenge was on his mind and at the tips of his fingers. It was time to grab hold.

"Very well," said the duke, interrupting Earnst. "Depart at once. Bring me the heads of Adalyn's captors. Show them no mercy."

"Yes, sir," said Earnst, bowing his head. "We will find her."

Roland waved his arm for the captain to leave and rolled his eyes. He also would depart soon, but there was one task of importance that he needed to deal with first. Trotting down the spiral stairs, he headed to the lower dungeons. His mood was fierce and his countenance bold. Etnah had betrayed him in the worst way, and now there was no changing his mind. The savages would pay.

There was a time when Roland would have entrusted the entire western region with his former servant, but those days were past. All bonds of friendship had been shattered, and Etnah would soon be burdened with a wrath of vengeance that only few men would ever receive. A duke's fury knew no bounds.

Continuing into a corridor of cells, Roland paced straight through to the back wall. In the hold to his right, he saw his former ally, sitting casually on a thin recession before a small barred window. His cell was altogether claustrophobic, about six feet deep and four feet wide. Etnah appeared oblivious to the duke's presence as he gazed curiously out of the window before him, whistling his favorite melody.

"How are your accommodations?" asked Roland smugly.

Etnah continued to whistle until his song was finished. Never turning his head, he responded smartly, "Happy to have the one with a view. What brings you down here, friend?"

"I thought it was courteous to allow you to see me off before I leave to the Ashlands."

"Aye," said Etnah enthusiastically, "and I thought you had come to kill me."

Roland laughed, temperament failing. "I haven't come to kill you! First you must feel the same pain that I have! You must know what it feels like to lose those closest to you!"

"I have already felt that," said Etnah gazing up and into the bushes of the castle grounds.

"Killing you is far too merciful."

Etnah smiled and turned away from the window, looking at Roland for the first time. "Well I would never ask for mercy! What a fool that would make me!"

Roland scoffed, "You brought this upon yourself when you warned that boy in the mountains."

"Aye," said Etnah nodding, "but I suspect it will be the bird of the mountains that finds the princess, wherever she may be. He is Obah-a-Tou, Roland. He is the one!"

Roland rolled his eyes again, a smug grin stretching across his face. "Tell me where he is Etnah."

Etnah hopped down from his perch by the window and walked slowly to the bars where Roland stood. Holding a fearless gaze, the elf spoke slowly, "The bird still flies."

Roland mashed his teeth and gripped the bars until his knuckles were white. Fire had entered his eyes and seethed through his response. "Spare me your damn riddles. *WHERE IS HE!*"

The elf did not blink. "On his way to Adalyn."

Ripping his hands from their grasp, Roland turned his back and relented, "If my men cannot kill him, I certainly will, and then I am going to kill you, but only after I massacre every living soul in your god-forsaken clan."

The duke waved over the guard that was sitting on a stool down the hall. The jail-man promptly followed the command, clearly alert to the tension between Roland and the prisoner.

"Whatever you need, sir," said the guard loyally.

The duke fumed a passionate indignation. "I am off to eradicate this savage's people. Do as you will with him, but I ask that he still be alive upon my return. That is my *only* requirement, understood?"

The guard looked at him grimly, comprehending fully what the ruler had ordered. "I understand."

CHAPTER 60

L ancen galloped rhythmically beside Keira as they rode across the Grasslands. Since fleeing the bogs, they had travelled far and quick on the road between Rutledge and Calderon. It had been a week since their departure from Mozan-Garo, and the pressure to find Adalyn and stop the tyrant's ritual had never been so burdensome. Though the urgency was severe, Lancen was beginning to recognize the world around him, and unprecedented memories began to flow through his mind.

"This was my home," he told Keira as they slowed their horses. "I can smell the fruit of the wineries on the wind — must be their last batch before winter. We are nearing Calderon."

"This is a beautiful land," mentioned Keira, admiring the plains and fields of farmland. Every rolling hill and cluster of trees was new to her eyes. "I would love to live in a place like this."

Lancen laughed as they began to climb a gradual but lengthy hill. "Everything is frozen! You should see it in the spring. The grass is green, night-scented stock lingers in the air. Blue skies, clear horizons, it is truly a place of beauty then."

"I would like that," said Keira. "You know, this land was long inhabited by my ancestors. They did not leave until the Lurid War. On a day that the world is not so dismal, I'd hope to return. You can give me the tour."

Lancen had a hard time picturing that occasion. "It may be some time before I can show a Native through the city streets."

"Yes, well when we win the war, any who object will learn quickly enough."

Lancen nodded and tried to imagine a future world where the Natives and Nobles lived together peaceably, but it was so far from reality that he just couldn't believe it. The hate between them would be difficult to silence. Like any political movement, there would be certain resistance to every inkling of change.

"Can you actually picture our peoples coming together?" Lancen asked.

"I don't see it," answered Keira honestly, "but one day I might. I'm learning that there is at least some good in the Noble realm."

Lancen smiled quietly while they ascended the climb, Calderon coming into view at its summit. When their eyes had rested upon the great city of stone, Lancen looked it over, withholding emotion. In sight were retired farms of all kinds, hills baring exhausted vines and small houses that dotted the landscape around the massive walls. The city appeared magnificent yet miserable in the late afternoon, every stone-crafted structure lying quiet and gray. In the distance, just south of the eastern gates, was a large glen of trees, the humble lumber mill remaining just as he had remembered it.

Though little had changed in the land he had once called home, Lancen was not the same boy that had wandered those streets. To him, the city seemed foreign and unwelcoming, as if he were viewing it for the first time.

Snow-covered mountains created a beautiful backdrop, while the wide river wound from their depths and through the valley southward as far as the eye could see. Much to Lancen's fear, thousands of soldiers with their tents and horses could be seen lingering near the western banks. Smoke rose from a hundred fires while clinking armor and heavy voices carried faintly on the wind. They were undoubtedly setting off for the Ashlands.

Keira found them quickly as well and watched them through moistening eyes.

"Oh no," she muttered. "Somehow I had held on to hope that it would not be true."

"Most of them are on foot," said Lancen, choosing to calculate rather than panic. "Calderon has a standing army of ten thousand, and it looks like they are mostly there. It will take them a month to reach Obuthahn."

Keira shook her head, denying the estimate. "That can't be. The number of our warriors will be one drop in a pond. How long will Tomutah take to arrive?"

"I'd imagine about the same, assuming they can be convinced."

"What do you mean assuming?" Keira was rightfully upset. Hope was hard enough to come by without bringing up doubts and grim realities.

"It is no guarantee. You heard Motl."

"I also heard the saint! It was promised!"

Lancen's lips pursed. He wished he could provide comfort, but there was no sense in denying fact. "It was promised that they would trust *me*. Nothing was said of an alternative."

Keira glared at him, shocked and offended. "Then why did you not go there yourself? You could have sent the others for Adalyn! If Obuthahn stands alone, they have no chance, period!"

"They are not alone! Lena departed to call on Endwah. Bondor of Riverock may already be in the Ashlands. We are still outnumbered ten to one, but the Ashlanders are not alone."

"We will be obliterated," said Keira hopelessly. "You should send me to Obuthahn. I could prepare them to flee."

"Nothing has changed. We have assumed this end for weeks and Obuthahn will not run now!" ordered Lancen. "We must make it to the base of the mountains tonight. We will reach my mine in the morning and depart for Obuthahn as soon as possible."

"That doesn't leave us much time."

"We have never had time, and we would be better off assuming that we never will—save ourselves the stress."

Keira kept her head up and clicked her tongue. "I can only see defeat."

"Then I will die side by side with every Native in the Ashlands!"

Keira looked at Lancen with a serious and caring gaze. She pointed her head north, motioning in a sober confidence to proceed. "Then we had better keep going, while our horses still show signs of life."

Lancen dipped his head and whistled, kicking his horse sharply and taking flight down the slope toward Calderon. As they stormed down the road, he tried to block out the memories that swarmed his mind. His heart ached when he passed the eastern gates, and the mill where he had spent so many long but pleasant hours. Embracing the wind against his face, he vowed that he would soon return to the 'Pinnacle of the Grasslands.' He would return when the burden he continued to carry had been lifted, and he would bring riches for the orphanage. One day, everything that he had done there would be set straight, but that day was not yet.

In crucial haste he and Keira fled from the road and tore north across the great plain, their steeds seeming to swim, belly deep in the brown and yellow grass. The sun slowly fell behind the mountains while dark clouds rolled in to replace it. Before their day's travel was over, they were leading the duns through several inches of newly fallen snow.

With every step closer Lancen's worry increased, as did his confidence. He was truly a different person than he had been the last time he viewed his mountain home. Before, he was weak, lonely, and afraid, but now he was motivated, liberated, and capable. It would not be long before the Legion would fall, and everything would begin with Goldtooth. The Noble captain would no longer get the best of him, not this time.

Lancen continued to wait for revenge with patience. Like his hunger, it was an urge that lingered, always on the back of his mind, but before he could save Adalyn and stop the tyrant, he needed to rest, think, and plan. The morning would grasp him with the fierceness of a troll, and he needed to be prepared. He didn't know how many soldiers would accompany Earnst, if Hans would be among them, or in what state he would find the princess, but on the morrow, vengeance was his. There would be no glory. There would be no reward, only vengeance.

Adalyn's wrists were sore. It felt as though the ropes had burned through her flesh and rested on the bone. She was hungry, and her tongue was dry, curling in thirst. Sending shivers down her spine, the floor was eternally cold beneath her. The typical use of the word hell could hardly describe what she was experiencing. Where was Lancen?

Time did not seem to exist in the dark world where she lay. Machinery moved and metal clanked. By the panel of knobs and switches, Knave continued to tinker and grumble obscenities. Steam blew steady across the floor between she and him, causing him to appear as a faded silhouette, haunting like a ghost and illusively surreal. A few paces to his left, the wide gaping hole in the floor had begun to screech and moan in repetitive cries. It was like the sound of a sword scraping armor, but much louder and constant.

The dark figure, Ventok, had gone back into the shadow some time ago, and though Adalyn was glad to be relieved of his eerie tone and vulgar threats, she wanted him to return. When Lancen came, she wanted to watch the large skole die.

Her wish was granted as Ventok came back into sight, working his way through the other creatures around their various stations. Approaching Knave yet again, a look of sadistic satisfaction was worn on his face.

"The clouds have come in," he said proudly. "Morning will be here soon and the storm along with it. Let us kill the girl."

The cloaked Knave took his time to respond, fingering a strange circular recession in the panel before him. "The moment is soon," he said, "but do not be hasty. Everything must be perfect for this glorious day."

"Can we begin the preparations?"

Through the darkness, an atrocious white smile spread across

Knave's face, his teeth glowing like stars under shadow. "Bring me the relic and get her in position."

Adalyn fidgeted as fear began to awaken the fight inside of her. When Ventok approached, she wriggled and kicked. Where was Lancen? Where was her father? Where were the divines? As the evil creature groped, she rolled away quickly, fighting every motion he asserted.

Ventok stood up straight and looked to Knave, exasperated.

Without hearing a word, Knave knew exactly what his subordinate was thinking, and approved. "Go ahead."

With no holding back, Ventok turned again to Adalyn and struck her with force, his sharp claws cutting through her shoulder, drawing blood but not ending her struggle. She only needed to fight a little while longer. Lancen would come at any moment! She knew it! As Ventok tried to grab her again, she kicked fiercely and hit him hard in the shin. Recoiling, he grabbed his leg in a spurred fury.

"Biddy *witch*!" he spat before he strongly struck her across the face. The hit stung on impact, causing her ears to ring and blood to run down her cheek.

"What's wrong?" asked Knave darkly. "Can't you handle a little girl?"

Ventok scowled and struck her a third time, sending her into a torpor. "Just wasn't expecting the fight. We chose a good one."

As Ventok finally laid hold of her, he reached for her neck and tore free the emerald necklace that Lancen had given her. After handing it off to Knave, he dragged her mercilessly across the granite floor and released her right next to the large circular pit. She looked over the edge to see two giant metal turbines, spinning at an incredible pace nearly twenty feet below. Mysterious lights dotted the walls of the hole to an unbelievable depth. What was this place?

As Adalyn lay bleeding, Ventok grabbed hold of a cable that hung from an uncertain height above them and attached its cuff appendages to her wrists. Nearby, one of the nameless monsters spun a wheel and lifted her several feet above the floor. With a strong push, Ventok sent her gliding backward. A short cry escaped her lips as she swung out and over the deadly hole. Trepidation had quickly overtaken her as she looked down into the terrifying trap below.

Ventok remained still, chuckling in a demented amusement. Knave slowly left the panel and stepped over to the pit beside his comrade. Raising the emerald necklace over its edge he called out loudly, "In the name of Droth, I cleanse this —"

"Why the necklace?" interrupted Adalyn, forcing words through her dry throat and cracked lips. She figured that there were two options before her. She could either stall for time and be a nuisance, or she could be silent and helplessly wait for death. She chose the first.

Knave lowered his arm and growled in annoyance. "Death does not suit you as it does us," he stated calmly. "We handle it with grace, but you are choosing blemish."

"Why the necklace?" she repeated. "Why me?"

Knave shook his head pompously, seeing right through her plan, and again raised his arm over the pit. "In the name of Droth, I cleanse this temple and call upon the powers within this mountain! Awaken and come forth!"

Adalyn watched as the gift Lancen had given her slipped from the skole's grip and disappeared into the darkness below the massive contrivances. At once a frozen and chilling wind shot forth from the depths. The princess grimaced and fought were she hung, the cold seeming to cut through her like a thousand knives.

After a moment the effect ceased, and Adalyn hung, beaten and afraid.

"Listen closely, girl, for I will only say this once," said Knave coldly. "You were always meant to dangle above the well. The Master has called with anger clear. Repeat these words in your mind, for they are your destiny:

A mortal, pure, royal, young,
Added to the well.
With one of three, golden sung,
Unleashes fury, hell.

Bowels churn, roof crumbles,
A spire to the height.
Clouds dark, thunder rumbles
Behold eternal night."

Adalyn stared at the monster as he turned back toward his work. She didn't know what else to say. What darkness was she now a part of?

"It is time!" hollered Ventok. "Let us kill her!"

"Idiot!" cried Knave. "The storm must be undeniable! Go and watch. When it fully is upon us, I will pierce the heart."

Some amount of heathen joy was removed from the larger skole's face. "Yes sir."

Adalyn tried to control her breathing and formulate a plan, tears coming yet again to her eyes. She tried to deny them, but it was no use. She had never been so afraid. Where was Lancen?

CHAPTER 61

A calm snow fell lightly in the wooden traces near his mountain home. Scattered rays of the early morning light wove their way through the trees. With the soft ripple of the stream, the windless and frosty air, everything appeared untouched, but there was something about the stillness that was unnerving. It was too serene.

Stopping just before his clearing, Lancen gently stepped off his horse and invited Keira to do the same. Soundless, they left the animals and slowly moved into the vicinity of his homestead. His burnt cabin still stood, all but one wall now blackened and dismal. Would there be a trap awaiting them? He could sense that something was off.

Carefully, he pulled his bow from his back and held it tightly, his breath rising in clouds as he moved steadily forward. Did he hear something in what was left of his old home? Or was it just his imagination? Motioning for Keira to stop, he crouched low to the snow and scarcely breathed. He listened for the smallest hint of life. If they were not alone, he needed to find his enemy before they found him — and he and Keira *were not* alone. He could feel it with all his being.

As if hunting the agile mule deer of the north, he surveyed the ground for tracks and quickly found them. Large boot prints, a man's, led from Lancen's shed and up the far hill into the woods. As he searched further, he spotted more tracks all across the clearing. They were from a dozen different men at least, all of them staying clear of the mine. Lancen assumed they were the Legion's dogs, watching and waiting for this very moment.

Up the hill and out of the corner of his eye, Lancen saw a dark hand, gripping a bow that crept out from behind a tree — and it was all he needed.

With astonishing speed, Lancen aimed the Sacred Tare and released an arrow, shooting straight and lightning quick. Like a bird over water, the projectile flew just above the ground until it pounded into the man's fist. In agony, the armor-clad soldier flinched backward and out of cover just long enough for Lancen to send a second arrow through his naked head.

Without a moment to breathe, another man leapt out from behind the shed, set to hoist a spear. He cocked back and poised for the throw, but before his release, another worthy Darkwood arrow crunched into the man's chest, easily piercing the steel breastplate.

"Not bad for a dead boy."

Before Lancen could draw another arrow, an irritating and loathsome voice echoed from behind his cabin. He would recognize it anywhere. Goldtooth.

"I implore you to put down your bow," the captain continued. "I'd like to have a civil discussion about all this mess."

Lancen tried to control his stampeding anger. Should he listen? Or would Goldtooth shoot him and Keira down at the first opportunity. Earnst did not even deserve to breathe, so why would he be entitled to courtesy?

"Come on boy," prodded Goldtooth. "You know as well as I do that time is pressing. Put it down and we can talk."

Lancen hesitated before angrily refastening the Sacred Tare to his back. "Say what you will, quickly."

Laughing irksomely, Earnst stepped out from behind a burnt wall with arrogance. His sword was drawn, and his golden tooth gleamed from within a smiling mouth.

"Now you should either turn around or tell me where the princess is," he said. "Otherwise nothing but death will greet you here. I have a hundred soldiers crawling these hills, and all it would take is my call. They will come running."

"But at the moment there are two of us, and only one of you," said Lancen. "Start talking."

"He's lying Lancen," muttered Keira fearlessly.

"Ah, *Lancen*, that's right!" retorted Earnst. "What a pleasant name for the savage-loving bastard of the mountains! Now tell me how to find the princess, filth!"

"You and I both know you took her," said Lancen. "So you will tell me what you've done with her, or I will cut the words out of your throat!"

Earnst laughed an obnoxious hoot and began stepping closer. "Looks like we've stumbled upon a conundrum! You are here for Adalyn. I am here for Adalyn. But perhaps we are both too late. She's likely dead by now. Truth is, I could care less where she is. My first order was to kill you, and that remains my prerogative."

"Stay here," Lancen muttered quickly to Keira. "This is my fight."

Lancen's hand was steady as it drew Securis from his waist, anger present as he walked toward Goldtooth. It was a fury more damning than it had ever been. Now, rather than burning like coals, low and steady, it was hot as fire. This time, nothing would ruin his moment. The two stopped just across the creek from one another, both standing on muddy, snow-riddled banks.

"Did you kill her?" asked Lancen directly. "You killed Rune, and now Adalyn?"

"You're pathetic," growled Earnst. "I ought to ask you the same thing, but it makes no difference to me. I thought I might find you here. Time to finish this. Then I'll ride to Obuthahn, take care of your friends. But one scum at a time."

In a rage, Earnst leapt into the stream and lunged swiftly at Lancen, giving him just enough time to raise his axe and parry the strike. As the blades clashed, with his free hand Earnst blew a swift fist across the boy's jaw. Biting his tongue, Lancen felt the warmth of blood ooze in his mouth and swung back angrily.

Goldtooth was quicker than him and masterful with a blade. His years of training and experience were evident in his every strike, and it was all Lancen could do to block or evade the first several jabs from his opponent. Yet as his adrenaline increased, so did his focus and precision. Ducking his head and throwing low, Lancen was able to land a sharp strike into the captain's hip, 'the blade of the reaper's touch' spraying blood across the frozen banks as it withdrew. The weapon had truly been sharpened by Taylah of Toltgaro, proven instantly as it cut through the formed metal of the soldier's greaves.

Swearing, Earnst doubled his efforts and launched a fiery swipe. In a blur, Lancen narrowly avoided by diving sideways into the icy water. Immediately the cold stole his breath as Goldtooth struck again. Scrambling backward, he felt the air from the blade as it missed his face by inches. In reprisal, he threw Securis upward, landing a strong blow into Goldtooth's ribs, wedging it between the bones. Without a second for thought, he left the blade buried in flesh and went for the knees, forcing Earnst down into the water beside him.

The captain was strong, and pressed at Lancen's face, forcing him down under the icy current. Desperate for air, the boy found hold of the back of his axe and pushed it in, inching it further into the man's oblique.

Screaming, Earnst lost strength for a brief moment, and Lancen took advantage. With no hesitation, he wrestled atop the captain and landed punch after punch into his face. After several solid strikes, he went for the kill, pushing down into Goldtooth's neck with all his might. In a final and desperate struggle, Earnst released his sword and with both hands twisted at Lancen's wrists, somehow breaking their grasp.

"*HELP!*" Earnst rashly screamed. The cry echoed through the forest, magnified by the pain that it exemplified.

For a moment the two rolled in the mud just outside of the water, tossing punches and cutting with elbows. Finally, Lancen pounded hard into the man's jaw, hearing a pop and gaining the upper hand. Immediately, he pressed down atop his embedded axe, wedging it deeper still. Adjusting position, Lancen jabbed his elbow against his enemy's throat.

"What have you done with Adalyn?" Lancen demanded. "What of the ritual?"

Earnst choked and groped at his neck. Lancen raised his arm just enough for the man to speak.

"You tell me," Goldtooth forced.

"*WHERE IS SHE!*" Lancen screamed, infuriated.

"Lancen," said Keira from his side. He hadn't noticed her approach.

She held up Goldtooth's blade and extended the handle toward him. Taking it gladly, Lancen rose to his feet and pressed the pointed tip sharply against its owner's cheek.

"Did you kill her?" he questioned strongly, drawing blood. "Where is Adalyn?"

"I don't *KNOW!*" Earnst growled. "But her blood is not on my hands, boy. Killing me is murder!"

Lancen knew that Goldtooth was telling the truth. He had known the whole time. There were no footprints near his mine, and that was where Adalyn would be. No one had entered or left since the snow had fallen. No one had even gone near it, but that would not save Earnst.

"You're right. You didn't kill Adalyn," said Lancen tranquilly, "but you did kill my dog."

In a swift motion Lancen raised the Legion sword and thrust it strongly downward into the chest of Captain Earnst. Looking to the sky, the man grimaced and whimpered, choking on his own blood. Heavy snowflakes settled upon his face, golden tooth gleaming dully in the soft morning light. He looked up to Lancen with pleading and fearful eyes, took a final breath, and then was still.

CHAPTER 62

L ancen look out!" Keira cried, barreling into him and knocking them both to the ground just as an arrow flew past his head.

At once his gaze was ripped from Goldtooth, and he began to awaken to the world around him. A second arrow skid across the water near his feet and a third plummeted into the mud beside his face, splashing filth.

Ripping Securis from the captain's side, Lancen jumped to his feet and boosted Keira to hers. "Quickly, to the mine!"

Lancen would rest easier knowing that he had won at least one battle this day, but there was no time for celebration as dozens of soldiers came racing down the hills around him and into the clearing. The malice of skoles did not exist in their eyes, but the determination to kill was the same. Sheltering Keira as best he could, the two tore off desperately for the lonely mine on the western end of his homestead. The experience seemed almost dreamlike as they sprinted across the open space leading up to his hollow. Spears and arrows flew past them from several different directions. The legionnaires multiplied and hollered curses. Like the grain of a silo, they poured into the vicinity, suffocating the space.

Lancen made sure Keira entered the mine first, and in a rush, chanced a look at his pursuers. There were dozens, maybe fifty or sixty total, all either firing arrows or running full speed toward the mine.

Before giving himself a chance to breathe, he lifted Keira into his sliding mine cart and pushed it along the rails. As it gained speed he jumped over its side and flew down the opening tunnel. The railing was short, perhaps a hundred feet, with a gradual descent. Keira held his arm tightly as they dropped. Just before the end of the track, he pulled the iron brake, keeping them from flying off the rails, but not preventing fierce whiplash and bruises as they crashed into the large wooden stopper.

Enemies quickly swarmed the narrow entrance, blocking light. There was no time to think as Lancen whipped the Sacred Tare from his back, instinctively remembering a fragile wooden beam near the mouth. He had been meaning to fix it for ages as it remained rotting and weak. Loose nails and burnt sides made it dangerous beyond reason. Perhaps it would save them.

"Shoot the brace near the entrance," Lancen managed to articulate, at once launching an arrow up the tunnel and into the target beam.

"Is there another way out?" asked Keira, pulling her bow. She understood the plan.

There was no time for Lancen to answer as the soldiers clamored toward them. That Adalyn would be in his mine was nothing but a hunch. If he was wrong, then they would surely die, but he would rather suffocate in a dark hole than be fallen by a Legion blade.

Launching another arrow into the beam, he noticed Keira's fall far left, bouncing off the stone wall. *Elbow up*, he thought as he nocked and released another missile. It pounded hard into the target brace and pushed it backward.

The rumble proceeded the crash as Lancen had just enough time to grab Keira and get atop her before the rocks came thundering down. Beginning at the mouth, it seemed an unbroken boom as the roof came slamming like a wave to crush the legionnaires beneath it. The death machine raced violently toward Lancen and Keira, shattering supports and casting smoke. In an instant they were pounded by dirt and debris, but just before the bulk collapsed above them, the nearest posts lurched and shifted, somehow holding up the earth above it. After a moment when they had finally dared to open their eyes, all was black, but they had survived.

Lancen choked on the dust surrounding him. It burnt his eyes and shot up his nose as he cleared away the rocks atop him. Keira was moving beside him, groaning in pain, but alive. She struggled to her knees as he began to feel his way to the wall and follow it until the next post. To his dismay, there was no torch hanging on its face.

"Where are you going?" the girl asked. They couldn't see a thing.

"I'm trying to find a torch."

"Are you sure there are any down here?"

"When I first fled Calderon, I made sure to line this entire shaft with them, every five or six posts."

"Wait, stop," said Keira. "I see a light, on your coat."

As the smoke slowly settled, a soft glow began to emerge from Lancen's torso, and he remembered at once the saber appendages that had been tied there. Through the dusty air, the teeth and claws illuminated the small tunnel to a dull but operable light.

"Thank the divines," said Keira, now able to see around the glowing boy.

"Thank Avik," said Lancen, playing the devil's advocate. "How are you holding up?"

Keira smiled and wiped some dirt from her face. "Considering all that just happened, I think I'm faring pretty well. I just wish my head would stop pounding."

The girl scowled and poked in her ear, cleaning out dust. "How are you?" she asked. "Your head is bleeding."

Lancen felt the top of his brow and sensed the warmth of blood. It was nothing serious. "I'm worried, but I'm alive. Shall we?"

He motioned for her to join him, and they swiftly trotted further into the mine. Normally its depth was nothing to stress over, but this day was different. The underground structure consisted only of the main shaft they were now in, and a few side tunnels, all of which had certain ends. If there was not an exit beyond the spot where he had found the key, then everything was over. They would be trapped until death and the tyrant would succeed.

With the light of the saber pieces, he knew it would not take long for them to reach the end of the narrow wing where Lancen had broken into the hollow and found the key so long ago. The event had marked an end of his old life and the beginning of a new. Ever since, there had been stress, pain, excitement, and romance, but most of all, there had been purpose. Since that fateful day, his thoughts and opinions of the Natives had changed, his desires and priorities — even his body had morphed into something different. It forced the question of which life was better. Currently drowning in worry and destruction, he wouldn't know the answer until after Adalyn was saved and Obuthahn protected.

As they made their way down the main shaft and veered right into another, Keira found a torch on the wall and held it out before her. Lancen stopped to watch her as she held a hand over its face and wriggled her fingers, muttering a nearly incoherent phrase. "Mohto Lahknet."

Instantly a thick orange flame ignited the object and light flooded the thin passage.

"How did you do that?" Lancen asked, amazed by her use of magic.

"Etnah taught me," she replied. "It is simple magic but will only work in a darkness such as this, on a fitting subject like this torch. Watch."

"Mohto Lahknet." Before the words even made it past her tongue, the fire extinguished. "It is actually a curse. I think it means something like 'hellfire' in the Noble tongue."

Lancen whistled softly. "Can anyone do that?"

Keira laughed, "A baby could do it if taught. Want to try?"

Lancen nodded and took the device from her as she repeated the words for him to say. He focused as best he could, trying to channel his intentions into the torch. Allowing his hand to hover just above the tinder, he moved his fingers and said the words, "Mohto Lahknet."

Nothing happened. Shaking his head, he repositioned and tried again, recalling what Etnah had taught him about magic. 'It exists in many forms,' the elf had said, 'living in a reality parallel to our own, waiting to be roused. All we must do is find the appropriate keys to summon it. You must dig within yourself, where no other emotions lie, and drive the heat to your fingers.'

Lancen tried to clear his mind, focusing on nothing other than the torch and his will inside of him. When thoughts of Adalyn or Keira came, he pushed them out of conscience. Concentrating on his fingertips, he tried to channel every ounce of emotion through them. "Mohto Lahknet."

Still nothing. Puffing his cheeks, he handed the torch back to Keira, not sure what he was doing wrong.

"Some people do not have the touch," Keira mentioned,

"Maybe we can try again later," said Lancen. "We're wasting time."

Though frustrated, he knew that he must continue at once. Menial pursuits would be but a shadow until Adalyn was out of peril's wake.

Keira again told the torch to enflame and followed Lancen down the tunnel. His nerves brought sweat to his brow as the two moved forward. The scope of his mission and the uncertainty of Adalyn's location weighed heavy on his mind. He would soon know once and for all whether he had sentenced both Keira and Adalyn to die. Was his mine the answer to Eltou's riddle? There was but one way to find out, and it would greet them at the next bend.

Nervously, he stepped forward, trying to brace himself for the worst when he rounded the corner, but as he did, relief flooded him as they discovered a gaping hole where months ago he had found the golden key. Others had clearly been through this way, but as Lancen admired the tunneling, he was distraught to see that it had been dug by claws. There were few holes and chips, but rather slight ridges and terraces where a monster had carved the earth. Immediately the question of skoles crossed his mind. The Legion could not have done this.

The room beyond the freshly dug tunnel was small and square, with nothing but a narrow opening receding into its cobbled floor. As they approached, they discovered a circular staircase, crawling downward with deep steps, descending into a realm of mystery. From its depths emerged a strangely emanating light, one that wasn't bright like the sun and didn't flicker like fire but was dull and gloomy like the moons.

What awaited them at the bottom Lancen didn't know, but his heart was warm, and he struggled to contain his excitement. Smiling broadly, he playfully hit Keira on the arm. "Our journey goes on."

CHAPTER 63

"What do you think is down there?" asked Keira, alarmed by the dreary light.

Lancen's smile faded as an ugly paranoia overwhelmed his excitement. "Adalyn," he mentioned, "and that's what matters."

Questioning thoughts fought their way through the chaos of his mind. Eltou had said that the tyrant had Adalyn, but Lancen had thought that to mean Goldtooth. Earnst was a sleaze, but his voice had shown no waver when he said he didn't know where Adalyn was. So who had captured her? If not the Legion, then who was the tyrant?

Lancen grit his teeth and slowly took the first step down the stairs. Who had tunneled this? Was it the dwarves? The ancients? Who could have carved something so deep into the earth and just beyond his mine? It was as if he, and only he, was meant to find the key, like some sort of fate: a predestined occurrence, placed into the expanse of time. Was it the divines? The Master?

Lancen shook his shoulders to rid himself of the cold that came over him. Who was the Master anyway? Even with all of his dreams in cloudy recollection, he didn't know, and he resisted the urge to want to.

Keira grabbed his arm as they walked down the spiraled steps. She did not seem entirely afraid, but rather anxious to investigate what was ahead. There was no hesitance in her step nor sweat on her palm, just a curious and determined gleam in her eyes. It took everything Lancen had to mirror that courage.

The stairwell was tightly enclosed with stone steps, and at the bottom, an open archway preceded a thin corridor that was barely shoulder width. The dim light lingered at the end of the passage, and in preparation Lancen gripped Securis for all it was worth. If Adalyn was in this hall of light, he refused to stumble upon her captors unprepared.

As they descended the final step, their eyes were widened as they beheld a new world beyond the dreary hallway. At the end of the corridor, the tunnel enlarged to a massive space, the source of light found in thousands of glowing orbs throughout the area. The phenomena hung in the air at various intervals by magic and exuded soft but extraordinary lights of blue and white.

Moving quickly to the incredible hall, amazement could not describe the look on their faces. Everything around them was foreign and indescribable. Lancen could hardly believe that beneath his mountain home stood an enormous hall of unthinkable origin. The ceiling was dark and smooth fifty feet over head, supported by glossily rounded marble pillars. The floor under their feet appeared as a colossal crystal sheet, transparent and glittering only a few inches above a rocky ground. The stone walls were sheer and bits of ore and gems still shined on their flattened faces.

Looking around in awe, Lancen felt as though he were up in the stars, everything dim besides the fingernail sized orbs. Reaching out his palm, he tried to grab the nearest marble of light, but his hand passed through as if it were a ghost.

"I think this is a ruin of the ancients," said Keira in astonishment. "Etnah spoke of them on occasion, but I never could have imagined something so glorious!"

"How could anyone build this?" asked Lancen, closing his eyes and opening them again just to ensure that he wasn't dreaming.

"How could those who built it disappear?" added Keira. "And without leaving a single trail."

Lancen took another moment to look around, but the ache for Adalyn's wellbeing quickly came back to his thoughts. They had no time to stand and gawk, not until she was safe.

"Every wasted moment is one moment closer to failure," Lancen said aloud, recalling Sidna's words. "We need to keep moving."

Keira agreed, and the two continued forward across the hall. When they reached its end there were three doorways before them, a large archway in the middle with two smaller on either side. Each passage led to a separate corridor, all lined with a minimal amount of floating lights. They appeared daunting and dangerous, shadows consuming in their depths.

"Which do we choose?" asked Keira.

Lancen exhaled roughly. This was just what he needed. Adalyn was at the cusp of demise, and he was left to decide which path to follow. There was no time to waste.

Without saying a word, he risked stepping forward and moved into the large middle passage with resolve. His amazement was overridden by purpose as they wandered far and deep into bizarre and magnificent chambers. Incredible crafts of glass and metal lined the walls as riches of all kinds flooded from containers too numerous to count. Lancen did not waste time but couldn't resist filling a pouch with several handfuls of the amethysts, emeralds, and diamonds that were scattered like dirt across the ground. He wondered how a people so intelligent and wealthy could fall from existence. Perhaps rather than disappear, they had simply risen to the heavens, to become divines, or some other beings of superior power and influence.

When they had wandered far and deep into the ruins, Keira stopped in her tracks and grabbed Lancen by the shoulder. "Did you hear that?"

Lancen held his breath and listened intently for any sound. They had proceeded down a narrow corridor on a grated metal floor, resting above slightly disturbed water. Shadows dashed along the wall, reflecting the liquid beneath, and he watched its dancing nervously, waiting for any disorder. All he could hear was the soft laps of the water.

But then it sounded again.

It was a distant and dire scream, high pitched and agonized. Immediately a coldness in the air surrounded him and forced chills. The cry was not human but held a horrifying similarity.

"Lancen," Keira began, but she was cut off by another screeching yelp. Hairs stood up on end as they waited and listened, trying to determine if it was growing closer. The noise was shrill and tortured, an unquenchable scream of desperate pain. Lancen whipped his head back and forth, searching either end of the lengthy corridor. The lighting was dim and shadows deceiving, but there was nothing between them and escape in either direction. All was silent between screams except for nervous breaths. It was difficult to tell whose was shakier.

Horribly, the cry sounded again and was disturbingly closer. Keira looked around with a restless intensity, her long knife singing as she pulled it from its sheath.

"What is that?" Lancen whispered, fist clenched unbreakably around his axe's hilt.

"Crone," breathed Keira so softly that it was barely heard.

Sweat began to moisten Lancen's palms as he tried to remember everything that Etnah had said about crones. They were dark and horrific creatures — possibly a remnant of the ancients. Skoles paled in comparison...

Lancen gulped down his fear as instinct decided to take over. Hurriedly, he began to nudge Keira further down the hall, away from the direction of the last scream.

"We need to get out of here," he mumbled. He was desperate, and as he peered back over his shoulder, his fear of being too late was already realized. Hunched over in shadow, an oddly shaped humanoid hobbled into the corridor on all fours. It was little larger than a Noble child, but was ghastly thin, with five protruding spikes extending, bony and unsettling from its naked back. Greasy and straggled black hair leaked over its face like moss as it stared down the hall, curiously admiring Lancen and Keira with white and glowing eyes.

At once Lancen prodded her more urgently. A small squeak escaped her lips. "Do you see it?"

Suddenly the monster cringed and screamed another blood chilling cry. In unparalleled fury, hunger, or perhaps some other driving appetite, it tore off like lightning at full speed toward them. The two began running at once, but they were no match. In an instant the creature had caught them and leaped into the air like a saber pouncing to kill. Clinging onto Lancen's back, it dragged him to the ground and sunk razor-sharp teeth into his shoulder. Ripping free flesh, it bit again, this time deeper. Keira quickly turned and swung her knife, grazing the beast. Releasing Lancen, it leapt to the wall and sprung from its face, taking down Keira with speed and ferocity. Ignoring the pain it caused, Lancen reached out his wounded arm, taking hold of one of the creature's ankles, and pulled it roughly away from the struggling Shaharan.

Without missing a beat, the monster was back atop Lancen, clawing menacingly at his chest. The fabric of his tunic ripped, and the claws began to cut through skin. Looking into the crone's dark and malicious eyes, Lancen tried not to panic. Its face was evil and full of rage. It appeared gaunt and starved, with no pleasure or satisfaction in the fight, only misery. Yelling loudly, Lancen shook his gaze and grabbed his bony opponent by both shoulders to throw it strongly against the stone wall.

Keira leapt back into action with a flashing swing of her blade. This time, the strike cut deeply through the monster's arm, spraying a black and watery blood. The crone screamed violently and threw its head against the wall, breaking skin. In the distraction, Lancen gripped his axe and threw it forcefully, impaling the sad being in the torso. It jerked and resisted, but as Lancen withdrew the blade, it fell limp to the floor, twitching once before collapsing like a fallen puppet.

Lancen groaned and returned to his feet, taking a moment to

observe his wounds. His chest was warm, but it appeared that the cuts had scarcely broken skin. Placing a hand on his shoulder, he grimaced. Its pain was piercing within but nearly numb on the surface.

Before either of them could catch their breath, another curdling screech echoed through the passage. It came from the same origin as the first, and it was moving quickly.

"Run," said Lancen, his fear reaching a peak.

And run they did.

CHAPTER 64

Adalyn dangled helplessly over a spinning death trap. Defeated, she hung silently, arms numb and useless above her. Sweat rolled down her brow, and as time passed, it was becoming more and more difficult to breathe. She gazed hopelessly over to Knave, who still waited patiently beside the same wall of switches and dials. He hadn't moved an inch since Ventok had wandered off down the dark corridor yet again.

Suddenly, she watched the cloaked leader look up at her, anger enfolding at the sight of his wicked eyes glowing through the shadow of his hood. It gave her a headache, and she wished she could place a hand over her throbbing temple. Instead, she just chose to contort and struggle. Knave began to chuckle softly. Who was this pig?

"No need to fret, my dear," he said in a guttural voice. "You will not have to wait much longer."

"Do you have a plan for after I am dead?" Adalyn asked through a weak and broken voice. She refused to give up, finding a boldness within her that she never knew she had. "You wish to create an everlasting storm, flood the world?"

"The goal is not to flood the world, precious girl," he said ominously. "It is only to darken the sun, to cast a lasting shadow across Serondhel."

"And what will that prove? It will only kill the peninsula, all the trees and flowers. Is that what you want?"

"It is not about what I want!" Knave shot back, infuriated. "There is no honor or glory where I sit. There is only necessity."

"Why?" probed Adalyn. "What makes it necessary?"

"You do not understand the call, and you cannot! You are nothing but the sacrifice!"

"If I am nothing then why are you waiting to kill me?"

Knave lowered his head and shook it in disbelief. "Because you are pure, in high prestige, and you bore one of the cursed artifacts."

"The necklace?"

"Aye, you can't be naïve enough to believe that skoles were in the cavern of Nahabuk to battle Native children? They were after the artifact!"

Adalyn closed her eyes tightly, recalling what Lancen had said about his experience in the Hero's Trial. She tried to catch her breath, but it was growing more difficult. "Lancen will find me. And when he does, he will kill you."

"Lancen?" Knave retorted, amused. "Who are you referring to, the champion? You, the helpless damsel, believe that prophecy will save you? It is prophecy that put you where you hang!

"But speaking of prophecy, here is a line for you: *'the clues are restored which were bound by obstruction. As the land once was it again shall be.'* This will not be the first time that the sky has been darkened. Can you see this?" he asked, referring to the circular recession in the panel of switches. "There is space here for a key, although I will not need one to turn the lock. When I do, you will be released, and killed in the blink of eye. This magnificent chamber where we stand is the heart of divines. It reeks of them!"

Adalyn kept her eyes closed, trying to make sense of all he was saying. "But what if you can't turn the lock? What if you do need the key?"

The cloaked man laughed again, irritably. "Then the ritual will be void! But a flaming pillar will shoot up from beneath you nonetheless, and you will be incinerated to a crisp. *'With a message of fire for all to see.'*"

As Knave finished, the epitome of evil, Ventok, reappeared in the aisle across the hall.

"Finally!" Knave exclaimed, clapping his hands together. "Has the storm become fierce?"

Ventok answered exuberantly, "It is as severe as it will ever be."

The cloaked leader stood and withdrew two thin metal picks from his cloak, stepping over to the keyhole at once. Turning his head back with a sinister smile, he mentioned quickly, "I told you it would not be long, princess."

Adalyn began to hyperventilate, shaking from where she hung. Why was this all happening? It was never supposed to end this way! Where was Lancen? Why had he never come for her?

It was all over, and the realization would destroy her long before the flame.

"What's taking so long?" questioned Ventok anxiously.

"Patience! It is a stubborn blight, but I almost have it."

For the first time, the cloaked skole threw off his hood and attacked the lock more diligently. As Adalyn saw his face, she knew at once that there was a better name for him than Knave.

"How long will it take?" probed Ventok, impatient as a child.

"Seconds."

Lancen and Keira raced around a corner and into a high-ceiling hall, much like the one they had found near the entrance of the ancients' ruin. Three quick and ferocious crones tore recklessly after them in pursuit, bashing into walls and leaving trails of blood as they took no mind of their own physical conditions. Eerie and deafening screams were constantly stabbing at the ears. Was escape a possibility? Or should Lancen and Keira turn and fight, ending the chase once and for all?

Bouncing through a doorway and into an adjacent room, Lancen threw down a waist high pedestal in an attempt to slow their pursuers. The room looked like a former antechamber, bearing display cases and relics, and on its far wall was an open metal door. Sprinting desperately toward it, Lancen and Keira battled through their fatigue. The moment they reached the barrier, the two pulled on its crystal handle, trying to force it closed, but the door wouldn't budge. In a heartbeat the crones toppled and stormed into the room, barreling mindlessly toward the humans.

Finally, the door swung free and Lancen and Keira shut it with a bang, falling on their backs as soon as it closed. Immediately three solid thuds pounded into the other side. Screaming, the crones clawed and beat against the metal, not letting up nor losing energy, but the door did not open.

Completely out of breath, Lancen struggled to his feet, holding onto his knees, completely exhausted. With every inch of her glistening in sweat, Keira rose also, throwing her hair back and gasping for air. After she had recovered a moment, she placed a light hand on Lancen's back and moved it softly, showing affection.

When Lancen had a hold of himself, he straightened up and immediately placed his arms around her. He was incredibly grateful to have her by his side and knew that there was nothing they would not be able to accomplish together.

"We did it Lancen," said Keira in between breaths. "The darkness couldn't stop us, and it never will."

They embraced for a long moment, feelings of relief drowning out the sound of the crones' racket. But after they released, both of them knew that the objective still remained. Adalyn still needed them. The tyrant still needed to be stopped. Lancen tied his axe back to his waist and drew instead the Sacred Tare. The next monster that came their way, he wanted to take out from a distance.

Looking around, they were in a very small room, lit only by a single glowing sphere. Two magnificent double doors waited for them just a few feet away, opposite of where the crones pounded and scratched.

Looking first to his aching chest, Lancen noticed his tunic, red with blood, then his shoulder which throbbed in pain. Meeting Keira's eyes, she looked at him with confidence, giving him a power that could not be placed at will. Without saying a word, he stepped forward and swung open the double doors.

Beyond them was an enormous and intriguing hall. It was littered with pumping machinery, metals of all kinds, and troughs filled with various liquids. His eyes were drawn at once to a female prisoner, hanging over a spacious pit. His heart raced at the sight, and tears instantly flooded his eyes. It was Adalyn! They had found her!

But his attention was soon stolen by the other many figures throughout the chamber. Without delay, a feeling of darkness crept over him as he looked upon the skoles. Most he didn't recognize, but one of them looked ultimately familiar. It was Engle of Obuthahn.

CHAPTER 65

Adalyn!" Lancen shouted in angst, stepping toward her and pulling an arrow from its quiver. "What have you done, Engle?"

Keira remained in a complete shock at the doors, frozen in her tracks. Her eyes were glued to the young man that she had once expected to marry, but now he was nearly unrecognizable. She could have sworn that he was dead!

Engle moved slowly away from the strange lock he was fiddling with and turned to face his new guests. It was only then that they beheld the full view of the creature he had become. His eyes were sunken and glowed a disturbing white. He appeared starved, with bony features and blue lips. His skin was pale and teeth like arrow tips. He was a full-blooded skole.

It was now completely clear to Lancen that the Legion was not the tyrant. He didn't know why it had taken him so long to figure it out. Of course it was the skoles!

"Welcome my flesh of flesh, my blood of blood," greeted Engle darkly. His voice was low and broken, as if something were blocking his airway.

"I thought you were dead," Keira whimpered, shaking her head. Tears trickled down her cheeks in steady streams. The white-haired skole standing closest to Engle looked at her crookedly.

"Yes, you would believe I was dead, wouldn't you?" said Engle, watching her sharply, never blinking. "As I recall, you left me bleeding in a dark hole, as bait for the very beasts that I had just saved you from! But that is of little importance now. Besides, I wasn't talking to you. It is *The Champion* that shares my blood."

Keira fought emotion as she struggled to process what had just been brought to light. "What are you saying?"

"Go ahead, *Champion*," said Engle smugly, "tell her what I'm saying."

"Not until Adalyn is down safely," Lancen responded, surprised that his voice remained so steady, seeing as his gut was rolling uncontrollably.

"What!" Engle crowed. "Don't you want to chat? It has been such a long time! Just ask Keira, I am back from the dead. I thought that would make for great conversation!

"No? Then alright, I'll play your game. Official deal, on the table: you tell my girlfriend what you really are — and I'm sorry, but I do still consider her *my* girlfriend — and then I will tell you how to save *your* girlfriend. What do you say? Do we have a deal?"

"What is he talking about, Lancen?" asked Keira, unmoving in trepidation.

Lancen glared at Engle with dead eyes. He felt no animosity, for he knew what evil had caused the Shaharan to turn. He understood better than anyone the carnal temptations that Engle had clearly given in to, but just because he understood Engle did not mean that he would spare him.

"Why are you doing this?" Lancen asked. "What's in it for you?"

"Avoiding the question? Do you refuse my deal?" asked Engle threateningly. The other skoles left their positions and approached their leader's side, all of them staring ominously at Lancen and Keira.

Smiling at his dozen followers, Engle strolled casually to the edge of the pit and gazed up at a distressed Adalyn. "Do not worry, princess. They cannot stop the fire. In a few minutes you will be dead, and you will never have to deal with the pain of the one you love doing nothing to save you when you are in dire need! That pain would change anyone, and I would hate to see you tainted!"

Adalyn's eyes widened. She had clearly been through hell and could take no more. "Please, Lancen, just answer him."

But the champion held his tongue. How could he ever tell them the truth? They would hate him.

"Why are you my blood? *ANSWER ME!*" shouted Engle.

Keira looked at Lancen with fear in her denying eyes, but in them as well was an unquestionable clarity. "You're a skole," she muttered in horror. "It all makes sense now, why you won't eat, why you can't sleep! Ret…"

Even then he couldn't say it.

"Lancen, please!" Adalyn pleaded.

Clenching his jaw, the boy tried to block out Adalyn and Keira, concentrating completely on Engle.

"I am a monster like you," he said steadily, the world going black around his focus.

"A monster he says!" Engle hollered, throwing up his arms and flaunting for his cronies. "That is exactly right! You were given my blood and are becoming my flesh! You and I have the same mission, Champion. The Master calls, and I have followed. It would be wise for you to do the same."

Lancen could still feel Keira's eyes on him, even with the wall he had raised to keep her out. His face flushed in shame, but he remained centered on Engle. "We made a deal. How do I save Adalyn?"

"Fool," Engle smirked. "It is as poetic as I have ever seen! The princess dangles helpless in agony, and the champion comes rushing to her rescue. '*How do I save her?*' You *CANNOT*! In a moment she will be consumed by fire, and unless I pick that lock and drop her into—"

Engle suddenly gasped and put a hand to his mouth, mockingly. "Oh, I have said too much! But I suppose a deal is a deal. If you want to get her down safely, then you must swing her away from the pit and turn the lock." The skole walked back to the main panel and pointed at the circular recession. "But speaking of this, I must get back to it! So unless you have the key, we're finished here."

Lancen steadily raised a hand to his neck, pulling free the string. "I have the key."

Engle threw up his arms stubbornly, tossing the metal picks into the air. They fell to the floor and rattled to a stop. "Well why didn't you tell me sooner? If we don't pierce the heart now, then this whole ritual goes to hell!"

Lancen looked to Adalyn. She was already beginning to kick her feet, trying to swing her way out over the floor. Her face was red and sweat dripped on her brow. She could not hide her panic while great and intimidating blades spun like a whirlpool beneath her. Lancen now knew the way to save her, but he had to do it quickly. If he could just turn that lock, then it would all be finished.

Immediately he raised his bow and pulled back the arrow, launching it into the heart of a nameless monster. The creature dropped like a rock, and Lancen stepped forward unphased, notching another.

"Oh no," said Engle furiously, moving across the open floor toward Lancen. His minions followed him, menacing. "I'm not playing this game! Hand over the key, Noble! I do not want to force it from you. Ventok, kill his skank. I am tired of her loud breath."

As Ventok laid foot to charge Keira, Lancen released his Darkwood arrow into the monster's chest. Engle's righthand man shrieked and dropped to the polished ground.

Immediately the other skoles began to charge as a dangerous fire entered Engle's eyes. Lancen shot down two more skoles before he was forced to drop his bow and pull out his axe to parry the stampeding gang. In a fierce and unreal lucidity, Lancen cut through beast after soulless beast, taking them out one by one. As soon as he had room to run, he made a break for the panel. In the corner of his eye, he could see Adalyn, swinging back and forth with all her might, gaining momentum. Ripping the key from his neck, he was nearly to the lock!

But just before he reached the saving grace, Lancen was hit powerfully by Engle, knocking him from his feet. Tumbling to the glossy floor, Securis flew from his hand, landing a few feet away, and toward Adalyn slid the envied key as if on ice. It stopped just short of the refined pit.

Before Lancen could gather himself, he received a ferocious kick to the stomach that threw him up from the ground and back down roughly. Rolling over with a battle cry, he urgently stretched out for his axe, but in a moment his arm was pinned to the floor by one of Engle's sharp black boots. Picking up the axe, the monster laughed and tossed it aside.

"We will not be using anything like that," said Engle. "You are skolic, Lancen! You do not need these petty weapons of men! Fight with the tools the Master has granted you! Now get up."

Engle grabbed Lancen by the shirt and with one arm, lifted him to his feet. Swinging blindly, the Noble threw a punch, missing badly. Engle dodged and countered, landing a quick strike. Recoiling, Lancen again dove desperately for his axe, but was denied and strongly shoved back to the floor.

"If you are going to be the champion, then you had better learn to fight like one!" Engle snapped.

Enraged, Lancen returned to his feet and began swinging with new passion, but he remained one step behind his larger opponent. A rapid swipe burned through his already injured shoulder like a stick through sand. A moment later he was picked up and rammed into a hard metal piece of machinery. The brute strength of the skolic Shaharan was felt in every blow as strike after strike pounded into Lancen's torso.

The champion kicked and threw his elbows, finally landing a strong swing across his enemy's jaw. Immediately, Engle answered by shoving a stout forearm into Lancen's throat, pinning him up against a series of metal poles.

"Join with us, Lancen!" Engle shouted. "End the scum that has done us both so much wrong! Your loyalty is a waste and integrity a haze! You have no allegiance with men! The Natives hate you. The Nobles hate you! Join us and end the *real* tyranny!"

Lancen grit his teeth and squinted in pain. His stomach felt like it had been stabbed by a dozen arrows, while his throat ached, on the verge of being crushed. For a brief moment the skole let up so that Lancen could speak, and he managed to choke out strongly, "then do not kill Adalyn!"

Quickly Lancen glanced to Keira. She was battling two, and the only remaining, skoles. Another was dead at her feet. He had no time to be impressed, but she was holding her own, and that was more than he could say.

"I have to kill the princess," Engle spit, inches from Lancen's face. Drops of saliva sprayed against his skin, and rather than the warmth of breath, an odd coolness left the creature's mouth with every word. "She is the one, fair and pure. Her blood is royal, and untouched by you or I. But do not fear! There are more fitting women for heroes of our stature than these two. *Join us!*"

For lack of a better response, Lancen decided to feed the skole some of his own, and spit in Engle's face.

With more of a hiss than a scream, the skole answered by hitting Lancen in the stomach over and over with every word, "You. Are. Not. My. Enemy!"

Reaching down, Lancen remembered one tool still left at his disposal. At the end of his reach, he managed to grasp the hilt of his dagger from his pant leg.

"Well you're mine," he seethed as he threw the small blade upward and cut smoothly through Engle's arm.

Momentarily loosed, Lancen tackled the large skole to the hard stone. For a brief moment he connected several rapid punches, but the advantage was short lived. Engle was bigger and stronger than he and was swiftly able to wrestle to a commanding position atop him. Pulling at his fingers, Engle forced the dagger from Lancen's palm and threw it away toward the pit.

"I told you," the skole fumed lividly, "we are above that! Our nails are swords, and our teeth are daggers."

Engle leaned in and bit hard into the tip of Lancen's ear. Ripping free a small piece of flesh, the monster spit it out and flashed a disturbing red grin.

"Your blood still has a human taste. You have not changed because you have not accepted the call. Interesting that you were given the choice!"

Lancen shoved and fidgeted, narrowly removing the monster enough to roll away and jump to his feet. He was covered in Engle's blood, as his own flowed freely from his damaged ear. Engle scowled at him with a serious conviction.

"I don't want to kill you!"

"Nor I you," said Lancen coldly, "but I will if I must."

He could now see Adalyn swinging back and forth behind Engle, well enough to avoid the pit if released at the perfect moment. The metal turbines lurched louder than they ever had.

"The odds are stacked against you Lancen. A wise man would give in and accept me as his ally!"

"Or come up with a new plan."

Lancen shouted and charged Engle at full speed, catching the skolic Shaharan off guard. Keeping his head down, he sent the monster reeling backward, driving powerfully for several steps. With one final push, he forced Engle to stumble on his heels. With malice bleeding from his eyes, the skole yelled and reached out, but grabbed hold of nothing before he fell back-first into the deadly pit. The great blades made a horrible sound of grinding, and just like that, Engle was gone.

But time was too pressing for thought as Adalyn still hung in peril from the lengthy cable, and Keira fought two powerful and deadly creatures. Which could he help first? Did he even have a choice?

The golden key rested near him, and he snatched it quickly. Turning back to Keira, he watched as she slashed one of the creatures across the arm, and forced the other to the floor, swiftly sending her knife into its chest.

With a nightmarish swipe, the remaining skole surprised her and sent her twirling to the stone. It pried the short blade from her grasp, and in a quick and thoughtless motion, shoved it deep into her side. She struggled at once, thrusting upward and away from the monster, and then, the sharpened obsidian blade was pulled free.

CHAPTER 66

Countless emotions instantly boiled to the surface. The ultimate peak of Lancen's anxiety was reached as terror and disbelief overcame him. Instinctively, his body began to move without thought or control. He sprinted to the main panel of switches as the skolic fiend that had just stabbed Keira flew toward him with unparalleled speed. He could hardly process what was happening as he quickly pushed the golden key into its lock.

He could hear a distant and muffled cry as he turned to watch Adalyn swing. It was a far-off and foreign plea of pain and desperation, disaster evident in each of its changing tones. It took him some time to realize that the agonized sound was coming from his own mouth. Every appendage, morsel, and fiber of his body felt numb.

Though his awareness seemed to be hiding in some strange and distant world, his eyes continued to keep track of the princess as she swung forward over the granite floor. An unearthly and booming roar burst from the pit below. Thoughts entered his mind incomplete and then faded into a cold air like steam. *Turn. Key. Now.*

The moment he did, Adalyn and the cable dropped like rags to the stone, just as a lethal pillar of fire shot like a geyser from the rounded pit. The explosion of flame thundered up to the ceiling high above and thrashed against its surface. A scorching wave of heat barreled past Lancen. Though so close to the flame, Adalyn in inconceivable exhaustion could barely rise to her knees.

Attempting to split fragments of seconds, Lancen glanced to Keira and saw her climbing to her feet—alive. Turning back to the princess, he heard a sound different than the consuming pillar. Adalyn crawled toward him with a tenacious determination.

"Lancen!" he heard.

The call came from behind him. It was distant and urgent, but he didn't recognize the name.

"Lancen look out!" It was Keira screaming in angst.

But before he could react, a strong arm seized him from behind. Skolic claws were pressed tightly against his throat.

"Hello champion," seethed the dangerous voice in his ear. It was the skole that Keira had just been fighting.

The monster turned Lancen around to face the Native girl. She had managed to find a Darkwood arrow near her feet and stumble over to where the Sacred Tare rested.

"Move and he dies!" hollered the bleeding skole, shielded behind Lancen. The monster breathed heavily and put its weight on him. Clearly the Native girl had wounded it greatly.

"Don't listen Keira!" Lancen shouted over the explosion of fire. "Kill him!"

At once the razor-sharp claws on the skole's fingers dug into his skin, already beginning to cut. "I don't think so, savage!" It screamed. "There is only one way to save him! Push the princess into the great flame!"

Keira immediately looked at Adalyn, who sat weak and stricken in fear, still attempting to get her feet beneath her. Shaking with every breath, the Native's face writhed along with her inner debate.

"Shoot him!" Lancen fired.

"Push the girl or he's dead!"

Lancen felt the claws, sharp and icy against his neck. Keira had the bow ready with the arrow. Torment was plain in her expression.

"Shoot him!"

"I can't!" she cried back. "I'll miss!"

"Elbow up!" called Lancen, the claws were drawing blood.

"I'll hit you!" she lamented, adjusting her stance and form. "I can't!" She lowered the bow and again looked to Adalyn in deliberation.

Lancen searched his heart and mind for the right words. The fire behind him seemed to singe every hair on his body, and the racket was unbearable. He had to think!

The skole angrily shouted an inaudible curse and cut the side of Lancen's face, retracting for a moment before quickly returning its claws to his throat.

"Fine then! Princess, push the savage into the flame, she'll do!" the monster proposed. "If we wait any longer, we'll all die!"

Lancen's mind went back to the cavern of Nahabuk, to his first sincere moment with Keira. She had told him something crucial. He prayed to recall the exact words that she had used.

The skole behind him was bleeding profusely. Lancen could feel it, a touch of cold to the menacing heat all around him. The monster was weak, supporting nearly all of its weight on Lancen, but the deadly weapons at his neck were sure.

"Then you choose *death*, both strong and great!" shrieked the creature.

And then something clicked in Lancen's memory.

"*KEIRA!*" he yelled at the top of his lungs, pushing past the screaming flame. "Make more difference than the sun!"

A deafening crack sounded as the roof gave way and the pillar of fire shot upward, far and high into the cloudy sky above.

Keira breathed deeply, straightened her back, and released the bow string. Like lightning, the arrow flashed across the distance and into the skole's neck, only a hair above Lancen's shoulder. The creature stumbled for a moment, grasping at the shaft that blocked its air, and then it dropped flat.

Not a moment later, a horrible cry was forced from Keira's mouth as a Darkwood arrow pushed its way up and through her stomach, before being quickly pulled free. Rising behind her was Ventok, Engle's large and ugly skole follower.

In a panicked desperation, Lancen spotted his dagger a few steps away and exploded off toward it. With the room spinning around him, he laid hold of the blade and charged the final skole with all the energy of his soul. He could hardly process what was happening as the monster rushed equally aggressive toward him. With no time to waste, Lancen stabbed the weapon between the eyes of the white-hair fiend. And as he released his grip on the blade, the skole fell at once to its knees, and collapsed forward on its face.

But as the monster fell, so did Keira, the wound in her abdomen pouring blood. Lancen snatched up Securis and sprinted toward her. As he slid to his knees beside her, debris both small and great began to violently crash all around them. Keira had fallen unconscious.

"*ADALYN! LET'S GO!*" Lancen screamed inaudibly into the boom of the collapsing world around him. He placed his arms around Keira and willed himself to lift her. Adalyn finally battled up and rushed over to his side, pointing to the aisle where Ventok had come and gone so many times. Forgoing the Sacred Tare, she and Lancen raced through a hellish destruction, behind the main panel, and into the darkness beyond.

CHAPTER 67

Lancen slammed his back into a rugged wooden door and burst through it to the outside world. The wind howled fiercely as heavy snow fell thick and wet all around them. Lancen could see no soldiers, but somehow his two grayish-brown steeds had managed to find their way to await him at the door. The pillar of fire behind him burnt through the storm and far above to an unfeasible height as Lancen carefully laid Keira down into the soft and deepening snow. It immediately soaked-in a crimson red.

Lancen longed for some pit karp to place into the gash, anything that would help her recover.

"Put snow in the wound," said Adalyn urgently, crouching down beside him. "I've heard that it helps."

Lancen scooped a large ball of snow onto Keira's stomach. It rapidly soaked red and melted. Her face was pale, her lips blue, and her breathing came in slow and forced. He was losing her.

Tears rolled down his face in steady streams, a thousand unanswered questions storming through his mind, and unanswered prayers through his heart. How could this be happening? How could fate allow it? Keira had become his best friend, someone that he truly loved, and now she was dying before his eyes, and there was nothing he could do about it!

Or was there?

He remembered suddenly the state of Engle in the cavern of Nahabuk. The Shaharan had been broken and bleeding, but somehow rose and walked away. When they had met the Endwans, Ret was critically injured, but within days rose as if unscathed. Both of them had become monsters, but both had survived a dramatic crisis.

Lancen was a skole. He could do it. He craved it.

'The inner battle that I try to avoid,' Etnah's voice suddenly sounded in his mind, *'persists until I eventually bust.'*

Was this the only solution? Was there any other way to save her?

Keira's breathing turned to choked and broken gasps. Lancen needed to act now.

"Close your eyes," he told Adalyn softly.

She did what he said at once.

Lancen leaned over Keira and stopped just inches from the side of her neck, the smell of sage still wafting from her hair. Would he be able to go through with this? Would he be able to live with himself afterward? Etnah had taught him that a skole could only fully evolve after feeding for the first time. Was that something that he could handle? Would it be worth it for Keira to face the same curse? He had no other choice.

He now heard Keira's voice sound softly in his mind, *'One day you will get it through your head that there is always a choice.'*

Not this time, Keira.

With his tongue, Lancen felt along the bottom of his teeth. They were dull, but perhaps just sharp enough. He leaned in, opened his mouth, and pressed on, biting delicately into the girl's flesh.

Warm liquid touched his lips at once and entered his mouth. In a moment he knew with certainty that it was the best taste that he had ever encountered. It was sweet like honey and smooth as syrup, warming his throat as he allowed her precious blood in through his mouth. For the first time in months, he felt completely rejuvenated, the aching hunger that had plagued him for so long vanishing in an instant.

Eventually, and exhausting every ounce of will he had left, Lancen forced himself away from the bite. The pure nirvana that he had just experienced lingered, the scope of his actions striking no chord of conscience. He finally felt free, awake, and alive.

But after he opened his eyes, he watched Keira intently for improvement. He waited for some sign of stability, but none came. Her breath had grown shallow and quiet, and then, whether in reality or in the darkest corner of an unbearable hell—Lancen heard it stop. Keira was dead.

CHAPTER 68

There was no feeling, emotion, or propensity in the world that could ever describe the scar this moment would leave on Lancen's life. In a flash, he had lost one of the most significant companions that he would ever know. In a flash, it felt like the entire world had begun to crumble all around him, sending him falling into an endless and miserable torment. She was really gone.

He could feel Adalyn's arms move in tightly around him, but his mind could not process that she was there. The warmth of her embrace did little to melt the ice that had just entered his heart. Through fire and pressure, he knew that the ice would eventually turn to stone, but for now it was cold. In this moment, he would resolve an oath that would outlast the eternities. He would never allow something like this to happen again. She would be avenged. If it took him to his final breath, she would be! He would silence the tyrant. He would be Obah-a-Tou.

There was no telling how long he sat there in Adalyn's arms, the warm air of the fire pounding against his face on one side while a frigid wind scathed the other. It could have been minutes, but it felt like a lifetime. He knew that there would be no filling of the hole that had just been torn through his soul.

After a long time of silence, Adalyn spoke lightly, "Lancen?"

He wanted to respond, but he could scarcely breathe.

"Lancen, I'm freezing," she muttered.

His head felt thick and heavy, but an instinct of duty somehow drew him to his feet. Looking to the horses, he saw that a variety of supplies still remained strapped on their hinds. Keira's fur cloak had been rolled up and stuffed into one of the packs.

Some unknown driving force ensnared him as he wandered forward to retrieve it for Adalyn. A thousand words of wisdom and encouragement flooded into his mind, forming a pool deep enough to drown in. To move on, he must move forward. To survive, he must move on. To succeed, he must survive.

Finding the warm clothing, Lancen placed it around Adalyn's shoulders and embraced her once more. With each passing moment, the numbness within him dispersed, and an incredible pain of loss filled the empty spaces. He ached for some relief, for anything to soothe his troubled soul.

"Thank you," said Adalyn quietly. "Thank you for finding me."

She hugged him tightly, her icy cheeks like wells of encouragement against his.

He couldn't speak, but simply cried, burying his wet eyes into her coat.

"What should we do now?" she asked sincerely, unable to stop her own tears.

Lancen raised his head and closed his eyes, letting the tears continue to squeeze from beneath his lashes. "There is no way to bury her," he said solemnly. "We should cover her with sticks, then ride away and never return."

"Will we go to Calderon?"

The question burnt like a brand in Lancen's ear.

"No," he answered, "we must go to the Ashlands. It is my duty to return there. I will understand if you do not wish to join me."

"Lancen, I am beaten and exhausted," she said genuinely, "but it would take the power of a god to remove me from your side."

"It won't be safe there."

"But if it is there that we must go, then we will go."

Tears wouldn't cease to pour from Lancen's eyes as he looked from Adalyn to Keira. The more he wept, the more the princess did also. She had now seen as much pain through her incredibly blue and piercing eyes as he had, but they couldn't give up, even if every horror, evil, and insatiable power in the world was pitted against them.

Trying not to waste valuable time, Lancen somberly released Adalyn and walked the gloomy and painful steps to his incredible friend. Kneeling-down beside her, he leaned in and kissed her on the forehead.

"Goodbye," was all he could manage to say before rising and gathering sticks for a makeshift grave.

After a dazed and melancholy process, he returned to the horses and helped Adalyn into her saddle.

"My father used to tell me that life will sometimes beat you half to death, but it is only when you stop fighting back that it can kill you," mentioned the princess as Lancen climbed atop his horse. "We're going to fight back, Lancen."

The champion nodded, wiping cold tears that had frozen to his face. Kicking his steed, he led the march as they rode away from his mountain home. As he contemplated atop his horse, he knew that what Keira had once told him was right. He needed to compensate for the shame he had felt, and thanks to her, he knew how that was to be done. Though the present seemed unimaginably difficult, there would only be more trials waiting for him in the future.

The road to freedom was long, and his journey was far from over. Through all of the bends and rises ahead, he would need to be strong, for at the end of the path lived a universal peace that only he could provide. He was the champion of Serondhel. He was Obah-a-Tou, and he must now fight for the future of both the Natives and the Nobles. The skoles were rising, and the Master still called.

First, Obuthahn needed him, and though the pressure of a collapsing world was pushing on him from every angle, he was hell-bent on participating in a crucial and intimidating race against time. For when he finally reached his destination, the heirs of Serondhel would be free...at last.

END OF BOOK ONE

About the Author:

Jason L. Garner is an artist, author, and fantasy enthusiast who loves a good narrative regardless of the medium. Aside from writing, he enjoys spending time with his wife and family. He is a budding software developer, fantasy football connoisseur, and a die-hard Utah Jazz fan.

CPSIA information can be obtained
at www.ICGtesting.com
Printed in the USA
LVHW031130271019
635473LV00002B/465/P

11/19